TREADING ON DANGEROUS GROUND

"This is the whiskey talking," Matt said. "In the morning you're going to be sorry."

"Did you ever stop to consider that the whiskey has given me the courage to say what I've wanted to for a long time? And that in the morning I might be sorry for what we didn't do?" Courtney asked.

He wanted to believe her. "I would never turn you away," he said.

She rested her forehead on his right knee. "Sometimes it's hard to ask. Sometimes I want you to read my mind."

He traced the curve of her cheek and the line of her jaw.

Her mouth parted. He took that as an invitation and touched her bottom lip. Her tongue darted out to lick the tip of his finger. Everything disappeared except his need and the woman who offered herself to him.

Books by Susan Macias

Fire in the Dark
Honeysuckle DeVine
Courtney's Cowboy

Published by HarperPaperbacks

Courtney's Cowboy

⧏ Susan Macias ⧐

HarperPaperbacks
A Division of HarperCollins Publishers

This is a work of fiction. The characters, incidents, and dialogues are products of the author's imagination and are not to be construed as real. Any resemblance to actual events or persons, living or dead, is entirely coincidental.

HarperPaperbacks *A Division of* HarperCollins*Publishers*
10 East 53rd Street, New York, N.Y. 10022

Cover illustration by Aleta Jenks

First HarperPaperbacks printing: July 1996

Printed in the United States of America

HarperPaperbacks, HarperMonogram, and colophon are trademarks of HarperCollins*Publishers*

❖ 10 9 8 7 6 5 4 3 2 1

*To Ruben who already is the best kind of hero—
even if he doesn't believe it yet.*

1

Cheyenne, Wyoming—Present Day.

"I should have driven my car," Courtney Johnson-Stone muttered as her left foot slipped out of the stirrup and she started to slide off the saddle.

She grabbed for the pommel and pulled herself back into a semi-straight sitting position. Her rear end slapped noisily against the smooth leather. She tried hanging on with her thighs as she'd been instructed, but it didn't help. With any other horse, she would have blamed her troubles on her inexperience, but this animal was taking an unnatural interest in her predicament. Its ears twitched with pleasure each time she slid down, and Courtney was convinced it was deliberately making the ride as uncomfortable as possible.

"I don't like you either," she said, letting go of the saddle horn long enough to brush a strand of hair off her face. The new leather backpack that doubled as her purse and overnight bag bounced against her spine. She was going to be bruised and stiff in the morning. She wrinkled her nose. Forget morning. She was already in pain.

After taking a firm hold of the horn, she gave her mount a sharp kick in the side, hoping to urge it into a smoother gait. What was it called? Oh, yeah, cantering. But instead of lengthening its stride, the rental horse simply trotted faster until Courtney's teeth were clattering together.

"Matt," she called loudly.

The mounted figure in front of her didn't slow down.

"Matt, please don't make me chase you halfway to Colorado."

Her words came out unevenly and she bit the edge of her tongue on the last syllable. She winced and tasted blood. She'd had better days.

"Colorado is south. We're heading west." He spoke without turning around. "Go back to town."

"I can't."

"You're stubborn."

"Maybe, but the reason I can't go back to town is that I don't know how to make the horse turn."

She sawed on the reins, but nothing happened. The bone-crushing trot continued until she feared all her internal organs would become carbonated.

Matt slowed his mount. When hers caught up with him, he reached over and grabbed the reins. Instantly the rented animal stopped, digging its back hooves into the ground. Unprepared, Courtney found herself sailing over the top of the animal's head. Her backpack slid down her arms, her hat soared toward the heavens. She somersaulted gently in the air before landing flat on her back. The bare ground was mercifully free of rocks, but the semi-frozen earth was hard.

Matt was at her side in an instant. He helped her to a sitting position.

"Breathe," he said.

Between the way her chest tightened and the sharp pain in her lungs, catching her breath was her first priority, but she couldn't form the words to tell him. She could only gasp ineffectually.

At last she drew sweet air into her lungs. The pain lessened. Matt pulled off his gloves and touched her cheek. "You hurt?"

His fingers were warm against her skin. There was a tenderness in the faint caress that nearly brought tears to her eyes. Only she never cried.

"I don't think so."

Still supporting her in a sitting position, he ran his free hand down each of her legs. The brush of his palm ignited little fires all along her skin. Amazing how he could do that through her jeans. But he had always been talented that way.

When he started to unbutton her coat—she guessed to check her chest—she pushed away from him. "Nothing appears broken," she said brightly.

"Sure?"

"I see you're still worried about the Lord docking you for excess words," she said. "But maybe you could risk a complete sentence like us city folk use."

The familiar teasing produced the expected result. He smiled at her. Her chest started aching again, but this time it was because the man in front of her took her breath away. Handsome was such a feeble word to describe him. The first time she'd seen him, she had thought him beautiful. She knew him well enough to know that description would make him frown, and right now she needed to see him smile.

His tanned skin enhanced the deep blue of his eyes. His jaw was square, his mouth firm. The bulk of his sheepskin-lined coat emphasized his size and strength. Matt Stone was six feet two inches of black-haired, blue-eyed, Stetson-wearing cowboy.

He was also her husband.

He rose to his feet and held out his hand. She allowed him to pull her upright. He bent over and collected her hat. As he passed it to her, she took one last lingering glance at him and spoke.

"Please sign the papers."

As she'd expected, the humor fled his expression, leaving behind the stern countenance of a stranger. "No."

"But you promised."

His eyes always darkened with any strong emotion. She'd seen them burn hot with anger and shine with passion, but now they were cold. Deathly cold.

"You're my wife. We made a commitment to each other and this marriage. The way I see it, neither of us has given that a chance."

His uncharacteristically long speech warned her he was getting ready to dig in his heels as deeply as her rented horse had. If he decided to get stubborn about this, she would never sway him. No doubt she would end up being the one who changed her mind. And she would end up in the same position her horse had left her—flat on her back and out of breath.

She adjusted her hat, the one she'd bought especially for this trip, then picked up her backpack and shrugged it on. "In the two years since our wedding, we've spent exactly fifty-seven nights together. That's not a marriage, it's an affair."

"I wanted you to come with me."

"I have a life. A career."

"You have a husband."

"And you weren't willing to give up what you do, either. I don't want to spend my days in a truck driving from rodeo to rodeo."

She jammed her hands into her coat pockets and tried to control her temper. They'd been over this a hundred times already. There wasn't an easy answer.

"It's not that I don't care about you," she said. "I don't know you. You don't know me. A weekend of hot sex every few weeks isn't enough to sustain a relationship."

"That's not what you scream in my bed."

"Yes, well." Courtney cleared her throat. She'd been hoping he wouldn't bring that up. Matt was her fantasy. But she needed someone real in her life. Not a dream lover.

She stared at the toes of her boots, also purchased new for the trip, and tried to find the right combination of words. "I don't want to hurt you," she said slowly. "But I do want a divorce."

She had to swallow the lump in her throat. This was harder than she'd thought it would be. "In time you'll see it's better for both of us. You need someone who wants what you want—a ranch, life in the country. I like living in Los Angeles. I love my job. My little red sports car. My condo by the marina. We're too different. It's not as if you ever fell in love with me. When could you? We were hardly together."

That was the bottom line, she supposed. They'd never been in love. At least she was pretty sure they hadn't been. Everything had happened so fast.

She drew in a deep breath, tasting the sweet, crisp air. She had to admit, it sure smelled better up here than it did in the city. "Matt, I—"

She glanced at him, but he wasn't listening to her anymore. He was staring past her to something beyond her left shoulder. She turned slowly, shuddering at the sight of tall trees. There was too much wilderness up here for her comfort. At least a line of power poles reminded her that civilization wasn't all that far away.

Matt continued to stare at the horizon. She followed his gaze and saw that the sky was darkening to a brilliant shade of violet. She'd never seen anything like it before.

"What is that?" she asked.

"I don't know."

"But you know everything about being outdoors."

"I've never seen the sky turn that color, but I don't think it's good. Get on your horse."

"What? Are you serious?"

He didn't bother to answer. Instead, he glanced around. His mount, Jasper, was a prize-winning cutting horse, trained to stay in one place when the reins were dropped on the ground. Her rental horse had wandered off to sample the bright green spring grasses. Matt caught the animal easily and led it over to her.

"Get on," he said, lacing his hands together to form a step.

"We can't outride it," she said, looking up at the rapidly darkening sky. She followed the deep colors back to the horizon. Her mouth opened and she pointed. "W-what's that?"

A blue mist seemed to boil up from the ground. It exploded into a turquoise whirlwind that danced across the land. Where it met the violet sky, lightning erupted. She saw the bolts flash silently, but there was no accompanying thunder. Overhead, the sun disappeared. Instantly, the temperature dropped as day turned nearly as dark as night.

Matt grabbed both sets of reins in one hand and draped his free arm over her shoulders. "It's a tornado," he said.

"I didn't know you got them up here."

"Sometimes. But not like this. It's not sucking anything up." He pointed. "Look."

He was right. The tornado moved over grasses and bushes, leaving everything undisturbed.

"Listen," Matt said. "There's no sound."

That's when Courtney noticed the absence of noise. She couldn't hear a bird or a rustle of wind. Lightning flashed and the whirlwind swirled closer, but it was so silent, she could hear her own breathing and the rapid pounding of her heart. Fear clutched at her like bony fingers clawing up her spine.

"M-Matt?" Her voice trembled.

"This way." He quickly urged her forward toward a pile of large boulders. "We'll be safe here. It's low ground."

The whirlwind danced closer. Lightning continued to flash across the sky. The unnatural silence made her skin crawl. They should have had to shout, but instead they spoke in whispers. She glanced at the horses and was surprised to find them calm and still. There was something odd about their eyes, though, as if they'd been sedated.

Matt pushed her down on the ground. She slipped off her backpack and pulled it close to her chest, then huddled by the largest boulder. The time-worn rock jutted out of the ground, as if it had sprouted a millennium ago. It had survived tornados before. She prayed it would survive this one.

Matt settled in beside her. "Lie flat," he told her.

She moved the backpack, drawing her arm through the straps, determined that she wasn't going to lose her driver's license and credit cards. Matt stretched out on top of her. He was warm and solid, the only normal part of a world suddenly gone mad.

"Are we going to die?" she whispered, her words and breathing plainly audible in the oppressive silence.

"I don't know."

She squeezed her eyes shut, not wanting to see the violet darkness. The air grew more cold until the frigid chill seemed to seep into her bones. She could tell how close the whirlwind was by the stillness and dropping temperature. Her teeth chattered. Matt huddled closer. He must be freezing. At least she had him to protect her. She had the oddest feeling that even if she wanted to move, she couldn't.

Next to them, one of the horses stomped its hoof. The sound was painfully loud. Obviously the animals weren't constricted in their movement. Suddenly the air around them exploded into a brilliant white light. For a moment Courtney wondered if they'd died. Was this the tunnel people talked about?

But she still felt cold and she had no sense of being beckoned anywhere. As far as she could tell, she was still lying on the near-frozen ground in Wyoming. Matt was still on top of her and she could hear the wind blowing.

Wind? There were birds, too.

"You can open your eyes," Matt said, rolling off her and rising to his feet. "It's gone."

Courtney sat up more slowly. The sky was a brilliant blue with a few fluffy white clouds for contrast.

"What happened?" she asked.

"I'm not sure. I guess the storm just blew over."

"But that was so quick. It was only a few minutes."

Matt glanced at his watch and frowned. He shook his wrist. "According to this, it's been three hours." He sounded doubtful.

"What? That's not possible." She looked at her watch. It had been noon when she'd ridden out after him and they'd traveled for about half an hour. So it should have been no later than one. But her watch showed the time as quarter to four. Courtney watched the second hand sweep around the dial. She didn't like this one bit.

Matt checked the horses. They were waiting patiently, even the one she'd rented. She stood up slowly, then grabbed her backpack.

"It didn't feel like three hours," she said slowly. "Do you think we fell asleep?"

"No."

"Maybe we were abducted by aliens and they did

experiments on us. That would explain the missing time."

Matt glanced at her, then rolled his eyes. "I'm sure that's it."

"Then how would you explain it?"

"I can't, but we survived and we're fine. When we're back in Cheyenne, we'll find some answers. Until then, let's just ride."

Courtney turned away from her husband. Obviously he was as concerned as she, but he didn't want her to worry.

But she was worried. That storm. She shuddered. The silence had been eerie. However, until they got to town, they probably wouldn't find out what had happened. She glanced at the sky and squinted. She didn't *actually* believe in aliens.

Her gaze drifted down to the row of trees beside the trail. Her eyes widened. "Matt?" She pointed. "The trail's gone."

The well-used riding trail had disappeared and in its place was a carpet of new grass. The trees were different, too. They were thicker and taller. She didn't know what kind they were. Not pine. Some budding leafy thing. But there were more than she remembered. Something else was off, but she couldn't figure out what. It teased at the back of her memory. A detail.

"We're heading back," Matt said firmly. "Step up."

He bent over and laced his fingers together. She swung up into the saddle, wincing as her tender fanny settled on the unforgiving saddle. Matt mounted easily, then headed back the way they'd come.

"Is town still that way?" she asked. "I mean, everything looks different. Maybe we got blown somewhere else."

"The boulder is still there."

So it was. Matt's horse broke into a trot, and hers followed suit. She tightened her jaw so her teeth wouldn't chatter. Her thighs were too tired to cling anymore, so she just held onto the horn and did her best not to slide off the side.

All around them, the countryside had changed. The old barn they'd passed earlier was gone. If the tornado had blown it down, there should have been splintered bits of wood. If it had been blown away completely, there should have been a rectangle of dirt on the ground. Instead there was only the rolling meadow, undisturbed by any man-made structure.

Before the storm there had been only silence. Now birds were everywhere. They flew through the sky, filling the late afternoon with their chirping.

"This is too weird," Courtney said softly. There had to be a perfectly reasonable explanation for what had happened to them. She wondered if they'd been lifted up in the whirlwind and deposited somewhere else. That was it, of course. It was the only thing that made sense. Barns might disappear, but grass and trees didn't spring up out of nowhere in just a few hours.

If it was still the same day.

She looked at her watch again and was relieved to see it said the tenth. Friday the tenth. She'd flown out of L.A. yesterday to come and talk some sense into Matt. So they were missing a few hours. Worse things had happened. At least they were still alive.

They bounced along for another forty minutes. At least she bounced. Matt sat relaxed in his saddle as if Jasper used a smoother sort of step than her horse did. Her behind had gone from sore to completely numb. Her gloved fingers ached from holding on to the reins and the horn. And she was getting tired of looking at trees. At least on the way out she'd been able to stare at a few buildings. But since they'd started back toward town, they hadn't seen anything but trees and sky. No barns, no billboards, no power poles.

She jerked her horse to a halt. The animal dug its back hooves in the ground again, but this time she was prepared. She hung on to the saddle and managed to save herself. She stared at the trees again as ugly realization dawned.

"Matt?" she said. When he didn't slow down, she screamed, "Wait!"

Matt reined his horse in and circled the animal back toward her. "What's wrong?" he asked.

She was shaking. She tried to stop, but her body didn't listen. She wasn't cold. Since the storm had passed, the temperature was quite pleasant, at least for early May in Wyoming.

"We've been riding for forty minutes," she said, trying to stay calm. "We should have reached the stable by now."

"Agreed."

He'd pulled his hat low over his forehead so she couldn't see his eyes or know what he was thinking. "Why haven't we?"

"I'm not sure."

"Do you think we were blown somewhere else?"

"That's not possible. The boulder wouldn't have moved, too. And the horses were calm."

"But it was three hours. What happened?"

His mouth straightened into a thin line. "I don't know."

Apprehension thickened into fear. "There aren't any power poles. Right after the storm I knew there was something different, but I couldn't figure out what. It's the power poles. They're gone. And not blown away, either." She pointed to where the side of the trail should have been. "See. They aren't lying on the ground and there aren't any empty holes. They're just gone. Like they were never here." Courtney's voice rose with each word.

Matt urged his gelding closer to hers. "There's a logical explanation."

"Which is?"

"I don't know yet."

She shuddered and closed her eyes. "We're going to die," she moaned.

"We're not dead yet. We're going to head east until we hit town."

"We should have been there by now." She folded her arms over her chest and began to rock back and forth. "Something terrible happened. Maybe there was a bomb."

Matt didn't like this any more than she did. The skin on the back of his neck crawled. Something wasn't right; he'd known that the moment he'd seen the storm. He spent a lot of time on the road traveling from rodeo to rodeo and he'd never seen anything like that turquoise tornado before. And the silence.

She was right. They should have reached the stables. The buildings were missing, as were the power poles. He'd noticed that right off but hadn't said anything. He didn't want to upset her more.

Matt resisted the urge to gather her in his arms. He didn't think she wanted comforting from him. All Courtney needed from him was his signature on those damn divorce papers.

He stared straight ahead, in the direction Cheyenne should have been but wasn't. "Any kind of bomb would have made noise and killed birds. I've never seen so many flying around." He paused, knowing if he wanted to get her moving again, he had to make her more angry than she was scared. "Unless, of course, it was an alien bomb. Maybe the Martians have a silent bomb that puts people to sleep for three hours."

Her eyes snapped open and she glared at him. Her hazel eyes widened with temper. "I've never heard you string so many sentences together before. Maybe *you're* the alien."

"Maybe you're right and we never knew each other."

He'd spoken without thinking—something he almost never did—and instantly wished he could call the words back. Courtney hunched up inside her coat and tossed her head in that way she had of showing the world she wasn't hurt. But he knew she was.

He urged his gelding toward Cheyenne again. Despite the call of the birds and the rustling of the wind, he heard her rental horse fall into step. He glanced up at the sky and figured they could ride for another hour before they would have to find a place to spend the night. It might be May, but the temperature could easily dip below freezing. Besides, this was Wyoming, not Los Angeles. If they had been blown somewhere else, they could ride for days without finding a speck of civilization.

As they rode east, he continually studied the land around them. Everything was different, as if he'd never been here before, yet it was naggingly familiar. The shape of a rise, a cluster of rocks. But the air smelled different, and he didn't recognize several birds. Where had all the trees come from?

He didn't have any answers. For now, all they could do was ride.

Half an hour later, they came to a railroad track. Matt reined in Jasper and studied the first proof of man they'd seen since the storm. A trail curved up from the south and paralleled the track.

"We'll follow it to town," he said.

Courtney nodded without speaking. He could see the fatigue pulling her mouth straight. She sagged rather than sat in the saddle. Her face was pale and she didn't bother to brush away the strand of pale blond hair that settled on her cheek. He thought about doing it himself, but he knew he didn't have the right. He'd already overstepped his bounds after she'd fallen off her horse. But he hadn't been able to help himself.

Touching her cheek had been a harmless gesture; she probably hadn't even noticed. She was slipping away from him as surely as the light slipped away at sunset and he didn't know how to make her stop.

They kept the railroad track on their left and angled slightly southeast. Twenty minutes later Matt caught sight of a few buildings. It wasn't Cheyenne, but it was something. At least they wouldn't have to spend the night outdoors.

As they got closer, he could make out a few wooden buildings and some others built with brick. There were no paved roads, just dirt trails, some of them as wide as a regular street. He squinted and saw a man stepping out of a wagon. The man's clothing was odd. Old-fashioned. Then he realized there weren't any cars.

"Maybe we did get blown somewhere else," he said, slowing Jasper so Courtney could catch up with him. "I don't remember any reenactment village close to town, but it's here."

"Reenactment? What's that?"

"Where people live like they used to in the last century. Old clothes, old buildings."

She shuddered. "How awful. I like the twentieth century. Why would anyone want to live in the past? No electricity, no microwaves." She sniffed. "What's that smell?"

Matt inhaled, then wished he hadn't. It was a combination of rotting garbage and outhouse. "I'm not sure. Maybe they're having septic trouble."

"I'll say." She adjusted her backpack and brushed the strand of hair off her face. "I hope there's a hotel. I want a long, hot bath and something to eat. Let's hope your little reenactment friends are modern enough to accept my American Express card."

"I have money."

"Fine, be macho and pay for the room. I don't care. Just let's get there."

Were they going to sleep together? Heat boiled through him at the thought. Maybe he and Courtney didn't know each other as well as they could, but they'd never had trouble getting along in bed. Maybe if he loved her long enough and hard enough, she wouldn't leave him. Maybe he could figure out the right thing to say to keep her at his side.

He grimaced. Hell. She'd never been at his side.

She was right. They didn't have a marriage. She lived in California and he followed the rodeo circuit. When they had time, they met up somewhere in between. A weekend in Colorado, a week in Texas. It wasn't a relationship. But he didn't want to let her go. He was close to getting his own place. With another couple of winning seasons, he could buy that land and start building something of his own. If Courtney would just hang on until then, he would give her the ranch. It wasn't L.A., but it would be theirs.

The daydream was familiar. When the separations grew long and the nights were unbearable, he imagined what it would be like when he had his own spread. The promise of a better future got him through the rough times. If he couldn't convince Courtney to give them another chance, the dreams would get him through losing her. At least that was the plan.

"Look at that woman," Courtney said, pointing to the right.

Matt glanced over and saw a middle-aged woman dressed entirely in black from the top of the hat set high on her curls to the bottom of her full skirt. The woman looked at them. He tipped his hat. "Ma'am."

The woman greeted them with a regal nod, then disappeared up the steps of a small house and closed the door behind her.

"Did you see her dress?" Courtney asked. "Wow. It was amazing. She must have had at least three or four petticoats under that skirt. And the top part was tight.

I've never seen a woman with such a tiny waist." She sat up straight and placed her hand on her side. "Maybe she was wearing a corset. Yuck. If you ask me, they're taking this reenactment stuff way too seriously."

The trail they were on widened into a street and seemed to lead into the center of town. Shadows lengthened as the sun drifted down toward the mountains in the west. Matt studied the buildings and fought against a feeling of uneasiness. Everything was *too* authentic. There were no power lines, no telephone lines, no fire hydrants. Most of the buildings they passed fronted the street without so much as a sidewalk. A few had wooden planking stretched over dirt that would quickly become a sea of mud in the rain.

Everywhere he looked were horses and wagons, or horses and carriages, or horses saddled and hitched. Too many horses for authenticity. Too many carriages and wagons to add flavor. He wondered if there was a religious group like the Amish nearby who refused to keep up with technology, but he knew he would have heard about them.

They passed a saloon, then another. Up ahead was a wide street, with the town's tallest buildings hunched beside it. He paused at the intersection and looked to his left, then his right.

This was a working town. There were a couple of hotels, a restaurant, a laundry. People hurried about their business. A wagon full of goods had pulled up in front of a mercantile. Young men in shirtsleeves, aprons, and hats unloaded the goods.

"Where are the tourists?" Courtney asked as she reined her horse in next to his. "Everyone is in costume." She fingered the long braid hanging down her back and leaned close. "People are staring at me."

She was right. Matt should have noticed that sooner. Nearly everyone around them stopped and stared at her.

Their gazes flickered over him, then dismissed him, but she was interesting. So she had to be different. How?

He studied his wife. Her Stetson was pale, the color of a fawn's belly. It was obviously new, but that wasn't too unusual. Her sheepskin-lined coat was also light-colored and purchased for the trip. So she looked like a greenhorn. But he didn't see practiced amusement on the faces around them. He saw shock.

"Maybe it's because you're so pretty," he said, not able to figure it out.

"Oh, yeah, right. That's it." She shook her head. "Pick a hotel. Any hotel. I can't wait to get off this horse."

He motioned to the largest one, about a hundred yards up the street. "We'll get a room, then I'll find a stable."

"Fine." She shifted on her saddle and winced. "Maybe there'll be something on the news about the storm. We can't be the only people who noticed it."

Matt tied Jasper to the hitching post in front of the three-story hotel. There was another horse there already. He touched the old-fashioned saddle before circling around to help Courtney dismount.

"You're going to be sore," he told her as he tied her horse to the railing.

"You know, I already figured that out." She swung her right leg over the horse and down toward the ground. Before she could slip her left foot free of the stirrup, her knee buckled. Matt caught her under the arms.

She staggered a step, then steadied herself against the horse. "I'm fine."

He didn't want to let her go. He was close enough to inhale the scent of her body and the sweet smell of her floral shampoo. They mingled with the heady aroma of her perfume. For as long as he lived, that unique combination would remind him of Courtney.

Finally he stepped back. She led the way into the hotel. Inside, lanterns hung from hooks in the cross-beams and glowed from small tables. Matt sniffed. Kerosene lamps. He glanced around at the walls and floorboards. He didn't see any electrical outlets at all.

There were three men sitting in the lobby, reading newspapers. A long desk stretched across one side of the room. Behind it, cubbyholes held keys. The man at the desk was tall, with long sideburns. His white shirt looked starched, as did his collar. His gaze flickered over Courtney, then his mouth straightened in disapproval.

"May I help you?" he asked.

Courtney slipped her backpack off her shoulders and set it in front of her. "You sure can. We want a room. Something with a nice big tub. Oh, a fireplace would be nice." She unbuckled the backpack and dug around for a moment. "Is there room service? We're starving."

She pulled out her wallet, then handed the man her American Express card. "Did anyone here notice a really weird storm a few hours ago? Violet sky with a kind of turquoise tornado?"

The desk clerk stared at the card, then at her. "Madam, what do you expect me to do with this?"

Matt's feeling of uneasiness grew. He walked toward one of the small tables by the front door. The three men had abandoned their reading and were watching the drama unfolding at the registration desk.

"I'm checking in," Courtney said, starting to sound frustrated.

"Rooms here are eight dollars a week. A bath is a dollar extra. The dining room opens in fifteen minutes. However"—he stared disdainfully at her jeans—"*you* can't go in without being properly dressed."

She obviously couldn't believe what she was hearing. "This is hardly a five-star place with a dress code." She glared at the man behind the counter. "This is a joke, right? You want me to wear a dress and you're only charging eight dollars for the room. Sure. Are you crazy? I mean I know this is a small town and all, but—" She turned to him. "Matt, what's going on?"

He didn't answer. He stared at the man closest to him, then reached for his newspaper. "Excuse me, sir. May I look at this for a moment?"

"What? Oh, certainly." The man handed it to him.

Matt straightened the sheets of newsprint and looked at the front page. "Courtney, come here."

"Can you believe this? They won't let women in the dining room in jeans. This is Wyoming, for God's sake. All cowboys wear jeans. But not a woman." She stepped toward him, then glanced at the clerk. "We are still in Wyoming, right?"

"Yes, madame. Cheyenne."

"Cheyenne? As in the city of? No way. I mean, what happened to everything? Matt? Do you know what's going on?" Her hazel eyes were wide with confusion and the beginnings of fear.

"No. But maybe you'd better take a look at this." He looked at the clerk. "Is it today's paper?"

"Of course, sir. We keep current." He was still holding Courtney's American Express card, turning the small piece of plastic over and over in his hands as if he'd never seen anything like it before.

He probably hadn't.

"Is the storm mentioned in the paper?" she asked, then frowned. "This isn't today's paper. I read it with breakfast. It didn't look anything like this."

"Read the date," he told her, then pointed to the line at the top of the sheet.

May 10, 1873.

2

"*It's a joke,*" *Courtney said,* staring at the date on the newspaper. "It has to be. It adds flavor. You know, like the horses did."

Her voice was calm. That pleased her because deep inside her chest, the urge to shriek was growing stronger and stronger.

Matt didn't say anything. She forced herself to look at his dark blue eyes and the unreadable expression on his face.

"You can't believe this is real," she insisted. "This is a reenactment village. These people are paid performers."

"There are too many horses," he said.

"What? How can there be too many horses?"

"You only need one or two for authenticity, but we saw dozens. Look at the lamps, at their clothes." He turned to the clerk, who was staring at them as if they'd just been released from a mental institution. "Do you have a phone? Or electricity? Television?"

The man's bushy eyebrows drew together. "I think

you two had better leave. We don't want your kind here."

Courtney snatched back her American Express card and waved it. "You know what this is, right? Right?"

"Never seen anything like it before in my life." He was curious despite his snooty behavior. "What's it for?"

"This can't be happening," she mumbled. "It doesn't make sense."

"It makes just as much sense as being abducted by aliens," Matt told her.

"But I was *kidding* when I said that. I swear I was."

She could feel the panic flaring inside. Her chest tightened and she was having trouble breathing.

"Come on," Matt said, heading for the door. "We'll figure something out."

Courtney snatched up her wallet and backpack. She tucked her credit card into her jeans' pocket. On her way out, she noticed that all three men sitting in the lobby were wearing old-fashioned suits with hats. The floor was scarred; the old stove in the corner actually produced heat.

She caught up with her husband. "I don't like this one bit. Why was that man so strange? Okay, if they want to be authentic, that's fine, but why would he pretend he didn't know what my credit card was? That's going to lose them a lot of business."

"Maybe he wasn't pretending."

"You can't believe that. Are you telling me this really *is* 1873?"

He didn't answer.

Courtney had to hurry to keep up with Matt's long-legged strides. He crossed the dirt road at an angle, heading to the mercantile. The sun had fallen behind the mountains and the small town was in shadow. There were a few dim lights from storefront windows, but no streetlights. The temperature had dropped considerably. She stumbled over something steamy and damp in the middle of the street but didn't stop to investigate. She didn't want to know what it was.

When they reached the wooden building, Matt pushed open the front door. A bell tinkled.

"Next you'll be telling me every time a bell rings an angel really does get its wings."

She wasn't surprised when he chose to ignore her.

The proprietor looked up as they entered. He was an older man, with a pair of glasses settled halfway down his nose. A white apron covered most of his clothing.

"'Evening, folks," he said pleasantly. "How may I help you?"

"We've been traveling for a few days," Matt said. "Could you tell us the date?"

"It's May tenth."

"1873?"

The man smiled. "It's been that long, has it? Yup, still '73."

"How long have you been in Cheyenne?"

"Oh, about five or six years, now. I grew up north of here, at Fort Laramie. My family was traveling west to Oregon, but my pa got sick and died, so Ma settled us there."

Courtney moved away from the two men and their conversation. So the store clerk had learned his lines. She wasn't impressed. She hadn't liked history in high school or college and she still didn't like it. Old things were just that—old.

She glanced around the store. It was a jumble of merchandise. The smells combined into an overwhelming perfume of spices and brine, tobacco and fish. A big stove sat in one corner and she instinctively moved toward it for heat. They sure kept the temperature of the building authentic for the time. She stuffed her wallet into her backpack and slung the leather bag onto her shoulders.

Against the closest wall were bolts of fabric, stacks of dishes, and gardening and farming tools, most of which she couldn't identify. Down the center of the store were several display cases. Under one of them was a coffin. She shuddered.

She could see barrels of food, tins stacked past her head, glass jars filled with odd-looking lumps and leaves. There were Bibles, books, playing cards, kegs of nails, wooden tubs, buckets, institutional-sized crocks. On the counter in the back were jars stuffed with striped candy.

"Who buys all this stuff?" she wondered aloud. Matt was still busy with the store owner, so he didn't answer.

The heat from the stove seeped into her clothing and warmed her. She could still feel the flickering of panic, but it wasn't as strong as it had been. Okay, something weird had happened. She was willing to concede that. Maybe they'd stumbled into some secret cult that worshiped all things old. But there was no way she was going to believe they'd actually gone back in time.

Her stomach growled. She glanced around but didn't really see anything she would risk eating. All the foodstuffs were so raw looking. She'd never understood the appeal of natural food. Her idea of a perfect meal was anything she didn't have to cook herself.

"Thanks," Matt said to the store owner as he walked toward her. "Let's go."

"Where are we going?" she asked, allowing him to take her arm and lead her outside. "What did you find out?"

It was dark back on the street. Feeble light spilled out of the glass windows, but didn't illuminate more than a few feet of darkness. Once the store's door had closed behind them, Matt turned and placed his hands on her shoulders.

"I think this is real," he said slowly. "I think we're really in 1873. I can't tell you how it happened, or why, or even how we're going to get back, but I believe we're here and we're going to have to find a way to survive."

She wasn't sure which shocked her more: his words or the length of his sentences. "Something hit you on the head. Are you dizzy? How many fingers am I holding up?"

He ignored her raised hand. "Listen to me, Courtney. That man didn't know anything about electricity or credit cards. Did you see how much inventory was in that store? It's not for show, it's real. The reason people have been staring at you is that you're a woman wearing jeans. You should be in a dress."

She stepped back from him and folded her arms over her chest. The temperature was dropping, and her breath came out in puffs of fog.

"If I'd been in a dress I would have shocked them more. I don't think something that ends just above the knee is what they had in mind."

"You've got a point."

She glared at him. "What is wrong with you? I was kidding. Making a joke. You know—humor. Damn it, Matt, we're not in the past. There's some logical explanation for what's happened here." She could feel the first hint of burning at the back of her eyes, but she refused to give in. "I just want to get to Cheyenne. I don't care how. I want something to eat and a hot bath. If this is all some elaborate trick to make me forget the divorce papers, then you've gone to a lot of trouble for nothing."

His face was in shadow so she couldn't tell what he was thinking. Not that she would be able to anyway. He was an expert at keeping his thoughts hidden. He loomed large above her, his masculine body dwarfing her and making her feel both intimidated and protected.

"If we had money, we could check into a hotel," he said.

"I've got cash." She started to slide off her backpack. "At least enough for a couple of nights."

"I've got cash, too, but it won't help. We can't use it here."

"Why not?"

When he didn't answer, the fear returned, and with it a sense of being helpless. "Don't do this to me," she said softly. "Please, Matt, if you're punishing me, please stop. I can't handle this much longer. Everything is strange enough without you acting crazy."

He moved closer to her. He removed his Stetson and the faint light from the store illuminated his face. His mouth twisted downward. "You think I want to believe what's happening? I'm just as confused as you are. Nothing makes sense. I can't say how or why, but as near as I can tell this is 1873."

She drew in a deep breath and stomped her foot on the dirt. "Stop talking like that."

"What else do you want me to do?"

"Make it all go away."

He pulled off his glove and touched her check with his hand. His fingers were warm and familiar. "I'm scared, too."

It was all she needed to hear. She rushed toward him and wrapped her arms around his waist. Through his bulky coat, she felt the hard planes of his body. She knew this man, trusted him. She might not want to be married to him, but that didn't mean she didn't still like and respect him.

He pushed her hat aside and stroked her hair. She wished his coat were unbuttoned so she could hear his heartbeat, but she contented herself with listening to his steady breathing.

"Swear to me you didn't plan this," she said.

"You have my word."

He was an old-fashioned gentleman, someone who honored a promise, no matter the price. She would risk her life on his word. She shuddered.

"I don't want this to be real," she said, afraid to look up and see the authentic wooden buildings.

"I know." He touched a finger to her chin, urging her to meet his gaze.

She raised her head reluctantly. The mercantile still loomed behind them.

"Are you wearing your gold chain?" he asked.

"Yes, of course. Why?" The necklace had been her first Christmas present from him. The thick individual links locked together in an intricate pattern. The chain was a quarter-inch wide and at the time, she'd been afraid he'd spent far too much on the gift.

"It's solid gold. We can use it for money."

She drew back and placed her hand on her throat, as if protecting the necklace. "You want to barter my jewelry?"

"Just a piece of it. If I cut a couple of links off—"

"Cut it? Are you crazy?"

"You'll get the links back."

"How? You think the hotel is going to return them in the morning?"

"I'm going to use them as my stake in a poker game."

Her hat threatened to slip off. She grabbed it and stared at him. The laughter started low in her belly. She drew in a breath and let it out. Her amusement sounded loud in the still night. She laughed until she could barely stand and had to lean against the rough side of the mercantile.

"You about done?" Matt asked.

"A poker game? Be serious. This isn't another

remake of *Maverick*. You seriously expect me to believe you're going to walk into the nearest saloon, put down part of my necklace, and walk away with a fortune?"

"Not a fortune. Just enough to get us a hotel room and some food."

"Why not just sell the necklace?"

"In a poker game I can win back the stake. We might need it later."

Besides, Matt wanted her always to have the necklace. It had cost him nearly a quarter of his winnings that year, but it had been worth it to see the look on her face that Christmas morning.

She stared at him. Her face was in shadow, but he sensed her mistrust. She still thought he was playing some kind of trick on her. Or that he knew something and was holding back. If only that were true. Instead he was just as concerned as she was—with one large difference. He *believed* they had gone back in time.

He glanced around the now-dark town. He'd seen plenty of reenactment villages before. They were usually small, one or two blocks of refurbished buildings with people in period costume. This town went on for blocks. As he'd already noticed, there were too many horses. There was also a lack of tourists.

None of the shops sold burgers and sodas. There weren't stands of "authentic" crafts. The displays in the mercantile had been practical, not educational. No souvenir shops.

He couldn't explain the silent tornado, the blinding white light, or the missing three hours. He could only do his best to help them survive.

Courtney shivered. "If we're going somewhere, then let's go now. Maybe it's warmer inside."

He led the way across the street. They collected their horses. He helped her mount up, noticing the way she winced when her fanny came in contact with the saddle. She wasn't much of a rider and he knew she had to be hurting bad. Instantly his mind was filled with the image of easing her pain. His hands tingled at the thought of rubbing warm oil into her aching muscles. He could see her smooth, pale skin and feel the taut curves of her buttocks and thighs. In a matter of seconds, his hands weren't the only part of him tingling.

There was a time he would have offered a rubdown and she would have accepted. The slow, sensual massage would have turned into something else, something hot and smoky as their bodies moved with the fiery passion he'd never experienced with anyone else. But not anymore. In the last few months things had changed. They hadn't slept together since the holidays. Of course they hadn't seen much of each other, either. And now Courtney wanted a divorce.

He refused to think about that. They had more immediate problems—like how to get enough money to get them a room and some food.

He swung into his saddle and urged Jasper down the street. The lack of streetlights reduced everything to shadow. Most of the businesses were dark, making the ones that were still open shine brightly in the dimness. They passed several saloons before he found one he liked the look of. It was big enough; they could blend in. Even from the street, he could hear the laughter of the crowd.

There were several horses and a couple of wagons parked out front. Matt smiled slightly. *Parked* probably wasn't the right word.

"We're stopping here?" she asked as he reined Jasper to a stop and stepped out of the saddle.

"Yeah."

"Ah, you're back to your monosyllabic answers. The aliens have left your being."

She waited until he'd tied his gelding, then she slid down into his waiting arms. She sagged against him briefly, as if she didn't have the energy to stand. She smelled of horse and leather, and sweetly of herself.

Her perfume was a floral scent, more nighttime sin than daytime innocence. She had it made to order in some little shop by the beach. She'd taken him there once on one of his rare visits to her world. She'd wanted him to pick a scent for himself, but he hadn't been interested. But he'd snatched one of their business cards when she wasn't looking and later had called the store and asked them to send him a small bottle of her perfume. When the nights got too lonely, he would pull it out of his shaving kit and inhale her fragrance. For that moment, she would be with him and he wouldn't be so alone.

"From what I remember of history," he said, pulling off her hat and reaching for her long, blond braid, "women don't spend much time in saloons."

"Except dancing girls and hookers."

"Something like that."

"What are you doing?"

He grabbed the back of her coat and pulled it away from her neck, then dropped her braid under the heavy garment. "Disguising you. Keep your coat buttoned and your head down."

"So I'll pass for a man?"

"That's not likely, but maybe no one will bother to look too closely."

"Terrific."

He bent down and grabbed a handful of dirt. "Close your eyes."

"Oh, no. You're not putting that on me." She tried to back up but her rental horse was behind her.

"You're too pretty and you smell too good. I'm not armed. I don't want to have to fight for you."

She glanced up at him and he had to bite back a groan. Even in the half-light from the saloon, he could see the perfection of her features. She had wide cheekbones and big eyes. The corners of her mouth tilted up slightly, as if she was about to do something bad enough to drive a man to his knees . . . or to paradise.

"You'd fight for me?" she asked.

He nodded, then started smoothing dirt on her cheeks. She tilted her head and studied him.

"I should be appalled, but I'm not. In fact, it's kind of exciting."

"Courtney." He growled her name. "We don't have time for this right now. I'd rather leave you out here, but I don't know how dangerous it is. So keep your head down and keep quiet."

"If I really can pass as a man, what do I do if one of the women comes on to me?"

"Tell her you don't have any money." He dusted a streak of dirt down her small nose, then stepped back and brushed his gloved hands together. "Ready?"

"I guess. Oh, wait. You forgot the most important part." She reached up behind her neck and fumbled with her necklace. After swearing under her breath, she pulled one of her gloves off with her teeth, then unfastened the catch. "Here." She held out the chain.

The gold shimmered in the darkness. He remembered how beautiful it had looked on her bare skin that Christmas morning. How she'd worn the chain and nothing else. He closed his hands tightly, wishing the links were sharp enough to cut through his gloves and hands, so the physical pain could distract him from the aching in his heart.

He pulled a penknife out of his pocket and pried several links apart. They fell into his palm like pieces of a puzzle. He clicked the knife closed.

"Let's go," he said, heading for the saloon.

The noise assaulted them even before they stepped inside. Tinny music, laughter, drunken shouts, calls from faro tables and card games. Empty glasses thumped on the long wooden bar and patrons called for more liquor.

Matt paused and blinked at the surprisingly bright light. Chandeliers hung from a beamed ceiling. There were lamps behind the bar and on all the walls. Tables filled the center of the large room, with a stage on the left and the gambling area on the right.

Men outnumbered women about twenty-five to one, but the hostesses, or whatever they were, made a brave show of circulating through the room. They wore their hair piled high on their heads. Low-cut dresses offered a view of their cleavage, and ruffled skirts were pulled nearly to their knees. Matt wondered how scandalous that was and could only imagine what Courtney was making of all this.

She stood directly behind him. With the stench of unwashed bodies, tobacco, and spilled liquor he couldn't smell her anymore, but he sensed her presence.

They stood there for a couple of minutes. He tried to take everything in. His hat was shaped differently, as was the cut of his coat. Most men were wearing dusters, while his lined jacket ended at his hips. The other men wore wool trousers; he and Courtney were in jeans. But the differences were subtle and someone not looking for them might not even notice.

"Can I help you?"

He stared at the petite brunette who sashayed to a stop in front of him.

"You're new around here, aren't you? I never forget a face."

"Ma'am." He tipped his hat. "We are new to these parts."

The woman glanced at Courtney. A frown drew her delicate eyebrows together as she studied his wife.

He put his hand on the woman's bare arm to draw her attention back to him. "We're a little short on cash, although we've got a bit of gold. I thought I might try my hand at some poker."

She moved close and smiled. Her brown eyes softened with promises. "How much gold, darlin'? I'm expensive, but I don't get any complaints."

"Let me parlay my stake into something worthwhile, then we'll talk."

She leaned close enough to brush his upper arm with her breasts. "My name's Marie, darlin', and we'll do much more than talk." She pointed to a round table at the end of the saloon. "Jonathan Hastings runs a fair game, though he's lucky more often than not." Her smile widened. "Of course, this time, I'll be offering a little prayer that you're even luckier."

Matt could feel Courtney stiffening behind him. He gave Marie a little push to send her on her way. She blew him a kiss, then moved off slowly, her hips swaying seductively.

"That woman's a tramp," Courtney whispered, her voice low and angry. "I can't believe you fell for that act. She's probably got diseases we haven't even heard of. Need I remind you that if you're right and this is 1873, there isn't any penicillin?"

"I'll keep that in mind."

He started to make his way around the tables. Cigar smoke swirled through the room. There were little details he would never have thought of. Spittoons arranged strategically, with stained flooring to attest to a certain lack of aim. Bowls of pickled eggs circulated among the patrons. Whiskey wasn't the only thing people drank, although it was strange not to see familiar bottles of beer or have a game of some kind blaring from a television mounted near the ceiling.

At the far end of the room, there was a round table

that seated eight. Currently six men were playing cards. The dealer, a dark-haired man in a white shirt and tapestry vest, worked the cards with the skill of a professional.

"If you run off with Marie, I'm taking up with that gambler," Courtney whispered, nodding at the dealer.

"You do that. I'm sure he took a bath sometime in the last month or so."

Even with her hat pulled low over her forehead, he could see the humor dancing in her eyes. She'd pulled up the collar of her jacket to hide the length of braid slipping down her back. Even with the dirt smudging her cheeks and her jeans, no one who bothered to look closely would mistake her for anything other than what she was: a beautiful woman.

"Stay against that wall there. Don't say or do anything to call attention to yourself."

"But I'm hungry and thirsty."

"As soon as I win some money, I'll take us back to the hotel and get us some food."

"What if you lose?" she grumbled, but didn't bother waiting for an answer. She stepped back into the shadows and tugged on the brim of her hat. If she pulled it any lower, she wouldn't be able to see where she was going.

Matt returned his attention to the card game. An oil lamp hung above the center of the table and illuminated the players. Except for the dealer, all the men had full beards that looked as if they hadn't seen a trim in several years. Dirty fingers held cards close to jacketed chests.

The dealer glanced up at him. "'Evening."

"You Hastings?"

The gambler smiled. "That's right. You and your friend want to join us? We're playing a little poker here. Nice and friendly."

"My friend's not lucky with cards, but I don't mind sitting in."

He chose the empty seat across from the gambler, then reached into his pocket and pulled out three links of the necklace. Jonathan Hastings reached for one of them.

Unlike the other men, his hands were clean, his nails trimmed. "May I?" he asked, then picked up the link. He turned it over, then tested the gold with the edge of a small knife resting by the peel and core of an apple. "Very nice, although I've never seen workmanship like this before. Where did you get it?"

"California," Matt said, remembering the elegant jewelry store in an exclusive section of town.

Hastings balanced the link in the palm of his hand, then collected several wooden chips from the pile in front of him and passed them over. Matt didn't touch them. Hastings smiled again and passed over six more.

"That's my final offer," the gambler said.

Matt nodded. Each of the seven men anted up a chip. While Hastings dealt, Matt fingered an intricately carved wood chip. The edges had been painted a bright green. He didn't know how much it was worth. A dollar? Five? Twenty? He'd always been able to catch on to games quickly and he'd always been lucky. Unless changing times had affected that.

He picked up the five cards he'd been dealt and was pleased to see they were using a regular deck. The kings and queens looked a little different, but he knew what they were supposed to be. He was so busy being relieved, he almost didn't notice he was one card away from a full house.

"I'm in," the man to the right of the gambler said, and tossed in a green chip. When it was his turn, Matt tossed one in as well. His luck hadn't deserted him after all. Now if only it would last.

* * *

Courtney had never understood the thrill of playing cards. She thought it was boring, especially when she was cold, tired, and hungry. About an hour into Matt's game, when her feet were sore and her back was killing her, the players at the next table stood up and left. She dragged one of their wooden chairs into her little corner, sat down, and settled her backpack on the floor by her feet.

It helped some, but not enough. She was still tired and hungry. Every few minutes her stomach sent up a growl of protest. She was getting light-headed. She leaned her head against the wall and tried to doze, but the loud sounds of bad piano music, laughter, and conversation kept her awake. Not to mention the smells.

If she pulled the edge of her jacket collar over her face and drew in shallow breaths, she could avoid the worst of the stink in the room. It was a nasty combination of damp wood, unwashed bodies, liquor, and horse manure. There was an unattractive green stain on her new boots and she didn't want to think about how it had gotten there.

Her eyes drifted closed and she tried to shut out the noise. As she relaxed, her elbow slipped off the arm of the chair and slammed into the wall. A jolt of pain shot up her arm. She straightened in the chair and sighed.

How much longer was he going to play poker? Courtney stared at Matt, willing him to remember she was there. Her gaze lowered to the table and she felt her eyes widen. She must have dozed off for longer than she'd thought. There was a large pile of chips in front of him. An even bigger pile was in the center of the table and they were down to four players.

A ratty-looking man whose dirty blond hair stuck out from under a dark sombrero laid a piece of paper on the table. He said something Courtney couldn't hear. She leaned forward, straining to catch the words exchanged. There was something that sounded like cattle. The other three men nodded. Courtney bit back a groan. Perfect. What exactly were they going to do with a cow? Use it for milk?

She had to turn away to hide her laughter. When she glanced back, the dealer was staring at her. His eyes were so dark, they were nearly black. He had hawkish features and looked very dangerous.

She hadn't known she was still smiling until she felt her lips straighten. She looked away quickly and spent the next several minutes staring at the wooden floor. She counted scars and pits and tried to imagine the origin of some of the more colorful stains. Only when she heard the words, "You're a lucky man," did she risk glancing up again.

Matt was raking in the pot. The gambler had done well, although not as well as Matt. Matt handed over his chips and got bills and coins in return. The other two men got up, grumbling.

The gambler rose to his feet and started toward her. Courtney didn't know what to do.

"Good evening," the man said. "Your friend was very successful."

She didn't dare speak. She might be able to keep her hat pulled low, but there was no way she was going to *sound* like a man.

"My name is Jonathan Hastings."

Courtney stared at her lap.

"I believe this is yours." His hand came into her field of vision. In the center of his palm was a link from her chain. "I'd like you to have it back."

"Why?"

"Because it's as beautiful as its owner."

Before she could stop herself, she instinctively

glanced up. "I thought as much," he said, as his gaze searched her face. "Your friend is lucky in more than gambling. But he should dress you in silks, not try to pass you off as a man."

"We've been traveling," she said softly.

"I hope you'll stay here for a time."

"I don't know what we're going to do."

The handsome gambler reached for her bare hand. He dropped the link onto her palm, then closed her fingers around it. "What's your name?"

His touch was warm and confident, but it didn't send shivers up her spine. She glanced at Matt, who was deep in conversation with the blond man wearing the sombrero. They seemed to be making a deal of some kind. She hoped it involved food.

"Mr. Hastings, I'm married."

The gambler's mouth straightened with disappointment. "A great loss to all of us, if you don't mind me saying so." He brought her free hand to his mouth and softly kissed the back of her fingers. "I hope to see you again."

She watched him walk away. Men were certainly more gallant in this century. Not that she was willing to believe Matt's insane theory that they really were back in 1873. She was still sure there was another logical explanation for everything that was going on.

She fought back a yawn, then rose to her feet. Matt and the other men were still deep in conversation. Then, as she stared on in horror and before she had a chance to do more than suck in a breath, he handed over nearly a third of his winnings. The man with the sombrero grinned broadly and left.

"What do you think you're doing?" she asked when she could breathe again. "You just *gave* that man our money?"

Matt walked over and caught her up in his arms. He

swung her around in a circle, then set her back on her feet. She grabbed at her hat to keep it from falling.

"I won," he said, fanning out the bills with one hand and jingling the coins with the other. "Over two hundred dollars. Do you know how much money that is in this time?"

"Don't start that back-in-time stuff with me, and don't try to change the subject. Why did you give that man our money?"

Matt grinned. His eyes brightened as if lit by an inner fire. She'd only seen him look that happy twice before in their married life. The first time was when she accepted his proposal and the second had been when she'd thought she might be pregnant. The light had died when it turned out she was just late.

"I bought a ranch," he said.

She opened her mouth, but no words came out. All the blood rushed to her head. She heard a buzzing sound, then the room began to spin as the blood drained away. He was still talking.

". . . cattle coming north. It's one of the first herds. Do you know what this means?"

"Huh?"

"The late 1870s and early 1880s were the prime era of the cattle baron. With this herd"—he waved a sheet of paper excitedly—"we now own two thousand longhorns. I bet there's plenty of cattle here already. Ones that people took West. Herefords or Durhams. We can crossbreed them. Make our fortunes."

"You bought a ranch?"

"Where else would we put the cattle? Besides, it's got a ranch house. We need a place to stay."

"You bought a ranch?"

"You asked that already. What's wrong?"

She noticed they were collecting a crowd. Several people at nearby tables had stopped to listen. Marie, the resident slut, had caught sight of Matt's wad of money and was sashaying her way over, no doubt to make good on her promise of a shared evening.

"Let me see if I've got this straight," Courtney said, poking her finger into Matt's chest with each sentence. "You won a lot of money and some cattle who are probably in Texas and never leaving Texas, then you turned around and used that money—all that's between us and starvation—to buy a ranch. Is that correct?"

"I didn't use all the money. Come on, Courtney. Don't you see how great this is? We're going to get rich."

"I'd rather get home. Is there at least enough for a hotel for the night?"

"Sure. The man said it was eight dollars a week, plus a dollar for a bath."

"Fine." She plucked a ten-dollar bill from his hand and started to walk out of the saloon. Matt trailed behind. She knew she'd hurt his feelings, but she didn't care. He was insane. Buying a ranch for Texas longhorns. It was ridiculous.

When she reached the door, Matt grabbed her arm. "You don't understand."

"I understand perfectly. Someone in your past, a great-great—I don't know how many greats— grandfather was named Jack, wasn't he? His idea of a good time was selling his cow for a few magic beans. Well, Jack, have a great time battling your giant or with your cattle, but I don't want any part of it."

3

Courtney pulled the quilt up over her shoulders and snuggled deeper into the soft mattress. Its contents shifted to accommodate her body. From the tips of her toes to the top of her head she was toasty warm.

She knew it was morning. She could see the light, even with her eyes closed. She didn't know what time it was and she didn't care. She wasn't going to get up until she was good and ready. After all, she was on vacation.

A flicker of memory stirred, but she pushed it away. She didn't want to deal with reality. She knew she was on vacation because the bed was strange and the scent of the room was different from her condo. There she could inhale the smell of the Pacific Ocean, some potpourri she kept on her dresser, and a pleasant comingling of her perfumes.

This combination of scents was interesting. Woodsmoke from a nearby fireplace. Coffee. Mildew—

a smell she wouldn't have minded missing. From the street outside the window she heard bits of conversation and the whinny of a horse.

A horse?

Courtney's eyes snapped open, then she groaned out loud. It hadn't been a dream, or if it was, it hadn't gone away yet. She was still here. Caught in some weird time-displacement nightmare that had put her smack in the middle of 1873.

The room was much as she remembered it from the night before. In the light of a lantern, she'd caught the shapes of large pieces of furniture, the faded fabric of the drapes at the window, and the puffy feather mattress in the middle of the too-high bed. In the light of day she could see the drapes weren't really faded. The pattern was muted, as was the wallpaper. And the print there wasn't exactly even, as if it had been done on a faulty machine. Assuming one printed patterns on wallpaper by machine. For all she knew, in 1873 they imported small children from foreign lands and set them to work coloring the strips of paper by hand.

She pushed aside the quilt and sat up slowly. The mattress hadn't been what she was used to but it was very comfortable. She'd slept well. Her clothes were wrinkled, but she hadn't been too sure about the sanitary requirements of hotels and had preferred not to risk her bare skin. Now she smoothed her blouse, then stood up and stretched.

Her stomach growled. By the time she and Matt had made their way to the hotel last night, the dining room had been closed. They'd managed to scare up some bread, but it hadn't been enough. She hadn't had a decent meal since breakfast yesterday. Or was that breakfast a hundred and twenty-something years from now?

"Oh, Lord, this is too complicated for me."

She moved to the window and pushed aside the drapes. The morning was bright, the sky a brilliant shade of blue. She squinted down at the people moving along the edges of the dirt street. Everyone was in costume. The women wore long dresses and bonnets. The men had on ridiculous tall hats or sombreros. A few were wearing what she guessed to be an early style of cowboy hat, but it was too round and not very attractive. She thought of her own pale Stetson purchased especially for her trip to Wyoming, then turned to glance at her pitiful piece of luggage sitting by the dresser. All that she owned in the world was in her leather backpack. If they didn't find their way back to their century soon, she was going to run out of some things very quickly.

She crossed to a pitcher and basin. They were as close to a bathroom as she was going to get in this small room. She splashed water on her face, then brushed her teeth. The small mirror on the wall showed her that her braid was coming undone. She pulled off the rubber band, then finger-combed the strands. When her hair was loose on her shoulders, she dug around in her backpack for a brush. Five minutes later the worst of the tangles were gone and she was expertly weaving a tight French braid. It hung down to the center of her back. When she was done, she tossed the brush back in the pack, then pulled the quilt over the now-lumpy mattress.

That finished, she glanced around the room. It was small, with only the single bed, dresser, and fireplace to furnish it. There wasn't even a chair to sit on. She wondered if Matt's room was any different. The clerk had handed them two keys and she'd grabbed one without saying a word to anyone.

Courtney sat on the bed and sighed. Okay, maybe she'd acted like a bitch, but what had he been thinking of? Buying a ranch was insane. They weren't staying here. As soon as the storm came back, they could return to their time.

Or could they? Was this even real? And if it was . . .

Before she could try and figure out the logistics of time travel, there was a knock on the door. She crossed the hardwood floor in two steps.

"Who is it?" she asked.

"Matt. I've got breakfast."

Her stomach gave a mighty growl. "Good, I'm starved." She opened the door and glanced at her husband.

Matt looked rested. There weren't any dark circles under his eyes. He'd shaved, too. Her fingers itched to trace the smooth line of his strong jaw. As always, his handsome features took her breath away. No one man had the right to be so attractive. It gave him an unfair advantage in the world. Whenever they were together she felt other women staring at them, judging her, wondering how she'd gotten so lucky.

She didn't have the answer to that question. Every time she saw him after being away from him for a few days or weeks, she was startled by his good looks. In the time they were apart, she managed to convince herself she simply imagined his attractiveness. But it was real. To this day, she didn't know why he'd wanted to marry her. For a while she'd been flattered, then curious, then sad. The latter emotion came from the knowledge that it was never going to work out.

"They won't let you in the dining room," he said and motioned to an open door a few feet down the hall. "I brought you a tray. It's in my room."

"Thanks." She stepped in front of him and moved toward the door. "Wow, this is huge," she said as she walked into his bedroom.

He had the same too-high four-poster bed and a long

dresser with a basin and pitcher. But in front of his much larger fireplace were two chairs and a small table. She made a beeline for the tray sitting on the table and moaned as she inhaled the scent of fresh coffee, eggs, and biscuits.

"I'm starved," she said, grabbing one of the biscuits and taking a bite. It was fluffy and still warm. As she poured coffee from the small pot into a cup, she finished the first biscuit and reached for another. "These are great. They taste like they're homemade." She glanced at him and grinned. "I guess they are, huh?"

"Yeah."

She took a seat and motioned to the other chair. "Did you eat yet?"

"Downstairs." He sat. "I figured you'd still be sleeping."

"I only woke up a half hour ago," she said, and glanced at her watch. It was barely after eight. She took a sip of coffee and grimaced. It tasted stronger than she was used to, bitter, almost raw. "I suppose chocolate shavings are out of the question."

Matt smiled.

Her heart fluttered a little at the sight. Her toes curled inside her new boots. Dammit, he'd always been able to do that to her. One smile and she melted. It wasn't fair.

"We need to discuss our options," he said.

"What options? Are you sure this is real?"

"Aren't you?"

Instead of answering, she started in on the eggs. They tasted about the same as she was used to. Not that she ate many eggs. She usually grabbed a bagel and coffee at the deli around the corner from her office. Lunch was often a salad and a sandwich or cup of soup sent up from the little cafe across the street. Occasionally she went out with coworkers, but not often.

Sitting here in front of a fireplace that was actually

burning coal, using a fork that was obviously silver and not some cheap flatware, glancing around at antique furniture complete with feather mattresses, she wasn't sure she believed.

"I haven't decided what is real," she said at last.

"Your lack of acceptance doesn't change the truth."

"Which is?"

"It's 1873 and we're going to have to deal with that."

"I have a tremendous ability to delude myself, Matt. I might decide to pretend this is just a dream."

She was teasing. Matt could see it in the way her eyes crinkled slightly at the corners as if she was fighting a smile. A shaft of sunlight filtered in through the window and angled across the room. It highlighted the side of Courtney's face, turning her skin to porcelain and her hair to white gold. He knew every inch of her body, yet he didn't know her at all. She'd complained yesterday that they didn't have a marriage, they had an ongoing affair. She was right. He couldn't predict how she would react to their present circumstances.

"I did hope it would all go away while I was sleeping," she admitted, then took another sip of her coffee.

"I didn't."

"Why? You *want* to be here?"

"I'm a cowboy. This is where I belong. There's a herd of two thousand longhorns coming north from Texas. Over the next ten years the price of beef is going to soar. With the railroad expanding, the cattle can get to market faster. There's a fortune to be made here. This is what I've always wanted. This is my chance."

"To do what? Smell bad and eat raw food?" She shook her head. "I just don't get it. Can't you do all this in the future? What's so exciting about being here? I mean, really. Did you use the bathroom last night? It's probably more frightening during the day."

Without thinking, he reached toward her. His fingers grazed her cheek. She wasn't wearing any makeup. Her skin was soft and warm.

"I've played cards before," he said. "But I've never been that lucky. I won the cattle and enough money to buy the ranch."

She leaned back in the wingback chair, moving her head away so he couldn't reach her. "Are you saying it was a sign or something?"

He didn't want to answer that. He wasn't sure. He didn't believe in signs. "I'm as confused as you are. I don't know how we got here or how to get back."

"We could go looking for that storm."

"Where?"

She set her coffee on the small table. The surface was inlaid with different shades of wood. They combined to make a checkerboard pattern.

"I don't know," she said. "You're the Boy Scout. How do you track a storm? Maybe we did something to call it to us. Maybe it was a magnetic freak of nature. If we re-create that moment—"

He didn't want to. He had cattle and a ranch. And he had Courtney. From the moment he'd proposed to her, he'd known that one day he would lose her. He'd been waiting for her to walk away, because a woman like her would never stay with a man like him. He'd been right. Those damn divorce papers were still in her backpack.

"I'm not sure I could find the exact spot," he said, lying to her for the first time in their marriage. "There isn't a trail anymore. Even if I could, who's to say it would help? Lightning never strikes twice in the same place."

"Some cowboy you turned out to be. Can't even find a little tornado." She picked up the last biscuit and took a bite. "You like it here, don't you?"

"I have everything I've ever wanted." Including her.

She rose to her feet and crossed to the window. She raised the glass and inhaled. "Oh my God. What is that stink?" She slammed the window down and turned to him. "Are they really going to make me wear a dress if I want to eat in the dining room?"

"That's what they told me."

"Sexist pigs." She rested her hands on her hips.

The action pulled her sweater tight across her breasts. He felt a stirring of desire. They hadn't made love in months. Of course they hadn't been together since the New Year. He wondered if she was ever tempted to stray when they were apart. He never was.

"Let me guess," she said. "You want to go to this ranch of yours and get ready for your cattle visitation."

"We're stuck here for now. We need to make the best of the situation. Staying at the ranch will give us time to figure out what we're going to do. We could ride out in the countryside and try to find the storm."

"When we find it, maybe I'll go back on my own and leave you here where you obviously belong." She shook her head. "I can't believe this is happening. You know, it probably isn't. It's probably like that television show and we'll wake up in the shower or something."

He wanted to ask if they were going to wake up in the shower together, but he didn't.

She sighed. "All right. The ranch can't be any worse than staying in town. At least there I can wear jeans without people refusing me service."

He stood slowly and reached for his hat on the dresser next to the water pitcher. "We're going to need supplies. I'll take care of that."

"Fine. I'll just read in my room. I have a book I started on the plane." She glanced over her shoulder toward the window and laughed. "Can you imagine what the locals would say if I tried to describe a plane? On second thought, never mind. I don't think I'd enjoy a visit to a mental hospital. They probably keep everybody chained and subdue them with electric shock therapy."

He walked toward the door. "I don't think so."

"Why not?"

"They don't have electricity yet."

Instead of smiling, she bit her lower lip. "I'm sorry," she murmured. "About . . . everything, I suppose. I'm scared. That's why I acted like a bitch last night. I didn't mean to call you Jack or say bad things about your family. I don't understand what's happened to us. I just want to go home." She squeezed her eyes shut.

He crossed the room in three long strides.

She stepped into his embrace and clung to him. "I'm being such a baby."

"You're very strong," he said. "Most people would have fallen apart."

"What do you think I'm doing right now? Clinging to you like a motherless monkey is hardly a sign of strength."

"We're going to be fine."

"Are we?" She tilted her head back and stared at him. Her hazel eyes darkened with questions. He could feel the heat of her. Her breasts flattened against his chest. He wanted to hold her forever and never let go.

The bottom of her braid brushed against the back of his hand. He fingered her hair. He wanted nothing more than to kiss her, make love to her. Instead he tugged on her braid once, then stepped away.

Circumstances had trapped him and Courtney in the past. They were together, but that didn't change anything. As soon as they returned to their time she would want her divorce. It was too late for them. It had probably always been too late.

"I'll see about the supplies," he said, and left.

*　　*　　*

Matt looked down the sights of the rifle. The barrel had been polished until it gleamed.

"That's new," Alfred, the owner of the mercantile, said proudly. The older man adjusted his glasses on his nose. "A Winchester 1873. Try the lever action. It's real smooth."

Matt did as he suggested. He couldn't believe he was holding a gun this old and it was brand-new. He felt like a kid in a candy store. "You got the cartridges?"

Alfred pointed to a shelf behind the counter. Dozens of small boxes were stacked neatly. "Take your pick."

Matt set down the rifle. "I'll take this one, and one just like it. And give me ten boxes of cartridges." There was no telling what kind of danger they might run into on their way to the ranch. At least Courtney knew how to shoot. He'd taught her when they'd had a week together in Texas.

"What else are you going to need?" Alfred asked.

Matt looked at the pile of foodstuffs already stacked by the door. There were hundred-pound bags of flour and sugar, a few ten-pound sacks of coffee, canned food, dried beef and fish, seeds for a garden, and some tools. "It's two days to the ranch," he said. "We're going to have to camp out."

Alfred's bushy gray eyebrows drew together. "I thought you'd been traveling. What happened to your supplies?"

When in doubt, tell the truth, Matt thought. "We lost everything in a tornado."

"Oh. I hadn't heard about one near here." He crossed the crowded store to the far side. From there he pulled down what looked like folded canvas and several blankets. "Oilcloth'll keep the damp from you. Here's blankets. You got a lamp?"

"No."

"Need at least one of those and some kerosene."

"Make it two."

Alfred smiled at him. "I just might close a little early today."

Before Matt could answer, the front door opened. The little bell attached to a string tinkled and announced Jonathan Hastings's arrival.

The gambler swept into the store, his long black duster flapping behind him. He was nearly as tall as Matt's six feet two. They both had dark hair, although the gambler wore his long, nearly to his shoulders.

The two men stared at each other. Matt had the feeling that Hastings had been looking for him. Alfred collected a coffeepot and said, "I'll start figuring your total."

Matt walked toward the gambler. Hastings paused in the middle of the store. He glanced at the pile of supplies. "You heading out today?"

Matt nodded.

"Is your wife going with you?"

"Yes."

Hastings grinned. "Aren't you going to ask how I knew?"

"It wasn't a very good disguise."

"It fooled plenty, but that's because we're not used to seeing a woman in trousers. You're not from around here, are you?"

"No." Matt picked up the rifle and rubbed the smooth barrel.

Hastings leaned against the counter, apparently unimpressed by the weapon. "What are you going to do with those cattle? Two thousand head coming from Texas? They're going to be a scrawny lot when they arrive. If they arrive."

"They'll get here," Matt said. "If not them, then others like them. Cattle's going to be big business here."

Hastings narrowed his gaze. "For a man who had to

use his wife's jewelry to ante up in a poker game, you sound mighty sure of yourself."

"I am."

Alfred glanced up from his column of figures. "I'm done with those bags, if you want to start loading up."

"Thanks." Matt put the rifle back on the counter and grabbed a hundred-pound bag of flour. He set it on his shoulder and started for the door. Hastings was right behind him balancing a sack of sugar.

"Most folks think it's pretty silly to drive cattle all that way," the gambler said. "Who's going to eat the beef?"

"People in the East." Matt lowered the sack into the back of the wagon he'd purchased. Hastings set his on top. They walked into the store together. "With the train service getting more regular, beef can get to where the population is. New York, Boston, places like that."

Hastings frowned. "What do you know about cities?"

"More than I want to."

"So what happens when the cattle arrive?"

Matt picked up a case of tinned tomatoes. Hastings did the same with the peaches. "Fatten 'em up. Breed them with whatever bulls I can find here. Herefords, Durhams. Longhorns are strong, but the meat is stringy. Combine the two and in a couple of generations you'll have the best beef known to man."

"You know cattle." It wasn't a question.

"Been around 'em all my life."

Hastings leaned against the wagon. "Two thousand head are a lot for one man to take care of on his own."

Matt hadn't thought that part through. Hastings was right. He'd need a dozen or so cowboys.

"What about barns, fences, a place for the men to sleep? How you going to feed them and pay them? I know what you won at the poker game last night."

Hastings motioned to the wagon and the two horses pulling it, then to the supplies. "You're not going to have enough of a stake left."

"What's your point?"

Hastings tugged on the brim of his hat. "I earn my way by knowing men and what they're thinking. There's something different about you, Stone. I suspect you've got an interesting story to tell, but I'm not asking to hear it. I also suspect you know more than most about those longhorns coming north. I think you might see something the rest of us can't. I've got some money put away and I've been looking for an investment. What I'm proposing is that we throw in together. I don't want to be bothered with your cattle. I'll give you money and you give me a decent return."

"You don't look like a money man," Matt said.

"A what?"

"Never mind."

The year might have changed, but not the way business got done. Hastings was right. Matt was going to need capital to get the ranch going. He'd thought about coming back to town and trying his hand at cards, but he hated to press his luck more than once. There'd been something odd about last night, as if no matter what he did, he couldn't lose. As if someone or something wanted him to get the cattle and the ranch.

He shook off the fanciful thoughts. He didn't have time to speculate. The day was slipping away and he and Courtney had a long journey in front of them.

"I haven't even seen the ranch," Matt said. "Give me a week or so to get settled, then you come on out and we'll talk. I have some good ideas about running cattle. I know they can work. Maybe we could both get rich."

"I'd like that." Jonathan Hastings held out his right hand. The two men shook on the deal.

Matt finished loading the supplies, then paid Alfred

and climbed onto the wagon. He flicked the reins and headed for the hotel. He was surprised how easily he slipped into the rhythm of the town. He found himself nodding back at people who greeted him.

The road was damp without being wet, so the wagon rolled easily. Matt knew that come summer, there would be a cloud of dust hovering over the buildings.

He felt as if he was caught up in some strange movie. He kept expecting to see cars and buses, but there were only wagons and men on horseback. A large stagecoach crossed in front of him. The people inside looked like costumed extras, but they were real. He was the one out of time.

The sun was bright and warm in the clear Wyoming sky. The worst of winter was over. Soon the prairies and meadows would darken with green grass. Then the cattle would arrive. If he and Hastings worked together, the ranch could be a success its first year.

He found himself urging the horses to go faster so he could hurry and tell Courtney what had happened. Then he realized there was no point. She wouldn't want to know. She didn't understand his dreams and he didn't understand hers. They'd always wanted different things. It should have been easy to let her go, but nothing about her had ever been easy for him—except maybe falling in love.

4

Courtney strolled down the stairs. Several men were sitting in the lobby of the hotel. All conversation ceased as she slowly descended to the main floor. The morning had warmed quickly, so she wasn't wearing her jacket. It was draped over one arm. She had her backpack slung over her shoulder, and her cowboy hat sat back on her head. There was nothing scandalous about her trim-fitting jeans or button-down shirt—unless of course one was wearing them in 1873.

Matt leaned against the open door in the lobby and watched his wife bring commerce to a halt. She was slightly on the tall side for a woman, just a hair over five feet six inches. She had enough curves to drive a man wild. He knew. They drove *him* wild on a regular basis. Her plain shirt neither emphasized nor concealed her generous breasts, but that wasn't what caught the men's attention. Instead they stared at her legs.

Her jeans hugged her small waist and rounded hips. The thick fabric more than hinted at the lean length of her thighs. She wore her new cowboy boots tucked under her pants so the curves of her calves were hidden, but a man didn't need much imagination to picture how they would look.

When she reached the bottom of the stairs, the men turned as one to watch her walk out. Matt knew they were studying her round behind, watching the firm curves tilt and sway with each step. Several men had to clear their throats. A man in the corner adjusted his trousers and the desk clerk still had his mouth open.

"Are we ready?" she asked, smiling up at him.

He could see twin spots of color in her cheeks. She knew she was the center of attention and it embarrassed her.

He nodded and placed his arm around her shoulders. She snuggled close. "I feel like the main attraction at a freak show," she whispered.

He bent toward her. "They aren't used to seeing a woman in pants. Remember, this is the nineteenth century. I don't know if women are even allowed to own property."

"Fortunately you're the only one with the burning desire to own land." She softened her words with a smile.

The morning was bright and warm. Several people were out on the street. They stared at Courtney. Some politely turned away. Others gaped.

As they crossed the dirt road to where he'd left the wagon, a young boy flew out of the building next door. "Look, Mama, you can see that lady's legs. Why's she dressed like a man?"

His young mother, her long dress sweeping the dirt, her bonnet quivering with indignation, grabbed her son's hand and tugged him along in the opposite direction. She never once glanced back at them. "I'm sure I don't know. Stop looking at her."

"I've been snubbed," Courtney said. She broke free

of Matt and started after the other woman. "I'm not the enemy," she shouted. "Liberate yourself. Don't be shackled to a man. Be independent. We women can do anything we set our minds to if we band together."

The woman darted a quick glance over her shoulder, shuddered, then ducked into the post office. Courtney paused a few feet away and looked around at the scowling people on the street. Several women sniffed in distaste, then turned away. An older man with bushy white whiskers frowned. Only a young man bothered to tip his hat to her. Matt suspected it was simply because that made it possible for him to stare at her legs.

"You about done?" he asked, untying the wagon.

She walked toward him. "I guess. Looks like I'm not going to rally these women into marching on Washington. I never was much of a leader."

While he made sure that their supplies were secure, she approached the horses harnessed to the wagon. She patted the right one on the nose. "I see my now-stolen rental horse is tied to the back, as is your horse. Two *different* horses are attached to the front of the wagon. Can you explain this?"

"Jasper and your horse aren't used to pulling anything. These horses are. I bought them with the wagon."

"Ah, so we own the wagon, too." She nodded slowly, then tossed her backpack and coat into the back, before climbing up onto the seat. Matt settled next to her and reached for the reins.

"Tell me one thing," she said.

"What's that?"

"We've been in this time, or whatever you want to call it, for about thirty-six hours. That's not even two days. Yet you've managed to accumulate one ranch, one wagon with supplies, two extra horses, and two thousand head of cattle. How come when we were back in our own time you never wanted to go shopping?"

He grinned. "Never had anything worth buying."

She smiled back. "All right, cowboy. Let's get this show on the road." She raised her hat and shook it. "Hi ho, Silver. Away!" she called, then smiled at the startled people around them. "Stop looking at me like that. Haven't you ever heard of the Lone Ranger? Don't you watch television?"

"Courtney."

"I know." She plopped her hat back on her head. "Okay, I'm ready."

He flicked the reins and the horses moved forward. At the end of the street, the town ended abruptly as buildings and pedestrians gave way to open land. There was nothing but wilderness for as far as the eye could see.

Without thinking, Matt slowed the horses.

"It's like falling off the edge of the world," she said softly from her seat next to him.

He gathered the reins in his left hand and squeezed Courtney's forearm with the other. She placed her fingers on top of his.

"What do you think?" she asked.

"It's beautiful."

"And scary. Maybe there's a mall just up ahead. A big one with six anchor stores."

"Ten movie screens."

She smiled at him. "A hotel and five restaurants."

Her hazel eyes were bright with humor. He could feel her fingers stroking the back of his hand. The gentle, almost innocuous touch began to heat his blood.

"You don't seem as upset," he said.

"I've decided to simply accept the situation as it exists. It's not as if I really have a choice in the matter, although I must tell you I have a strong suspicion it's not really happening. I've never done drugs, so this isn't a flashback of some kind. I haven't completely ruled out aliens abducting us, but this doesn't seem like anyone's idea of an experiment. So here we are. I can't whine all the time." She wiggled her behind. "Except maybe about the seats. Could they be more uncomfortable?"

He pulled his hand free and flicked the reins. "Grab one of the blankets from the back and sit on that. It'll help."

She did as he suggested, turning around to dig through their supplies. She collected two blankets and folded them. He sat on one, while she took the other.

The horses walked along in a steady northwest direction. Courtney sniffed the air. "It's cleaner out here. I won't miss that stench in town. The olden days sure had some nasty smells." She folded her hands on her lap and glanced around. "Okay, now what? Is there an in-flight movie?"

"Sorry. The projector's broken."

She shifted in her seat. "There's really nothing to do. We can't even play the license plate game."

Matt liked the quiet. He glanced at the sky and tried to recognize the birds he saw overhead. He squinted, then pointed. "Look up there."

"What?" She craned her neck back. "I don't see anything."

"Way up high. That black speck. It'll come closer. It's an eagle."

"No way. Really?" She tossed off her hat and brought her hands up to cup around her eyes. "I've never seen one before. Except maybe at the zoo. Cool." She fluffed her bangs. "You know a lot of stuff about the outdoors, don't you?"

"Some."

"What are those?" she asked, pointing to some trees in the distance.

"Pine and probably cedar. Further up the hill you'll find spruce fir."

"Maybe *you* will. I wouldn't know a spruce fir

from a rose bush even if it came up and bit me on the butt."

"A spruce fir is a lot taller."

"Thank you very much. You think you're so smart just because you fit in in this time. Maybe you were born in the wrong century."

"I've thought that myself." He'd never cared for the fast-paced life of the big cities. His best days had been spent working on a ranch. He liked the quiet, liked working with his hands.

"Oh my God! Look!" She half rose to her feet and pointed off to the right.

Matt was already reaching for the loaded rifle he'd tucked behind the seat when he saw a small rabbit dart between two bushes, then disappear into the grass.

"Did you see that?" Courtney grabbed her hat and set it on her head. "It was a rabbit. Running loose."

"That's what most animals do."

"Not the animals in my world. My neighbor doesn't even let her cat go outside." She peered toward the bushes, but the rabbit stayed hidden. "Maybe we'll see another one."

"I'm sure we will." He thought about pointing out the fact that they might be dining on Mr. Rabbit, but figured Courtney wouldn't react well to that.

She bounced in her seat a couple of times. "Do you know where we're going?"

"I have directions." They were vague at best, but he figured he could find the ranch. There weren't going to be that many houses out where they were headed. "It'll take nearly two days to get there."

"Okay."

Her lack of concern continued to surprise him but he figured she was experiencing denial. Still, he wasn't going to complain. He liked this Courtney. Bright, funny, and full of questions. Exactly how she'd been when they'd first met.

He still remembered that night. It had been during the rodeo finals in Las Vegas. He'd never understood how a big event like that had come to be held in a town like Las Vegas. He'd never seen the appeal of gambling in a place where the house odds were stacked against him, and when he was riding the circuit, he didn't drink. City people, especially women, came to see how the other half lived.

He was used to the buckle bunnies, the young women who traveled with the circuit. They racked up time with cowboys the way the cowboys racked up points—both hoping for a big score.

Matt steered clear of them. He'd reached his present height when he was sixteen and at eighteen, he'd started filling out. He'd inherited his blue eyes and dark hair from his mother. At least that's what her pictures told him. She'd died when he was born.

Sometime during his senior year of high school, women had started noticing him. The attention had come too late. In his mind, he was always the poor, skinny kid of a drunken day laborer. He'd grown up going to school without breakfast much of the time. He'd had Christmases and birthdays with no presents, summers with no shoes.

The rodeo circuit had been his way out. He'd hoped to win enough to buy his own place, raise cattle and maybe a few cutting horses. He hadn't wanted to get involved with anyone. Until that evening when a pretty lady stopped him as he walked through a bar.

Matt flicked the reins and grinned. He could still remember everything about the moment. The noise of the crowd, the lounge act who'd given up trying to make anyone take notice, the scents of perfume and liquor, and the faint frown drawing Courtney's delicate eyebrows together.

She'd been wearing a gauzy white dress that hung off her shoulders. Her long hair had been loose and tempting enough to make a man forget what mattered. He'd come in third in the bareback bronc riding and had a nice chunk of money to put aside for his ranch.

"Excuse me," she'd said as he walked past her. "May I ask you a question?"

He'd heard nearly every line, so he barely slowed as he said, "You just did."

"What? Oh." Then she'd laughed. Her eyes had crinkled at the corners and he'd seen her white teeth and the tip of her tongue. It was like being slugged in the gut with a sledgehammer. He'd had to fight to keep from going down on his knees.

"What's your question?" he'd asked when he could speak again.

"Are you a cowboy?"

His first reaction had been disappointment. He'd hoped for a better line than that. Something that would tempt him to forget his policy of never getting involved with a buckle bunny.

"Yes, ma'am." He touched the brim of his hat and prepared to move on.

"Why are you here? There must be twenty cowboys on every corner. I've been to Las Vegas a couple of times before, but I've never seen this many cowboys. Are you having a convention?"

Her smile was as sweet as spring rain. The genuine confusion in her hazel eyes made him want to kiss her.

"It's the rodeo, ma'am."

"Oh. I've seen signs and posters about that. It must be a big one if there are so many of you. Are you with the rodeo?"

He nodded.

"You do that for a living?"

He nodded again.

"Why?"

He'd laughed then and introduced himself. She'd told him her name and had explained she was from Los Angeles. She was a graphic artist who helped design movie posters. She lived in Marina del Rey, drove a convertible, and had an American Express card. He was a rodeo cowboy who mostly lived out of his truck, although he kept a couple of cutting horses in Wyoming. Nothing should have happened. Matt had fully expected to end the conversation and walk away. Instead he'd bought her a drink and they'd escaped the bar to find somewhere quiet to talk—not an easy task in Las Vegas.

They'd ended up at the far end of the dining room for a cheap buffet. They stayed up until dawn. He gave her tickets to the rodeo and the next day she showed up to watch his event. When they met up later, after he'd managed to stay on his bronc for the required eight seconds and had scored high enough to guarantee he would stay in the competition, she cut right to the heart of the matter.

"You're crazy," she told him. "There have to be easier ways to make a living."

"It's all I know."

Her sweet lips had pulled into a straight line. "What if you get hurt?"

"Want to see my scars?"

But she hadn't smiled. Instead she turned away, but not before he saw the concern in her eyes—and the fear.

"Courtney?"

She'd glanced up at him, her emotions firmly under control. He meant to ask if she was all right, or tell her that he would be fine. Instead he pulled her close and kissed her. In that moment, when their lips touched and their hearts beat in unison, his life had been irrevocably changed.

It wasn't just about the passion, although it had taken every ounce of his self-control not to bed her right there outside the holding pens. It was about connecting. For the first time in his life, he felt whole. As if he belonged, as if he mattered. He'd known then he would marry her. He'd known then he would love her for the rest of his life. He'd known then she would be the death of him.

But he hadn't said anything. Instead he'd made a joke and they'd gone on talking. He'd—

"Matt? Are you listening to me?"

Her question drew him back to the present. The image of the crowded rodeo disappeared and was replaced by wide open spaces, although he could still feel her in his arms.

"What?"

"Could you please stop the wagon? I want to ride my horse."

"Aren't you sore?"

She grimaced and as the wagon stopped, she grabbed the sides and jumped down. "Everything hurts, but I think the wagon is making it worse. Anyway, I prefer to alternate my instruments of torture."

She bent her knees several times, then walked around the uneven ground as he saddled her rental horse. When he was done, she grabbed hold of the reins, put her foot on the step he made with his laced fingers, and swung up onto the animal's back.

"Oh, this hurts," she said as she shifted on the saddle.

"You want to come down?"

"No, I'll ride it out. It's going to get better, right?"

He stared at her, at the pale Stetson shading her eyes and the way the corners of her mouth tilted up even when she wasn't smiling.

"Why are you looking at me like that?" she asked. "Do I have dirt on my cheek?"

"I was remembering the first time I took you riding." It had been during a week together in New Mexico, the spring after they were married.

She wrinkled her nose. "My arms got sunburned, my hands got blisters, and my thighs felt as if they'd been stretched for a mile."

He'd spent the next two days taking care of her, soothing her burns, blisters, and sore muscles, and tenderly making love with her.

She glanced at the gloves she wore, then down at him. "That was a long time ago, but I learned my lesson." She wiggled her free hand.

He headed back to the wagon.

"Matt?"

He paused and looked at her.

"I—" She ducked her head until the brim of the hat shielded her face from view. "I had a good time that week we were together."

"Me, too."

"I was thinking—"

His gut clenched tight. "Courtney, don't. We've got enough to handle trying to survive here. When we figure out what's going on, we can deal with the rest of it."

She nodded.

He knew she was hurt. If she raised her head, he would see the pain in her eyes. But he couldn't bear to hear her talk about maybe trying again. Not yet. She was just reacting to the situation, to being afraid. He was the only familiar part of her life. In time, she would remember all the reasons she'd wanted a divorce and once again he would be faced with losing her.

She nudged her horse closer to the wagon. "I'll race you to that rise up there," she said, pointing to a high point on the horizon.

"Wagons don't race."

"Good. That means I win by default."

Her smile was contagious. He didn't bother trying to resist.

"Is there a bathroom?" she asked.

"Pick your spot," he said, pointing to the trees and bushes around them.

"That's what I was afraid you were going to say. I hated that outhouse back at the hotel. I don't think I'll enjoy the great outdoors any more." She urged her horse into a trot. "I'll hold it."

"For how long?"

"Until we're back in the right century."

Unfortunately her bladder wasn't willing to cooperate. Courtney stepped out from behind the bushes and grimaced. This was worse than camping. At least then there was the promise of a quick return to civilization. Here she was at the whim of some mutant storm. She didn't trust weather with a sense of humor.

She paused by the stream and rinsed her hands, then made her way to the small camp she and Matt had set up.

"We have to start a shopping list," she said as she grabbed her backpack. "Number one is toilet paper."

"I don't think they have that here."

Matt had collected several large pieces of wood, along with a few smaller ones and some twigs. He sorted them by size, then started to pile them inside a ring he'd made with stones.

"I don't want to think about what they use instead," she said, "but I guess we're going to have to find out." She dug into her backpack for a small notepad and a pen. "I'm sure we've forgotten other things, too."

"Town is a two-day ride away."

"Time seems to be our greatest commodity." She watched as he flicked on his lighter, then held the small flame close to some wood shavings.

They caught instantly. The fire crawled up to the splintered twigs and burned brighter. In less than three minutes, the entire pile was ablaze.

"Very impressive," she said. "What are you going to do when your lighter runs out of fuel?"

"I bought matches."

Matt squatted in front of the fire. The temperature was dropping as quickly as the sun, but he hadn't pulled on his coat yet. The dancing flames cast uneven shadows over his face and body, highlighting his broad strength and drawing her gaze up his powerful legs to the apex of his thighs.

He wore button-fly jeans. The men she used to date were either executive types who wore flannel trousers or beach bums in ragged shorts. She still remembered the first time she'd watched Matt undress. It hadn't been the first time they'd made love. That afternoon and evening were still a sensual blur in her mind. It had been later.

There was something incredibly erotic about a man's arousal testing the strength of the buttons. The act of unbuttoning seemed more conscious than simply slipping down a zipper. There was more contact. Sometimes when she unfastened his jeans, her fingers brushed against his arousal. The heat of his need enveloped her, making her clumsy.

The cold evening breeze blew against her suddenly heated cheeks. She looked away, but not before a sharp pang of longing stabbed her chest, longing not only for what they'd lost, but for what they could have had.

"You want to get the water for coffee?" he asked, holding out the coffeepot.

"Sure." She walked down to the stream and filled the pot. The water was icy, probably spring runoff. It felt frozen in her hands. She pressed her damp fingers against her cheeks.

When she returned to the fire, the sun had nearly set behind the western mountains.

"What's for dinner?" she asked as Matt scooped coffee into the pot and set it on a flat rock he'd put near the center of the fire.

Lunch had been wonderful: fried chicken and biscuits purchased from the hotel dining room before they left.

"There's beef jerky and some canned vegetables."

"Oh, sounds yummy," she said, determined not to complain.

"Can you make bread?"

"Sure. With a breadmaker and a mix."

He frowned.

"Oh, you mean like from scratch." She knelt on the ground and looked at the dried beef and single can that would make up their dinner. "I've never tried. You need flour and water. Oh, yeast."

"Yeast?"

She grabbed for her list. "Let me add that. We'd better get a cookbook, too. Neither of us was very useful in the kitchen."

"Maybe not, but you dial a mean takeout."

She smiled. "I know. I already miss that little Chinese place around the corner. They had the best ribs."

"Don't think about it."

He handed her a piece of dried beef, then started opening the can of tomatoes. She tried not to grimace when she tasted them. They were way too salty, almost as if they'd been pickled instead of canned. Dessert was canned peaches that weren't too bad.

By the time they finished eating, night had fallen. The temperature kept dropping. Courtney fastened her coat, then pulled on her riding gloves. The light from the flames barely extended three feet past the fire.

"It's sure dark out here," she said.

"The stars will be out soon."

"Great. I can read by their light."

Matt collected an armful of blankets. He tossed them to her, then set a folded cloth on the ground. "Why don't you make our bed while I see to the horses."

"Our bed?"

A shiver raced through her, but it had nothing to do with the temperature and everything to do with the man in front of her.

"It's going to get close to freezing tonight. We're going to have to share a bed to stay warm. Oh, and put on an extra pair of socks."

Extra socks. That was romantic. She set the blankets on the ground and spread out the oilcloth covering to protect them from the damp.

"What do we do about pillows?" she called into the darkness.

"You can use my shoulder."

"And of course you're too manly to need a pillow," she muttered, then grinned.

She smoothed down the blankets, then sat on top of them, not sure what to do next. As Matt had promised, the stars had come out. Her eyes adjusted to the lack of light. She was able to make out trees and brush. She could see the wagon, just beyond the fire, and the horses beyond that.

She could hear the crackle of the wood and Matt's low, soothing voice as he spoke to the horses. She found herself relaxing and her eyes drifting shut.

A sharp yipping cut through the night. It was followed by a chorus of howls.

She sat up straight. "Matt?"

"I'm right here." He stepped into the circle of firelight. "There's an extra rifle. You remember how to use it?"

"Yes. There's nothing like the sound of a wolf pack to jog my memory."

He paused by the wagon and pulled out both rifles, along with a box of cartridges. He walked over to the makeshift bed and handed her the firearm. She shifted onto her knees, turning toward the fire.

She turned the barrel away from him and the horses. "Check to see if it's loaded, make sure the action isn't stuck, put in a cartridge. It goes in bullet first." His instructions came back to her as she matched actions to her words.

When she finished, she handed him the loaded rifle. He checked it. "Looks fine." He handed it back. "Keep it next to you, but don't shoot without making sure it isn't me or one of the horses."

"I think I can tell the difference, but I'll ask before I pull the trigger."

She put the rifle on the ground and started to get under the covers. She couldn't see her watch, but she doubted it was much past seven. Still, the long day of traveling—first riding in the wagon, then on horseback, then in the wagon—was exhausting. Everything hurt. She would take jet lag over wagon butt any day.

"I feel like I've been beat up," she said, struggling with the blankets. They tangled around her legs.

"Here, let me do it." Matt stood up and smoothed the covers. When she was settled, he slipped in next to her. His heat beckoned and she moved close.

"I'm freezing," she said.

"Let me get my arm around you. Lay on your side."

She shifted on the hard ground, turning until she pressed against him from chest to knee. Her head rested on his shoulder, her legs nestled against his. She could hear his heartbeat. The slow, steady sound soothed her.

"Better?" he asked.

"Much."

The campfire warmed her back, Matt warmed her

front. In a few minutes, she stopped shivering. In another hour or so, her feet would thaw. She closed her eyes, but they popped open. She knew why. The vastness of the open land made her nervous.

They'd heard the wolves calling. What other *silent* predators were out there?

She glanced around. The trees were tall, awkward silhouettes against the starlit sky. Bushes moved for no reason. Every time something rustled, she tensed, waiting for some carnivore to pounce on her.

She could hear night sounds. Bugs and birds. The soft hoot of an owl. They were the only two people around for miles. She wasn't sure she'd ever been this alone before.

"Matt?"

"Hmm?"

"If we don't get back, is anyone going to miss you?"

The arm around her tightened. "Sure. Some guys on the circuit. My friends."

"The stable is going to think I stole that horse. If we go back, will they want to hang me?"

She felt as well as heard his chuckle. "Horse stealing isn't a hanging offense anymore. Especially not for a woman. Besides, you didn't really steal it."

"Do you expect me to tell them the truth?"

"No."

He moved his hand until he touched her hair. His fingers stroked her head. He always knew how to make her feel safe.

"I don't think anyone is going to miss me," she said softly.

"But you have a lot of friends."

"Do I? I know people at work. I go to lunch with them. And there are a couple of single women in my condo building. But I don't have any really close friends. No one who's going to wonder about what happened to me. Allison will be thrilled when I don't show up for work."

"Who's Allison?"

"A new graphic artist. She's just out of college and has these ideas for posters. She's convinced she's the best thing since sliced white bread. I hate her."

Matt tugged on her braid until she looked at him. "You don't hate her. It's not your nature."

"Maybe hate is too strong a word. I hope she gets a really big wart on the end of her nose."

"Better."

His coat was soft against her face. She snuggled closer. "Do you know I don't even have a plant to miss me. I never bothered to get a pet. My parents are gone. I never had any brothers or sisters."

It was a little disheartening to realize that she could disappear and almost no one would notice. The only person who would really care was Matt. He would have noticed and been worried. He would have missed her. Except two days ago she'd been chasing after him demanding that he sign divorce papers. If she was trying to get rid of the one person in her life who cared about her, she was doing something very wrong.

"And here I thought I was so bright," she murmured.

Matt's chest rose and fell rhythmically. She liked the feel of him next to her. It had been too long between weekends together.

"If I had to go through time with someone, I'm glad it was you," she whispered.

Silence.

"Matt?"

His breathing deepened. He'd fallen asleep. She smiled, then closed her eyes. The wolves howled again, but this time she wasn't afraid. With Matt around, she felt safe. He'd always looked after her, been good to her. Even when she didn't deserve it.

5

The countryside was stunningly beautiful, but eventually the scenic vistas began to blur together. Matt shifted on the hard seat of the wagon and envied Courtney her place on horseback. At least he was used to being in a saddle all day.

He figured they'd traveled about eighteen miles. Something they could have done by car in a half hour to forty minutes. It had taken them nearly two days.

He remembered hearing about pioneers who traveled overland across the country. At different rodeos there were often reenactments of those times. He'd seen the wagons. A couple of times he'd ridden along for a day or two on horseback. But it hadn't been real. When he was tired, he went to a motel and crashed for the night. He could stop at any number of diners or fast-food places and get something to eat. It wasn't like this—endless open land with no people.

What shocked him the most was that they weren't far from the city. Not that Cheyenne was much of a

city. Still, population expanded up toward the fort, as
well as due north. But in this direction, there wasn't
much of anything.

Courtney reined in her horse and tilted back her hat.
"Are we lost?"

"No."

He had general directions to head northwest for a
day and a half then turn due west. They'd already done
that. In another hour or so, they should come to a spe-
cific cluster of trees. They were to go northwest again
until they found the ranch.

"What would you give for an Autoclub map right
about now?"

He smiled. "You got one you want to sell?"

"Wish I did." She glanced at the sky. "Still clear in
all directions. Not even a hint of the storm."

He didn't tell her that he was glad. He wasn't ready
to go back. Not when he was so close to getting everything he'd ever wanted.

"Why don't I go scout out a nice place to take a
break?" she said.

"Don't go too far out in front. If you get lost, you
can't call home for a ride."

She arched her pale eyebrows. "See, Matt, you do
have a sense of humor. I've always thought it was one
of your better qualities."

"Thanks for the vote of confidence."

Courtney kicked her horse. The animal started to
trot. She slipped in the saddle and made a grab for the
horn. Her body bounced with each bone-jarring stride.
Her braid flapped furiously against her back.

"Get him into a canter," Matt called.

"You're so helpful," she said, her words uneven. She
kicked the horse again. Instead of breaking into a
smoother gait the gelding trotted faster.

"When we get back to civilization, I'm going to turn

you into dog fo—ouch!" She reined in and cupped her jaw. "I bid my tongh."

Matt swallowed the chuckle that rose in his throat, forcing his mouth to stay straight. He drew the wagon to a stop beside her.

Courtney glared at him. "You're waughing at me."

"You're talking funny."

"I can't help it."

He leaned back in the wagon. "When he tries to trot faster, rein him in, then kick him hard. If he doesn't move into a canter, rein him in again. He's playing with you, trying to figure out who's in charge."

"I think we both know the answer to that."

She circled the gelding around and kicked him. The horse started trotting.

"Rein him in, then kick," Matt said.

She pulled back on the reins until the animal's trot slowed, then she kicked him again. He broke into a smooth canter.

"I did it!"

Matt stood up and cupped his mouth. "You're going the wrong way," he called to her, then pointed northwest.

She bent low over the gelding and gradually turned in the right direction. In a few minutes, she disappeared over a rise.

Matt swore under his breath. She was going to get lost. He could feel it. Then God knows what would happen to her.

He urged the horses on, wishing he were on horseback instead of stuck in the wagon. He wouldn't be able to keep up with her. Why had he taught her how to get that stubborn gelding to trot?

Before he could decide whether to saddle Jasper and go after her, she reappeared, still on her horse. Her cheeks were flushed, her eyes wide. A few strands of hair had escaped from her french braid and danced around her face.

"Oh, Matt, come see what I found."

He didn't know whether to expect a mountain lion or a snake. "Are you okay?"

She nodded. "I think this horse was just being stubborn. I bet he learned if he acted badly, he wouldn't get rented much, or if he did, no one would stay out very long." She bent over and petted the horse's neck. "He was the last one in the stable when I came after you. I didn't even ask his name."

"Call him what you like, then."

The gelding was rust colored, with black stockings. Courtney tilted her head as if considering possibilities. "I'll call him Rocky."

"Fine. Now what did you have to show me?"

"Oh. I almost forgot." She smiled as if she'd just discovered a new form of chocolate. "You're not going to believe this. Follow me."

She turned Rocky in a tight circle, then led the way through a grove of trees. The afternoon sun was starting its slow descent toward the mountains to the west. While it was warm in the sunshine, as soon as they got in the shade of the budding trees, the temperature dropped. Before he could grab his coat and shrug it on, they reached the top of the rise and broke through the trees.

Matt didn't remember reining in the horses or securing the brake. The next thing he knew, he was standing next to Courtney, staring at the valley below.

It stretched out for miles. A narrow stream of spring runoff cut through the center of the green grass. Trees lined the stream, and marched up the far side. But it wasn't the grass or the trees that captured his attention. It was the huge shaggy beasts dotting the landscape.

"Buffalo," he said quietly. "Hundreds of them."

"There are a bunch," she agreed. "Are you surprised?"

"Stunned." His ears were ringing as if he'd gotten bucked off the horse and kicked in the head on the way down. "It's not possible."

"Of course it's possible. If this really is 1873, why wouldn't there be buffalo?"

"They were hunted to near extinction." He took a step closer to the edge of the rise. "I guess that hasn't happened yet. But it will. Within the next few years, these buffalo will be gone."

Courtney moved closer to him. "They're sure big. Did they kill them for the meat?"

"No. The hides. They left the carcasses to rot."

"Yuck. Haven't these people heard about recycling?"

"Not yet." He sat on the fresh spring grass and stared at the herd. Most of the animals were eating. A few stopped to drink at the stream. A couple of calves teetered alongside their mothers. It was like watching a movie, only he could hear them and smell them. If they stampeded, the ground would tremble.

"I wish I could save them," he said.

"Why don't you?"

He looked at her. Courtney had settled next to him. She'd pulled off her hat and set it brim up, next to her. A few smudges of dirt stained the once-crisp fabric of her shirt. They both needed a shower, but she was still beautiful. At least to him.

She turned her head until their gazes locked.

"Why are you looking at me like that? My Lord, you bought a ranch and are expecting a couple thousand cows to live there. What's a few buffalo going to matter?"

He grinned. Without thinking, he started to lean forward to kiss her. Her eyes widened, but she didn't move away. Then he remembered the reason she'd come after him two days before. She wanted to leave him; she wanted a divorce.

He straightened and returned his attention to the buffalo. They were larger than steers. Their thick hides were still woolly from winter. They looked like great prehistoric beasts roaming a virgin land.

"That's a great idea," he told her. "Once we figure out where we're going, I'll cull out a small herd and keep them close to the house."

She leaned back on her elbows and stared up at the sky. "Think of all the other things we know that everyone else doesn't. What's going to be invented? Who's going to win the World Series? We could make a killing."

"The World Series doesn't exist yet."

"Details. What else is there? Are there any big horse races we could bet on?" she asked.

"I've never followed horse racing."

"Me either." She exhaled slowly. "I never liked history. Everything between the Civil War and World War One is sort of a blur."

"Don't look at me," Matt said, holding up his hands in surrender. "I hated school."

She collapsed onto the ground and giggled. "This is horrible. Bad history students travel through time and get lost. We don't know enough to take advantage of the situation." She rolled toward him, propping her head on her hand. "At least you know about cattle and horses. I probably don't even get to vote."

"You could rally the women in town like you tried yesterday."

"Somehow I don't think they'd listen to me. I don't even know who the president is right now."

He thought for a moment, trying to remember. "I don't know either."

She started to giggle again. He grinned.

"At least we're together," she said. "I'd hate to be doing this alone."

Her words made him hope, though he knew it was futile. If they made it back to their own time, Courtney would leave him. If they didn't, she would grow to hate him. But he pushed the thoughts away, because for now laughing with her was more than enough.

Courtney felt like a four-year-old. For the last hour she'd been asking "Are we there yet?" every fifteen minutes. Now they were here and she was sorry.

When Matt had said he bought a ranch, she'd pictured something large, like in the movies. Maybe a two-story house with a well-tended garden. Some outbuildings, a barn. Several corrals. She also pictured rows of something growing in the background, which was more farmlike than ranchlike, but hey, she'd never done the rural thing before.

The house in front of her was small and dark. Except for a half-built structure that might have once been the beginnings of a barn, it stood alone in a shallow valley. There was a stream to one side of the house, several trees just beginning to bud, and little else. No horses, no cattle, no neat rows of anything growing.

As she pulled Rocky to a stop, she could hear the wind and the call of a bird somewhere in the sky. As the sun fell, so did the temperature, but her shiver didn't come from the cold. Instead it was the isolation that frightened her. They had reached the end of the earth and taken a step off the other side.

For the last two days, ever since they'd left the hotel, she'd been playing a game. In her heart, she knew this wasn't real. She and Matt hadn't traveled through time, this wasn't 1873, she wasn't stuck in the middle of nowhere. She'd ridden ahead of the wagon with the firm expectation that around the next bend, behind the next rock or across the next stream would be the way home.

She'd searched the skies, fully expecting to see the beginnings of the odd storm that had swept them here. At night, she'd gone to sleep believing she would wake up with a blinding headache and Matt telling her she'd just lived through some new strain of the flu.

But behind the next rock and tree, across the next stream, there had been only wilderness. In the mornings she'd awakened with sore and stiff muscles brought on by too much time on a horse and sleeping on too-cold ground. But she hadn't worried because eventually it was going to be all right.

She'd been wrong.

Matt stopped the wagon in front of the house and walked toward the front door. There wasn't a porch, just a narrow track in the dirt. He didn't have a key, but apparently he didn't need one. He touched the latch and it gave. She watched him step into the darkness.

Courtney continued to sit on Rocky and stare at the house. She couldn't believe it. Even when Matt came out and said, "It's not much, but it's a roof over our heads."

"Unless it's a lot nicer on the inside, I think I'd rather sleep outside."

"I doubt that," he said, pointing to the western horizon.

She squinted against the setting sun. Much to her dismay, dark clouds billowed up against the mountains beyond, then began to spill over one by one. For a moment, her heart leapt in her chest. Then she realized the clouds weren't the violet hue of the mysterious force that had swept them back in time. These were normal clouds, no doubt producing a normal storm.

"Rain?" she asked, eyeing first the clouds, then the small, dark house.

"If we're lucky."

"If we're not?"

"Snow. I'm going to see if there's a back door." He circled around the building.

Courtney slid off her horse. As her feet hit the ground, her knees buckled. She was used to the phenomenon and had already grabbed hold of the saddle. It took her a couple of minutes to get her "land legs" back after riding all day.

Once she could support her weight, she walked forward slowly, slightly afraid of what was behind that open door. She couldn't see because the inside of the house was black. Which made sense. There weren't any windows in front.

"Perfect," she muttered.

She pushed opened the warped, wooden door. It squealed a protest.

"I feel like I'm in the middle of some B horror movie. Any second a masked guy with a knife is going to leap out and stab me."

Talking to herself might have helped if the subject matter was more pleasant. But instead of feeling relieved by the sound of her voice, she felt a flicker of fear whisper up her spine. She drew in a deep breath and stepped inside.

Her left hand brushed against the wall as she instinctively searched for a light switch. There wasn't one. Just as well, she thought, knowing the room would look better in little or no light.

The house didn't smell as bad as she'd feared. Musty, but not as if something had died in here. The room was much cooler than the afternoon had been. She supposed it wasn't sunny long enough to heat up the air inside.

As her eyes adjusted to the dimness, she was able to make out individual features. She stood in a good-sized room, nearly half again as long as it was wide. There was a stone fireplace in one corner. Wood had been left piled neatly on the grate, as well as on the floor. A couple of uncomfortable-looking chairs faced the fireplace,

with a small table between them. Some sort of white
paint or wall covering had started peeling and bits of it
covered the furniture like dandruff.

She took another step inside. To her right was a
short hallway; to her left, in front of her, was an opening to another room, probably the kitchen. The toe of
her boot caught on something. She glanced down.
Instead of carpet, or wood, she saw a stained grayish
fabric that might have once been white. It reminded
her a little of the canvas cloths they slept on. Only Matt
has said they weren't canvas, they were oilcloth. She
wasn't sure of the difference and she didn't want to
know.

She could hear Matt moving around and she started
toward the sound. She stepped through the narrow
doorway into what was obviously the kitchen. Only it
wasn't like any kitchen she'd ever seen before.

On the left-hand wall was a small window. Matt had
propped it open with a stick. Despite the dirty glass,
sunlight filtered in and illuminated the room. Courtney
turned slowly, taking it all in. Instead of bleached pine
cabinets and gleaming Formica countertops, she saw
open shelves, some of them crooked. The kitchen's
inventory consisted of bits of crockery, a few oddly
shaped pots, and a tray filled with tarnished flatware.
The counters were made of filthy, scarred wood. A
table and four chairs sat in front of the window.

She glanced down. Dust and dirt covered what
looked like a hardwood floor. The right side of the
kitchen was dominated by a large black stove. Rust
coated the top. A pipe rose to the ceiling. Soot stained
the wall, the dark circles marking places where the
chimney leaked smoke.

Next to the stove was a small counter, and next to
that sat a large sink with a pump.

Matt came in from the back entrance to the kitchen.

He held a lantern in his hand. The wick gave off a steady glow.

"The other rooms are dark," he said. "This is the only window."

Courtney tried to speak but her mouth wasn't working. She could only follow silently as he went back into the living room, then down the short hall toward the back of the house.

There were two bedrooms. The front one was small, with a single bed and a chest of drawers. Three shelves had been nailed against the far wall. The linens stored there had been dinner for some unknown, unseen creature. The bed itself was all wood, but higher than modern furniture. There was a small block of stairs pushed against one side, as if that were needed to climb onto the mattress. Courtney knew she wouldn't need it because she had no intentions of sleeping in that bed. Even from the doorway, she could see the mice scampering across the straw, squeaking as they ducked out of sight. She didn't scream. She didn't react at all. She simply followed dumbly as Matt went into the back bedroom.

It was nearly twice the size of the first bedroom. The bed was wider, the mattress just as suspect. Instead of a small dresser and open shelves, there was a large armoire. It was the only nice piece of furniture in the place.

Matt led the way back to the kitchen. "I know it's not what you expected."

"Obviously. This must be someone's idea of a joke. There's no way I'll believe that people really live like this. You can't mean for us to stay here."

"Where else are we going to go? There's a storm coming. There's going to be rain, maybe even snow. At least in here we'll be dry."

"If the roof doesn't leak."

"I don't see any water stains on the floor."

She glanced down at the dust and dirt. "How could you tell?"

"There's no mud."

She looked at him, not sure if he was teasing her. His expression was blank, his eyes hidden by the brim of his hat.

"I'd better go check on the barn. Part of it looks completed. I want to get the horses taken care of and the supplies out of the rain."

He left the lantern on the table and started toward the door at the rear. She followed behind. "What am I supposed to do?"

"Get started cleaning up the kitchen. We're going to need the stove to stay warm." With that he stepped through a long skinny room and opened the back door. It slammed shut behind him, plunging her into darkness.

If she'd been holding something, she would have thrown it after him. She didn't want any part of this and she sure wasn't going to try cleaning up anything in this house. They should just torch the place and start over.

As her eyes adjusted to the dimness again, she realized she was standing in the pantry. There were large barrels and more open shelves. A few tins of food had been stacked haphazardly. She saw another lantern, as well as several candles. She reached up for them.

They were fat and uneven, and they didn't smell pleasant at all. What she would have given for a little lavender potpourri right now. She carried the candles into the kitchen, then realized she didn't have any matches.

She stared at the mess around her and wasn't sure where to start. Everything was dirty and nothing was familiar. She didn't know how to work the stove or the lantern. She'd never seen the appeal of camping. She liked hotels. Her idea of a good time was a heated pool and room service, maybe an in-room movie.

She walked over to the sink. Something had dried to the sides. She grimaced, then noticed there wasn't a drain. That didn't make sense. Why would there be a pump and no drain? Didn't they have plumbing?

She remembered her hotel room and figured they probably didn't have plumbing, which made her wonder what the outhouse looked like.

"I'm being punished," she said quietly. "Obviously I've committed some heinous crime. We died and I'm in hell. It's the only explanation."

After blowing off the worst of the dust, she gripped the pump handle firmly. She raised and lowered it over and over again until her arm ached. There wasn't a drop of water.

"Which explains the lack of a drain."

Her chuckle of humor ended in something that sounded suspiciously like a sob. Courtney drew in a deep breath and reminded herself she never cried. It didn't accomplish anything and left her with puffy eyes. Maybe she would have better luck with the stove.

She approached the huge black monster feeling as if it was a dragon and she was one of the more puny knights. She couldn't light it without matches, but maybe she could figure out how it worked.

There were two doors in the front, one lower than the other. Fuel probably went in the lower one, she thought. And whatever was being baked went in the other. She opened the top drawer.

Something much larger than a mouse raced toward her. She flung the door shut and screamed. In her haste to get out of the house, she misjudged the turn to the back door and slammed into the rear wall. Large tubs hung on nails crashed down around her. She felt dirt and something that wasn't dirt and had way too many little legs fall on her shoulders and hair.

Still screaming, she raced outside.

"Matt!"

He ran out of the makeshift barn. "What's wrong?"

She was trembling and could barely speak. "There's rats in the house and bugs and no water and I can't live here." She sucked in a breath.

Instead of the reassuring embrace she'd expected, he placed his hands on his hips. "The house has been empty all winter. What did you expect?"

"Nothing like this. It's horrible."

"It's great. Don't you see?" He moved close and took her hand in his. As always, his touch soothed her. "Look over there."

She turned toward his outstretched arm. A small stone building stood several feet from the stream. "What's that? The local movie theater?"

"It's a springhouse. There's a spring right here. It means we'll always have fresh water. Better than that, it's cold, so in summer we can keep food fresher."

"Great. I was wondering what to do with my frozen entrees. Now if only we could find a microwave."

He ignored her. "There's great drainage all around the house. The trees block the worst of the wind. It's an ideal location. I know the house needs a little work, but—"

She snatched her hand away. She didn't want to be soothed anymore. "A little? Are you crazy? There's Lord knows what living in the mattresses. There are rats in the stove and crawly things in the pantry. I don't dare open the barrels. I'm sure there's a new life-form breeding even as we speak. The candles stink, the house is dark, and there's no water in the pump."

"Did you prime the pump?" He asked the question as if he were speaking to a two-year-old.

"No, I didn't prime the pump. I don't know what that means. I've never had to pump water before and I don't want to start now."

"Courtney, it's not all that bad." He reached up and placed his hands on her shoulders. "We're going to have to work together to get this place livable. We're stuck here and we need to make the best of it."

Those earnest blue eyes of his were working their magic. She could feel her anger and frustration drifting away. In another few minutes she would be begging him to let her clean the house.

She jerked free of his touch. "I don't want to make the best of it. I don't want to be here. It's easy for you because you're finally getting everything you want. Your precious longhorns are on the way. You've got horses and a ranch. You're in cowboy heaven. Maybe this is your time, but it isn't mine. I hate it here. I hate the open land, the silence, and most of all I hate not having a flush toilet. This isn't my time. I want to go home. I want to go find the storm."

All emotion fled his face. His features turned to stone. "Fine," he said. "Go find your storm. I won't stop you."

6

The cold wind whipped around her, tugging at her jacket and threatening to sweep off her hat. Clouds moved closer, overtaking the setting sun and leaving the valley in shadow.

Courtney sat under a tree, huddled against the trunk as if the slender sapling could protect her from the elements.

"I want to go home," she said, staring up at the darkening sky. "I want to go home!"

There wasn't a response to her plea, no turquoise tornado, no flash of white light, no eerie silence. In fact, there was plenty of noise. The creaking of branches, the wind, some birds. Her own voice pleading to go home. But they were the wrong sounds. She wanted to hear street traffic, cars, airplanes, a radio, anything that would give her hope of returning to where she belonged.

She glanced back at the house. It was still small, dark, and ugly. Matt hadn't left it. She wondered what he was doing inside. She didn't want to return, but the cold and the dark clouds didn't give her much choice. It was going to start raining soon. She couldn't stay outside.

She wasn't sure how long she'd sat by the tree but when she stood up, her legs screamed in protest. Her muscles had cramped. She might do an aerobics class a couple of times a week, but it hadn't prepared her for the rigors of nineteenth-century travel. Her inner thighs felt as if they'd been ripped apart like a wishbone, then loosely reassembled. The tops of her legs were on fire, the muscles burning with each step. She didn't even want to think about her rear end. Between the wagon seat and the saddle, her behind was one giant bruise.

She slowly made her way back to the house. As she neared the barn, she saw the horses had been left in makeshift stalls, while the wagon had been pushed to the rear of the finished section. Their supplies would be safe from the elements. Courtney went inside the partially constructed building and peeled back the protective tarp. She gathered up her backpack, then smoothed the cover back in place.

As she walked the few feet to the house, she wondered what she was supposed to say to Matt. She didn't like being difficult, but he expected too much from her. Traveling had been an adventure. While they were moving, she had been able to believe it wasn't real. But this was different. Rats in the stove were difficult to ignore. For reasons she didn't understand, through circumstances she couldn't explain, this was 1873 and she didn't belong here.

The back door was propped open with a piece of wood from the stack beside the house. At least there was plenty of fuel. If all else failed, they could burn the building itself.

She walked through the pantry into the kitchen. The window was still open and the cold breeze had chased out most of the smells. The floor had been swept and

Matt was adding a log to the stove. She could feel heat coming from the black monster. The flicker of warmth gave her hope.

"What are you doing?" she asked.

Matt glanced at her. He'd removed his hat so she could see his face. A single lock of dark hair slipped onto his forehead. He straightened and brushed it back with a familiar gesture.

"The stove works," he said, not answering her question. "And there's water. The pump just needed priming. But there's no drain in the sink. We'll keep a bucket under the pump to catch any spills."

"What happened to the rats?"

"They've been relocated." He was stating a fact, not making a joke.

A flicker of guilt licked up her spine. He was taking care of business and she was acting like a spoiled child. Okay, maybe she'd overreacted when she'd first seen the house. It was small and dark, and moldy, and ugly, but people lived in worse. She glanced around at the open shelves, at the dirty dishes, the lack of plumbing, and remembered the outhouse in the backyard.

On second thought, no one *she* knew lived in worse.

"We have to talk," Matt said, holding out one of the chairs and motioning for her to take a seat.

She sank down and placed her backpack on the ground next to her. He took the seat opposite.

She didn't know how she looked, but she suspected it wasn't especially glamorous. She'd been on a horse most of the afternoon. She pulled off her hat and smoothed down the loose strands of hair. She hadn't had a shower since arriving in this century. Nor had she changed her clothes. Not that she had all that much to change into. Her real luggage was back at the hotel. The *real* hotel with running water, a big jacuzzi tub in the bathroom, and in-room movies.

Matt had been through the same ordeal, yet he looked gorgeous. He'd rolled the sleeves of his shirt up to his elbows, exposing strong hands and forearms. He was tanned, his skin weathered from the elements. His blue eyes studied her. She didn't want to think about what he was seeing. She didn't want to think about anything, or have this talk, but there was no way to avoid it.

"This is a kerosene lamp," he said, pointing to the lantern at the end of the table. The steady flame gave off a surprising amount of light.

"About once a week, they need to be cleaned, filled with oil, and have their wicks trimmed. There's plenty of fuel and two more lamps, so that's not a problem. You control the height of the flame with this here." He pointed to what looked like the end of an ornamental metal key. When he turned it to the right, the flame rose higher.

"Let there be light," she murmured. He ignored her.

"There's a couple of hooks in the beams in the ceiling. You can hang the lantern from those and see what you're doing."

"Great."

He leaned forward, his expression earnest. "I know you don't like it here, Courtney, but we're stuck. We don't know why the storm brought us here, or how. We also don't know if it's going to take us home."

She sagged back in her chair and glared at him. "I'm glad you're still referring to that time as 'home'. After the way you've adapted to everything here I would have thought this was your home."

"I'm not the enemy."

She hated that his voice was so calm. She felt like screaming. She wanted to jump out of her skin. She wanted to go home. "Then who is? Where do I complain about what happened? This isn't right. It's not natural. People don't just fly through time."

"How do you know?"

She opened her mouth, but no sound emerged. He had a valid point. How did she know this wasn't normal? Maybe people traveled through time on a regular basis. She shuddered, not wanting that to be true. There was a consistency to the thought of life flowing forward in time and she would prefer to keep her world that way.

"We can't know for sure," Matt said. "But we *are* here and we have to make the best of it. We need to assume we can't get back. We have to make plans to survive. We can build a life here. I don't want to spend the next twenty years waiting for something that might never happen."

She looked away and stared out the window. It was already dark outside. She couldn't see more than a few feet from the house. The barn was just a hazy shadow. The air smelled damp, as if the rain would fall any moment.

She hadn't thought they couldn't go back. In her mind, it was just a matter of when. "I don't want to think like that," she said. "I am going back."

"When you find a way, let me know."

"You're just going to accept this, then?" she asked, sweeping her arm in front of her, motioning to the antiquated kitchen. "You want to live like this?"

"It's not so bad."

She stared at him, at his familiar features, and knew that she'd never really known her husband. Why would she? They'd never spent any time together.

Outside, she heard the cry of a single wolf. It went unanswered in the early evening. Her heart pounded in her chest. Under the table, her fingers twisted together, turning over and over restlessly. There was nowhere to go; they were trapped.

A combination of panic and sorrow tightened her throat. She didn't want to be here. She couldn't be here. Did he understand? She already felt lonely and it had only been a few hours. What would happen after days or weeks? She would go mad.

Before, when she felt lonely, there were places to go and people to call. Oh, she didn't have a lot of close friends, but there were a collection of acquaintances who would gladly join her for brunch, or dinner and a movie. She'd had her weekends with Matt to plan for. When the silence got too difficult to bear, she would think about where they were meeting and decide which clothes she would take. She would pore over guide-books and make notes about places to see. It didn't matter that in reality they would spend most of their weekends together in bed. The planning gave her some-thing to do.

"I have to get ready for the cattle," he said. "The barn needs finishing. We need fence lines, outbuild-ings, a bunkhouse for the cowboys. I want to ride the land and figure out the best pastures. The cattle will need to graze when they arrive."

"Sounds like a fun day."

"There's work for you, too. It's probably late, but we need a garden."

"Why?"

"For food next winter. Wyoming winters can be tough. There aren't any snowplows out here. You'll have to learn to cook on this stove, take care of the house, look after the chickens."

"Chickens? I didn't see any chickens."

"I'll buy some."

"Don't get them for *me.* I'm happy to do without."

"You'll need eggs for baking."

"Baking?" She stood up and walked over to the win-dow. The wind banged the wooden frame against the side of the house. She stood there for a few minutes let-ting the rapidly dropping temperature cool her cheeks.

When her skin was cold, she grabbed the window and pulled it shut. The latch made an audible click when she secured it.

"Baking?" she repeated and turned to face him. "I've never baked anything in my life. Wait." She held up her right hand. "I take that back. I've made brownies a couple of times. From a mix." She walked over to the large black stove. Heat poured out of it. Summer was going to be a bitch in this small kitchen.

"I can't tell you the last time I used my oven," she continued, "let alone a monstrosity like this. I don't know the first thing about cooking or raising chickens, and frankly I don't want to learn. This is your dream. Horses and cows haven't changed that much in the last couple of centuries, but homemaking has. You want too much from me, Matt. This isn't my idea of a dream. It's a nightmare."

"We can compromise," he said. "I need your help. There's so much work with the cattle, I can't take care of the house, too."

"I'm not asking you to do everything," she said. "Don't make me sound like a selfish brat. I'm just pointing out that you're expecting miracles."

"Spend your mornings inside," he said. "In the house. Then spend your afternoons looking for the storm. Maybe it will come back."

"And when it does, what will you do?"

He looked at her for a long time before turning away. Her stomach tightened. "You're not coming back with me, are you?" she asked.

"I don't know," he said, and rose to his feet. He started toward the back door. "I want to check on the horses. Why don't you start coffee?"

"Fine."

He grabbed his coat and a lantern, then went out, leaving behind silence. Courtney stood alone in the room, not knowing whether to cry or just start throwing things. Matt wanted to be sensible and plan for the future. She wanted to run until she left this nightmare behind. Nothing made sense.

She doubted it was ever going to, so rather than continue to make herself even more depressed, she collected the coffeepot Matt had left on the counter and walked over to the pump. He'd said it had needed priming, but it worked now.

She raised and lowered the pump handles. Water gushed out. "Cool," she said, and filled the coffeepot. She set the metal container on the stove, then decided to heat some water for washing.

The full bucket was heavy and she didn't know which part of the stove top was the hottest, so she just slid it on the side. The thought of adding fuel to the fire crossed her mind, but she didn't know how much, nor did she know which of the doors in front to open. She shrugged and returned to the table.

After sitting in a chair, she reached down for her backpack and unsnapped the fastener. Then she turned the bag upside down over the table. The contents spilled out.

Everything she owned in the world was in this bag. It had been a combination carry-on and purse. She sorted through the contents.

First she picked up her red leather wallet. Inside was about a hundred dollars in cash, some change, her California driver's license, an AT&T calling card, and several credit cards. All useless. She pushed the wallet aside. There were three pens. She frowned. What did they write with in 1873? Those feather things she'd seen in old paintings? Perish the thought. Did they even have pencils? She realized she didn't know which had been discovered first—ink or lead. Not that she was going to be doing a lot of writing. Who was there to write to?

A shimmering green nightshirt caught her attention. She picked up the bit of satin. It was sleeveless and barely came down to her thighs. She'd brought it just in case. Stupid really. Had she expected Matt to want to make love after she asked him to sign the divorce papers? And if she was so intent on leaving him, why had she wanted to have sex? Speaking of which . . .

She sorted through the backpack's contents until she found the smooth plastic container of birth control pills. She had just started the cycle, but was at least two pills behind. Or was it three? She got up and found a cup made out of some sort of smooth material. It didn't look rusty or too dirty. She filled it with water and rubbed it clean with her fingers, then tilted the cup to pour the water down the drain. Only there wasn't one.

"Damn," she muttered, then looked around for a place to dump the cup. Finally she crossed to the window, unlatched it and flung the contents outside. She was going to have to find something more practical. She couldn't use the kitchen window as the county sewer system.

She filled the now clean cup and took three pills, just to be safe. She knew what happened to women who had babies in this century. They all died. That was not part of her master plan.

She returned to the table and the contents of her bag. She had three pairs of cotton underwear and a spare bra. At least she could wash what she was wearing. There was a paperback book, a portable hairdryer—she picked up the plug and fingered it with disgust—shampoo, conditioner, a hairbrush, hairspray, sunscreen, and a small zip-up bag with her cosmetics. Amid the usual bag lint and assorted rubber bands and paper clips were a small radio, some Tylenol, and a bag of M&M's.

She fingered the latter, liking the way the paper crinkled. If she were a nice person, she would share her find with Matt. After all, they'd both been living on beef jerky and canned food. Instead she carefully drew her nightshirt over the wooden table and tore open the bag. She spilled the candies onto her nightshirt.

There were fifty-seven all together. Four each of the orange and blue, seven green, twelve red, fourteen yellow, and sixteen brown. She'd never really thought about M&M's before. They were something she took for granted in her life—like electricity or drains or central heating. She'd grabbed a bag at the airport, but hadn't eaten them on the plane. So here they were, who knows how many years before their time.

The colors of the candies glowed in the light of the lamp. She touched them gently, noticing for the first time how perfectly round they were. She picked up a brown one and put it into her mouth. Turning it over and over with her tongue, she sucked until the hard shell began to dissolved into little pieces. The chocolate melted, leaving a lingering sweet flavor.

She reached for another one, then realized she didn't know how long they were going to be stuck here. What if they didn't get back to their time? She would be in a world without M&M's.

She scooped up the candies and put them back in their bag. There had been a couple of rubber bands in the pile of junk from her backpack. She dug one out and, after twisting the top of the candy bag, used the rubber band to close it securely. When she'd put everything back in her backpack, she realized the kitchen wasn't as warm as it had been before. Had the fire gone out or did it need more wood? She eyed the large black stove and decided to let Matt figure it out.

Matt was halfway back to the house when the back door opened. Courtney started to step outside, saw him, and paused.

"There's something wrong with the stove," she said.

"Like what?"

"It's not giving off heat."

"Did you check the fire?"

"I don't know how."

She held the door open for him, then followed him into the kitchen. Outside the temperature continued to fall. It would get close to freezing, he thought, but it was unlikely the rain would turn to snow. It was a little late in the year for that, although not impossible.

"See these two doors?" he said, pointing to the front of the stove. She nodded. "The fuel goes on the bottom." He opened the appropriate door. "There isn't much left to burn. I started with very small pieces of wood in case the chimney was clogged. But there isn't any smoke in the kitchen."

He showed her how to pick the right-size log and where to put it. The new wood caught immediately. He closed the door. Courtney took off her jacket and hung it on the hook by the back door. He did the same. Then they stood awkwardly in the room and avoided looking at each other.

He didn't know what to say to make it better for her. She was upset about the house. He couldn't blame her. He'd hoped for something better. But while she only saw the flaws, he could see the potential. They could make it here. With a lot of hard work and a little luck, the ranch could be a showplace. But Courtney didn't want to know that.

"There's clean straw in the barn," he said. "I can restuff the mattresses."

"Good. I'd like mice-free straw in mine, please."

"I'll do my best." He kept his voice friendly, even as he felt a stab of disappointment. They'd spent last night in each other's arms. It had been strictly to share body heat, but he'd enjoyed having Courtney close to him again. He missed her, being with her. He'd hoped once they were in a house together that she would turn to him. Instead she turned away.

"I guess I can start dinner," she said, sorting through the cans he'd left on the counter. She opened a small sack. "Oh, look, there's beans. Do you know how to cook them?"

"You soak them all night, then cook them all day."

"Not exactly fast food."

"Life is slower here."

She grimaced. "Not that slow. I'm hungry and you must be, too." She picked up a couple of cans. "Corn or green beans with our beef jerky?"

"Either."

"Corn." She put one of the cans down. "At least we can have it hot tonight." She bent down and searched through the pots until she found a small one. It was dirty, coated with something that might have been burned into the bottom.

"I saw some soap in the pantry," he said, walking into the back room. There were several jars on the top shelf, along with homemade candles. Judging from the stink, he knew why they'd been placed away from the foodstuffs.

Courtney took the jar and opened it. She sniffed once, then shrieked. "What is this?"

"Homemade soap. It's a lye base, I think. I saw it during a reenactment. It comes from ashes."

She held up her left hand and stared at her fingers. "I guess I can kiss my last three nails good bye," she said, then plunged her hand into the soap.

After pulling out a small amount, she pumped water into the pot, then glanced around. "I don't suppose there's a sponge or even a cloth for me to clean this with?"

"I'll get you something."

He quickly walked through the living room into the

first bedroom. Most of the linens folded on the shelves had been both home and food for some creatures. He tore off a strip of cloth and took it back to her. She attacked the pot with the determination of a conquering general.

"I hate this," she said as she scrubbed. "Cold water and lousy soap, just so we can eat a horrible meal. I'm tired, I smell, I'm hungry. I don't want to use the outhouse. I don't want to eat corn canned by God knows who and die of botulism. And where the hell am I supposed to drain this?" she asked, finishing with the pot.

He grabbed a bucket on the floor and stuck it in the sink. "Use this. I'll dump it later."

He didn't know what to do. Courtney was hurting and that in turn hurt him. Tentatively, he moved closer to her and brushed his hand against her arm. She jerked away from him.

"Leave me alone," she said. "Go take care of the mattresses. I'll handle dinner. After all, it's women's work, right?"

She sniffed, but he knew she wouldn't cry. Courtney never cried. It was one of the things that confused him about her. He'd always thought all women cried. But she never had.

He reached out to touch her again, then lowered his hand to his side. "I'm sorry," he said. "I didn't mean for this to happen."

She drew in a deep breath. "I know you didn't, but hearing you say that doesn't make me feel better right now. I can't discuss this. Please, just leave me alone."

He left her because she asked him to. He went into the front bedroom and pulled out the mattress. It was light and filled with rotting straw. A brown mouse jumped out of a small hole and ran across the canvas covered floor, then disappeared under the dresser. They would need traps. Or a cat.

He took the mattress out the front door and into the barn. After pulling the old straw out, he shook the mattress to remove any stubborn visitors, then filled it with new straw.

Like Courtney, he didn't understand what had happened to them or why they'd been transported back in time. Unlike her, he felt as if a mistake had finally been made right. He couldn't escape the feeling of belonging. Not just to the time but to the land.

He glanced up at the half-finished barn and knew what it would look like when it was done. He could see himself driving in nails, then standing back and admiring his handiwork. He could see the cattle grazing on the land. Success meant enduring hard times and hard work, but he wasn't afraid. He could do this. He could make something of himself here. In the past he could finally lay to rest the demons who haunted him and branded him a failure by virtue of his birthright.

Yet without Courtney it would mean nothing.

He carried in the mattress and went to collect the second one. Sleeping without her meant more than not making love. It meant not being close. He'd lain awake for a time last night and listened to her breathing. The weight of her head on his shoulder, the feel of her hand on his chest had made him remember the good times in their marriage. The times when they'd been—

A loud shriek cut through his thoughts. He dropped the mattress on the floor and raced into the kitchen. Courtney stood in the center of the room holding her left hand cradled in her right. Steam rose from the top of the stove and the smell of doused fire filled the room. There was an overturned bucket on the ground.

"What happened?" he asked, coming up beside her.

"I went to pick up the bucket," she said, her voice laced with pain. "By the handle. I got burned."

He looked closer at the bucket. The thin handle was

metal. It would have been as hot as the water. He looked at her palm. A narrow band of burnt flesh cut down the center. It was one long, red, blistering strip.

No doubt there was a damp ashy mess in the bottom of the stove, but he didn't care about that. He grabbed both their coats, shrugged into his, and placed hers around her shoulders.

"Where are we going?" she asked as he picked up the lantern and led her out of the room.

"To the springhouse. The cold water will help the burn."

He put his arm around her. Instead of pushing him away, she snuggled closer. "It hurts," she murmured.

"I bet."

The stone building was small and set on higher ground than the house. Inside, it was cold and damp. She shuddered. He wondered if she was at risk of going into shock, but figured he would deal with that when it happened.

Stones surrounded the small bubbling spring containing the water, then provided a route down and out of the building. There was a pipe leading into the house. Matt settled Courtney on the stone ledge and lowered her injured hand into the cold water. She sucked in her breath but didn't cry out.

He sat next to her and held her close. She shook but was silent. There was only the gurgle of the stream and the sounds of the night beyond the small room.

"I ruined dinner," she said.

"Just some canned corn and coffee. I'll make more."

"I'm not very hungry."

She pressed her head against his chest. He stroked her silky hair, wishing it wasn't tightly bound in a braid.

"I'm sorry," he said.

"It's not your fault."

"I know, but I want to make it better."

"You can't. No one can."

She looked up at him. In the lamplight he saw the unhappiness and lingering pain in her eyes. Without thinking, he leaned forward and pressed his lips to hers. She didn't respond, but she didn't pull away, either. She simply accepted the kiss.

Her lips were as soft as he remembered. He moved back and forth slowly. The first spark of desire made itself felt low in his belly. It flared out in all directions, sending blood rushing to his groin. In seconds he was hard and wanting.

The fire still burned hot. He still loved his wife, but he didn't understand her, and he sure couldn't give her what she wanted or needed.

He broke the kiss. She closed her eyes and rested her forehead against his chest. "I just want to go home, Matt. Make this all go away."

He tightened his arms around her. That was the worst of it. He loved her enough to let her go. No matter how much it would hurt. He would have done anything for her, but he didn't have the answers either.

"You have to come with me," Matt insisted two days later. It was barely dawn. The horses were already hitched up to the wagon. The only reason he hadn't left was Courtney refused to go with him. "You can't stay here alone."

"Watch me," she said, and poured another cup of coffee. She took a sip and grimaced at the bitter taste. She might have conquered the stove, but she wasn't having much luck with the coffee. "I have one of the rifles and I know how to use it. There's enough beef jerky and canned vegetables. Besides, if you leave me here, I can look after Jasper and Rocky."

"They'll be fine on their own," he said. He'd rigged up a water trough that was fed by the stream. There was plenty of grass and he'd fixed the corral. They had sun during the day and could go under cover at night.

He studied his wife. Courtney had dark shadows under her eyes. She didn't sleep at night, she simply paced. In the morning, she ate some jerky and then left to spend the day on a knoll about a quarter of a mile from the house. She returned at dark. He'd checked on her several times over the last two days and she'd always been sitting in the same place. She took a rifle with her, didn't speak, just stared in the distance as if willing the storm to come to her. So far it hadn't obliged.

A part of him was afraid to leave her on her own. Not only because of the danger, but because she might slip more and more into herself. He'd hoped that a trip into town would help snap her out of her determination to find the storm.

"We need more supplies," he said. "And a housekeeper. Without someone who can cook, we'll starve."

She took another sip of her coffee and glanced out the window. "I already told you I think it's a great idea. You're right. We do need someone to cook. So go. I'll be fine."

He fought down a wave of frustration. "I could drag you out to the wagon."

"But you won't."

She took a last drink of her coffee, then rose to her feet and collected her coat. "'Bye, Matt. Have a safe trip." She grabbed her rifle on the way out.

He followed and watched her head for the knoll. Her determination unnerved him. He wondered if she was slipping into madness and what he could do to stop it.

"She just needs time to adjust," he told himself as he

closed the back door. He didn't lock it. There wasn't anything worth stealing. Besides, neither of them had a key. After one last look at Courtney walking away, he climbed into the wagon and took the reins. As the horses started toward town, he wondered if she would be at the house when he returned. He didn't fear predators. Instead he dreaded the mysterious storm.

Six hours later he spotted a rider on horseback. He hailed the other man. As they drew closer together, he recognized Jonathan Hastings. He slowed the wagon to a stop.

Jonathan grinned. "Neighborly of you to come welcome me."

"I was going into town for supplies."

Jonathan glanced at the wagon. "Without your wife?"

"We decided it would be better for her to stay at the ranch."

"Did you think about my offer?" the gambler asked.

"Some."

"Favorably, I hope." He reached into his jacket pocket and drew out a large wad of bills. "I brought this to prove my earnestness."

Matt studied the other man. He usually let his gut tell him whether he could trust someone.

"I wouldn't mind talking," Matt said. "But not right now. We need supplies from town and I want to hurry back as quickly as I can."

"I understand why a man wouldn't want to leave a pretty woman like your wife all alone." He drew his eyebrows together for a moment. "Why don't you tell me what you need and I'll go back and get it? You take my horse out to the ranch and I'll bring along the wagon."

Matt only hesitated a second. "You got yourself a deal." He pulled the list out of his pocket. "We need all this, plus anything else you can think of. Oh, we also need a housekeeper."

Jonathan swung down from his horse and took the list. At first he seemed more interested in the paper than what was written on it. Matt wondered if the small notebook sheet was considered odd for this time.

"Nothing too difficult here," Jonathan said after he'd read the list. "And I know someone looking for a job as a housekeeper. An older woman. Her husband passed on a while back. She's been living with one of her daughters, but she wants more independence. She's got a seventeen-year-old son. He could help with the cattle."

"It sounds great," Matt said. He reached into his jeans pocket for his money.

Jonathan waved to stop him. "Consider this the beginning of my investment," he said. "I'll be back with your provisions and Hallie in four days." He held out his hand.

Matt stared at the other man. They were the same height and about the same build. Jonathan Hastings sensed that Matt was different, but wasn't sure what it all meant. He was trusting his gut, too.

"We'll be waiting," Matt said, and shook the man's hand.

While Jonathan settled on the wagon seat, Matt swung up onto the gambler's horse. The old-fashioned saddle was more uncomfortable than his, but he didn't mind. He would be home before dark. Home and back to Courtney.

If she were still there.

7

Courtney sat on the top of the knoll and stared out into the distance. She felt as if she'd spent her whole life in this one spot. Actually it had been more like a week, but it felt like a lifetime. She wasn't used to sitting and doing nothing.

She knew this wasn't the most mentally healthy thing she'd ever done. She'd become obsessed with the storm, even dreaming about it at night. During the day she sat under a tree and waited for it to return and take her back. She could feel her brain turning to sludge. Matt was worried. She saw it in his eyes. But it was too much effort to reassure him, or to participate in this bizarre world. It was easier to do nothing.

She gazed at the now familiar horizon. She knew every bush, every tree. She could sketch this landscape from memory. There was a family of rabbits who lived in a small burrow just a short distance away from her tree. She'd watched them come out to play. The babies were still small enough to stay close to their mother. Courtney had found if she stayed perfectly still, the rabbits didn't even notice she was there. Sometimes, when she didn't think she could stand it for another second, the rabbits were all that kept her sane. They were so alive; they reminded her that she was a living creature, too.

This afternoon, however, the rabbits weren't around. There was only the bright blue sky with not a cloud in sight. Spring had arrived and summer wasn't far behind. She could tell by the way leaves burst out on the tree limbs. There were wildflowers everywhere, and the first hint of berries.

She closed her eyes against the colors and tried not to breathe in the sweet scents. She didn't want to be distracted from the place she'd found inside herself. It was so much easier just to go there.

She heard footsteps on the soft grass. They stopped beside her, but she didn't look. She didn't have to.

"I brought you some lunch," Matt said.

"I'm not hungry."

"You have to eat something."

"I don't have to do anything," she snapped, then felt a flush of shame heat her cheeks. She was acting like a brat. She knew it and yet she couldn't seem to stop herself. She didn't want to be here and she was making Matt pay for that. It was a childish gesture. He deserved better, but she just didn't have the strength.

"How long are you going to wait for the storm?" he asked.

His voice was closer now. She opened her eyes and saw he'd squatted down in front of her. He'd brought some jerky and a bowl of peaches. Her stomach turned at the sight of the familiar fare. They'd been living on jerky and canned fruits and vegetables for more than a week.

"For as long as it takes."

"And if it doesn't come back?"

His blue eyes held her gaze. He was clean shaven.

He'd found an old straight-edge razor and sharpened it. Every morning he shaved using soap and a small mirror from her backpack. He worked on the barn, prepared their meals, pumped water, did all the tasks that needed doing. At night, he tried to get her to speak or eat. She did neither. She simply sat by the window and waited until morning.

He needed to know she was going to be all right, but she couldn't reassure him. "If the storm never comes back then they'll find my bones up here, bleached white by the sun."

Worry pulled his mouth into a straight line. He was so damn handsome. If he smiled, her heart would still beat a little faster and her toes would curl in her boots. But he had no reason to smile, so her pulse remained slow and steady.

"Courtney, you can't—"

But she never heard what she couldn't do. Instead of finishing his sentence, he rose to his feet and stared toward the distance. "Finally," he said. "They're here."

"Who's here?"

"Jonathan Hastings. I told you I met him on my way to town. He's the reason I wasn't gone for three days."

"Oh." She sort of remembered Matt returning more quickly than he'd planned. But the days had blurred until she couldn't tell them apart. "You said 'they'."

"There are two wagons heading this way. He's brought supplies and a housekeeper. Come on."

Before she could stop him, he bent down, grabbed her hand, and pulled her to her feet. She found herself walking beside him. Protesting would require too much energy, so she returned to the house long before sunset. She had a fleeting thought about the storm, then sighed. It hadn't come back. There wasn't even a hint it was going to. In her heart, Courtney suspected they were stuck here. Or maybe her original thought had been right: She and Matt were both dead. This was his heaven and her hell.

They reached the house at the same time as the wagons. Courtney pulled her hat low and squinted against the bright sunlight. She recognized the gambler from Matt's night of playing poker. He was dressed in a black coat and trousers, with a brightly colored vest worn over a white shirt. His flat, dark hat looked as if it had been borrowed from the prop department on an old Hollywood back lot, but it was the genuine article. She and Matt were the ones out of place.

The gambler, Jonathan Hastings, met her gaze and smiled. There was something about his dark eyes. Something dangerous. It made her uneasy.

Matt walked over to the first wagon and shook hands with Jonathan. The gambler set the brake and climbed down. When the two men were standing side by side, she could see they were about the same height and build. Both had dark hair, although Jonathan's was longer. Unless Matt found a barber in the next couple of weeks, his hair would commit the unforgivable sin of actually touching his collar.

The men looked about the same age. They were both strong. Matt was better looking, although it was more than that which made her prefer him. From the first moment they'd met, she'd known Matt could keep her safe from anything, and he was capable of giving back. Jonathan Hastings was the sort of man who hadn't yet discovered the value of life's softer side.

She turned her attention to the second wagon. The driver wasn't much more than a boy, maybe sixteen or seventeen, with bright red hair and freckles. He stared at Courtney as if he'd never seen a woman in jeans before.

His passenger was a woman. Her large bonnet shaded most of her face. She wore a simple long dress in a blue calico print. Courtney tried to judge her age, but she couldn't. Nor did she care. If the woman could do more in the kitchen than heat canned green beans, she was welcome to stay as long as she liked.

Jonathan walked toward the second wagon. "Matt Stone, this is Mrs. Hallie Wilson and her son, Roger."

Matt shook hands with the boy and tipped his hat to the woman. "Ma'am, we're much obliged to you for coming out here. The house isn't much, but I have plans."

"Plans are one thing, young man. Do you intend to do the work to see those plans through?" Hallie's tone was sharp.

Matt thought for a moment, then smiled. The smile wasn't directed at her, but Courtney's toes curled on cue anyway. The other woman didn't seem as affected, though. She just sat still as a statue until he spoke.

"Words are cheap, ma'am," he said. "Why don't you wait and judge for yourself?"

Hallie Wilson sniffed, but Courtney thought she might have been a little impressed by Matt's answer. Her husband had a way about him. Lord knows the first time they met, he'd charmed her in less than fifteen minutes and up until that moment she had assumed she was immune.

Hallie poked her son in the arm. The young man jumped down, then went around to the other side and assisted his mother. When Hallie was on firm ground again, she walked up to Courtney and stared at her.

Courtney was just over five feet five inches tall. Hallie had to be at least three inches shorter, although with the large bonnet nearly circling her face, it was hard to tell. There were faint wrinkles around her light brown eyes and freckles on her nose and cheeks. Her gaze was steady as it held Courtney's.

"She touched in the head?" Hallie asked.

It took Courtney a moment to realize the woman meant *her.* "What a ridiculous question."

"Crazy people don't bother me much," Hallie went on as if Courtney hadn't spoken. "Unless they get violent. She's kind of skinny, but I won't stay if she throws things or hits me."

Courtney opened her mouth, then closed it. She was too stunned to think of any words. Matt quickly came to her side and put his arm around her.

"My wife isn't crazy, Mrs. Wilson. Why would you think there was a problem?"

"She goes around dressing like a man. Exposing her lower half to all the world. Even the whores aren't that brazen. So I figured she has to be touched in the head."

"Where we come from," Matt said, "women often wear trousers instead of long skirts. It's more practical."

"It's a scandal, if you ask me."

Courtney jerked free of Matt's arm and stared at the other woman. "I don't recall anyone asking you. If you don't like what you see here, then just get back in your wagon and—"

"Hallie, I told you Mrs. Stone lost everything in a tornado," Jonathan Hastings cut in smoothly. "Besides, you can tell from looking at her and listening to her talk that she's not from around here. People have different standards."

Hallie shook her head. "You'll never convince me wearing men's clothing is normal, but I said I'd take the job and I'll give it a try." She narrowed her gaze. "Just don't you be trying your fancy ways on my son. Roger's a good boy and I don't want him influenced by the likes of you."

With that, Hallie picked up a small bag from the rear of the wagon, turned, and went in the house.

Courtney sucked in a breath. "That woman is a—a—"

"Housekeeper," Matt said. "She can cook and clean. As you pointed out to me, it's not fair to expect you to cope with everything at once."

If Jonathan Hastings hadn't been standing right there, she would have told Matt what she thought of his throwing her words back in her face. But one person on the ranch was already questioning her sanity. She didn't need anyone to know they were from the future. Not only wouldn't they be believed, her humorous statements about an insane asylum might come true. And that was not how she planned to spend the rest of her life.

She glanced at the saintly Roger and was faintly embarrassed to realize he was still staring at her legs. For the first time she understood that she *was* different from any woman in this time. Not just in how she dressed, but in how she thought and what she expected from the world in general and her husband in particular.

She looked at Matt, then at Jonathan Hastings. On the outside they were very similar, but on the inside, they couldn't be more different. Matt had been shaped by the same forces she had. He would understand her sensibilities. Imagine if she'd come through time on her own. How would she have survived? How could she have ever talked with anyone? Perish the thought.

"I brought everything on your list," Jonathan was saying. "There's more food, linens, bedding, chickens." He went on with his list.

Courtney eyed the two wagons. They were both overflowing with supplies. For the first time since they'd arrived at the house, she felt a slight lifting of her spirits. She grabbed an armful of linens and went inside.

Hallie was in the kitchen, examining the stove. She glanced up and frowned. "This thing needs a thorough cleaning and blacking. It looks like it hasn't been used in months."

"It hasn't. The house was deserted for the winter, maybe longer."

"I thought you'd been here a week."

"We have."

"Well?"

Courtney flushed. "I'm not from around here. I don't know about stoves like this."

"Or cooking," Hallie said, pointing at the piles of empty tins on the counter. "Is that all you've been living on?"

Courtney nodded.

Hallie untied her bonnet and pulled it off. "No wonder you're so skinny. Don't worry, Mrs. Stone. I'll fatten you up."

"Call me Courtney."

Hallie seemed to consider the request. Her hair was a stunning shade of auburn and had been pulled up on her head in a bun. With her old-fashioned dress and the bonnet hanging from her hands, she looked as if she'd just stepped from the pages of *Little House on the Prairie.*

"All right," she said at last. "And I'm Hallie. If we're going to be living in the same house, there's no call for being formal. Those are linens," she said, pointing to the fabric in Courtney's arms. "They go in the bedroom."

Hallie led the way through the living room. "This place needs a good dusting. I wonder if there's wood under the canvas, or just dirt." She stomped her foot. "Wood. We can take up the cloth and polish the floors. After a couple of days we'll have them shining like window glass."

She stopped in the doorway to the smaller bedroom. "I'll take this one," she said.

"You can't. It's Matt's room."

Hallie glanced over her shoulder. "Are you telling me you and Mr. Stone aren't married? Because if you aren't, I'm marching right out of this house and not coming back."

Courtney sighed impatiently. "Of course we're married. But that's—"

Hallie cut her off. "Near as I can tell there are only two bedrooms in this house. Roger will sleep in the barn with the horses. My pay includes a private room. If you don't see fit to provide one, I'm marching right out of this house—"

"And not coming back. Yes, I can figure out that part of the speech." Courtney stared at the other woman. She hadn't thought about a housekeeper, but now the idea intrigued her. "You're very bossy," she said without thinking.

Hallie surprised her by smiling. "I do enjoy getting my way from time to time."

Courtney was even more surprised when she found herself smiling back. "Can you really cook?"

"Put those linens down and come with me. I'll prove it."

In the kitchen Hallie unfastened her small bag and pulled out a white apron. After slipping the narrow straps over her shoulders, she secured the ties in back. The apron covered her down past her knees.

While Matt and Jonathan unloaded the wagon, Hallie put Courtney to work peeling potatoes. Courtney sat at a kitchen chair and scraped the old-fashioned peeler against the vegetables. The scraps fell into a bucket.

Roger was sent outside with the barrels of rotting food. He dumped everything, then scrubbed the insides with a dry brush. Hallie inspected his work and pronounced the barrels clean enough. A hundred-pound sack of flour was dumped into the first barrel. Sugar went into the next.

Jars of mysterious dried plants were left on the kitchen counter. Suspicious-looking tins were thrown away, and the shelves in the pantry were dusted and new foodstuffs put away. While this was going on, Hallie put some dried beef in water for a stew. She rummaged through the jars of spices and pulled out leaves and cloves and pellets. Using a mortar and pestle, she ground them up and added them to the water. Canned tomatoes went in next.

"Do you have any beans?" she asked.

"There's a sack of them in the pantry," Courtney said.

"I meant cooked."

"I don't know how. Matt said I needed to soak them first but I never got around to it."

Hallie raised her eyebrows. "Where exactly are you from?"

"Los Angeles."

"Where's that?"

Courtney sighed. "A long way from here. It might as well be on another planet."

Hallie considered that for a moment. She had delicate features—a small nose and mouth with almond-shaped eyes. Most redheads Courtney knew bemoaned their lack of eyelashes but Hallie's were thick and a shade or two darker than her auburn hair. She was actually quite attractive. Courtney wondered what had happened to Hallie's husband. The woman wore a simple gold band on her left hand.

Before she could ask, Hallie took the peeled potatoes from her and began slicing them into the stew. "You don't know how to cook beans. What else don't you know?"

"Let's go with the shorter list: what I do know how to do. I can shoot a rifle and I can boil water." She thought about mentioning the fact that she could make perfect espresso, but didn't think that would impress anyone.

"You don't know how to cook?" Hallie was incredulous.

"Not on that thing." She pointed at the big black stove. She hadn't made peace with it yet. So far, their relationship was one of respect. At least she respected the stove. She didn't know what it thought of her.

"And you a married woman. It's shameful."

"I'm sure that's what Matt thinks."

Hallie finished slicing the potatoes and stared at her thoughtfully. "You swear you're not touched in the head?"

Courtney smiled. "Sometimes I wish I were, but no, I'm perfectly sane."

"This is the oddest household I've ever seen. Go grab me a couple of handfuls of beans. Rinse them in water, then put them on to soak."

"Why?"

"So we can have them tomorrow. The first thing you need to know about cooking is that you have to plan ahead. Beans need to soak overnight, then they cook all day."

Courtney did as she requested. She grabbed two handfuls of beans and dumped them in a bowl. She pumped water over them, then, not knowing what else to do with the water, drained it into the bucket with the potato peelings. She found a reasonably clean pot, filled it halfway with water, then added the beans.

"Now what?" she asked.

"Cover them so nothing falls in and leave them in the corner. We'll cook them in the morning. It'll have to be beans and dried meat for a day or two. The chickens won't lay for a few days."

"Live chickens?"

"You prefer another kind?"

"Lay as in lay eggs?"

Hallie stirred the stew and nodded. "They've been upset. They need to calm themselves before they get back to laying. Once we're all settled down here, your Mr. Stone and my Roger can go kill a buffalo. That'll give us fresh meat, plus plenty for smoking."

"Smoking?" Courtney knew her vision of buffalo cigarettes had to be wrong.

Hallie wiped her hands on her apron and smiled kindly. "I'll show you. It's easy. A strong woman like you shouldn't have any trouble taking care of this house."

"Sure."

Hallie walked to the small window and glanced out. "We'll need to start a garden. It's late in the season, but we'll get a few things in the ground. Winter lasts a long time out here and no one takes kindly to starving."

Courtney felt as if she were Alice and had followed the white rabbit down a hole to Wonderland. She was talking to a living, breathing woman who had lived a hundred years before she, Courtney, had even been born. They were discussing smoking buffalo meat as if it were the normal way to spend the afternoon.

In the pantry were foods she'd never seen before, at least not in their raw state. They were cooking on a wood-burning stove and Hallie thought *she* was crazy?

"I'll get started on some biscuits. I don't suppose you have any sourdough starter?"

Courtney stared at her blankly. "What?"

"Never mind. I'll make baking powder biscuits. We don't have time to bake bread today."

"If you say so." Courtney glanced at the bucket of potato peelings. "What do I do with these?"

"Give them to Roger and he'll throw them out. While you're at it, tell Mr. Stone he needs to get himself a pig. It's a shame to let good food go to waste."

Courtney felt as if her mother had come back to life. "Yes, ma'am," she said and picked up the bucket.

When she stepped outside, she saw Roger, Matt, and Jonathan building what looked like a small one-room house. Off to one side sat several chickens in makeshift cages. All three men looked up when the back door slammed behind her. Jonathan and Roger instantly stared at her legs. She held the bucket in front of her thighs and told herself she was foolish for feeling self-conscious.

"Everything all right?" Matt asked, coming toward her.

"Fine. Hallie said to tell you we need a pig." She motioned to the potato peelings. "I guess for scraps and stuff. Personally, I'd rather have a garbage disposal."

Matt grinned. "Me, too. I've never liked pigs. But I'll see what I can do. You want me to get rid of this?" he asked, taking the bucket.

"Sure. Thanks." Their fingers brushed. She felt a spark of electricity jump between them.

"It's good to see that light back in your eyes," he said. "I was worried."

"I know." She glanced up at the knoll, but it didn't seem so important to be there right now. She was losing faith in her ability to will the storm to return.

"Mrs. Stone?" Jonathan Hastings approached, carrying two large packages wrapped in paper. "Your husband mentioned a tornado as the reason you've been forced to wear men's clothing. Not that you don't look completely charming."

The man was too smooth for her. Courtney had always been wary of men who knew women better than they knew themselves. She glanced at Matt. He winked at her. "Yes, there was a storm, Mr. Hastings." She bit back a giggle when she realized she'd instinctively fallen into an old-fashioned, formal way of addressing people. Maybe she and Matt should start calling each other Mr. and Mrs. Stone.

"I hope you're not insulted, but I took the liberty of buying you a few things." He handed her the packages. "There are two dresses and well, other things."

"I won't be insulted that you bought them if you won't

be insulted when I don't wear them." She could just imagine what the other things might be. Those weird long pantaloon-thingies and a corset. She glanced at Matt. "I don't care what you say, I'm not wearing a corset."

Roger was close enough to hear. His eyes widened in shock. Jonathan fought a grin, but Matt didn't bother even trying. He laughed out loud. "No one's going to force you to do anything, Courtney."

Her toes curled on cue. She stared at her husband for a moment, then smiled back at him. "Then why do I suddenly feel something tightening around my ribs?"

Matt leaned back in his chair and sighed with contentment. "This was the best meal I've had in days."

"High praise for throwing a few things in a pot. Any fool could have—" Hallie paused for moment, then cleared her throat. "What I meant was, I didn't mind the trouble."

Courtney picked up the dirty dishes and carried them to the dry sink. "Don't worry about insulting me, Hallie. I agree with Matt. Dinner was terrific. We've been living on jerky and canned tomatoes for a week."

Courtney grabbed a thick cloth, then took a bucket off the stove. She poured half the contents into another bucket and pumped cold water into both of them. After opening the jar of soap, she wrinkled her nose at the smell, then started washing dishes.

Jonathan Hastings had started back to town several hours before, so there were just four of them for dinner. Roger pushed back his chair, mumbled a goodnight, and left the house to sleep in the barn. Matt had offered him the living room floor, but the boy had shyly insisted he preferred to sleep outside unless it was snowing.

After watching the teenager trying not to look at

Courtney's legs, Matt couldn't say he was sorry to see the kid go. Roger's hyperawareness of her made Matt notice her, too. Even now, as she washed dishes, her body flexed and moved in a graceful dance designed to bring a man to his knees.

There was no where he would rather be. Kneeling in front of her, touching her, loving her everywhere, with his fingers, his lips, and his tongue. There wasn't a part of her he hadn't kissed and tasted.

Her jeans emphasized the feminine curve of her hips, the narrowness of her waist, and the length of her legs. Sometime during the day, she'd abandoned her Stetson. He could see her long blond braid hanging halfway down her back. He knew what her hair would feel like if he loosened the rubber band. Thick, silky waves would slip through his fingers. Every part of him ached to be with her.

He wanted to take her into his arms and hold her. Just hold her. They didn't have to do more. He'd gone without before.

"I envy these dishes," Courtney said as she rinsed the plates and handed them to Hallie, who was drying.

"Why?" he asked.

"They're getting clean. I would kill for a bath."

Hallie frowned slightly. "There's no call to end a life just to indulge yourself. If you want a bath, then have one. Though if you ask me, bathing at night is flirting with a chill."

Hallie set down the plate she was drying and collected several large pots. She shooed Courtney out of the way, then quickly filled each pot with water and set it on the stove.

"When you're done here, go outside and bring in the largest wash tub," Hallie told her.

Courtney looked doubtful. "That's my bathtub?"

"If it cleans clothes, it'll clean people just the same.

If you ask me, people are a mite simpler to clean. They don't take to stains as easy."

Courtney dumped the silverware into the bucket and scrubbed each piece. "I probably don't want to know, but where will I take my bath?"

"Right here," Hallie said, sounding surprised. "Where else would you take a bath?"

"Where else?" Courtney echoed.

"It's the warmest room in the house."

"Why didn't I think of that?" Courtney glanced at Matt over her left shoulder. "You're pretty quiet, Matt. What do you think of all this? I'm going to take a bath in the kitchen."

He wanted to ask if he could watch, but figured she wouldn't appreciate the question. "Women's ways have always been a mystery to me."

"Ah, the politically correct answer." She plunged the last of the silverware into the rinse water, then dried her hands on a spare towel. "I'm off to get my wash tub. If I'm not back in five minutes, send the cavalry." She disappeared out the pantry door.

When she was gone, Hallie turned slowly and looked at him. "What's wrong with her, Mr. Stone?"

He'd been expecting the question. He'd seen the way Hallie looked at Courtney and couldn't even begin to imagine what the older woman was thinking. Courtney didn't know how to do the simplest domestic tasks. He wanted to tell Hallie that Courtney designed movie posters combining a painting, computer-generated pictures, and text to create something that not only promoted movies but was an art form of its own. But she wouldn't understand that.

"Courtney isn't from around here," he said, hedging.

"She told me she was from a place called Los Angeles."

"She is."

"She doesn't know how to do anything." Hallie picked up several pieces of silverware and started to dry them. "She must have had servants all around her."

"In a way," he said, thinking of the microwave oven and portable phone in her condo. "She has a lot to learn, but she's very smart."

"I don't mind teaching her things. I just wondered." Hallie's light brown gaze rested on him. "You're not from around here, either."

"No."

"But you're not from this Los Angeles. You're used to working."

"I've been around cows my whole life."

"I heard that you're expecting longhorns all the way from Texas. A bunch of nonsense, if you ask me." She set the dry silverware on a tray, then gave him a quick smile. "Of course, you didn't ask me, did you?"

"The cattle are going to thrive here. You wait and see."

"Oh, I will, Mr. Stone. Tell me one more thing, then I'll mind my business for a while."

"What's that?"

"If you love your wife so much, why are you keeping separate rooms? Women don't want a man who gives them their way. They want their men to be strong. I was married nearly twenty years. We had our fights, it's true, but I knew in my heart Mr. Wilson wanted what was best for me. Courtney knows that, too."

"I'll give that some thought," he said, then wondered what his wife would think of nineteenth-century marriage counseling. If anyone tried to tell Courtney what was best for her, she would have that person's hide hanging in strips.

The back door banged open. "I got it," Courtney said as she dragged in a large wash tub.

Hallie tested the water on the stove, then looked at

him. "We're about ready here, Mr. Stone, if you'd care to take a turn around the barn."

It took him a moment to realize he was being thrown out of his own kitchen. Not that he'd expected to watch. Okay, he'd *hoped* to watch, but he known it was unlikely. He grabbed his hat and coat and left by the back door.

The night was clear and cold. He was familiar with the evening sky, recognizing the constellations from the time he'd spent on the road. He often pulled his truck off the interstate and slept in the middle of nowhere. He would wake up hours before dawn and stare at the sky. That hadn't changed.

He checked on the horses. Roger was still awake and came out from the last stall.

"'Evenin', Mr. Stone," the teenager said.

"Call me Matt."

"You sure? I don't want to show disrespect."

"I know you don't and I appreciate that." Matt walked outside and leaned on the corral fence.

The boy followed. "Mr. Hastings said you're going to be bringing up cattle from Texas. Is that true?"

"Yes. Nearly two thousand head. They'll arrive late in the summer." At least he hoped they would. He wanted to get the herd settled on the lower grazing land before the first snows set in.

"I worked on a dairy ranch for a time, but I've never seen me no longhorns."

Matt started to explain the differences, then realized he was talking about the longhorns of his own time. How had the generations of breeding changed the animals? He grinned in anticipation. "I haven't seen any like these, either. I guess we'll learn together."

"I appreciate you giving me this job. My ma was worried about me being on my own, away from her. I think she was thinkin' she'd be lonely. There's five of us. I'm the youngest. Anyways, with both of us on the ranch together, it'll be better. I'll work real hard for you, Mr. Stone, ah, Matt."

"I know you will, Roger. It's getting late. You go turn in."

"Yes, sir. 'Night."

The boy disappeared in the darkness of the barn. He was about five or six inches shorter than Matt and he hadn't filled out much yet, but the promise of strength was there. He seemed to take to the animals, which would make working with the cows easier.

There were so many decisions to be made. Which outbuildings to construct first, how to set up the breeding program, whether to take Jonathan Hastings on as a partner.

The gambler wanted to be a part of the operation, and he was willing to pay for the privilege. Matt knew he could use the cash right now. When the herd arrived, he was going to need cowboys, fences, holding pens, more horses, and about two dozen other things he couldn't think of right now. All of them would take money he and Courtney didn't have.

Jonathan had already paid for some of the supplies. Unless Matt paid him back with interest, the gambler would own a piece of the ranch. Matt didn't want to make that decision without talking to Courtney, and he didn't think it was a conversation she would want to have. After all, she didn't want to be here at all. Why would she discuss the day-to-day workings of the ranch?

He glanced up at the stars winking down at him. The night was inky black. The sky stretched on forever. Instead of feeling insignificant, he felt part of a larger whole. As if he'd found his place in the cycle of life. Unlike Courtney, he didn't want to search for the storm. She was right, he belonged here.

Is that what the storm had been doing? Setting something to rights? But if he'd been born in this time, he would never have met her. Being with Courtney was worth any price. Even the ranch.

"Mr. Stone?" Hallie called from the back porch. "Your wife is done with her bath. Seems a shame to waste hot water. You want to come and set in it a spell?"

He was feeling a little grubby himself. "Sure. I'll be right there."

He crossed the yard between the barn and the house. The light from the small kitchen window illuminated his way. When he stepped inside, it took a moment for his eyes to adjust to the brightness of the lanterns. Then he blinked and everything came into focus.

His heart clenched tight in his chest and he couldn't catch his breath. Courtney sat on a low stool brushing her hair in front of the stove. A white cotton gown covered her from neck to ankles. Her unbound hair tumbled nearly to her waist. She combed the damp strands, fanning them with her fingers.

She looked as innocent as a bride. In his mind, she'd never been more beautiful. She glanced up at him and smiled shyly.

"Hallie didn't approve of my nightgown."

"That little slip of fabric wasn't bigger than a handkerchief. It's a scandal." The housekeeper poured more hot water into the tub, then set the empty bucket on the floor. "Leave the water until morning. Roger will empty it when he starts the fire." She started for the door.

"'Night, Hallie," Courtney said.

"Good night."

With that the housekeeper disappeared into the living room. A few seconds later her bedroom door closed.

They were alone.

8

The lantern on the table cast a soft glow of light through the kitchen. The room was steamy and warm and smelled of woodsmoke. As Courtney raised her arms to smooth her hair, her body straightened. He could see the movement of her bare breasts under the cotton gown. The fabric stretched slightly, outlining the small points of her nipples. His gut clenched as his hands balled into fists. He tried to control his breathing and his reaction. Both quickly burned out of control. As she turned slightly, he caught the shadowy outline of her narrow waist and curved hip. He had to fight back a groan.

"Hallie let me use some of her soap," Courtney said, tilting her head so that her hair slipped off her shoulder to hang straight down like a cascade of blond silk. "I've started a new list of supplies and soap is at the top of it. That homemade lye stuff is awful. Anyway, she left it for you."

He glanced down and saw a square of soap resting on a folded cloth next to the metal tub. "Thanks."

His voice was low and hoarse. He knew why. He also knew what was going to happen the second he unbuttoned his trousers. She would know exactly what he'd been thinking.

He didn't know whether to turn away or flaunt his condition. After a moment of indecision, he stayed where he was. She could look or not. It wasn't as if she hadn't seen him aroused before.

He unbuttoned his shirt, then sat on a kitchen chair to pull off his boots. Socks came next. While he was still seated, he shrugged out of his shirt. Jeans were next. As he rose to his feet, he noticed Courtney darting little half glances at him through the curtain of her hair. She was about to get an eyeful.

He reached for the first button. His erection strained the fly. He wanted to cross the few feet between them and pull her close. He wanted to bury himself deep inside her, touching her and teasing her until she could barely pant his name. He wanted to make her writhe and scream, then have her give herself up to the pleasure. His favorite memories of their lovemaking were the ones when she was out of control beneath him, clawing at him, moaning, then climaxing so violently, he had no choice but to come himself.

When he ached for her, that was what he remembered. Echoing shudders, breathing returning to normal, sweat-soaked skin brushing and the sound of her voice as she whispered. It had never been like that before for her. It had never been like that before for him, either. He didn't take advantage of all the buckle bunnies offered, but he'd been with women before. He'd known pleasure. But nothing like what he found with Courtney.

He unfastened the last buttons and pushed the jeans down his legs. His reminiscing had only aggravated the condition. With a quick tug, his briefs joined his jeans. He stepped into the water.

He didn't sit down right away. There was no point in hiding the obvious. Courtney moved her head slightly to glance at him. Their gazes locked for a second before hers slipped away. She dipped her chin and continued brushing her hair, but not before he saw a faint flush on her cheeks.

For some reason that pleased him. He sat in the hot water.

"This isn't the most dignified way to take a bath," he said as he tried to stretch out. The tub didn't accommodate his legs and he was forced to keep them bent at the knees.

She giggled. "I know. But it's better than anything we've had all week. At least I feel clean again. But I miss my shower."

He reached for the soap and lathered it slowly. "I've hated seeing you so unhappy," he said as he washed his arms and chest. "I wish there were something I could do to help." He thought about the storm and the way she'd spent her days waiting for it to come back. "I could take you back to the boulder where we first showed up. I told you before I couldn't find it, but that's not true."

She turned on the stool until she was facing him. Her long hair glowed in the lamplight. Her eyes darkened, her mouth tilted up at the corners. "I know you could find it, but I don't think it would help. For now, we're both stuck here. I'm feeling better. Maybe it's having other people around. They've convinced me this is real. I'm going to have to learn how to adjust." She smiled. "At least I can learn how to cook. Hallie promised to teach me."

"There's a lot of work for both of us."

"Hallie says she's going to send you and Roger out to kill a buffalo for meat. Is that true?"

"It makes sense. A buffalo could feed us for a long time."

She leaned forward. "I hate to rain on your parade and all, but we don't have a freezer. Where are you going to put it? Hallie said something about smoking it, but she wasn't serious, was she?"

"Afraid so."

"We're going to need five hundred and one ways to serve buffalo then. I wonder if she knows how to make fajitas?"

"I don't think so. Maybe you can teach her."

"The blind leading the blind. What do you think is in corn tortillas? Corn meal and something else. Maybe we could make them. Oh, we could make them really thin, then cut them up and fry them to have our own chips." She closed her eyes and sighed. "I miss Mexican food."

"Me, too."

She opened her eyes. "What else do you miss?"

He soaped his legs and splashed water to rinse them, then he looked at her. "I miss you."

"Matt—"

"I miss being friends and being lovers. I miss being married to you."

All traces of humor faded from her face. "How can you miss what we never had?" She set her brush on the counter and began braiding her hair. Her fingers moved swiftly, separating her hair into three strands, then quickly folding them, one over the other. "We were never married, not in the real sense of the word. I don't know that we were ever friends. How could we be? We don't know each other. A week here, a weekend there. It was always new. We never had to deal with the day-to-day problems of being married. We never worked through the tough times and came out stronger."

She was right, but he didn't want to think about that. "Then I miss what could have been."

He ran his fingers through his hair, dampening the strands, then lathered up the soap. Courtney tied off her braid and used a towel to lift a bucket off the stove. She pumped in cold water, then tested the temperature.

"Scoot forward and tilt your head back," she said. "I'll rinse your hair."

He did as she asked, moving to the front of the small tub and holding on. He arched his head back. She poured the water over his hair, holding the bucket with one hand and shielding his eyes with the other. The gentle touch made him ache with longing. Not so much for sex as for affection.

When she was done, she handed him a length of cloth. "Towels, nineteenth-century style."

As she returned to her stool, he stood up. The water and their conversation had combined to ease his condition. She glanced at his midsection, dipped her gaze lower, then looked away.

He dried off, then wrapped the towel around his waist and sat in the chair nearest to her. There was still the width of the kitchen table between them. The room was silent, except for the snapping of the wood in the fire. He could smell the smoke, the lingering odor of their dinner, and the fresh, clean scent of the soap. He smoothed his hair back with his fingers, then asked the question that had haunted him since she'd first mentioned wanting a divorce.

"Is there someone else?"

Her eyebrows arched up as her eyes opened wide. Her lips parted. "What?"

He had to swallow hard. He didn't want to know, but he had to find out the truth. "Are you seeing someone else? Is that why you want a divorce?"

He'd braced himself for several reactions, but not for her smile. "There's no one else," she said. "We haven't had much of a marriage, but I've been a faithful wife. I don't want the divorce because of another man but because of me." She stood up and crossed to the table, then took the seat opposite him.

"I remember feeling abandoned and alone when my parents died," she said. "I went to college, got a good job, had lots of friends, but no matter what I did, that feeling of being alone was always there inside me. It's taken crossing time for me to realize it's still there. I've always tried to fill my life with sound and people and activities. Once they were all gone, I could still hear the echo of that empty place." She leaned back in her chair.

They'd both lost their mothers. It was a connection and they'd never talked about it. Were there other missed bonds? Had he lost Courtney because he didn't pay attention?

"I married you because of how you made me feel," she said. "When I'm with you, I feel like I belong. That's what I've always wanted. But it's not enough." She leaned forward and rested her hands on the table. Her gaze sought his. "I want the divorce because I want more than a part-time relationship. I want something real where I'm forced to be with someone day after day. I want to know every intimate detail of my husband's life. I want to bare myself the same way. I want to risk it all in the hope of something wonderful together. And if it fails, it won't be because I didn't try my best."

Her courage awed him. She was willing to expose every layer in the name of love. The thought chilled him to the core. He knew what was underneath his facade of confidence. He knew the truth about himself. If Courtney knew, she would turn away in disgust. He wasn't good enough; he'd never been good enough, but for a while he'd been willing to pretend.

"Our collection of long weekends and vacations

wasn't a real marriage," she said. "Neither of us was willing to change and we both knew it. My life is in the city and yours is on a ranch somewhere." She stretched her fingers toward him. "Did you notice that we always fought at the end, just before we said good-bye?"

"Yes."

"I always wondered why."

"I thought it was because we didn't want to be apart." At least that was the reason he said things to her. He wanted her to stay with him, not to return to her life in the city. "I never felt I had the right to ask you to stay."

"And you wouldn't offer to come with me."

"Live in L.A.?" He shook his head.

"I always thought we fought because we both knew the truth," she said. "Our time together was limited. It hurt so much to be apart that each time we were together we fought, hoping the other would be strong enough to end it."

His heart ached. The pain in his chest grew until it hurt to breathe. He couldn't speak, he could only stare at her mutely, wishing it wasn't so damn painful to love her.

The light from the lantern made her skin glow. He knew every curve of her cheek, the shape of her mouth, the length of her neck. He knew her body, yet she was right—he didn't know *her.* Perhaps he never had. He'd been kidding himself. Loving Courtney was a unique form of torture. He'd allowed himself to believe he might have the only woman he'd ever wanted. But he'd been doomed from the start.

"Where do we go from here?" he asked.

"I don't know. Everything is different. I didn't mean to say all that. I guess I wanted you to know there was never anyone but you, Matt. Not from the moment we met." She smiled slightly. "Frankly, the thought never crossed my mind. Who would have thought I'd be such a sucker for a cowboy?"

He tried to smile, but his face felt frozen. The pain in his chest made it hard to concentrate on what she was saying.

She tossed her braid over her shoulder. "It's getting late. We should go to bed. Hallie has taken the front room."

"I figured that."

"That leaves the back bedroom for us." She stared down at the table. "I don't mind if you don't."

Did he *mind* sleeping next to her, feeling her body press against him? He must be a masochistic jerk because he couldn't think of anything he wanted more.

"No problem," he said, rising to his feet. He collected his clothing while she picked up the lantern and led the way into their bedroom.

The mattress didn't look wide enough for the both of them, unless they slept touching. More than his gut tightened at the thought.

He waited until she extinguished the lantern before dropping his towel and sliding onto the mattress. The linens were new. The straw rustled. Their legs brushed as she turned on her side. Her skin was smoother than the cotton, a soft heat that tormented him.

"Sorry," she murmured, and tried to move away. There wasn't anywhere to go.

He lay on his back and stared at nothing. Even after his eyes adjusted, he couldn't see much of anything. There were no streetlights, no car headlights, nothing to illuminate the complete blackness. But he could hear.

Her breathing was slow and rhythmic, as if she were trying to convince him, or maybe herself, that she was asleep. His heartbeat sounded loud. She stirred slightly and the straw again rustled. He heard cotton slide over linen, skin over cotton.

The need in his belly moved lower until his arousal throbbed with the rush of heated blood. It would be so easy to take her in his arms and make love to her.

Easy . . . but wrong.

Their odd journey to this place had changed everything, yet one important fact remained the same. Courtney wanted a divorce. As soon as they returned to their own time, she would ask him to sign the papers. Then she would disappear from his life. Making love with her now would make it harder to leave her later.

So he ignored the desire and the hunger. He touched her shoulder, tugging her toward him.

"Matt?"

"We can't not touch," he said. "We might as well be comfortable. Use my shoulder for a pillow."

She turned over and settled next to him. Her right leg rested on his, her arm draped across his belly. He wondered what she would think if he pushed her hand down a few inches. What would she do?

He didn't bother to find out. It was better this way. She wouldn't move her hand lower, so she would never know what he wanted. This position was safer than curling up behind her playing spoons. In that pose he wouldn't have been able to disguise his erection.

She sighed, her breath fanning his bare chest. He bent his arm so he could stroke her hair. She whispered his name. For now, it was enough.

There wasn't a window in the bedroom, but Courtney had the impression of daylight. Maybe it was the shadows she could make out in the hallway. Maybe it was because Matt was gone and the sheets where he'd slept were cold. Maybe it was the faint pounding she heard from the direction of the barn.

She sat up and reached for her watch, but she

couldn't read it in the dim light. She got out of bed and fumbled for her clothes.

They were gone.

"I left them right here," Courtney muttered, feeling around the armoire. There was a pile of something but it sure wasn't jeans.

She felt her way around until she got to the lantern. The little drawer at the bottom opened easily. She drew out a match and lit it. By the light of the flame, she removed the chimney and touched the match to the wick. Instantly it caught and the room lightened.

As she replaced the chimney, she blew out the match and glanced at the pile of clothing. Several white puffy things sat on top of a dark green thing.

She had a bad feeling about this.

A thorough search of the room didn't turn up anything. Even her panties and bra were missing. She checked the hooks behind the door, then grabbed the lantern and started for the kitchen.

Hallie was stirring something on the stove. Her auburn hair had been pulled neatly back in a bun. She still wore her blue calico dress from yesterday, but the apron was clean and looked freshly pressed.

"Where are my clothes?" Courtney asked from her place in the doorway.

"Well, now, I see you decided to get up. The sun and a few people around here have been working for nearly two hours."

Courtney glanced at her watch. It was barely eight. "I was tired," she said, then realized that for the first time since arriving at the ranch, she'd slept the night through. In fact she didn't remember anything from the time she'd rolled into Matt's arms until she'd awakened a few moments ago.

She felt rested and full of energy. Ready to take on the world, including one slightly stubborn housekeeper. She narrowed her gaze. "I want my clothes back," she said. "Where are they?"

Hallie put down her spoon and brushed her hands on the front of her apron. "I'm not about to let you prance around in men's clothing. I've got Roger to worry about. I saw him staring at your legs last night. Heaven knows what kind of thoughts filled his head. He's a good boy and I won't have him ruined."

The woman was serious. Courtney stared at her in disbelief. "You're acting as if my wearing jeans is a crime. I assure you it's very common."

"Maybe where you come from, but not here. I'm not going to spend my days worrying about Roger having evil thoughts."

Their gazes locked in stormy competition. Courtney felt she had to stand firm on this or heaven knows what else Hallie might coerce her into. Besides, it was ridiculous to think that poor Roger would be plagued by evil thoughts just because he could see the outline of her legs.

Hallie turned away first. She grabbed a towel and bent over the oven. After pulling open the door she drew out a tray of cinnamon rolls. They didn't look exactly the same, but Courtney recognized the smell. Her mouth watered and she was suddenly ravenous. She took a step forward.

"Not so fast," Hallie said. "If you're going to eat my food, you're going to have to dress accordingly."

"That's blackmail."

The other woman shrugged. "It's my final offer. If you don't wear a dress like a proper woman, then I won't work for you."

It was a battle of principles and hunger. Her stomach growled and hunger won. "I'll wear your stupid dress, but I won't wear a corset and I want my bra back."

Hallie frowned. "We don't wear corsets, except on special occasions. You can't do work in one. What's a bra?"

"It's with everything else you stole. White cotton, with straps and cups—" She motioned to her breasts.

Hallie laughed. "Is that what it's for? I couldn't figure it out. Silly-looking thing, if you ask me."

"I didn't, did I? Do we have a deal?"

"As long as my Roger doesn't have to see your bra, I don't mind if you wear it."

"How gracious of you." But instead of being angry, Courtney found herself smiling at the other woman.

She ate two cinnamon rolls to give herself strength, then went to tackle getting dressed. Her panties and bra were back sitting where she'd left them. She put them on, then picked up the first garment. It looked like a sleeveless blouse with lace around the scooped neck and hem. It slipped over her head easily. She tied the ribbon at the center, just above her breasts.

"This looks useless," Courtney muttered.

Next were four identical petticoats. They fell to the floor with ties at the waist. She held them all up, then started for the kitchen. "I have to wear four of them?" she asked, stepping into the warm room.

Hallie looked up and gasped. "Lord have mercy, child, get back to your bedroom." Hallie flapped at her with her apron. "The purpose is to get dressed so you don't go showing your parts off."

"It's not like I have anything you haven't seen," she grumbled, heading down the hall. "I really have to wear four petticoats? How can you walk around?"

Hallie stood in the doorway and tilted her head to one side. "All right. Start with two. That should be enough to keep everyone from seeing the shape of your legs."

"Oh, is that what this is all about."

"That and looking nice. Here, I'll help you with your dress."

Hallie moved into the room and picked up the dark green calico garment. "It's lovely," she said. "Mr. Hastings has excellent taste."

Courtney was shimmying into the second petticoat and smoothing it down. "If you ask me, he spends a lot more time getting women out of their clothes than into them. I know his type."

She glanced up. Hallie was staring at her. Two spots of color stained her cheeks.

"What did I say?" Courtney asked.

Hallie cleared her throat. "Nothing. I'm just not used to your modern ways. Speaking about men like that."

"This is hard." Courtney reached for the dress. "I can't show my legs and I can't talk about anything interesting. Any other rules?"

"Plenty. You'll have to learn as you go."

Hallie pulled the dress over her outstretched arms, then down over her petticoats. It fell to the floor. Courtney began to fasten the tiny buttons up the front. "I'm going to have to get up an extra half hour early just to get dressed."

"You'll get faster."

"Maybe. What I want to know is how I use the outhouse in this dress."

Hallie cleared her throat.

Courtney looked at the other woman. "I can't say outhouse?"

"No. It's not polite to mention it at all."

"But sometimes you have to say *something*."

Hallie glanced around the room, then leaned forward and whispered, "It's 'the necessary'."

"Okay, and sometimes it's more necessary than others. What do I do about the dress?"

"That's why you want pantaloons." Hallie picked up the pair Courtney had ignored. She stuck her hands through the waistband, turned them over, then wiggled her fingers through the slit that would run from mid-thigh to mid-thigh. "They make it easy to squat."

Courtney stared at them for a minute. "I'm not really the squatting type. I'll figure out something." She smoothed down the front of the dress. "How do I look?"

"Almost like a lady. You need this to finish." Hallie handed her an apron.

"Perfect. I'm a domestic drudge. Lead on," she said as she slipped her arms into the apron. While they walked into the kitchen, she tied it in the back.

She was wearing a long dress, two petticoats, and cowboy boots. Who would have thought?

"The first order of business is to make bread," Hallie said. "We'll start today, then finish tomorrow."

"Two days? My breadmaker can do it in about four hours. I miss my breadmaker. I miss a lot of things."

Hallie looked at her strangely, then shook her head. "Get a little water from the bucket on the stove and mix it with some cold until it's just warm."

"How much is a little?"

"Use that cup there. About half, maybe a little more."

Courtney did as she was instructed, dissolved a square of yeast into the water, then added "a little" sugar. The mixture was covered loosely with a cloth and left to ferment.

"I wish we could do something about the smell in here," Courtney said. The odor of last night's dinner, the spices and foods, yeast, and a moist mustiness that was probably from their bathwater combined to create an unpleasant scent.

Hallie frowned. "It's easy enough to get rid of. I thought you didn't mind the smell."

"Hey, I forgot my Glade freshener. Tell me what to do."

"Put vinegar in a pan with a little water. Let it simmer. It'll freshen the room right up."

"No one told *me,*" Courtney said, grabbing a small pot from the lower shelves. "Do we have vinegar?"

"In the pantry." Hallie showed her the glass jar with the cork stopper, then stepped back and watched her pour. "You've never spent time in a kitchen before."

It wasn't a question, but Courtney answered it anyway. "Not really. I never saw the point."

"Do you know how to sew?"

"No. I'm not familiar with any of the domestic arts."

Hallie placed her hands on her hips. "You are the most peculiar woman I've ever met."

"I'm not surprised, Hallie." She put the pan of vinegar and water on the stove. "Now what?"

"You mind if I ask you a question."

"Sure. What?"

"How old are you?"

"I just turned twenty-nine."

"And you've got no babies of your own?"

Courtney thought about her near miss. For two days, she'd thought she was pregnant. She hadn't known what to feel, although Matt had been thrilled when she'd confessed her fears to him. When she'd finally gotten her period, he hadn't said anything for a long time, then he'd just held her close and promised they would make a baby soon enough. Only that hadn't happened. And now they were getting a divorce. Well, they were getting divorced if they ever made it back to their own time.

"No, I haven't had children."

"What do you do with yourself all day?"

Courtney burst out laughing. "You wouldn't believe me if I told you."

Hallie sniffed. "Probably not. And if you're wearing your trousers while you do it, I don't want to hear a word."

"How old are you, Hallie?"

"Why, I'm an old woman. Nearly forty."

"Forty's not old."

"I've got three grandbabies already, with more on the way. Roger's my youngest. Three boys, two girls."

"Five kids?" Courtney shuddered and made a mental note to keep taking her birth control pills. "That's too many for me. Now what do we do?"

"Go talk to your husband about a garden."

Hallie led the way outside. The sun was bright in the morning sky. There were only a few clouds to the west. The air was already warming and it was going to be a beautiful day.

Hallie marched toward the barn. Courtney trailed after her. Her legs kept tangling in her long skirt. It was a giant pain but worth it for Hallie's cooking.

The housekeeper reached the barn before she did. The sound of hammering stopped abruptly. Courtney wondered what it must be like to have raised five children and have three grandchildren, all before the age of forty. She wasn't sure *she* was ready for children and she was already twenty-nine. It must be the times. What else was there for a woman to do but have a family?

As she rounded the side of the barn, she heard Hallie talking with Matt. "Cows are fine, Mr. Stone, but we need some vegetables. It's late in the season, but we'll be able to get something in."

"I agree," Matt said. He leaned against the corral and braced one foot on the lower rail. "Take Roger and show him where you want the garden. He can do the digging."

The boy had already picked up a shovel. He followed his mother, giving Courtney one long disappointed look before disappearing around the barn.

Courtney shaded her eyes as she glanced at her husband. "How's the building coming?"

"Slow, but we'll get there. How are you feeling?"

"Great. I slept well."

"I know."

She winced. "You say that like you spent the night awake. Did I snore or something?"

"No. You just looked like you'd slept well when I got up."

His attention seemed fixed on her skirts. "What are you staring at?" she asked. "You've seen me in a dress before."

"Not like that."

"Tell me about it." She glanced around to make sure Hallie and the ever-innocent Roger were out of sight, then raised her skirt slightly. "I'm wearing two petticoats, if you can believe that. It's hard to walk, let alone try to do work. I feel as if I'm in a costume production of *Oklahoma!* or something."

"You're not going to break out into song, are you?"

"I don't sing that badly!"

"Yeah, right." He grinned.

Her heart and toes responded right on cue. She swore to herself that one day Matt Stone would smile at her and she wouldn't react at all. The phrase *when hell freezes over* drifted through her mind, but she ignored it.

His smile faded. "Jonathan Hastings wants to throw in with us. He wants to be a partner in the ranch. The cattle are coming soon and we don't have the cash to pay for cowboys, build outbuildings, or buy supplies. What do you think?"

"Why does my opinion matter? The ranch was your idea."

"As long as we're married, it's our ranch. I don't know how long we're going to be here, but for as long as we are, I think we have to act as if it's permanent. We can't put our lives on hold indefinitely."

She was torn between pleasure over his saying the ranch was half hers and fear that he was right and they were stuck here forever.

She glanced to her right, toward the knoll where she'd spent the last week waiting for the storm to reappear. Waiting hadn't helped. Matt was right; they had to get on with their lives and hope for the best.

"If you want to go into business with Jonathan Hastings, I don't mind."

Matt tugged on the brim of his Stetson, a sure sign he was nervous about something. "Do you want to go live in the city instead of here? There would be more modern conveniences there."

"Not enough so I could notice," she said. "I'd rather stay here with you. Besides, here I'm closer to the storm."

"Just thought I'd ask."

She searched his face, hoping for a sign of relief that she wanted to stay, but his eyes were shaded and she couldn't tell what he was thinking.

"I appreciate that," she said. "I'd better go back inside. Cooking seems to be an all-day task here."

She gave a little wave, then turned toward the house. As she strolled over the green grass and inhaled the sweet smell of the air, she glanced at the few clouds in the sky. They were white and puffy and looked completely normal. She was surprisingly pleased not to see a hint of a storm . . . of any kind.

9

Courtney pulled the cover off the bowls and stared at the results of her handiwork. Two smooth, round mounds of dough waited to be formed into loaves. She smiled as she unfastened her cuffs and began to roll them up to her elbows.

In the two weeks since Hallie's arrival, the women had made bread several times, but this was Courtney's first attempt on her own. Yesterday she'd combined yeast, sugar, and water to ferment. Just before lunch she'd added flour to make a batter. The batter rose. After dinner she added more flour and lard to make a smooth dough. Now, this morning, she would shape it into loaves and bake it.

She floured her hands and dumped the first bowl of dough onto the marble pastry board. "If they could see me now," she said softly, then shook her head. No one would believe it. She didn't believe it herself.

When had living here become real? She didn't have the answer to that. Somehow she'd gotten used to long skirts hampering her ability to walk. She'd started adjusting to the quiet, although she missed electricity and modern appliances, and no matter how long she

lived here she would never get used to that damn outhouse or the lack of running water.

She wanted to take a shower.

But she was willing to admit there was a certain comfort in the sameness of the routine of day-to-day life.
And serving a meal that she'd made herself gave her a
feeling of satisfaction. Not that she wanted to stay and
go native, but it wasn't as hideous as she'd first thought.

She put more flour on her hands and patted the
dough into place. After grabbing a thick cloth, she
opened the oven door and let some of the hot air drift
over her. Hallie could tell just from that how hot the
oven was. Courtney felt a dial to standardize the temperature would be a terrific improvement, but Hallie
had stared at her as if she'd suggested slicing off a bit
of the moon to serve with supper. The housekeeper had
shown her the paper trick instead.

Courtney reached for a small piece of torn newspaper kept next to the stove. She flung the paper inside
the oven and watched. It swirled around in the heat,
darkening quickly to a medium brown.

"Perfect," she said, and put the bread in the oven.

If the paper burned, the oven was too hot. If the paper
turned yellow or a very light brown, it wasn't hot enough.
Not exactly a digital readout, but it got the job done.

After closing the oven door, she tossed down the
towel. It was time to feed the chickens.

They kept the feed in the pantry. She scooped out
the necessary amount, holding up the corners of her
apron and using it as a container, then opened the back
door and stepped outside.

The morning was crisp and clear, with a bright sky
that promised another perfect day. They'd had wonderful weather since "arriving." Rain every two or three
days. Just enough to make everything grow but not so
much that it slowed the construction.

She glanced around. Almost overnight the trees had gone from budding to thick with leaves. There were flowers and lush grasses everywhere. The threat of frost was over. She and Hallie had planted the garden. Everyday she stopped by the patch of earth and stared hopefully, but so far they hadn't seen a sign of life. Something had better grow fast. She was tired of eating tinned food.

She walked toward the chicken coop. To her left stood the completed barn. Matt and Roger were now constructing a bunkhouse. Without plumbing and electrical wires to worry about, the building went quickly. They should be done by the end of the week.

"Courtney!"

She turned and saw Matt jogging toward her. It was nearly nine and they'd both been up for three hours. He'd abandoned his jacket and was working in shirtsleeves. The first couple of buttons were undone, exposing a bit of his tanned, muscular chest. Dark hair reached down and brushed against his collar. One lock fell over his forehead. As he neared her, he pushed it out of the way.

Eventually she would stop reacting to his good looks. At least that was her plan. Living with him like this was doing a number on her nerves. Every time she saw him, her heart got all flappy in her chest. If he dared to smile, which seemed fairly likely, her toes curled and her stomach felt funny. It drove her crazy. They'd been living together in very close quarters for over three weeks—the longest they'd ever been together—but the symptoms weren't going away. Maybe she was allergic to him.

She walked toward him, stopping on the house side of the corral fence. Matt leaned against the same fence from the other side and smiled at her. Her body reacted; she bit back a groan.

"Hi," he said, resting his forearms on the top rail.

"Hi, yourself."

"What are you doing?"

She glanced at her apron. "Feeding the chickens. What did you think I was doing?"

He shrugged.

"You called me over," she said. "Did you want to ask me something?"

"No."

Then why are you bothering me? Only those words never left her lips. There was an odd light in Matt's blue eyes, something playful and friendly she didn't get to see often enough. While her toes were in the curl mode, she might as well make him smile again. If she still remembered how. When was the last time she'd made an effort in her marriage?

He bent low and stepped through the railing. When he straightened, he placed his hand on the small of her back and urged her forward. They strolled toward the chicken coop.

"How's it going?" he asked.

"Good. I'm baking bread."

"I can't wait to taste it."

Their mundane conversation seemed to be a conduit for something else, something important. Courtney just wasn't sure what it was. She glanced at her husband out of the corner of her eye. He was tall and handsome, a fantasy come to life. How many times had she watched him and wondered why he'd chosen her? She was sort of attractive. She didn't have to wear a paper bag on her head, but she'd never stopped traffic. She was smart, but not supersmart. She had a good job, but she didn't make tons of money. What combination of features or traits had made Matt choose her?

Before she could ask, they reached the chicken coop. The birds squawked at the sight of her. She glared at them.

"I don't suppose I could convince you to go in there and feed them?"

Matt surprised her by raising his hands in a gesture of surrender and backing up. "Not me. I'm scared of chickens."

She laughed. "You'll ride a bucking horse bareback but you won't face one itty-bitty chicken?"

"That's right." His gaze narrowed as he stared at the birds collecting by the gate. "They're mean little buggers."

"Tell me about it." She shooed the birds back and stepped inside. "I always feel like they want to trip me, then peck me to death."

She flung the feed out a handful at a time, then flapped her apron to get rid of the last few grains. While the birds were busy eating, she ducked into the small, smelly henhouse and collected still-warm eggs. Again she used her apron as the carrying device.

When she backed out of the coop, Matt was still standing by the fence. She went out the gate and stopped in front of him. "The long dresses are a pain, but I like the apron," she said, motioning to the collection of eggs. "It's like always having a really big pocket whenever you need one."

His gaze searched her face, then he smiled slowly. This wasn't his everyday smile, but the one he used to make her knees tremble. Damn him, it still worked fine. Didn't he know he was endangering the eggs?

"I know you hate it here," he said, reaching up and tucking a strand of hair behind her ear. "I appreciate everything you're doing. You didn't have to pitch in, but you're doing it anyway."

She felt herself flushing. "I couldn't stay up on the hill forever. Besides, it's getting easier."

His fingers lingered, brushing gently against the side of her neck before resting on her shoulder. Even when she was wearing her cowboy boots, he was taller than her by several inches. She could see his features clearly, the firm line of his mouth, his clean-shaven jaw, the dark hairs peeping out of the V of his shirt. She had an almost uncontrollable urge to press her lips against that spot and taste him. Her legs were still weak. Need coiled low in her belly before moving higher, to her breasts.

Their gazes locked. She saw the fire in his eyes and knew it was matched by the flames flickering in her own. Heat blossomed, spreading from him to her.

"The land gives back," he said. "All that we're putting into it will be returned to us."

Was he really talking about the land? "I don't understand."

He took a step closer. His thighs brushed against the apron she held out. The eggs shifted. Instinctively she stepped to one side to protect her cargo.

He looked down. "Sorry."

When he glanced back at her, the fire had been banked, the mood broken. She wanted to stomp her foot in frustration. Her hunger still flared.

"I'd better get back to the framing," he said.

"Wait." She didn't want him to go just yet. Something had almost happened between them. Something she wanted to hold on to. "Why is this so important to you? The land, the ranch, all of it? You've always wanted something like this. Even before . . ."

"Before we were abducted by aliens and thrust back in time?" The last of his desire disappeared as amusement filled his eyes.

"Something like that."

He stared past her toward the horizon. "It's not something I can explain."

Courtney suddenly needed to understand. "Try."

He continued to look into the distance. She watched emotions slip across his face like ripples across a pond. Amusement turned to thoughtfulness which turned to regret. Then the emotions disappeared altogether, leaving his features set and unreadable.

"I grew up on ranches. My father worked them, when he could get work. After a few weeks, he'd quit or get fired. He drank." He glanced at her and shrugged. "I saw the big spreads, all the cattle and horses, and wanted the same for myself. Big dreams for a little kid."

"I didn't know."

"No reason you should. It happens all the time. I grew up determined that I would have more, *be* more, than my old man."

What had started out as a hasty device to keep him at her side turned into something else. She ached for him. She knew what it was like to be alone in the world, to feel lonely, to want something. He'd hungered for the land, and she'd dreamed of not being alone.

"You're making that happen," she said.

"Here. When we go back, I'll have what I started with. Nothing. I've got a few thousand saved, but it's not enough to buy the land, let alone the cattle. The rodeo isn't a great way to make a living." He drew in a breath. "But it's all I know."

"You know a little bit more than that," she pointed out. "You're building a bunkhouse with raw lumber and antiquated tools."

"Yeah, and I've got the blisters to prove it." He held out his left hand. His palm was callused. Three raw-looking blisters sat at the base of his index and middle fingers.

"That's nothing," she said, shifting the apron corners so she could hold the eggs steady with just her right hand. "I've got more."

She held out her left hand, palm up. The thin line of the burn was healing, but she would probably always be scarred. Her palm was red, the skin dotted with blisters, like a strange case of the measles. They were in different stages of healing, some still puffy and filled with fluid, others raw, and a few nearly faded.

"When I think of what I'd give for some hand lotion right now. Do you know how much money I'd make if I could get an Avon concession back to 1873?"

He took her hand in his and gently stroked her fingers. His soft touch sent electricity racing up her arm.

"I'm sorry," he said. "I never meant—"

"Neither of us meant for this to happen," she said, cutting him off. "It just did. We have to make the best of it."

She found it difficult to think while he touched her. Her heart rate increased, as did her breathing. Her hands trembled and the apron wobbled precariously.

Matt's hand was bigger than hers, his fingers longer, thicker, his palm more broad. Yet he brushed back and forth with the gentleness of a mother touching her newborn . . . or of lovers discovering each other for the first time. He cupped her hand in his and brought her palm to his mouth. His lips pressed lightly against the burn. She felt the moist heat of his breath a split second before the sensual contact of his lips.

Her legs trembled, her breasts ached, and the fire inside her exploded to life. Again and again, he kissed her hand, not moving from the palm, not touching her more intimately, although she felt the passion with every fiber of her being. He closed his eyes as if he, too, were being swept away by awareness. She longed to be closer to him.

She cupped her hand until her fingertips touched his cheek. She felt the faint prickling of stubble.

"Matt," she whispered.

"You do this to me every time," he murmured against her skin. "Damned if I know how."

The back door opened. "Your bread's close to burning," Hallie called.

Matt released her at the same moment she pulled her hand back. She grimaced. "I'd better see to that."

"I've got to finish the framing."

They both lingered for a moment, as if neither

wished the moment to be over. Courtney knew she didn't. She wanted to stay with Matt, to have him really kiss her, the way he used to. She wanted to make love with him. But that would complicate everything. Wasn't she the one who wanted the divorce?

But the thought of living without him didn't seem so right anymore. Especially not here. Where would she go? How would she exist in this time? Most importantly, how would she survive without being with him? In a world of modern conveniences it was easy to go from day to day with her work and her few friends, but here she couldn't imagine looking at the vast Wyoming wilderness and not knowing Matt was nearby.

"I think my nose is sunburned," Courtney said as she washed up the dishes from lunch. It seemed as if every time she turned around there was another meal to prepare for or dishes to be washed. That's all women did in the olden days. Wash and cook. And if it was Monday, they not only washed dishes, but they washed clothes.

She shuddered at the thought of the large tubs in the lean-to out back. Now that she'd actually experienced wash day—the boiling hot water, the backbreaking scrubbing, the skin-burning soap, and the wringing that made her arms feel like they were going to fall off—she understood why people didn't change their clothes very often. She'd begged Hallie to tell her that someone somewhere had invented a washing machine, but the housekeeper had simply stared uncomprehendingly at her.

"If you don't want to get sunburned, then wear your bonnet," Hallie said from her seat at the table. She was darning one of Matt's shirts. He'd ripped the sleeve with a nail.

"The sunbonnet is ugly."

"So's a sunburn."

Courtney smiled. "That's why I like you, Hallie. You're not afraid to say what you're thinking."

The older woman glanced up at her. As always, her auburn hair was neatly piled on top of her head. Not even a single wisp dared to escape. Courtney wore her long hair in a braid and she couldn't get that to behave. There had to be a trick.

"Why should I be afraid of my own thoughts?" Hallie wanted to know. "I'm a God-fearing soul."

"Hmm, I think bad things all the time. If I said them, no one would like me."

"What makes you think people like you now?"

Courtney was so startled, she dropped the plate she was washing. It slipped to the bottom of the pan and landed with a thump. She stared at Hallie as the housekeeper made impossibly small stitches. One corner of Hallie's mouth tilted up.

Courtney smiled in relief. "You're teasing me. For a moment I thought you were serious."

"You're not so bad. At least you learn things quickly. I still don't understand how you came to be as old as you are and not know one useful thing about cooking."

"I never had to know before. I just heated prepared meals."

"So who prepared them?"

"I bought them that way. At the grocery store." They'd been frozen, but Hallie didn't have to know that.

"A lot of foolishness if you ask me. There's no reason why a strong, healthy woman can't cook for herself."

"I didn't have time."

"What were you doing with it then?"

"I had a job." Courtney turned back to the dishes and fished out the plate she'd dropped. "I spent my day working there, so there wasn't time to cook."

She hated that Hallie constantly found her wanting when it came to domestic duties. She didn't know how to do the simplest tasks. At first it had been a novelty, almost like taking a class. "How to Survive in the Past." But gradually she grew tired of always asking. How do I clean out the lamp? How much kindling is enough? How long do I bake the pie? It was getting embarrassing.

"Where did you work?"

"At a design firm." She picked up the last dish and plunged it in the soapy water. "I designed posters, um, large pictures to be put in theaters." And video stores. Some of her posters actually became the design for the videocassette holder.

"So you draw?"

"Not exactly. I assemble other people's drawings, or photographs, put words on them."

Hallie looked skeptical. Courtney didn't know how to explain it without telling the other woman she was from the future. She and Matt had decided it was better if no one knew. If they were stuck here forever, they didn't want to be labeled as crazy, and if they went back, well, people would find some way to explain it.

Once again she was grateful Matt was in this time with her. If she didn't have someone who understood her situation, she would have gone crazy.

She finished with the dishes and took the bucket of soapy water outside. Matt had designed a shallow ditch for a drain. Every time she used it, she flinched.

"I've sent hundreds of dollars to conservation organizations and here I am dumping waste directly into the river. They'd shoot me if they knew." Unfortunately, there wasn't anywhere else to put the water. Sewage treatment plants were a couple of generations up the road.

After putting the bucket back in the dry sink, she pumped herself a glass of water and left the kitchen. This had become her routine, so Hallie no longer asked what she was doing. Courtney went into her bedroom.

After lifting her backpack off its hook, she sat on bed and unbuckled the fastener.

"Alone at last," she murmured as she pulled out the bag of M&M's. They were nearly half gone. Carefully she shook one out and placed it on the spread. Next she found her birth control pills and popped out the day's dosage. There weren't that many left.

The first couple of times she'd come into the bedroom, Hallie had followed her. She'd told the other woman she was taking medication a doctor had given her. Hallie hadn't questioned the information. The poor woman probably hoped it was for Courtney's mental health rather than any physical condition.

Courtney swallowed the birth control pill first. She studied the empty plastic pockets, then counted the number left. Unless they went back to their century really soon, she was going to be without protection. Not that she and Matt were having sex. But they could. The physical side of their relationship had always been intensely satisfying.

She picked up the single M&M and placed it on her tongue. She closed her eyes as first the candy shell, then the chocolate itself dissolved. Life would take a serious turn for the worse when her candy stash was gone. Did they even have chocolate yet? She would have to remember to ask Hallie.

She put the M&M's and the pills in the backpack, then had a horrible thought. If her pills were almost gone, she was close to getting her period. Oh, Lord, she didn't even want to think about that! She dug through her personal possessions and found one lone tampon still wrapped in plastic. She stared at it.

"This isn't going to be enough," she said, and grimaced. What would she use? Something hideous, that was sure. She shuddered. This century was certainly a trial for women.

10

Matt nailed the support beam in place and wondered what they were going to put there for a window. He'd left the opening, then realized getting glass wasn't as simple as driving to the hardware store. He'd probably have to take the dimensions to town and order the window special. While he was at it, he might as well order another one for the bedroom. He was getting tired of waking up in the dark.

"Matt, look!" Roger called, pointing south of the house.

Matt saw someone on horseback, pulling a cow behind him. He recognized the man and the horse. "Go tell Hallie and Courtney that Jonathan's here," he told the boy. "He'll be staying for dinner."

Roger grinned, then took off for the house. The teenager liked the gambler. And they shared a common attraction toward a certain blonde.

Matt finished securing the frame, then set down his tools. By the time he reached the barn, Jonathan was dismounting. Roger ran over and grabbed the man's horse.

"Hastings," Matt said, holding out his hand.

"Stone." The two men shook hands.

"A relative?" Matt asked, pointing to the cow.

The gambler's dark eyes flashed with humor. "A milk cow. I thought you could use her for milk and butter."

"Part of your share of the ranch?"

"Have you decided to accept my offer?"

"Yeah." Matt untied the cow and led her toward the barn. Jonathan followed. "I spoke with Courtney. She wants me to do whatever I think is best."

"You discussed this with your *wife?*"

"Where we're from, women make decisions, too. They're smart and we like them that way."

"You don't mean to imply that women think and reason like men?"

"No. They think and reason in ways no man can understand. But don't underestimate them, Hastings Courtney went to college."

"Really?" He glanced thoughtfully toward the house. "She doesn't look like a bluestocking."

"A what?"

"It's just an expression. A bluestocking is a woman who has too much education. She thinks too much and has opinions. Usually about men and how they treat women."

"Sounds like you're speaking from experience."

He shook his head slightly. "I've known a bluestocking or two in my time."

Matt saw the haunting sadness in the gambler's eyes, but didn't comment on the fact. He suspected he had the same look about him when he worried about Courtney. She'd always been able to tie him up in knots.

"We're grateful for the cow," he said. "I think I saw an old butter churn in the lean-to. I'll clean it up and make sure it works." He figured Hallie would know how to use it. What would Courtney say when she found out about the work involved in making butter?

There was a large airy stall on one side of the barn. He smoothed straw over the dirt floor and led the cow inside. After leaving her a bucket of fresh water, he latched the half-door behind him. Roger was busy at the other end of the building with Jonathan's mount. He'd already removed the animal's saddle and was brushing him down.

"How long are you staying?" Matt asked as he and Jonathan walked outside.

"That depends. You been out hunting buffalo yet?"

"No. There hasn't been time. But we need the fresh meat."

"I'll come on the hunt with you, if you like."

Matt raised his eyebrows.

The gambler grinned. "I'm a decent shot and not too bad with a knife."

"Then we'll leave in the morning."

"Sounds fine."

The back door of the house opened. Hallie stepped out, followed by Courtney. His wife had changed in the last couple of weeks. She forgot her bonnet as often as not, so her cheeks were tanning, her nose sunburned. The sun bleached her hair nearly white around her face. At night, when she unwove her braid, the different colors of blond shimmered and shifted like the changing image of a kaleidoscope.

Sometimes, when he could bear the torture, he watched her undress, shedding her layers like a chrysalis, her lithe body emerging from beneath her long dress and petticoats. The physically challenging chores had honed her already slender body to toned leanness, although the generous curves of her breasts and roundness of her hips left no doubt as to her femininity. Even after she pulled her nightgown over her head and doused the light, he could see her. Those nights were the longest. He lay awake next to her, hot, hard, and aching.

"I supposed you'll be staying for a few days," Hallie said by way of a greeting.

"If it's not too inconvenient."

"More food, more work, but you're not so bad." She smiled at the younger man.

"Are you enjoying your employment?"

Hallie glanced over her shoulder at Courtney. "She's not so bad either."

"I thought you two might get along."

"Did you, now?"

Courtney moved closer. "Mr. Hastings. How nice of you to visit us again."

"My pleasure, ma'am."

He reached for her hand. She didn't resist as he brought it to his mouth. He kissed the back of her fingers, then frowned and turned her wrist. "You've been working hard," he said, staring at the calluses.

Matt felt a surge of irritation. He remembered those few minutes he'd spent with her by the chicken coop not three hours before. He didn't want anyone else looking at Courtney's hands and noticing the changes. They were for him alone. He swallowed the irrational thought and met her gaze. She stared at him as if she could read his mind. As if she, too, shared the memory as well as the moment. His anger faded.

Roger came running out of the barn carrying two bulging saddlebags and a cloth. "Did you want these, Mr. Hastings?"

Reluctantly, Jonathan released Courtney's hand and reached for his belongings. "I took the liberty of bringing some things in from town. Including"—he nodded at Hallie—"a milk cow."

"Wonderful," the housekeeper said. "We can have butter, cream, and fresh milk."

Courtney grimaced. "Milk fresh from a cow? Eeeuuu, that's gross. It wouldn't be pasteurized or anything. Do you know how much fat is in whole milk, not to mention cholesterol, germs, antibiotics? Well, I guess you wouldn't have antibiotics, but still. We could all die."

Roger, Hallie, and Jonathan stared at her as if she'd grown horns. When she noticed, she stopped talking and drew in a deep breath.

Matt stepped closer to her. She glanced up at him. "Milk from a cow. It's so primitive. I miss plastic."

"Me, too," he said.

Jonathan recovered first. "Who is Plastic? A pet?"

She bit on her lower lip, he suspected to keep from laughing. "Not exactly," Matt said. "It's a way of storing food, including milk. Very convenient."

"Another one of her citified ways," Hallie said. "You wouldn't believe me if I told you all the things that girl didn't know how to do before I got my hands on her. I don't know how she survived long enough to grow up."

Hallie started for the house, with Jonathan and Roger on her heels. "Next time you come out this way, Mr. Hastings, why don't you bring us a sow and a boar? There's plenty of scraps to keep them and their babies going. I make a pork roast that'll make you think you're on your way to meet St. Peter at the pearly gates."

The back door closed behind them. Courtney glanced at Matt. "Is there really a milk cow?"

"Sorry."

"I'm going to have to learn how to milk it, aren't I?"

"Probably."

She took a step toward him and bent her head until it rested against his chest. "I really do miss plastic."

"I miss french fries."

"Yeah, and thick creamy milk shakes. Any flavor, even strawberry."

"We have that cow now. You could make a milk shake."

She shuddered. "That's so disgusting." But he heard the smile in her voice.

Without thinking he placed his hands on her shoulders, then slid his fingers under her thick braid. The skin on the back of her neck was warm and soft. She wrapped her arms around his waist. "What else do you miss?" she asked.

"The rodeo. I'm used to being on the circuit."

"Do you miss television?"

"No. Movies."

"Oh, movies." She sighed and he felt her warm breath against his chest. "I miss the radio and my CD collection."

She leaned fully against him, her slight weight teasing him with a quick brush of breasts and thighs. "Don't you miss chocolate?" he asked.

She hesitated slightly before answering. "Um, sure I do."

He tugged on the end of her braid, forcing her to tilt her head toward him. Her wide hazel eyes tilted up at the corners as she smiled.

"You've got freckles," he said, touching the tip of her nose.

"I ran out of sunscreen."

"You should wear your hat."

"That's what Hallie tells me. I don't think it's the sort of fashion statement I want to make."

"It doesn't matter what you wear, you're always beautiful."

She blinked several times, as if fighting unexpected tears. Only Courtney never cried. "Matt, that's so sweet."

"I didn't say it to be sweet. I said it because it's true."

Her slow smile made his heart beat faster. She rose on tiptoe and brushed her mouth against his. "You're not so bad yourself, cowboy," she murmured, then stepped back.

He released her reluctantly, holding onto her braid until she tugged it free. "We'd better go inside," she said. "We've got company and I have to help with dinner."

She started walking away from him, then she paused until he caught up with her. Without saying anything, she took his hand in hers and squeezed his fingers. He returned the pressure.

By the time they stepped into the kitchen, Jonathan had emptied the contents of his saddlebags onto the kitchen table. He'd brought several lengths of cloth, a pair of hair combs that looked as if they were made out of gold, a large bottle of whiskey, and a small one of brandy.

"These are for you," he said, handing Hallie three small jars of spices. One was filled with a dark yellow powder.

She pulled out the cork top and sniffed. "Saffron. It's almost too dear to cook with. But I'll do my best." She winked.

He gave Roger a slim bound book. The teenager took it and stammered his thanks.

"I thought we could use these to celebrate our partnership," he said, giving Matt the two bottles of liquor.

Matt stared at the intricately printed label. The brandy was from France, the whiskey from Scotland. Not exactly the cheap stuff, even in this day and age. "It'll go down smooth," he said. "Thanks."

The gambler shrugged as if to say it was nothing, then turned to Courtney. His dark eyes burned brightly as he stared at her. "I'm glad the dress fits so well."

She smoothed down the front of her apron. "It's very nice. I never did thank you, did I? Actually I hadn't planned on wearing it, but Hallie gets all huffy if I even mention wearing my jeans."

"It's a sin, same as stealing," the housekeeper said.

"You know, I don't remember seeing that listed as one of the Ten Commandments. *Thou shalt not wear jeans.* You must show me where that is in the Bible."

"If we had a Good Book, I would."

"Sure you would. Even if you had to write it in yourself."

The two women smiled at each other. Matt was pleased they'd become friends. For the first couple of days, they'd existed through an uneasy truce. Then Hallie had realized that even though Courtney didn't know anything about the household, she was willing to learn. That her strange ways were just that—strange—not evil or dangerous.

Jonathan cleared his throat. "I thought you might want to make something more to your liking," he said, picking up the fabric and holding it out. The cloth shimmered in the light from the window. It was a deep blue, shot with black and red. He'd brought along lace for trim and buttons.

Courtney took the fabric. "It's lovely, but I can't accept this."

"I want you to have it. These, too." He placed the gold combs on top of the pile. "Your husband and I are partners now. It's almost like family. You lost everything in the storm, Mrs. Stone. I want to replace a few things."

"This is beautiful." She fingered the material. "Of course it would be better if I could sew." She glanced at Hallie. "Do you know how?"

"Of course I can sew. I'll teach you. It's not that hard. In fact it's a lot easier than laundry day."

Courtney smiled. "Nearly everything is."

"Let's see how it looks." The housekeeper took the combs, lace, and buttons and set them on the table.

Then she shook out the length of cloth and held it close to Courtney's face.

The color brought out the hazel color of her eyes and the pink in her mouth and cheeks. She touched her hair self-consciously. "Do you like it?" she asked Hallie, but her gaze sought Matt out.

"Oh, land's sake, yes, child. You'll be as pretty as a spring garden," Hallie said.

Matt simply stared at her, wondering how he'd been lucky enough to win her.

She flushed and he realized she'd read the longing in his gaze. As she glanced away, he saw Roger and Jonathan also staring at her. The gambler's eyes burned with a hunger and need that made Matt both angry and resigned. Jonathan couldn't help how he felt any more than Roger could control his adolescent crush. In their way, they adored Courtney. If something happened to him, they would take care of her.

Perhaps he should have worried that one of them, especially Jonathan, would speak out of turn to her, perhaps even try to tempt her away. But she didn't notice their attention. She never saw the way Jonathan carefully controlled his features or Roger's awkward shuffling as he struggled to conceal his sudden erection. He held the book in front of himself, then mumbled an excuse and bolted for the barn.

"I want you to have a blouse from this," Courtney said, pushing the fabric toward Hallie. "It looks great on you, too. And you have that black skirt."

"An old woman like me doesn't need new things."

"You're not old. You're not even forty, and there isn't a speck of gray in your hair."

Hallie smiled. "I've got grandchildren. That makes me old."

"Then I guess you are old." Courtney grinned. "But you still get a new blouse. I insist."

"Thank you," Hallie said. "That's very nice."

He could see the housekeeper was touched. Courtney had won them all over. He'd never doubted her. Courtney always came through.

After dinner Matt and Jonathan cleaned out the fireplace in the living room. By the time Hallie and Courtney finished in the kitchen, the two men had a bright fire going. It chased away the musty chill and added light to the darkness. There wasn't much furniture. Just a couple of chairs, a low table, and a stool. Matt took one chair, Jonathan the other. Courtney brought in a tray with several glasses and the bottles of liquor.

"I'm in the mood to get drunk," she announced. Matt started to stand up to offer her his seat. She waved him back. "I'll be fine on the floor. Less far to fall."

Courtney didn't handle liquor well. He'd only seen her really drunk once and she'd been sick as a dog the next day. Usually a single glass of anything gave her a buzz and she was done for the night.

"So you're going to have a second glass of brandy?" he teased.

"I'll live life on the edge." She knelt in front of his chair and set the tray on the low table, then glanced at Jonathan. "Whiskey, brandy, or both?"

"Brandy."

She poured an inch or so into one of the squat glasses and handed it to him. Roger had already retreated to the barn, but Hallie hovered just inside the room.

Courtney looked up at her. "What would you like, Hallie?"

"Oh, my, well, I probably should just turn in. It's getting late."

"Nonsense," Courtney said. "Come sit by the fire.

You've worked hard. Now I'm sure alcohol is a sin, but are you willing to tweak the devil's tail?"

"I might have a drop of that whiskey," the house-keeper said as she moved into the room and settled on the stool by the hearth.

Courtney poured for her and gave her the glass. She glanced over her shoulder. "I know what you like, Matt, and I'll join you." She gave them each a generous portion of whiskey.

As he took it, their fingers brushed. Electricity raced up his arm, while heat settled low in his groin. He'd been close to her for too long, sleeping next to but not sleeping with. He needed her. He wanted her.

In the light from the lantern in the corner and the fire itself, Courtney was as elusive as a shadow, flicker-ing close to him, then darting away. He could physi-cally touch her arm or her shoulder and she wouldn't run. But she didn't come to him, needing to be taken. He wanted that. He wanted her to want him.

"To us," she said, raising her glass.

"To us and those like us," he said, echoing an old toast they'd teased each other with.

Jonathan and Hallie clinked glasses with them. Everyone sipped in silence.

"This is nice," Courtney said, leaning back against his chair. She rested her head on his knee. He could feel the heat of her.

"You've done a lot with the ranch," Jonathan said. "It hasn't been that long, but you've made progress."

"We need to talk about that," Matt said. "If we're really going to be partners and you have the cash, then there are several things that need doing. We need to hire men to help with the construction. As soon as the outbuildings are done, we can start on the fences. I'd like to get some hay planted so we have enough for the horses and to tide us over for the winter. It's too late for this year, but we can get the ground ready for next season."

"Cowboys to help with the cattle," Jonathan said. "More horses."

"Windows," Courtney murmured from her place on the floor. "I'd like a window in the bedroom. Maybe even one in here."

"While you're doing all that building outside, you should add a room on here," Hallie said.

"For what?" Matt asked.

"Guests." She nodded at Jonathan, who would be again sleeping in the barn. "Or babies."

Courtney stiffened. He felt her muscles tense and heard her quick intake of air. Regret burned hotter than the whiskey in his belly.

There would be no children because Courtney was on the Pill. She'd had that scare once and had been diligent ever since. Even if she went off the Pill, they didn't make love. Unless something changed, there weren't going to be any babies.

Funny, he'd always assumed he would have children. His childhood had been grim, but instead of convincing him not to bother, his past made him determined to give his children better. Not in terms of having money, although he didn't intend to send them to school in hand-me-down clothes, but in the stability of a home. His kids wouldn't go from ranch to ranch while their father searched for work. He wanted them to know the land was there. That they were a part of it, of its history.

He'd never loved Courtney more than when she'd confessed she might be pregnant. She'd been worried about his reaction. He'd held her close and prayed it was true. But she hadn't been. And since then, she made sure there weren't any accidents.

"A guest room would be nice," Courtney said slowly and reached for the whiskey bottle. She poured herself another generous splash, then downed it quickly. Matt thought about saying something but figured she was old enough to know what she was doing.

"Unless you want the cowboys eating with you, they'll need a cook," Jonathan said quickly, as if trying to change the subject. "Mrs. Stone and Hallie have enough to do without worrying about feeding them."

"I agree," Matt said.

"Oh, while you're at it, get someone to do their laundry, too," Courtney said, then shuddered. "It's bad enough just doing ours."

Hallie set her empty glass on the table. "It's getting late and morning comes early. Good night."

She rose and moved down the hall. Jonathan swallowed the last of his brandy and also stood up.

Courtney protested. "You don't have to leave, too. The night is young and so am I." She giggled.

Matt touched her head. "You're already drunk."

"Yes, and it's lovely."

Jonathan bent over and raised her hand to his mouth. "Good night, Mrs. Stone."

"Courtney," she said firmly. "Just say it. You can't sleep in the barn, then call me Mrs. Stone. It's ridiculous. Loosen up, Jonathan."

His dark eyes held her gaze. Matt saw the flicker of desire, then the gambler blinked and it was gone. "Good night, Courtney."

"See, that didn't hurt so much, did it?"

Matt could hear the smile in her voice. She waved until Jonathan was out of sight, then she collapsed back against his chair.

"Oh, Matt, I feel glorious."

"In the morning, you're going to feel like hell."

She rose up on her knees and reached for the whiskey bottle. With unsteady hands, she poured an inch or so of the liquid, then collapsed on the floor facing him. "Hell's not bad enough. I'm going to feel like shit." She giggled and covered her lips briefly. "I have a potty mouth. What would the ever-proper Hallie say? Or worse, Jonathan?"

"He would be enchanted."

"Ha! I doubt that. I shock him. I shock them all."

He set his unfinished drink on the low table and rested his elbows on his knees. "Jonathan has a crush on you. So does Roger."

Her eyes widened. "A crush? On me? You think so?" She glanced around the room as if to confirm the rumor. "But I was never popular with boys. I'm too outspoken." She swayed toward him. "I was sort of a nerd in high school. My grades were just good enough to keep me from being accepted. Not that I was supersmart. I mean I studied hard. But the boys never noticed me. I wasn't very pretty."

"You're beautiful now," he said, staring at her, at the way the fire highlighted the shape of her face.

"I think you're prejudiced," she mumbled, the words slurring.

"And I think you're drunk."

He reached toward her to take the glass, but she held it out of reach and giggled. "Not so fast," she said. "I like being drunk."

She downed the whiskey, then wiped the back of her free hand against her mouth. Slowly, carefully, as if she had to plan every movement, she set the glass on the table. She scooted closer and rested her hands on his forearms. They were inches apart.

"Do you really think I'm pretty?" she asked, as her mouth turned up in a come-kiss-me smile.

"What do you want, Courtney?"

"You. Always you. Why is that, Matt? No matter what happens, I always end up wanting you. Is it fate?"

"I don't know." His throat was dry, his palms damp. Her words conjured an image of them together.

Instantly he was hard and hot, his body ready to take what she offered.

She slid her hands up his arms to his shoulders, all the while moving closer. She was still on her knees. She pulled his head to hers and kissed him.

Her lips brushed his, then opened, and her tongue traced the seam of his mouth. She sighed his name. "Are you playing hard to get?"

"This is the whiskey talking," he said, reaching up and pulling her hands from around his neck. "In the morning you're going to be sorry."

"Did you ever stop to consider that the whiskey has given me the courage to say what I've wanted to for a long time? And that in the morning I might be sorry for what we didn't do?"

He wanted to believe her. "I would never turn you away," he said.

She sank down until her fanny settled on her heels, then rested her forehead on his right knee. "Sometimes it's hard to ask. Sometimes I want you to read my mind."

He touched the top of her head. Her hair was smooth. When she looked at him, he traced the curve of her cheek and the line of her jaw. Perfect feminine features.

Her mouth parted. He took that as an invitation and touched her bottom lip. Her tongue darted out to lick the tip of his finger. He felt the quick, damp caress all the way to his groin. His blood pumped double-time, his heartbeat kept pace. Everything disappeared except his need and the woman who offered herself to him.

"Matt," she whispered.

He grabbed her shoulders and pulled her to her feet. In the same fluid movement he rose, then bent his head to hers. Her eyelids closed as her hands reached for him. Their mouths brushed together. Warm waiting heat enveloped him. She trembled in his embrace and he was lost.

11

The room spun around her, or maybe she was spinning. She wasn't sure. In the end, Courtney knew it didn't matter. Matt held her close to him and in his arms she would be safe.

His mouth teased her with slow, gentle touches, as if he needed to explore her to remember. His large, strong hands moved up and down her back, rubbing, enticing, making her want to squirm and submit, to be naked under him, feeling him against her, inside her.

The whiskey made her fuzzy-brained, but she didn't mind. Being unable to focus on anything meant there was nothing to distract her. She could concentrate on the taste of heat, on his tongue as it circled her lips. She could sigh his name and notice how that made him surge against her.

She tilted her head and parted her mouth, silently signalling her need for more. He dipped inside, then withdrew only to dip again, as if he were a hungry bee and she the sweetest flower. Did she taste of honey? He did. Honey and passion spiced with whiskey.

She clung to his shoulders, then moved her fingers

up through his hair. The short strands reached his collar. She slipped through them, moving to his ears, then following the curve down to his neck. Once there, she found the edge of his whiskers where beard gave way to smooth skin. She lingered on that path to his chest, on the V of his shirt exposing the first hint of dark hair.

He was as she remembered. Hard and broad. Strong. Strong enough to make her feel protected. Strong enough not to be intimidated by her. Strong enough to admit she was bright and to take advantage of her intelligence.

His tongue at last plunged into her mouth and all rational thoughts fled. His thrust sent shivers of delight skittering along her already sensitized skin. She met him and circled him, tracing his shape and textures.

Blood pooled low, at the apex of her thighs. Each labored breath brought her swelling breasts agonizingly close to his chest. His hands on her back swept lower to cup her behind and urge her closer to him. She arched into him, brushing his groin with her belly. But the layers of petticoats and dress frustrated her. She could feel nothing.

She whimpered and pressed harder. His tongue tormented her, plunging and withdrawing, mimicking the pleasure that was to come. She caught him gently in her teeth, then suckled him. He stiffened and groaned low in his throat.

She moved her hands across his chest, searching out buttons and popping them free. The whiskey blurred the edges of her mind, allowing her to be bold where in the past she might have allowed shyness to make her cautious. She tugged the cotton shirt tails free of his trousers and parted the fabric.

A pattern of dark, curly hair, wide at his shoulders, tapering down to a narrow line before disappearing beneath his jeans, tempted her. As much as it pained her to release him, she broke their kiss and placed her mouth on his chest. He tasted salty sweet. His skin was smooth, the curly hair tickled her tongue. She nibbled his flesh, feeling a hunger that had nothing to do with food.

"God, Courtney, do you know what you're doing to me?" he asked raggedly.

She didn't answer. She found she was starved for him. For all of him. Her hands traced frantic patterns on his chest and she attempted to follow them with her mouth. She pushed the shirt away and gripped his shoulders, then drew her hands down his arms. Her tongue traced a straight line to his belly.

She bent her head and bit his side, quickly licking away the faint mark of her teeth. Her legs trembled. She gave up trying to stand and sank to her knees.

His arousal strained against the button fly of his jeans. She stared at it for a moment, remembering how he felt in her hands, her mouth, and her body. Moisture dampened her panties. She ached for him.

His arms hung at his sides and she might have thought him unaffected by what she was doing if she hadn't seen that his hands had balled up into tight fists.

She clutched his narrow male hips and pressed her mouth against his erection. The hard length flexed against the denim. Her hot breath quickly heated the fabric and he groaned. Again she bit down, gently this time, raking her teeth against the side of him. She moved lower. His legs parted, exposing his groin.

She shook. Her fingers fumbled on the buttons of his fly.

"Help me," she murmured frantically.

He reached for the belt and unfastened it. She glanced up and his dark gaze locked with hers. The fire burning there made her catch her breath. Need tightened his features into a mask of raw masculinity.

Without breaking their eye contact, he pulled the belt free and let it fall. The metal buckle clinked on the hardwood floor. He undid the buttons, each snapping as he pushed it open.

She continued to look in his eyes as she brushed his hands away. His jeans gaped open. Her unerring fingers found the sensitive tip and trailed down to the thick base. He surged against his briefs. She tugged the jeans down his hips, then pulled back the waistband of his briefs. He sprang free.

Still holding his gaze, she opened her mouth. Her fingers encircled him, angling his erection toward her. She stuck out her tongue and licked the very tip of him. His body jerked in reflex as his eyelids drifted shut. She smiled.

Before she could lean forward and take more of him into her mouth, he pulled his jeans back into place.

"Two can play at this," he said, and drew her to her feet. Her legs would barely support her weight. It didn't matter. Matt bent over and swept her up in his arms.

Every fiber of her body vibrated with awareness. The rapid thundering of his heart was exquisitely loud as she pressed her ear to his chest. He held her firmly, and she clung to him more because of how it made her feel than because she feared he would drop her.

He quickly walked the few short steps to the bedroom, then kicked the door shut behind them. The darkness was complete. At the side of the bed, he lowered her to the straw-filled mattress.

She sat on the edge, her feet dangling, while he found and lit the lantern.

The light cast shifting patterns on the walls, making it appear that something mysterious was afoot. His shadow dwarfed hers, and as he loomed over her in life, so their reflections repeated the actions.

Working quickly, he pulled off her cowboy boots and socks, then his. He shoved his jeans and briefs down and stepped out of them. He was naked before her. She reached for him, but he brushed her hands away. So she contented herself with looking.

He was beautifully built, as if the Lord had taken extra time to fashion a perfect male. His broad shoulders were muscled, although not overly so. His wide chest tapered to a slim waist and narrow hips. Several scars from run-ins with horses' hooves, fence posts, and a knife added to the texture of his skin. She followed the hair on his belly as it became a single dark line below his belly button before flaring out to crown his maleness in a wreath of curls.

When he reached for the buttons of her dress, she sat as obediently as a child. But her stillness belied the life swirling inside her. Every pore of her body was on fire for him. Every cell swelled in anticipation. Her breasts ached so fiercely that when he accidently brushed her nipple with the back of his hand, she had to bite her lip to keep from crying out with pleasure. She wanted to squirm, to rip the buttons free, to pull off her skirts, drag down her panties, and beg him to take her. Instead she drew in shallow breaths and waited.

The buttons reached past her waist, nearly to her thighs. She'd given up wearing the camisole top, so when he pulled the front of her dress apart, he exposed her bra. With one quick jerk, he pulled the open dress down to her elbows . . . and left it there, trapping her arms at her sides.

She could have easily shrugged free of the garment, but she didn't. A ripple of anticipation shot through her. He'd never done anything like this before, but then she'd never bitten his arousal, either. Was it the whiskey? Was it the shift in time? Or was it simply them? Was this adventure the sensual by-product of spending so much time together? She decided it didn't matter, as long as it didn't stop.

Matt nudged her legs apart and stepped between her knees. Reaching behind her, he grabbed her braid and began unfastening it. She pressed her mouth to his belly and sucked, drawing up the taunt skin and muscle. Her bra-clad breasts brushed his bare skin and made them both shiver.

He finger combed her hair until it fanned out over her shoulder. Days of wearing it in a braid had left the strands wavy. They bounced and slipped against her skin.

He pushed on her shoulders until she lay back on the bed. Her feet dangled. He knelt before her and grabbed her ankles. He placed her bare feet flat on his thighs. She felt his taunt muscles. He pushed her skirt up high and began to nibble on the inside of her knee.

Courtney sucked in a breath. Sharp little nips set her nerve endings on fire. Her thighs quivered, her breasts engorged even more, and the aching dampness between her legs made her want to scream for release. She was hot and cold at the same time, empty and full. Needing. Desperately needing.

His mouth ascended her leg. She wanted to weep with frustration. Her panties would provide a barrier to paradise. She squirmed beneath him and when she couldn't stand it anymore, she fought against the layers of fabric to reach them and pull them down.

"Impatient, aren't you?" he asked, his voice husky.

"Yes," she breathed as she tried to free her trapped arms. "Please, Matt."

But instead of helping, he pushed her hands away. He continued to move up her thigh until he was so close, she could feel his breath against her. She caught a sob before it escaped, then shuddered as he moved past her throbbing center and worked his way down her other leg.

When he reached her knee, he rose to his feet and bent over her. His erection pressed against her, meeting the resistance of her panties. She squirmed to get closer, to let him enter, but he barely seemed to notice.

In the lamplight, his blue eyes looked black. Twin

flames burned hot. He left the dress in place as he unfastened the front clip of her bra. She shook her breasts free. He stared down at the generous curves. She wanted to beg him to touch her there. Anywhere. She was damp with perspiration and willing to do anything to find release.

He brushed his flat palms over her nipples. The pleasure was so intense that had he continued the stroking, she could have come right there. Instead he circled around, then cupped her breasts. The tension in her chest eased, only to tighten between her thighs. Long fingers circled her curves. As he lowered his mouth to hers, he took her nipples between his thumbs and forefingers. His tongue dipped inside her mouth. She moaned and drew her legs even more apart, trying to urge him closer. Again the panties defeated her.

She wiggled slightly and the head of his penis brushed her most sensitive spot. The pleasure was instant and exquisite. She held her breath, praying he would shift and do it again. Nothing happened. His hands continued to caress her breasts, his mouth excited hers, but between her legs was only the empty ache of unfulfilled desire.

He raised his head slightly. Black eyes burned into hers. "Touch me," he commanded.

Instantly she stretched as far as the dress would let her, reaching until she found and encircled him.

"Where do you want me?" he asked.

She didn't understand at first. When she moved him lower against her panties, he flexed impatiently. "Not there," he said. "Where do *you* want me?"

She understood then. Despite the fact that he'd seen her and touched her in every intimate way, she felt herself flush.

"I—I can't."

He didn't answer. He brought his mouth back to hers and invaded. His fingers continued to move on her breasts until she thought she would go mad from the wanting. But none of that eased the ache between her thighs.

Hesitantly, hoping he wouldn't notice, she inched his arousal up until the tip pressed against that small point of pleasure. He flexed in her hand, stroking the spot. She was so close already. It wouldn't take much. She wanted him to move again, but he didn't. Tentatively, she tipped her hand up, then down. He brushed against her again. Nerve endings jumped as her body focused on her potential release.

Suddenly she couldn't stand it. She wiggled free of him and rolled over, coming up on her knees. Her hair tangled around her face. She pulled her arms free of the confines of the dress. The fabric bunched around her waist. Dragging at the material, she pulled it up and got a hold of her panties. She jerked them down to her knees, then sat back and pulled them off.

The long dress and petticoats twisted. She couldn't see and she couldn't get her balance. After pushing her hair out of her way, she reached behind her for the ties to her petticoats.

"I'm caught," she said.

Matt joined her on the bed. He brushed her hair off her face, then stilled her hands. She was half reclining against the pillows, a mess of skirts and undergarments. Instead of helping her free, he placed his mouth on her right breast. He drew the taut nipple into his mouth and sucked until she didn't care about anything but making him continue. His hand stroked her other breast before moving lower and reaching under her skirt for her bare skin. He caressed her hip. She raised on one side so he could stroke her fanny before slipping his hands between her legs. She parted instantly.

He released her nipple and drew his mouth down her breast to her belly. He pushed the skirt and petticoats up higher and kissed the small triangle of blond hair between her legs. She couldn't see what he was doing, but she could feel it. The heat of his breath as he moved closer and closer, then at last the brush of his tongue against her point of desire.

She'd been ready since she asked him to make love to her. With a single stroke, he brought her to the edge of release. Her muscles tightened, her breath came in pants, and her fingers curled into the mattress. A second stroke had her biting back a scream. He plunged his finger inside, as if testing the tightness of her opening. She clamped around him and drew her legs back more.

The third stroke, a quick flick, followed by another and another, sent her tumbling out of control. Her body rocked against him, giving him that which he demanded. He continued to touch her until she was still. Only then did he raise himself onto his knees and plunge home.

Her hips arched off the bed, tilting so she could take all of him. His hands caught hers and pulled them above her head. He stared first at her face, then at her breasts, which bounced in time with his thrusts. His face tightened as the pleasure caught him in its grip. She braced her feet on the bed and met him each time, tightening around him, forcing him to surrender as she had done.

At last his body stilled for a heartbeat as he gathered himself for the final assault. He returned his gaze to her face and, as he convulsed into orgasm, hoarsely whispered her name.

Later, when her clothes were finally removed, they cuddled together under the covers. Courtney lay on her left side, Matt tucked behind her, like spoons in a drawer. His right hand roamed over her belly and breasts, teasing sensitized skin, making her squirm with delight.

They didn't speak. They didn't have to. The familiarity of the ritual was enough. She felt safe and contented. But her body knew the next part and began to tense in anticipation.

His fingers crept toward her feminine place.

"I couldn't," she murmured.

"Of course you can."

She'd never understood this odd quirk of his. After they made love, he liked to make her come again. Gently, unhurriedly, with just his fingers touching her. If she was satiated it could take nearly half an hour, but he always claimed he didn't mind.

"Why do you do this?" she asked, as his index finger slipped between her slick curls. "I'm perfectly happy."

"It's just a bad habit," he whispered, his breath fanning her shoulder. "Like not picking up my socks."

He found the sensitive place, but didn't touch it. Instead he circled around. She ignored the tingling starting at her toes and working up.

"It's a better bad habit than socks," she admitted. "But I still don't know what you get from it."

"When we make love, I'm usually too aroused to notice what you're doing," he said. "I can't pay attention to the little things. When I do this—" He stopped moving long enough to make her wish he would start up again. And bless his little male heart, he did. "I get to pay attention more. I listen to your breathing. I feel the heat of your skin. When I roll you over"—he moved away and she obligingly shifted onto her back—"your nipples are hard. I like that."

His conversation was just as erotic as the movements his fingers made. She spread her legs and let her eyes drift shut.

He always seemed to know if she was tender from their lovemaking. He moved slowly, almost as if he wasn't concentrating on what he was doing. There had been times when they'd had intense conversations until her attention was finally captured by what his fingers did between her legs.

Once he'd whispered dirty jokes until she was laughing and coming all at the same time. Once he'd described an erotic fantasy in such detail, they'd quickly brought each other to orgasm. But most of the time he touched her without talking at all.

The tension began to build and she gave herself up to it. She knew he watched her, but she didn't mind. He'd watched her before. She had no secrets from him.

When the release came it was deep enough to shake her very soul. He held her through the aftermath, when her body wouldn't stop shaking. Then he smiled with contentment and went to sleep.

Courtney couldn't find the same escape. After a few minutes, she gave up and slipped out of the bed. She grabbed Matt's shirt, pulled it on, then walked quietly down the hall and into the living room where she grabbed the bottle of whiskey. There was enough light from the fire to show her the way into the kitchen. Once she lit the lantern on the table, she settled in one of the wooden chairs and poured herself a drink.

The liquid burned as it went down. She swallowed, then gasped. The rest of her body was relaxed and satiated, but her stomach was on fire.

In a few minutes the flames became a tingling as the alcohol seeped into her bloodstream. She felt herself drifting into that half-awake, half-asleep phase when nothing was real. Abandoning the glass, she picked up the bottle by the neck and took another swig. This time the burning only lasted a second before turning into a mellow glow.

"Matt Stone, you're going to be the death of me," she murmured.

They'd made love tonight, but what of tomorrow and the next day? She was nearly out of birth control pills. When they were gone, she would be unprotected.

Then what? She didn't dare get pregnant. She knew what happened to women in this time. They all died giving birth. She didn't want that. Besides, making love with Matt only confused things. It made her remember the good times and made it too easy to want to forget the divorce. It made her want to settle.

She took another swig and closed her eyes. The lingering warmth from the stove chased the night chill. She swayed in the chair, hearing music in her mind. Music from the night she and Matt first met, when they had talked, then danced together. She remembered how well she'd fit into his arms. She'd never met a cowboy before. She'd thought he might be uneducated and crude, but Matt danced like a gentleman and treated her like a lady.

Picturing the crowded dance floor in her mind, she was instantly transported back. She could feel Matt's arms around her and the soft pressure of his hands on her back. He'd held her close, but not too close. And he hadn't tried anything. He hadn't even kissed her at her hotel room door.

When he'd offered to see her to her room, she'd been sure he would want to come in. She'd never had a one-night stand before, but he'd actually tempted her. Instead she'd been left standing alone. The next day she'd gone to see him at the rodeo. She'd watched him ride the bareback horses and win his go-round. She'd cheered with the crowd and had smiled proudly when two women in the row in front of her had moaned about his good looks. There, by the horses and steers, he'd kissed her for the first time.

Later that week they were still together. He hadn't kissed her again until their fourth date. She took another drink. They'd walked together, gone on drives; he'd even taken her riding. He'd touched her until she wanted to scream, but he hadn't taken it further. Even though she'd wanted him to. And then, on the Friday, he'd told her they had to talk.

She still remembered the tight feeling in her chest, as if her ribs were squeezing out all her air. He was going to tell her that he was gay, or already involved, or worse, although she couldn't figure out what could be worse. He'd taken her back to his room and seated her on the bed while he paced the plush carpeting. In his jeans and cowboy hat, he'd looked out of place in the luxurious room. She'd plucked nervously at the bedspread, sure she was about to have her heart broken.

"You've probably wondered why we haven't made love," he'd blurted without warning.

She'd blushed, then nodded.

She'd expected a lot of things, but not for him to drop to his knees in front of her. He'd removed his hat, placing it brim up on the floor next to him.

"You're the kind of woman a man dreams about. On those long drives from rodeo to rodeo, or sleeping in the back of my truck, I'd try to imagine what my life would be like five years from now. I sort of figured I'd have my own spread. Maybe in Wyoming."

He'd taken her hand then, staring at her fingers at if he'd never seen them before. "You're funny, pretty as hell, and smart. I don't deserve to ask, but I can't imagine just walking away from you."

He stared at her then, all earnest and nervous, his blue eyes dark with an emotion she was afraid to label.

"I don't want to lose you," he said.

She'd grasped his hand firmly and scooted to the edge of the bed. "I don't want to lose you, either," she told him and smiled. "I never thought I'd fall for a cowboy, but I guess I did."

But he didn't smile in return. Instead he swallowed hard. "Then marry me, Courtney."

She'd expected an invitation to his bed, not his life,

so she'd answered without thinking, without trying to picture what their future would be like. She'd never stopped to consider their differences. Instead she'd said yes and they'd married that afternoon. They'd spent the next three days in bed, discovering that while their lifestyles might be out of sync, their bodies had been designed for each other's pleasure.

Courtney took another swig of whiskey and was surprised to find herself fighting tears. She sniffed loudly, then blinked until her eyes were dry again. Matt had learned a hard truth. She wasn't the perfect princess he thought her to be. She was stubborn, demanding, and determined to have a relationship that was just that . . . a relationship. No part-time romance, no torrid affair. She wanted a marriage. Or did she?

She drew in a deep breath and admitted it would be easier if she weren't so afraid. Of him. Of being in love. Of this damn time. What the hell was she doing in 1873?

She stared at the rustic kitchen. It was difficult to believe that she'd begun to conquer that hideous stove in the corner, but she had. She'd changed since being here. But one thing remained the same. She was holding herself back from Matt because of the fear.

She'd known from the beginning they were destined to failure. Okay, maybe not the very beginning, but within the first month or so. She'd known it wouldn't last forever. Maybe in her heart she'd always known and that was why she'd married him in the first place. Because a temporary relationship kept her from having to deal with the real thing. Only, sometimes, when she let herself admit the truth, she knew Matt was the real thing. She was just so scared. Of caring, of not caring. Of trust. Of being alone.

She raised the bottle again and was surprised to see it was empty. When had that happened? Her mind was getting slow and she suspected if she tried to speak only gibberish would come out.

The bottom line was, neither she nor Matt was willing to compromise. Therefore their marriage was never going to work. Therefore they should get a divorce. Very simple. At least it had seemed simple . . . until now.

She rose unsteadily to her feet. The room tilted and spun. As she slowly made her way back to the bedroom, she wondered why what had seemed so logical a few weeks ago suddenly didn't make sense at all. After coming through time with Matt, she couldn't imagine life without him. So she had to make it work. Only she couldn't because their relationship had always been a way for her to hide.

She staggered into the bedroom and half fell onto the bed. Matt barely stirred. As she pulled the covers up around her shoulders, she told herself she would find a way to resist him. As she slipped into unconsciousness, her last thought was that it was pretty stupid to lie to herself.

The light from the hallway was ugly and painful and Courtney hadn't even opened her eyes. She could feel the individual rays piercing her eyelids and spearing for her brain. Her head already felt as if some small but very angry men had taken up residence inside. They were currently having a boxing match, with most of the blows landing on the inside of her head.

She wanted to die.

Please, God, she prayed silently. Make it quick.

But instead of relief from the Lord, she heard footsteps on the hardwood floor. Each thud made her wince. Even her eyebrows hurt. She knew exactly what was going to happen when she opened her eyes. She could feel it. Her stomach would start to spin in time with the room and she would toss her cookies.

"How are you doing this fine morning?" Hallie sounded disgustingly cheerful.

"Go 'way," Courtney mumbled, trying to get the words out without actually moving her lips. Someone had cranked her skin a notch too tight. Her teeth felt as if they'd been extracted, then shoved back in place. Some furry animal crouched on her tongue.

"I didn't think you'd want to face food," Hallie said. "I brought coffee."

Coffee? She risked opening one eye. The house-keeper didn't come into focus, but Courtney could see the mug, tauntingly out of reach.

She raised her arm slightly and her stomach lurched. "Oh, God, I just want to die," she moaned, and buried her head back in her pillow.

"The good Lord is busy with more important things than your condition. What were you thinking of, finishing the whiskey by yourself?"

"I wasn't thinking. Obviously."

Hallie moved closer and bumped the bed. Courtney clutched her midsection. "Turn toward me and I'll help. The coffee will make you feel better."

It took every bit of reserve strength, but she shifted onto her back and pushed herself up against the pillows. When she was reclining, Hallie held the mug to her lips.

Courtney inhaled the bitter smell and sighed with relief. Maybe she wouldn't die. She took a sip and nearly gagged. But the warm liquid washed away the fur on her tongue and as she swallowed, her stomach seemed to settle.

After a couple more sips, she managed to hold the mug herself. By the time the coffee was gone, she felt surprisingly better, except for the too-tight skin and the pounding in her head.

"If I just lie here and don't move at all, I might sur-vive," she told Hallie.

She heard more footsteps in the hall, but these she recognized. Matt.

She wanted to sink under the covers and never be seen again, but settled for just closing her eyes. What was she supposed to say to him? Most of last night was a blur in her mind, although she vaguely remembered begging him to make love with her. She recalled incredible passion, if not the details.

Guilt fueled her hangover. Guilt because there were only a few more birth control pills in her little plastic case and she wasn't going to risk having a child. Not here. And guilt because nothing had changed. He'd always driven her wild in bed, but that didn't affect the rest of their marriage.

"How's she doing?" he asked quietly as he stepped into the room.

"No need to whisper," Hallie said. "She's awake. She just finished a cup of coffee and seems to be feeling better."

"Good." He moved close to the bed, then sat on the mattress. "Courtney, how do you feel?"

"Horrible," she muttered, still not looking at him.

Hallie left them alone. When the housekeeper was gone, Matt leaned close and kissed her check. The brief caress made her want to throw herself in his arms. Instead she deliberately pulled away.

"Don't," she said.

"Sorry. I know you don't feel well. Why did you get up and finish the whiskey?"

She risked opening her eyes and looking at him, then wished she hadn't. She felt like something that had been run over by a bus. He'd never looked better. He'd shaved, exposing the sharp line of his jaw. Dark hair tumbled onto his forehead. She had to curl her fingers into her palm to keep from pushing it back in place. There were no shadows under his eyes, no hint of a hangover. Just the faint smile of a sexually satisfied male.

She told herself the pain in her chest was part of the hangover, but she knew it was something else. "I drank to forget what we'd done," she said bluntly.

His smile faded as his mouth straightened into a line. "Why?"

"Because it was a mistake and we can't do it again. I wasn't thinking. Neither of us was."

He stood up, his arms hanging loosely at his sides. "I knew exactly what I was doing."

"Good for you. I didn't. But I've thought about it. Nothing is real here. It's easy to pretend we're both something we're not."

"This is very real," he said. "Maybe more real than that other world we've been living in."

"I'll admit it's real enough that we can't make love again. I only have a few pills left and I don't want to have a baby."

"My baby, you mean."

She glared at him. It increased the pounding in her head and she just wanted him to go away. "No. Anyone's baby. I'm not willing to bleed to death or whatever happens to women in the middle of nowhere. There's no doctors, no medical care."

He stared at her for a long time. Finally she took the coward's way out and turned away. She shifted on the bed and her body screamed out in protest.

"This isn't about sex at all, is it?" he asked.

"No. It's about everything else. That's why I got drunk last night. Because I kept remembering. You thought you married a fairy princess and I'm not her."

"What were you marrying, Courtney?"

She didn't want to think about that. She waved her hand. "This isn't really happening. Or if it is, it's some alternate universe, a fluke of nature. It's summer camp all over again. We're both pretending."

"I'm not."

His words stabbed at her, piercing her heart and making her bleed. "I just want to go home," she whispered.

"Home? This *is* your home."

"No, it's yours. I never wanted this."

She finally risked glancing at him again and was stunned by the rage in his eyes. His whole body radiated anger. He glared down at her.

"Not 'this,' Courtney. Me. You never wanted me." His voice vibrated with dark, ugly emotion. "So why did you marry me? Was it a joke? Were you giving some dumb cowboy the ride of his life? Is that what it was all about? Did things get too serious for you? Are your feelings at risk? Is that why you're acting like this?"

"No! I never pretended—"

He cut her off with a harsh laugh. "According to you, this is all pretend. None of it's real, not even the fact that I—" He caught himself then and stalked away from the bed.

That he what? Cared about her? Loved her? She closed her eyes against the pain. Matt didn't love her. She didn't inspire those kind of strong emotions, especially not in someone as good and honorable as him.

He paused in front of the wall next to the door. Her backpack was hanging from a hook. He stared at it for a moment, then grabbed it and carried it to the bed.

In that second, she knew exactly what he was going to do.

"Matt, don't."

"Why not? Isn't this what you've wanted from the beginning?"

"Don't do it like this."

"You mean there's a nice way to get divorced?"

He dumped the contents onto the bed, then

searched until he found a thick legal-looking envelope. He pulled out the papers and thumbed through them to the last page. Grabbing her pen, he set the papers down and quickly signed his name.

"Congratulations," he said, straightening and tossing the pen down. "The marriage is officially over."

12

Eventually Courtney forced herself to get out of bed. As she buttoned the bodice of her dress, she stared at the thick sheets of paper. He'd signed them. She couldn't believe it.

As the ache in her chest deepened, she knew this was all her fault. Instead of being honest, she'd assigned blame. She should have told Matt she was afraid. Of this time, of getting pregnant, of her feelings for him. She should have reminded him of her short-comings, not that he was likely to forget them, and tried to find some kind of middle ground. He might not have understood, but he wouldn't have gotten so angry.

Surely he wasn't surprised that she didn't want to stay here. Okay, maybe life wasn't as bad as she'd thought it would be, but would anyone actually *choose* to live here instead of in the future? Anyone other than Matt?

She gathered the papers together and put them back

in their envelope. What was she going to say to him? First she would apologize for what she'd said. After that . . . she wasn't sure. Maybe they could find an emotional place that didn't involve sex or feelings, although that didn't sound like very much fun.

With her head still splitting, she made her way into the kitchen. Hallie took one look at her and poured another cup of coffee. Courtney took it gratefully and sank into one of the chairs. When she'd finished half of it, she felt slightly more human.

"Where's Matt?" she asked.

"Gone. Mr. Hastings and Roger are with him. They're off to track the buffalo herd. In a few days we'll have enough fresh meat for months."

"Without a refrigerator, it's not going to stay very fresh," Courtney muttered.

Hallie stood at the counter, rolling out dough. "What was that?"

"I was just wondering how we kept the meat fresh."

"We'll smoke it, of course."

"Naturally."

"You're the strangest person I've ever met," Hallie said as she picked up the piecrust and set it in the dish. "You wear trousers like a man, you've been educated at college, you have the smallest, fanciest timepiece I've ever seen." She turned around and nodded at Courtney's wrist. "But you don't know something as simple as how to make bread or smoke meat."

Courtney glanced at her watch. Both Hallie and Roger had been amazed by it. Matt had told them it was from Europe and they'd both accepted the explanation. Her inexpensive Timex traveled through time and kept on ticking, bless its little mechanical heart. Although when the battery ran out, she was going to be in trouble.

"I know it's difficult to understand," she said. "I

wish I could explain it. Things are different where I'm from." She thought about her birth control pills. They had revolutionized the 1960s; imagine what they would do in this era. Speaking of which . . .

"Hallie, what do you do about your, um, cycle? What do you use?"

"What?" Hallie whirled to face her. Her brown eyes widened and her mouth dropped open. "You don't know what to do about *that?*"

Courtney felt a blush crawl up her cheeks. She ducked her head and took a sip of coffee. "I didn't bring anything with me. Where I'm from, we have special things we use and I haven't seen them here. So I wondered what you did."

The housekeeper drew her eyebrows together. "It's just plain odd that a woman your age doesn't know to use rags."

"Rags? Rags! Please tell me that you throw them out when you're done."

"Don't be silly. You wash them out and use them again."

Courtney slumped on the table and rested her forehead on her arm. "Anything but that. It's disgusting. I don't want to be here now, and if I have to be here, couldn't I be a man?"

She was surprised to feel a hand on her shoulder. She glanced up. Hallie was staring at her, concern obvious in her features.

"You miss your family," the housekeeper said. "Your neighbors. If your ways seem strange to us, then ours must seem strange to you. You've been working hard and doing a fine job for someone raised with servants her whole life. The men will be gone for a few days. We can relax. Without them around, there's almost nothing to be done."

Courtney brightened. "Really? I guess the cooking

will be easier. We still have the chickens and the horses."

"Don't forget the new cow."

She grimaced. "Oh, goody. The cow." So instead of a million things to do with their day, there were only a couple thousand. "What will we do with our free time?"

Hallie gave her shoulder a squeeze and returned to the counter. She'd been soaking dried apples and spices overnight. Now she poured the mixture into the piecrust.

"I thought we could start working on your new dress."

Courtney had almost forgotten about the material Jonathan had brought. "You probably won't be surprised to find out I can't sew. I mean, I took a class years ago, but I didn't do very well."

"No, I'm not surprised. I'll start you with something simple."

Hallie opened the door to the oven and slid the pie inside. After cleaning up her mess, she washed her hands, then disappeared into her room. She returned with a basket full of scraps of material and sewing supplies.

"I'm going to cut out the dress," she said. "Then I'll piece it together. I'm a passable seamstress, though I don't do fancy work well. I never had the time. I thought you might want a dress like mine. Maybe with an overskirt so you can wear it for best."

Courtney studied the other woman. Her blue calico dress had long sleeves with cuffs at the wrists. The small collar lay flat and a row of buttons marched down nearly to her thighs. It was exactly like dresses she'd seen during their brief stay in town.

Hallie had added a few of her own touches with tucks at the waist, giving the dress a more fitted look. On the back, several rosettes clung just above her apron tie.

"What's an overskirt? And don't roll your eyes at me before answering," Courtney said.

Hallie grinned. "It goes over the regular skirt, but is usually shorter and more decorative. If this were my overskirt, I could have gathered it like this." She took hold of the hem at one end of the apron and pulled it up several inches, then did the same at the other end. In between, the fabric curved in a scallop. "You hold the gathers with ribbons or a rosette."

"I like it," Courtney said. "Can the overskirt be removed if you don't want to wear it?"

"If that's how you would like the dress designed."

"Great." She reached for the scissors sticking out of Hallie's basket. "Where do we start?"

"*We* don't start anywhere. I'll work on the dress. You can start on my quilt." Hallie fished out a twelve-inch square of layered fabric. There was a cloth top and bottom, and soft batting stuck out from the sides. One side was a calico print in red, the other was ivory.

"This is a square for a quilt," Hallie said, handing it to her. "See those long stitches going from corner to corner?"

Courtney nodded.

"They'll hold the three layers together. Your job is to replace the big stitches with small, even ones. A quilt is only as good as the seamstress who makes it."

Courtney stared at the square. "You want me to sew another *X*? Can I do something else?"

"Like what?"

Courtney turned the square over and studied the calico print. The printed flowers seemed to form a larger pattern in the shape of a teardrop. "What if I outline this?" She traced the path with her finger. "Hmm, they almost make the petals of a daisy. I could do the whole square like that."

"If you'd like. Remember, keep the stitches small

and even." She pulled out thread and a needle from the basket.

Courtney angled her chair close to the window so she could take advantage of the light. Her stomach had settled from nauseous to faintly queasy and the banging in her head was no more than the rumble of a train. She figured she was probably going to live.

Hallie spread the material out on the table, then dug around in her basket. She came up with several worn pieces of cloth that looked as if they'd once been part of a dress. After studying the weave of the cloth and the direction of the pattern, she placed the individual pieces down and started cutting.

"We're nearly the same size through the midsection," Hallie said. "Once we've basted everything, we can fit it to you. The skirts will have to be longer, of course."

While Hallie cut the cloth, Courtney struggled to keep her stitches small and even. What had sounded simple, even obvious, in the abstract was not too easy in practice. The thread tangled, she poked herself in the finger, and her first attempt to sew in the shape of a petal yielded a slightly lopsided oval that had a sharp indentation on one side.

She held it up for inspection. Hallie shook her head. Courtney sucked in a breath and pulled the stitches out, one by one.

"Where's your family, Hallie?" she asked.

"Here and there. My oldest daughter lives in Cheyenne. Her husband works on the newspaper. One of my sons works on a ranch. Elizabeth married a doctor and moved to Kansas. Albert is in New York City. He wants to be a writer, if you can imagine such a thing. And Roger, my youngest, is here with me."

"But he's seventeen. You must have been a child yourself when you started having babies."

"I was a year younger than Roger is now." She stopped cutting and stared off into the distance. "I met Mr. Wilson at a barn raising back in Ohio. You know where that is?"

"Yes," Courtney said, then frowned. She'd done as poorly at geography as she had at history. She was pretty sure Ohio was east of here, somewhere between Wyoming and the Atlantic Ocean.

"He swept me off my feet. After that first dance—" She glanced down and smiled. "Well, I just knew."

"So you married him?"

"That I did, and started west with him. My mama was heartbroken to lose me. Now that I've got grown children of my own, I understand her feelings. But I was young then and didn't know better. We spent time around Fort Laramie. Three of my babies were born there." Her smile faded. "One of them died there."

"You lost a child? I'm so sorry."

Hallie nodded. "A little girl. Such a pretty thing. A fever took her. It was quick. But I've got five healthy children, and grandchildren."

Courtney stared at her. "I can't believe you're only thirty-eight and you have grandchildren and everything. I didn't even get married until I was twenty-seven, and I thought that was young. I guess times change. If you don't mind me asking, what happened to your husband?"

Hallie sighed. "Mr. Wilson was killed when his wagon turned over. It was nearly five years ago."

"You must still miss him."

"I do." She glanced at Courtney. "Time makes it better. I'm strong and healthy. I found work to take care of myself and Roger. Soon it will be just me."

"Will you go live with one of your daughters?"

"No. They think I'm stubborn and bossy."

"Really? I don't think that."

"I can be, from time to time."

Courtney grinned. "I'll try to notice when it happens."

She bent over the sewing. This time the petal actually looked like a petal. She showed it to Hallie. "Better?"

"Much. Do that five more times, then I'll give you another square."

"How many are there, or don't I want to know?"

"Enough to make a quilt."

Courtney sucked on her pricked index finger, then shook it. "Maybe this could be a baby quilt."

"You'll want it for your bed. Winter can be long and cold up here."

"That's hardly a news flash."

Hallie looked at her quizzically.

"Never mind," Courtney said. "Just an expression from my other life." She stared at her hands. "My skin is so dry. It's that soap."

"Use grease on them before you go to bed, and cover your hands with an old pair of gloves."

"That would work if I had old gloves, but I don't." She wrinkled her nose. "Let me guess. It's bear grease."

"Don't be silly. Bear grease smells bad."

Courtney laughed. "How foolish of me. Of course. I should have guessed that."

Hallie laid several cut pieces of cloth over the back of an empty chair. "I'll find you an old pair of gloves. When Mr. Stone returns, tell him you want some milled soap. It's not so hard on your skin."

"Thanks, Hallie. That's nice of you."

They worked together in silence. Courtney found herself relaxing in the chair. The sewing was restful, in a domestic sort of way. It wasn't the same as curling up on the sofa and watching old movies, but it was better than doing the washing.

Life was different here. Pleasures were simpler, but

people appreciated them more. She wondered what her friends would think if they could see her now. Then she remembered she didn't really have a lot of friends. People at work would notice she was gone, of course, but she would be easily replaced. The neighbor down the hall would have to find someone else to watch her cat when she went out of town. But close friends?

Her long-distance marriage required her to be gone frequently, traveling on weekends to be with Matt. She couldn't get together with people regularly. She didn't go out much with her single friends because they were usually interested in finding men. But she didn't have a husband to bring to events with her married friends. She'd been on the fringes.

She glanced at Hallie and realized they couldn't be more different. Yet they were finding ways to get along. People needed each other more in this time. Petty complaints didn't matter when compared with getting enough food to survive the winter.

She glanced out the window at the vast open land that was their ranch. Matt and Roger were gone, but she wasn't afraid. That was because she knew how to shoot and Hallie knew how to do everything else. They would be fine. She probably would have been fine on her own, but it was better this way.

"I'm glad you're here with me," Courtney said, feeling suddenly shy.

The housekeeper smiled at her. "I'm glad, too."

Matt rode Jasper over the rise and started down toward the house. Jonathan and Roger were an hour or so behind, their horses slowed by the weight of the buffalo. Matt had gone ahead because he wanted to see Courtney. Now that he could see the smoke from the chimney, he found himself reining in the gelding.

It had been nearly a week. What would she say when she saw him? What would he say? Their parting had been angry. If he could change one thing in his life, it would be the act of signing those damn divorce papers. Why had he done it?

Even as Jasper headed for the barn, Matt knew the answer. She'd wounded his pride. All her talk of wanting to leave, of not wanting to have a baby in these primitive conditions, had made him feel inadequate. With the wisdom of hindsight, he realized she was afraid. Everything was still foreign to her. Because she was fitting into this life so well, he sometimes forgot she didn't want the same things he did.

So what was he going to say to her when he saw her?

Jasper stopped outside the barn. Matt dismounted and patted the gelding. It had taken the three men two full days to find the buffalo herd. They'd shot two young animals and had kept the hides for blankets. Matt planned on giving one of them to Roger, though he hadn't told the boy yet.

He unfastened Jasper's saddle and took it into the makeshift tack room. When he came out, Hallie was waiting for him by the entrance to the barn.

"Welcome back, Mr. Stone," she said. "Were you successful?"

"We killed two buffalo."

"That's very good." Her slight smile faded. She held her hands together at her waist. Her knuckles were white, as if she clutched her fingers in a death grip.

A spring thunderstorm rumbled in the distance. The cool breeze tugged at a few loose hairs around Hallie's face. Matt realized it was the first time he'd seen her hair anything but perfectly tidy.

"Mr. Stone, I need to have a word with you."

"What's wrong?" he asked, then had to swallow hard. Dear God, not Courtney.

"It's about your wife."

It was as if something slammed into him. He couldn't breathe.

"What's wrong with Courtney? Did she have an accident?"

He started for the house. She grabbed his arm and held him in place. "She's not hurt. But I—" She drew in a deep breath. "Is she dying?"

"What?"

"She takes these pills every day. After lunch. I've seen her. She must be under a doctor's care. Is she dying?"

Pills? Matt placed his hand on Jasper's back and sighed in relief. "She's not sick, Hallie. She's taking—" How was he supposed to explain birth control pills to his nineteenth-century housekeeper? "The little white pills are temporary. She'll stop taking them soon." She would run out and be vulnerable to pregnancy. No wonder she'd been scared after they made love.

"What about the other ones? The big ones."

He stared at Hallie. "What are you talking about?"

She squeezed her eyes shut. "She takes a second pill. They're very large and brightly colored. She puts them in her mouth and just sits there. She gets the most peculiar expression on her face. Extreme pain or suffering." Her eyes opened. "When I first arrived, I was concerned about Mrs. Stone's odd behavior so I . . . watched her. I quickly realized she wasn't mad or dangerous, but I'd already seen her take the pills. She still does it every day after lunch." Worry drew her eyebrows together. She repeated, "Is she dying?"

Panic gripped him. "I don't know." He ran toward the house. "Courtney! Courtney, where are you?"

He jerked open the back door and raced inside. She was standing in the kitchen, staring at him. "Matt? What's wrong?"

He didn't care about their fight or the divorce papers. He crossed the wooden floor in three long strides and grabbed her upper arms. He gazed at her face searching for symptoms, but her skin was clear, her eyes bright. "What didn't you tell me?" he demanded.

"What?"

He shook her. "Those pills. Hallie says you're taking pills. What's wrong with you? What are you hiding?"

"Birth control pills. I take them every day."

"What else? Hallie says there's another pill. What's it for?"

He was prepared for several reactions. Maybe she would go pale or defiantly blurt out the name of some terrifying disease. She might cry, but with Courtney that was unlikely. Instead, she blushed.

The color started low, at the collar of her dress. It climbed up her cheeks to her hairline. She ducked her head.

"I'm not taking pills," she mumbled.

"You are, too." Hallie had followed him in from the barn. "I've seen you myself."

Courtney glanced from the other woman back to him. She shook her head. "They're not pills."

She pulled free of his grip and started for the bedroom. He followed, with Hallie trailing behind. Courtney collected her backpack and set it on the bed. She unbuckled it and reached inside. When she pulled her hand out, she was holding a familiar brown wrapper.

He stared at her. "M&M's?"

She nodded. "I've been eating one every day after lunch. I should have shared. It was selfish of me, but you know how I love chocolate."

He began to laugh. Fueled by relief, the sound started low in his belly and exploded up his chest. All the worry, the anxiety, and the concern disappeared.

Courtney joined in. Only Hallie was left staring in confusion, her hands planted on her hips.

"I'd like to know what's so funny," she said.

Matt caught his breath and pointed at the bag in Courtney's hands. "Not pills, Hallie. Candy. She's been eating candy."

Hallie opened her mouth, then closed it. She glared at Courtney. "You could have said something instead of worrying a body half to death."

Courtney sobered. "I'm sorry. If I'd known you were worried, I would have told you."

Hallie stared at her for a moment longer. "No harm done. I'd best see to dinner." She turned on her heel and left.

Suddenly he and Courtney were alone.

She started to put the M&M's away, then held out the bag. "You want one?"

He shook his head. "You keep them."

"Thanks." She put them away, then, with her back still to him, spoke. "How was the hunt?"

"Good. We killed two buffalo." He gave her a few details of the trip. "I made the mistake of telling Jonathan my plan to keep a small herd on the ranch. He thought I was crazy."

"Then we're even. Obviously Hallie thinks I'm crazy, too. The things I don't know, how I talk. All of it."

He shoved his hands in his pockets. He wanted to touch her, but he didn't have the right. Signing the papers hadn't made the divorce official, but it had changed things.

He took a step toward the door. "Jonathan and Roger will be back soon. I'm going to have to help them with the meat."

She turned toward him. "Wait, please. I—" She shook her head. "I don't know what to say. I guess the best thing is the truth. I'm sorry I hurt your feelings."

"I know. I'm sorry I signed the papers."

"Really?" She smiled faintly. "I'm glad. I don't think it counts anyway. You dated them 1873. But it's nice to know you don't mean it anymore." She held out her hands, palms up. "Where do we go from here?"

"I don't know." It would have been easy to step next to her and pull her close. She would have let him. He could have kissed her and tried to pretend it was going to work out. But he couldn't. He loved Courtney too much to lie to her.

"I saw the storm," he said.

Her eyes widened. "Where?"

"West of here. It was there for a second, then gone. Three days ago."

"What does it mean?"

"I guess that there's a way back."

She smiled in delight. "We can go home."

He heard voices from outside. "I'd better go help them," he said, and left the bedroom. She hadn't figured out the truth and he didn't know how to tell her. She might long for something else, but he *was* home and he didn't plan on leaving.

13

Courtney scooped chicken feed into her apron and stepped outside. The bright sunshine warmed her body as she drew in a deep breath.

"Don't forget your bonnet," Hallie called, tossing the hat after her.

Courtney laughed. "Yes, ma'am."

She held the corners of her apron together with one hand and set the bonnet on her head with the other. The long ties dangled and she pushed them over her shoulders, out of the way.

The sky was a brilliant blue. She looked up and squinted, then stared west, looking for the first signs of clouds pushing over the mountains. They'd had a couple of weeks of afternoon thunderstorms, but the last few days had been clear and beautiful. It looked as if today was going to be the same.

Humming softly, she made her way to the chicken coop. The birds heard her and came trotting out for their breakfast. She stepped into the pen and scattered the feed. A few kamikaze chickens dove for her toes, but she gently pushed them aside.

She ducked into the chicken coop and scooped up the eggs, then returned to the house. Hallie was working in the parlor, cleaning out the fireplace. Although it was already late June, the nights were still cool. Last evening they'd played cards in the front room and had needed a fire to take the chill out of the air.

Courtney left the eggs on the counter, then picked up the slop bucket and headed for the east side of the barn. There the large sow and her piglets lay in the shady moist mud. Jonathan had brought them a couple of weeks ago.

"Come on, Miss Piggy, breakfast," Courtney called as she dumped the bucket into the feed trough. She walked over to the pump Matt had installed next to the barn. After cleaning out the bucket, she filled it with water and poured that into the pigs' tire-size watering dish. Roger milked the cow, so she didn't have to worry about that every morning and evening.

Her next stop was the vegetable garden. Everything had sprouted. Hallie promised that in another month or so she and Courtney would be frantically putting vegetables up, but for now they waited for the plants to grow. Courtney bent over and raised the small wooden dam Matt had designed. She didn't have to carry buckets to the garden anymore. She lifted the barrier and water flowed down the shallow irrigation path to the neat rows of the garden.

While she waited for the watering to be completed, she glanced around at the outbuildings. Everything had changed in the last four weeks. The bunkhouse had been finished and several cowboys had moved in. They had their own cook, kitchen, and dining room so she rarely saw the men. A small two-room house had been built for Jonathan. He had taken to staying a few days at a time. The gambler took his meals with Courtney, Hallie, Roger, and Matt, but spent most of his time with the cowboys, learning all he could.

Courtney found herself liking Jonathan more, although he made her crazy with his opinions about women. He was willing to admit she had a brain and knew how to use it, but he was sure the female population in general wasn't so blessed.

"Men," she muttered, then bent over and pushed the wooden barrier back in place. If the temperature continued to climb, she was going to have to start watering the garden twice a day. She licked her lips and smiled. It was a small price to pay for fresh vegetables.

Her first round of chores done, she started for the house, then changed her mind and headed toward the corral. Matt worked Jasper in the main ring, preparing the cutting horse for the arrival of the cattle.

She set her bucket on the ground, then climbed the fence and perched on the top rail. Her long skirts didn't hamper her movement much anymore. She'd grown used to the extra weight of the skirts. Sometimes she longed for the freedom of jeans, but not as much as she would have thought.

Matt and Jasper worked together in the center ring. Clover, the milk cow, stood silently, chewing her cud. Matt urged Jasper forward. Man and horse thundered toward the milk cow who continued to stand placidly in place.

Courtney smiled. "She's not cooperating."

"Tell me about it. We both need the practice, but she doesn't care."

He turned Jasper toward Courtney and trotted over. She reached out and petted the bay's soft nose, then glanced at her husband. Matt had been working long hours getting everything ready. There were still miles of fencing to build.

"When will the cattle arrive?" she asked.

"I don't know. Could be next week, could be three months. They left Texas in the middle of last summer and holed up for the winter. Depending on how many survived the cold and how skinny they are, they might make good time, or they might be delayed. We'll have to wait and see. The north pasture is waiting for them. If they get here soon, they'll have a few months to gain weight before they face another winter."

"Will you send any to market this year?"

He squinted against the bright sunlight. "A few. We'll need the cash for supplies and a blooded bull."

He spoke as if they were going to be here forever. Sometimes Courtney was far less sure about what was going to happen to them. In the last month there hadn't been any signs of the mysterious storm that had brought them to this time. The first few days after Matt told her he'd seen it, she'd spent a part of each afternoon waiting on the top of the knoll. Eventually she'd had to give up the pastime. There was too much work to do.

"Why are you smiling?" he asked.

"Am I?" She laughed. "I was thinking about the rhythm of life. There's so much that has to be done every day. The chickens, the sow, cooking, cleaning. Soon we'll be putting up berries, then the garden. In the winter, Hallie says we do the sewing."

"Help me with my rhythm," he said. "Run around the corral for me."

"Are you serious?"

"Yeah. Jasper and I are rusty. Come on, just a couple of times. Give me a moving target to rope."

She scrambled off the railing and jumped into the corral. "All right, but no hog-tying."

"Fair enough."

Matt slipped his lariat off the horn of his saddle and slid the noose around Clover's neck. He dismounted and led the milk cow back to the barn, then returned to the ring. Courtney hovered by the railing, not sure what to do.

"You just going to stand there?" he asked as he settled in the saddle. "Clover could do that."

"No, I'm waiting for you to make the first move."

She didn't see the signal, but suddenly Jasper was heading toward her. She'd watched Matt and his gelding during a cutting horse competition several months before.

"Today the part of the steer will be played by Courtney Stone," she said in a low voice.

She picked up her skirts, ducked quickly to her left, and took off at a run. Her bonnet flew off, but she didn't stop to see where it landed. She could feel the pounding of the horse's hooves as he moved closer. She chuckled, spun to her left, ran several feet, turned left again, and came around behind Jasper.

"You *are* out of practice," she said, panting.

"We're going easy on you." Matt pulled his hat low and grinned.

Without warning, the horse lunged toward her. She shrieked with laughter and ducked away. She tried circling around them again, but Jasper had already figured out her trick. He turned in time with her. She'd barely run fifteen feet when she heard the warning whisper. Then a lariat dropped neatly over her head and tightened around her waist. Before she could get her balance, she was jerked off her feet and landed hard on her butt. The jolt made her teeth rattle.

"Matt!"

"Sorry." He was by her side in a heartbeat. "You okay?" He signaled Jasper and the rope loosened.

"I'm fine." She pulled it over her head and stared at him. "What happened?"

"Jasper is trained to keep the line taut, so he backs

up to counteract the cow. You weigh a lot less and he wasn't expecting that."

She glanced over her shoulder at the horse. "Maybe you'd like to feel Clover in that saddle. That would teach you the difference in mass distribution among mammals."

Jasper snorted.

Matt rose to his feet and held out his hand. She placed her palm in his and allowed him to pull her up. Dirt clung to the back of her dress. When he started brushing it off, she thought about telling him she would do it, but she liked the feel of his hands on her body. They might be sharing the same bed every night, but they weren't lovers.

She told herself she was glad. She'd been off the pill for nearly a month and if they had sex regularly she probably would get pregnant. But all the logic in the world didn't make her miss him less.

The hard work of keeping the ranch running left them both tired at night, but there were times when physical exhaustion wasn't enough. Often she would lie awake and listen to his breathing while every fiber of her being burned for him. Her muscles trembled, her breasts ached, her secret place dampened in readiness. There were mornings when she awakened with the sleepy memory of Matt spending a restless night. They slept in the same bed separated by a few inches neither of them could cross.

She told herself all she had to do was ask. If the words were too difficult, she could tell him what she was thinking with a touch. But she was still afraid of so many things. Besides, *he* hadn't asked either—a childish bit of logic she couldn't seem to escape.

"Walk around," he said when he finished brushing away the dirt. "I want to make sure you're all right."

"I'm fine." She took several long, exaggerated steps to prove her point, then rubbed her fanny. "I've got plenty of padding to protect me."

Jasper took a step toward her and sniffed her neck. He blew hot air against her skin, tickling her.

"I know you didn't mean it," she said, and stroked his face.

Matt stood next to her. He didn't speak, he just watched her. They could talk about the ranch for hours, but they never discussed anything personal. Maybe he was afraid, too, but of what? The signed divorce papers lingered between them. They might not mean anything legally, but the deed couldn't be undone. There had been a change in their relationship and until one of them was willing to do something about it, until one of them was willing to acknowledge it and start the healing process, they were going to remain strangers.

"Hallie's going to try making potato chips again for lunch," Courtney said when she couldn't stand the silence. "She even had Roger sharpen the knife so she can cut the slices really thin."

Matt came around her and coiled the lariat. He placed it over the saddle horn. "I appreciate the effort, but I suspect there's some spice or something in the oil. They just don't taste right."

"I know. It's probably some chemical that hasn't even been invented yet. I think we're doomed to failure in trying to recreate junk food."

Matt shifted his hat back on his head. She could see his eyes. The warm expression there confused her. She felt the connection, the awareness swirling around them. Should she say something? Maybe acknowledge her feelings? But she didn't know what they were. They'd rushed into marriage already and had paid a price for that. This time she wanted to be sure. This time she wanted to know exactly what she was getting into. She wanted to know they planned to spend the rest of time together, wherever that might be.

"Does Hallie know how to make cheese?" he asked.

"I'm not sure. Why?"

His mouth turned up in a slow smile. On cue, her toes curled. That, at least, hadn't changed. "Pizza. Dough is easy, and so's the tomato sauce."

"What a great idea," she said quickly, catching his enthusiasm. "As soon as we have fresh vegetables. Sausage—" She shuddered. "I don't even want to think about making sausage, but I bet we could buy some in town. But you're right. It's the cheese. I don't know how they make them come out different from each other. Butter is butter, but cheese? We'd need some mozzarella." She tilted her head. "Do you think we have any Italian neighbors nearby we can ask?"

"I'll check with Jonathan when he arrives." His gaze narrowed. "He's due tomorrow."

"Oh. Good." She glanced down and saw her bonnet lying on the ground. She picked it up and brushed off the worst of the dirt, then plopped it on her head.

"Maybe we could—" She realized he was still staring at her. "What's wrong? Why are you glaring at me?"

He turned away. "I wasn't."

But he had been. Glaring at her as if—"Did I do something?" she asked.

"No." He collected the reins hanging on the ground and swung into the saddle.

"Matt, don't." She placed her hand on his knee. She could feel the heat of him through the denim. "Tell me what's wrong."

"Nothing." He drew in a deep breath and stared out at the horizon. "I'm being a jerk. Sorry."

"I can't forgive you until you tell me what you've done."

But he didn't respond to her teasing. She tried to figure out what had just happened. One moment they were connecting and the next he was angry about something. And they said women were complicated.

"Speaking of Jonathan, remind me to tell him that the next time he's in town I want him to see if there's a Sears catalog yet. I know they had them in the past. Well, the future." She shook her head. "You know what I mean. Anyway, I want to see what kind of modern conveniences we're missing out on. Hallie swears that sewing machines have already been invented, but I would rather have a washer and dryer."

"I think you're going to have to wait a little for the dryer, but we might be able to find you a washing machine. Once we see what the herd looks like, we might be able to afford to hire another woman to help around the house."

She smiled. "Who knew I'd have to travel back in time to be able to afford live-in help?"

"Maybe you should go to town with Jonathan and see if there's anything else you want."

There was something odd about the way he made the offer. Not in the words themselves or the tone, but she got this shiver along her spine.

"I don't think so," she said easily. "I'll wait until you have time to come with me."

Before he could say anything, the back door opened and Hallie called her.

Courtney grimaced. "I've got to start dinner."

"But we haven't had lunch yet."

"I know." She shook her head. "Don't ask. You don't want to know."

She walked to the corral fence and climbed through, then met Hallie by the hen house.

The older woman patted her shoulder. "It won't be so bad."

"Easy for you to say." Courtney pressed her hand to her already rolling belly. "What do I do?"

Hallie opened the gate and motioned her inside. "First you catch it."

*   *   *

Matt washed up at the sink he'd installed outside the house under the lean-to. With the main pipe in place, it had been easy to tap into it. The spring provided plenty of fresh water. He eyed the ground and wondered how hard it would be to put in a septic system. He could make do with the equipment he had available now. It was just a matter of adapting the technology.

He dried his hands on the towel left hanging by the back door and stepped inside. The smell of dinner made his mouth water. Hallie was setting the table. He frowned. His wife usually did that.

"Where's Courtney?" he asked.

"Lying down."

"Is she sick?"

Hallie grinned. "Not exactly. She's in the parlor."

Matt fought against the cold panic swirling in his belly. He crossed the room in three long strides and saw Courtney curled up in one of the chairs in front of the fire. Her face was pale, her eyes closed.

He walked to her, then sank to his knees.

"Honey, what's wrong?" he asked, smoothing away a strand of blond hair.

She opened her eyes and tried to smile. Her mouth trembled a little at the corners, then straightened. "Nothing," she said softly. "I'm fine. I threw up a couple of times, but I'll recover."

"Are you sick? Did Jasper and I hurt you?"

"What? No." This time she managed a whole smile. She touched the hand stroking her hair. Her fingers were cool against his skin. "I cooked dinner is all."

He glanced over his shoulder. Hallie was pulling a roasted chicken out of the oven.

He turned back to his wife. "Why would cooking a chicken make you sick? You've done it before."

"Oh, not like this. I didn't just cook it, I prepared it. I caught it, killed it, cut off its head, plucked it, and scooped out its little chicken guts." She swallowed hard and leaned her head against the chair back. "The cooking part is easy. I may never eat again."

He didn't know whether to laugh or applaud. Courtney was a hell of a woman. He brought her hand to his mouth and kissed her fingers. "You're very brave."

"Don't make fun of me."

"I'm not. I always knew you had strength, but I didn't know how much."

"Yeah, right. I'd make a lousy pioneer woman."

"What do you think you are now?"

She looked at him. "Hallie's the expert. Without her, we would have starved a hundred times over."

He rubbed his thumb against her palm and was pleased when she didn't pull away. He'd missed holding her and touching her. "Maybe, but look at all that you've learned."

She thought for a minute, then nodded slowly. "It's true. I can do a lot. I can plant a garden, milk a cow, disembowel a chicken, bake bread, even sew."

He'd always believed she was beautiful, but here in the faint light of the parlor, he knew she was the most stunning creature he'd ever seen. She wore no makeup yet her large eyes and full mouth dominated her face. She took his breath away.

"I don't deserve you," he said quietly, still holding her fingers.

She raised her free hand to his mouth and touched his lips. "Don't say that. You think I'm this fairy tale princess, but I'm not. I never have been. I'm a little selfish sometimes. I get stubborn and scared, just like everyone else. Don't think I'm perfect, Matt, because then I'll only disappoint you."

He stared at her. In the background he heard the kitchen door softly close. Hallie had left them alone.

"I've been thinking about what you said," he told her. "About us not knowing each other well when we got married."

She smiled. "It was the best week of my life, but we were still strangers."

"I know that now. Those long weekends together didn't improve matters. We never had a chance. But we've got it now. This is the longest we've ever spent together."

"I know."

He held her gaze. "I've finally got something to offer you. This ranch is going be a success. I know every-thing I need to. The cattle are coming. Nothing can stop us."

"What about the storm?" she asked. "Don't you want to go back?"

He didn't. In his soul, he admitted the truth. This was where he belonged. In this time. "You do," he said, indirectly answering her question.

She nodded. "I know." She drew in a breath. "I wish I could make you believe it was never about what you had. Did you ever wonder why a city girl like me mar-ried a cowboy like you?"

"All the time."

She shifted on the chair and leaned toward him. "I married you because you didn't kiss me the first night we met. I thought it was going to be a one-night stand. I'd never done anything like that, but you tempted me. Then you didn't try anything for days."

She smiled. "At first I thought there was something wrong with me. Then I figured there had to be some-thing wrong with you. Finally I realized you were some-thing I'd never met before: an honorable man. You didn't mind that I was a little shy and didn't always know the right thing to say. You're honest, trustworthy, hardworking."

"You make me sound like a good cutting horse," he mumbled, embarrassed by her praise.

"Not exactly. You make my toes curl when you smile. Why wouldn't I want to marry you?"

He desperately wanted to believe her. If she spoke the truth, then maybe they had a chance. He swallowed his pride and his fear. "Maybe we could start over," he said. "Be friends."

She bit her lower lip. "I'd sort of hoped we were friends. Don't you like me even a little?"

I love you. But he couldn't say the words. Not yet. "Of course I like you. We are friends. But we could be best friends. Maybe we could give the marriage a chance to work."

Her hazel eyes darkened with emotion. "You signed the divorce papers."

"You had them drawn up in the first place."

She considered that, then nodded. "I was wrong."

"Me, too."

"Then let's try." She licked her lower lip. Desire slammed into his gut, heating his blood and instantly making him hard.

"I've missed you," he said, lowering his head to hers.

Just before his mouth brushed her, a voice cut through the silence.

"Why you standing out here, Ma? I could smell the roast chicken clean to the barn."

"Roger, don't come inside yet."

But it was too late. The teenager stomped into the kitchen. Courtney paled at the mention of the bird and collapsed back in the chair. Matt chuckled. For the first time in months, he felt hopeful about the future . . . and about the woman he loved more than life itself.

14

As he usually did, Jonathan Hastings arrived with gifts. He brought Roger one of his precious books, Hallie received an embroidered silk shawl. For Courtney there was a set of brushes and combs, inlaid with mother-of-pearl. For Matt, a blooded bull he'd wanted to buy and news of the cattle.

"Three days, maybe four," Jonathan said as he led his horse into the stable. "According to the men who drove them all this way, they're mean and skinny, but they survived the winter."

"Hot damn." Matt slapped his hat against his thigh.

Courtney glanced up and smiled. "You're the only person I know who could get so excited about a bunch of cows."

"You won't be so unimpressed when I use the money we get from selling them to buy you whatever you want from the Sears catalog."

Her hazel eyes widened with excitement as she stared at him. "It really exists?"

Jonathan slipped off the saddle and handed it to Roger. "Of course it exists. I'll bring out a copy the next time I'm here. There's every modern convenience. Even a sewing machine."

Courtney brushed that off. "I want my washer and dryer. Or just a washer. Anything to get my hands out of that hot water. The soap burns my skin, I'm not strong enough to wring the clothes well, my back aches. All and all, wash day is a hideous experience. Sewing is easy. You're indoors, you take small stitches. Nothing hurts. I just know the sewing machine was designed by a man. Did he bother to ask women which chore they hated most?" She glanced around, then shook her head. "No. Of course not. He just assumed. Your gender is flawed that way."

Roger, who had stood perfectly still during Courtney's speech, nodded respectfully. "Yes, ma'am," he said, though it was obvious he hadn't understood a word of what she was saying. The teenager was used to her rambling on about things that made no sense. He didn't care. If the object of his affection spoke, he stopped to listen.

Jonathan was equally confused. "You don't want me to order a sewing machine?"

"Oh, go ahead," Courtney told him. "Hallie will be grateful." She smiled. "As I am for the brushes. They're lovely."

Matt watched her walk toward the gambler, then rise on her toes and place a kiss on his cheek. Jonathan stiffened at the brief contact, then looked at him. Matt turned from his friend's gaze before the other man saw the sympathy in his eyes. Matt knew all about loving Courtney. There was something about her that made a man want what he couldn't have. Jonathan brought her gifts and paid her compliments, and she never noticed his hunger or his love.

It was the same with Roger, although for the boy Courtney was simply a first crush.

In another time, he might have been more worried about Jonathan Hastings. Yet in 1873, the gambler would never be able to win Courtney's heart. Their differences were too great. He might acknowledge her intelligence, but he would never respect it or appreciate it. Courtney would never accept being thought less of because she was female.

A bellow of outrage swept through the barn. Jonathan recovered his control and stepped away from Courtney. "Your husband's bull seems to desire attention," he said.

"A typical male. You can't leave him alone for a minute or he starts whining." She came up to Matt and linked her arm through his. "Have you two come up with a name?"

"Why don't you think of one?" Matt asked.

"All right." As they strolled out to the pen on the far side of the bunkhouse, she offered several suggestions. "We have a Miss Piggy, so I suppose we could use Kermit, although that's not exactly a bull's name. We could call him Matt Junior."

"Thanks, but I'll pass."

Her laughter warmed him to his soul. He didn't even mind when she tugged him to a stop to let Jonathan catch up with them, then linked arms with the gambler as well.

"What about you, Jonathan? Any relatives you'd like to insult by naming a bull after them?"

"Only my Aunt Mary, and I wouldn't do that to the bull."

"There's always Ferdinand after that cartoon bull who liked flowers."

"Cartoon?" Jonathan asked.

"It's a—" Courtney stopped, then shrugged. "I can't explain what it is. Sorry. I like Ferdinand."

"Fine with me," Matt said.

"Then Ferdinand it is," Jonathan said.

The three of them stopped by the large pen. Several trees offered shade. The grass was thick, the drainage good. The bull stared at them warily, his dark eyes confused and faintly enraged. He hadn't enjoyed the trip from town but Matt knew the animal would settle down in a couple of days. Then he would be ready to start his duties.

"He's smaller than the bulls at the rodeo," Courtney said.

"There isn't the same sort of specialized breeding. He's more proportioned through the chest, and his hips and rear legs are bigger." He would have to be, Matt thought with a grin. In this time, there wasn't artificial insemination. Ferdinand was going to cover the cows the old-fashioned way.

She leaned close. "Bulls have very large testicles."

"Yes, they do," he said.

"I wonder why."

Matt didn't have to look at the gambler to picture the shocked expression on his face. He cleared his throat to keep from laughing.

"Why do you want to breed this bull with the Texas cattle?" she asked.

"To get better meat. Longhorns have been running wild since the time of the Spanish exploration. They're hearty, but their meat doesn't marble."

Both she and Jonathan frowned in confusion.

"The fat doesn't run through the meat," he explained. "That's what makes it tender. By breeding the more domestic bull with the longhorns, we'll upgrade the quality of the meat, while passing along the traits that help the cattle survive."

Courtney nodded slowly. "Ah, the life of a gigolo. Of course, all the female cows get out of it is babies to raise on their own. Where are the buffalo going to be?"

Jonathan leaned against the railings. "You're still going to go ahead with that?"

"There's a shallow valley up north of here. I'd like to put a small herd there. In the next couple of years, the buffalo will have to be fenced so they aren't all killed."

Jonathan stared at him. "Do you know many buffalo there are? Hundreds of thousands. They'll always be here."

"I wish that were true. As the value of the hides increases, more people will come to hunt them. In another fifteen years, the buffalo will be gone."

Jonathan's arched eyebrows hinted at his opinion of Matt's prediction, but he was polite enough to keep his thoughts to himself.

"It's important to protect the environment," Courtney said. "I always sent money to save the whales organizations, as well as to the World Wildlife Fund."

"What are you talking about?" Jonathan asked. "You're both crazy."

Courtney laughed. The sunlight caught her blond braid and made it shimmer like white gold. She released the gambler's arm and leaned against Matt. "I guess that's the reason we're married. We can be crazy together."

Matt draped his arm across her shoulders and knew he was crazy about her. They'd agreed to try and be best friends, to make the emotional part of the relationship work before confusing everything with the physical.

He held back because it was the right thing to do and because he sensed Courtney's fear of getting pregnant. He didn't blame her. What would they do, out here in the middle of nowhere? Despite modern technology his mother had died giving birth to him. Matt couldn't bear to lose Courtney. She was his world.

She stared up at him and smiled. "I've got to go start

lunch. See you two soon." She gave a wave, then moved toward the house.

Instead of watching her go, Jonathan gripped the sides of the pen. "You're damn lucky to have her."

Matt stared at the sway of her long skirts and the way her braid bounced with each step. He thought about her strong spirit and her willingness to try anything once. She could have made his life hell. Instead she pitched in and worked as hard as any of them.

"I know," he said, then wondered if he would be lucky enough to keep her.

The whole town arrived on the heels of the longhorns. It took nearly half a day to get the herd separated onto the various pastures and by the time that was done, the first of the wagons had appeared.

Courtney stood at the back door and stared. "What are they doing here?" she asked.

"Being nosy and neighborly all at the same time," Hallie said. "Folks like an excuse to break their routine. You and Mr. Stone haven't been in town since you bought the ranch. Folks is curious about you and your Texas cattle."

Courtney counted six wagons, all filled with families. She could see more in the distance. "What will we do with them all?" she asked in a panic. There weren't enough bedrooms or linens. Not nearly enough food.

"They'll take care of themselves," Hallie assured her. "Every one of them has their own ranch or business to attend to. They'll stay the night, maybe two, then head back. They'll have brought plenty of food, you'll see." She squinted at the wagons. "Of course, we'd best set up a few fires outside for cooking. Good thing we've got a fresh buffalo for meat."

"That will be gone in a day," Courtney said. She

glanced down at her apron. She'd been preparing meat for smoking and the fabric was stained with blood. She touched her neck and felt several loose strands of hair.

"I'm a mess," she said. "I'd better go clean up."

She raced into the back bedroom and poured water into the basin. After washing her face and hands, she quickly unfastened her braid, then brushed her hair. If only she'd taken the time to learn how to put her hair up. But she hadn't. She paused long enough to weave a French braid, then tied the end with a ribbon that matched her dark red calico dress.

She pulled a fresh apron out of the dresser and slipped it over her dress. As she started out of the bedroom, she caught sight of herself in the small mirror on the wall. If the colors hadn't been so bright, her reflection could have been mistaken for an old photograph. But unlike those women in antique pictures, she wasn't solemn. Instead her mouth curved up in a smile and amusement sparkled in her eyes. She was excited about her guests. Who would have thought she would actually have fun here?

She hurried through the house and out the back door. Several of the wagons had stopped by the barn. People swarmed everywhere, greeting each other, unloading food. Conversations, laughter, children's screeches, and the yapping of several dogs combined to create more noise than a stadium during a high school football game.

She caught sight of Matt shaking hands with some men. They were asking questions. He pointed to the barn, then the bunkhouse. The men nodded, then picked up tools they'd brought with them and started toward the partially framed outbuilding that would hold supplies and act as a second barn. Apparently the men had come to work.

"Courtney, here are a few ladies I'd like you to

meet." Hallie led a group of women as proudly as a mother hen leads her chicks.

Courtney stepped off the back porch and fought a sudden rush of nerves.

Hallie paused in front of her. "This," Hallie said dramatically, "is Mrs. Matthew Stone. She's from Los Angeles. That's in California."

"Hello," Courtney said softly, and tried to smile. She could feel her mouth trembling. Hallie gave her a wink as if to say she would be fine. Courtney wasn't so sure. "Please call me Courtney."

The women stared at her, studying her. She fought against the urge to check her hair and glance at her apron to see if she'd scorched it with the iron.

"Look at that pretty hair," one of them said. "How do you do that fancy braid? My three daughters would love it."

"Hallie tells me you used to have maids to do everything for you," another said. "That's what I've always wished for."

"I can't believe everything you've done with this ranch," said a third. "It's nearly a miracle."

"Did you see her handsome husband?"

"My Robert is talking about us getting our own herd of Texas cattle. They're mean looking, but I hear they're going to sell well back East."

The women surrounded her and drew her into their conversation. Introductions were a blur of old-fashioned names and unfamiliar faces. Nell, Pansy, Estelle, Elizabeth, Lavinia. She would never keep them straight. But it didn't seem to matter.

The women went to work, dividing up tasks. Several started a large fire downwind of the house. Soon pots were heating and delicious smells wafted through the hot August afternoon.

Pitchers filled with lemonade appeared. There were

pies and bread, rolls and cakes. Matt announced that one of the longhorns would be slaughtered so everyone could taste the meat. Two teenage boys, obviously friends of Roger's, went to work preparing a spit to roast the beef. Courtney was grateful they wouldn't be having chicken. The thought of it still made her squeamish.

A petite, obviously pregnant young woman came up and smiled at her. "I think we've overwhelmed you," she said.

"Just a little. I'm sorry, I don't remember your name."

"Pansy." Her dark eyes danced with humor. "We're your closest neighbors. Just a few miles east of here." She pointed in that direction, then stepped close and lowered her voice. "I shouldn't be here, what with . . . " Her voice trailed off as she glanced at her protruding stomach.

"You're not allowed to go out if you're pregnant?"

Pansy blushed. "It's so private."

"I guess." Courtney wondered what Pansy would think of a very beautiful but very pregnant actress posing nude for the cover of a magazine. The idea alone was probably enough to send the young woman into early labor.

"When are you due?" she asked.

"A month or so," Pansy said, then glanced around to make sure no one was close enough to hear what she was saying. "It's my first. Franklin is hoping for a boy. I just want an easy time and a healthy baby."

"That makes sense." She stared at the young woman, at her coal black hair and wide blue eyes. "I hope this isn't a rude question, but how old are you?"

"Eighteen. Franklin and I have been married for nearly a year." She blushed again.

Eleven months married and eight months pregnant.

The thought made her skin crawl. "Is there a doctor nearby? For the baby, I mean."

"Oh, I wouldn't want the doctor." Pansy glanced down in embarrassment. "Mary Frances will be with me. She's our midwife. And my sister's still in town. She'll come. Hallie, too. And you, of course."

"Me?"

"We're neighbors, Courtney."

Courtney glanced around, frantically looking for Hallie. There was no way in hell she was going to attend some frontier birthing ceremony. She spotted the housekeeper talking to a tall, spare woman. "Excuse me," she said to Pansy. "I must ask Hallie something."

"Certainly."

Courtney quickly walked across the yard and touched Hallie's arm. "May I have a word with you?"

The tall woman drifted off. Hallie patted her hand. "Everything is going just fine. A few of the women want to see the changes inside the house, if you don't mind."

"Whatever." Courtney stared at her. "Pansy is pregnant."

"Shh!" Hallie glanced around at the crowd, then pulled Courtney to a quiet spot by the house. "You can't say that out loud. She shouldn't even be here in her condition."

"I know. She told me. That's not the point. She said that when it's time for her to have the baby, she's not going to a doctor."

Hallie stared, uncomprehending.

"That's insane," Courtney insisted. "She'll need a doctor. Decent medical care, if you people have such a thing. She expects you to be there. Worse, she expects me! I've never seen a baby being born and, frankly, I don't want to start now."

Hallie shook her head. "You worry about the silliest things. You're Pansy's nearest neighbor. Of course you'll attend her. When your time comes, she'll be here with you. That's how we do things."

"I'm not getting pregnant."

"The Lord doesn't always listen to a woman's prayers."

Courtney didn't tell her the Lord had nothing to do with it. She wasn't getting pregnant because she wasn't having sex. In the last few weeks, she'd felt herself wanting to give in to her desires. It was difficult to share a bed with Matt and not make love. Her body ached for him. Every day they seemed to grow closer together. Sex was the next logical step.

Not anymore, she thought grimly. She wasn't going to get pregnant and die giving birth like some wild animal.

"Pansy and Lavinia want to see the house. Why don't we take them through?" Hallie said.

"Fine. I'm sure they're going to laugh at my quilting efforts."

"You're not so bad."

The women didn't laugh, but they did hide smiles behind their hands. They admired the dress and blouse made from the silk Jonathan had brought, then reverently touched the mother-of-pearl brushes. When Hallie opened a drawer in Courtney's dresser and pulled out her spare bra, there was a moment of silence, followed by an explosion of laughter.

"What's that for?" Pansy asked, clutching her rounded belly.

"You put your bosom in it," Hallie said.

"That's the oddest thing I've ever seen." Lavinia touched the bra, fingering the elastic strap. "What's this made of?"

Courtney snatched it away from her and stuffed it back in the drawer. "I'm sure I don't know. Laugh all you want, but a hundred years from now, women will be wearing bras and laughing at corsets."

"I'm trying to make one for her," Hallie said. "So when hers wears out she'll have another. But I'm having trouble with the shaping."

"It doesn't make sense," Lavinia said. "Women are different sizes. Not only their bosoms but around their bodies. Who could possibly keep track of all that?"

Pansy nodded. "Plus a woman changes when she's expecting. You'd have to keep sewing new ones. Corsets are much more sensible."

Courtney slipped away while they were still extolling the benefits of having one's internal organs smashed and ribs bent, all in the name of a feminine shape. She would take a simple bra any day.

Outside, the crowd had grown bigger. Several of the longhorns were in a pasture near the house. She started in that direction. Matt saw her and called her over. He was talking to several men she hadn't met.

When she reached him, he put his arm around her. "This is my wife," he said proudly.

The men greeted her. "What do you think of these Texas cattle, Mrs. Stone?" a tall, bearded man asked. "They're not much to look at."

Next to her Matt shifted uneasily. She glanced at him. He gave her a half smile. Her toes curled.

"If my husband says they're money on the hoof, then that's good enough for me," she said. "He knows ranching and he has great vision. I think that in a few years you're going to be wishing you'd brought a herd north."

The men laughed. Matt squeezed her arm. "Thank you for that," he said when their neighbors had moved closer to the pasture fence.

"I meant it." She motioned to the finished barn, the bunkhouse, and the cowboys working the herd. "You've built something here."

"You're not so bad yourself."

"I'm willing to admit I have a bit more pioneering spirit than I might have thought," she said. "I wouldn't want to travel the overland trail, but I can manage the odd chore or two."

She looked around at the wagons collected near the house, the children playing tag and other games she didn't recognize. Women tended the meal cooking on an open fire. The longhorn had already been strung onto a spit.

"I feel as if we're extras in some epic Western movie," she said. "All we need are some bank robbers with a posse hot on their trail."

"And die in a hail of gunfire?" He shook his head. "No thanks. Not unless I can get the girl at the end."

His hand moved up and down her spine, making her shiver with anticipation. "You can't die *and* get the girl," she reminded him. "You have to pick."

His face was close to hers. His hat brim blocked out the sun. "Which do you think I'll choose?"

A loud shriek interrupted them. They turned in the direction of the noise. Several small boys were bent over like bulls. They charged the girls playing with their homemade dolls. The girls scattered and cried. Hallie came out of the house and flapped her apron at the boys, who ran away laughing.

Courtney glanced back at Matt, but the mood had been broken. "I'd better see that those kids stay away from the cattle," he said.

"I've got things to do in the kitchen," she said. "Hallie wants me to help her with biscuits."

Matt gave her fingers a squeeze, then he walked away. She headed for the house. She glanced at her watch to check the time. Eight-fifteen. She stared uncomprehending, then realized the battery had given out.

There was a clock in the parlor but no one cared about precise time here. The day was measured by the sun and chores to be finished, not seconds and minutes.

She took off the watch and tapped the face, but the second hand remained stubbornly still. She slipped past Hallie, through the kitchen and into her now-empty bedroom. She opened a small side drawer and set the watch down. Next to it was her gold chain. Several links were loose, lying next to the rest of the necklace. Someday she would have to get that fixed.

She stared at the watch for a moment, feeling as if it were her last connection with her time, then she closed the drawer and returned to the celebration.

15

Matt was saddling Jasper when the boy rode into the stable yard. He was barely eleven or twelve, but there was a rifle strapped to his saddle and a knowing look in his dark eyes.

"What can I do for you, son?" Matt asked, trying to place the boy. He'd probably been on the ranch three weeks ago when the longhorns had arrived. During a week's period, nearly half the county had come by for a look-see at the Texas cattle. He couldn't be expected to remember one small boy.

The boy didn't bother dismounting. He urged his horse close to Matt and bent down. "It's my sister Pansy's time. She said for me to tell Hallie and your wife, sir. I can't stay and show 'em the way, though. I've got to get into town so our Alice can come be with her, too."

With that he straightened, touched his heels to his mount's flanks, and rode off toward Cheyenne. Matt stared after him, blankly. Her time? His brain filled in the missing pieces of information and he bolted for the house.

"Hallie, Courtney!" he called as he jerked open the back door and stepped inside. The women were finishing the breakfast dishes. They turned to stare at him.

"Pansy's little brother stopped by before heading for town to get their sister." He paused long enough to gulp a chest full of air. "Pansy's having a baby."

Courtney paled instantly. She swayed and clutched at the side of the dry sink. Soapy water dripped off her hands.

"I've been expecting this," Hallie said, unfastening her apron and folding it neatly. "I've got a basket prepared for the baby. We'll take some of the vegetables we've started putting up and the pies we baked. There's bread, too." She glanced at Matt. "You and Roger will have to eat with the other men while we're gone."

"I can't go," Courtney said quickly. "I've got too much work here. The chickens, the sow. The garden needs watering. Who's going to do that? There's more vegetables to be put up and the berries, too."

"Nonsense," Hallie said, collecting an empty basket from the corner of the kitchen and brushing past Matt as she walked to the pantry. "The men's cook can use the ripe vegetables. The rest will wait until we get back."

She disappeared for a moment. Matt heard her collecting food. He stared at Courtney. She was visibly shaking. "I can't do this," she murmured. "I don't want to watch her die." She raised her gaze to his face. Her hazel eyes were dark with fear. "Matt, don't make me go."

Before he could answer, Hallie returned and handed him the full basket. "You go hitch the wagon."

"Pansy's brother couldn't stay," he said. "How will you find the ranch?"

"I've been there a time or two. There was a barn raising after the wedding. Besides, when her mother died, I stayed with her and her little brother for a time. It won't take us half a day to get there. It's due east of here. Now get on with you."

She shooed him away as if he were one of the chickens. Courtney cast a helpless glance at him, but he didn't know what to do. Obviously if she didn't want to go, she didn't have to. Yet how much of her fear came from the unknown? Would she feel better or worse witnessing the birth?

Matt understood her concerns. There had been times he'd wanted to turn to her in the night. Unresolved emotions and worry about pregnancy had kept him on his side of the bed. If they had unprotected sex, she would probably get pregnant. Ignoring the medical dangers inherent in giving birth in this time, what happened later? What if they were thrust back into the future? Would she still want a divorce? He couldn't knowingly do that to an innocent child. Would she go without him, taking the baby? Until she committed to him—until they committed to each other—he wasn't going to risk it.

He paused by the back door. "Courtney, you can stay if you want."

She looked at Hallie's stern, disapproving features, then at Matt. She slowly shook her head. "I'll go," she said softly.

"We'll need ammunition for the rifle," Hallie told him.

"I'm coming with you," he said.

Hallie paused in the act of folding soft linen towels and placing them in the already overflowing basket. "You have plenty of work to keep you busy here. Courtney's a good shot. I've seen her. You'd waste a whole day taking us, then coming back yourself. Besides, how will you know when we want to leave?"

"I'd bring Jasper along for me. You can keep the wagon."

She smiled. "So what do we need you for in the first place?" She shooed him completely out the door this time. "We'll be fine, Mr. Stone. I promise no harm will come to your pretty wife."

Matt walked to the barn and called Roger. He instructed the teenager to hitch up the wagon, then went to collect the extra ammunition that Hallie had requested.

Jonathan came out of his horse's stall and frowned. "What's going on?"

"Our nearest neighbor's wife is having a baby. Courtney and Hallie are going to go be with her."

The two men watched Roger get the wagon ready. Jasper stomped impatiently, ready to begin the day, but Matt ignored him. Courtney was leaving.

The pain in his gut was familiar. He got it every time he and Courtney separated. He'd driven away or stepped on a plane countless times with the same gnawing sensation. Only this time was different. This time the pain was tinged with fear of losing the happiness they'd finally found together.

The two women came out of the house. Courtney had slung her backpack over her shoulder and held her rifle in her right hand. Both women carried baskets overflowing with food and linens. Matt and Jonathan relieved the women of their baskets and set them in the back of the wagon. Matt touched Courtney's cheek. Her skin was soft and warm.

"You don't have to do this," he said.

She swallowed hard and nodded. "In a way, I do. If we don't ever get back . . . " Her voice trailed off. She looked at him. She'd pulled on a bonnet and the wide brim shaded her face. As usual, the ties fluttered down her back. "If we stay here, then the time might come when I need this information. Besides, Pansy doesn't have anyone but us. There isn't going to be a doctor." She grew pale again.

"I can come with you," he said, lowering his hand to his side.

"No. Hallie's right. It's not that far and she knows the way. I'm not afraid to use the rifle." She patted the barrel of the gun. "We'll be fine." She smiled. "I wish I could call you when I get there, but I guess I can't."

"Think about me instead."

"I will."

Her gaze found his. He thought about all they'd been through in the last couple of months. No, longer than that. They'd arrived in early May and it was already the end of August. The warm days remained, but the nights were getting cool again. Soon it would be fall, then winter.

"All right," Hallie said, breaking in. "You've said your good-byes. Courtney, we've got to leave."

Courtney raised herself up on her toes and brushed his mouth with hers. The bittersweet contact intensified the ache in his gut.

"Roger," Hallie said. "You'll have to take over Courtney's chores with the chickens, the sow, and the garden along with your regular work. Water the garden every day, unless there's rain. You understand me?"

"Yes'm."

"Good. Mr. Stone, I'm going to count on you to make sure Roger gets it all done. Tell the cowboys' cook he's welcome to all the fresh vegetables everyone can eat. There's meat in the smokehouse. Don't let him have any of the chickens until we get back. I've got my eye on a couple that I'd like to keep." She thought for a moment. "Laundry is going to have to wait." She smiled. "Try not to get too dirty."

"We'll do our best," Matt said.

"A body can't ask for more than that."

Roger helped her into the wagon. Courtney was already in place. Hallie picked up the reins and flicked them once. The two horses started walking. She manueuvered them expertly until they were heading due east. Courtney turned her head to see him, then waved. He waved back. He watched until they disappeared over a rise.

From the moment the boy had ridden into the yard until now had been less than thirty minutes. She was gone.

Roger went back to his chores. Matt stood next to the corral trying to take it all in. The pain in his gut intensified. He realized this was the first time he and Courtney had been apart since they'd traveled through time. It was also the end of the longest period they'd ever been with each other. They'd spent the last three and a half months living and working together like a real married couple.

"God, I'm going to miss her," he said hoarsely.

"Me, too," Jonathan said, then grimaced. "Sorry, Matt. I didn't mean to say that. I would never—" He cleared his throat. "That is, your wife would never dishonor you. She's a very loyal woman."

"I know. It's okay."

Jonathan's smile was bitter. "Thank you for your generosity. Forgive me for saying I suspect it comes from the fact that Courtney thinks of me as a favorite brother."

Matt sensed that the gambler was right. At times he could even feel pity for the other man. Loving Courtney and not having her love back was a familiar place in hell. While their marriage might not be everything he wanted it to be, she never gave him reason to doubt her fidelity. Matt had come to realize that she did view the gambler as an adored relative. She handed out smiles and touches with all the indulgence of a master giving treats to a dog. There was no cruelty in her actions. Just ignorance. Courtney had never understood her power over men.

"I'd better get ready to head back to town," Jonathan said. "I'll make inquiries about that bull you're interested in, and see how much the Hereford cows are going for."

They'd agreed to invest most of the profits from the sale of the few cattle they'd cull this fall. The first big shipment would be next year. In the meantime, Jonathan had bought in with cash, allowing the ranch to afford more breeding stock and Matt to lay in supplies for the winter.

He stared at the spot where the wagon had disappeared and fleetingly wondered if he would ever see Courtney again. What if the storm showed up? He knew in his heart she would step into it without a second thought. She would want to go home, but now this land had become his home.

He turned to face the open pastures. Cattle grazed in the warm summer morning. The outbuildings were finished. Everything was falling into place. This was what he'd always wanted. In time, he would begin to buy up cheap federal land so his ranch would have a head start over the others. He would be rich and powerful, a true cattle baron.

Was it enough?

The question surprised him, but once it had been whispered, he couldn't ignore it. Was it enough? Was *he* enough? Money wouldn't change who he was. No wealth, no large house, no amount of power would erase his past. For as long as he walked this earth, he would hear those childhood taunts and remember watching his old man drink himself into unconsciousness. He would continue to feel the hunger pangs as the last few dollars went for whiskey. He would remember going barefoot in the summer, simply because he had no shoes, and he would hear his father's drunken promises that he, Matt, would never amount to anything.

The words had hurt more than the beatings. He'd sworn to do better, to *be* better. And he had. He'd finished high school, had even gone to a junior college. He'd had success on the rodeo circuit and was saving for his own spread. But in the back of his mind, the voice continued to scream out its filth. That he would never be more than the failure his father had predicted.

Which made Courtney a miracle in his life. She was the bright shining spark, the light. If he'd completed a list of appointed tasks, if he'd felt that he'd earned her, he might have believed he could hold her. But she was with him for reasons he would never understand, so the thought of her leaving was a constant fear.

Even now. Especially now. What would happen when the storm returned? And it would, one day. He could feel it.

Jonathan came out of the barn leading his gelding. "Anything you want from town?" he asked. "If the windows are in, I'll be coming right back."

Matt thought for a moment. "Yes, there is something you can do for me." It wouldn't keep her, but it might make her happy. Most of the time seeing her happy was more than enough.

"You don't understand," Courtney said from her seat in the wagon. "I don't know nothing about birthing no babies."

The funny line from a favorite movie did make her feel a little better, even if it made Hallie stare at her oddly.

"There's nothing *to* know," her friend told her.

"Pansy does all the hard work and Mary Frances is the midwife."

"So why are we going?"

"To give support, to help around the house. There may be problems with the birth."

Courtney's stomach rolled as it had when she'd been faced with killing and gutting the chicken. "That's what I'm afraid of. I have no experience at this. I wouldn't know what to do. I'll only be in the way."

"Then do what you can. Hold Pansy's hand and tell her it's going to be all right."

Ah, but that was exactly the problem. Courtney closed her eyes tightly together. "I don't want her to die," she said quietly.

She'd expected Hallie to voice similar concerns. Instead the other woman chuckled. "Do you always imagine the worst?"

"The worst? I remember reading about this. Women die in childbirth. It's a fact. I don't remember the exact number, but it's a lot. More than half, I think. Maybe all. I can't stand that. Watching her slowly bleed to death, screaming in agony. What if the baby is turned wrong, or it's in distress, or it's already dead inside her and . . . oh, Lord, I think I'm going to be sick."

She clutched her stomach and took deep breaths until the nausea passed.

Hallie was silent for a long time. Courtney studied the countryside. Hallie had told her to pay attention so she could find her way to Pansy's and home again on her own if she had to. It wasn't all that difficult. The sun moved from in front of them to directly overhead. Soon it would be behind them. Coming home would mean making the trip in reverse. She glanced over her shoulder several times, memorizing the terrain.

"Not all women die in childbirth," Hallie said at last. "Some do, it's true. Most don't."

"Name one woman you know who didn't die in childbirth."

Hallie glanced at her and smiled. "Me."

"Oh." Courtney hadn't thought of that. "Gee, you had five children and lived."

"Six," Hallie reminded her.

"Oh. Sorry." She remembered her mentioning a baby lost to fever.

"Most of the women who came to the ranch a few weeks ago already had children and they're all alive. Birth is a part of life. Children are the reward. Sometimes it's frightening, and yes, there's pain, but it's not what you think."

"Then what is it?"

Hallie smiled mysteriously. "You're going to have to wait and see for yourself."

Courtney was torn between wanting to know and wishing the journey would go on forever. But finally they reached the two-story house behind the stage station. Two other wagons were tied up in front of the house.

A pale young man in his early twenties came out of the stage office and ran to help Hallie down. "Mary Frances and Lavinia are already here. I'm sending some telegrams, then I'll see to your horses." Sweat beaded on his brow and upper lip. His hands trembled. "Mary Frances says Pansy's fine, but I can't see her. Do you think she's really fine?"

Hallie patted his arm. "This is a time for womenfolk, Franklin. You take care of your business and before you know it, you'll have a healthy new baby."

The young man clutched her sleeve. "I prayed for a boy. Do you think God will punish me for that?"

"Why would the good Lord punish you for wanting a child in his own image?"

"Oh. I hadn't thought of that." Franklin gave

Courtney a vague smile, then stumbled back into the stage office.

"He's even more scared than me," Courtney said, somewhat brightened by the exchange. She collected the baskets they'd brought.

Her good mood faded as soon as they stepped into the house. Thick drapes covered the downstairs windows, as if the building was prepared to mourn. Strange smells drifted down the staircase and made the air thick. Faint whispers of conversation led the way, but she grabbed hold of the bannister and refused to climb.

"You go ahead," she said. "I can't do this."

Hallie turned and glared at her. "Courtney Stone, you quit acting like a baby and come with me right now. Pansy needs all of us."

Hallie had never used that tone with her before, but Courtney responded instinctively to the voice of authority. She released the bannister and started up the stairs.

Her heart knocked against her ribs. Her thighs trembled and her knees threatened to lock. Still, she kept going until she reached the landing on the second floor. Here the voices were louder and the scent of herbs stronger.

The first door on the left stood ajar. Hallie moved toward it and knocked softly. "Pansy, we're here."

Someone opened the door and motioned them in.

It took a few seconds for Courtney's eyes to adjust to the dimly lit room. It seemed to be the bedroom, but the bed itself had been pushed to one side. Several chairs had been set up around the perimeter of the room. There was a puffy mattress covered in linens in the middle of the room, and an odd-looking chair positioned close to the floor. The chair seemed to be missing most of its seat. Light gauze curtains covered the windows. A screen provided privacy at one end of the room.

On a table by the strange chair was a metal bowl filled with smoldering leaves and powder. That was the source of the soothing odor. Next to it were several bowls filled with water and a stack of linens. Tins of leaves, bark, and seeds stood beside a cup. Unlit candles crowded every available surface. They were along the edge of the table, on the dresser, and collected in a corner.

Pansy stood awkwardly beside the mattress. She was wearing a huge white nightgown that completely covered her body. Her long dark hair had been pulled back in a braid. Her big brown eyes dominated her pale face.

"Hallie, Courtney, thank you for coming."

Hallie brushed aside her words. "Of course we're here." She walked toward her and placed a hand on her brow. "Nice and cool. How do you feel?"

"As if I'm being ripped in two." She gasped and clutched at her swollen belly.

Hallie turned toward the shadowy corner. "She seems well, Mary Frances. What do you think?"

A small-boned Indian woman stepped forward and smiled faintly. "I agree. The baby has turned. It should only be a few hours now."

A few hours? Courtney felt faint.

Hallie motioned her forward. "Mary Frances, this is Mrs. Matthew Stone. I work for her. Courtney, Mary Frances is here to help Pansy with the birth. Mary Frances is a healer."

Courtney smiled at the petite woman. Her hair was blue-black and hung in a braid nearly to her knees. Her features were so perfect, so beautiful, she looked otherworldly. When she smiled, a dimple appeared in her right cheek. She leaned forward and touched Courtney's stomach.

"I won't be visiting you for some time," she said. "No baby waiting in there."

Courtney flushed. "I know," she mumbled.

There were footsteps on the stairs. A tall blonde stepped into the room carrying a tray. Courtney recognized her as Lavinia, one of the women who had come to see the longhorns.

"I thought you might be hungry after your trip," the tall blonde said as she nudged aside some candles on a small table by the bed. Hallie moved to help her.

"Courtney, set the basket down. Pansy, we brought you some cloth for diapers, some canned things, and a few vegetables we put up."

"Thank you." Pansy had to pant the words. She bent over with the force of a contraction.

Courtney fought against panic. She hated to see anyone in pain. Mary Frances moved to Pansy's side and spoke soothingly to her.

While Lavinia and Hallie prepared plates of food and poured tea, Mary Frances helped Pansy walk around the room. When the contraction passed, the midwife moved to the low table and began grinding several seeds and a bit of bark together. She put the ground mixture into the cup, then poured in tea. After stirring it together, she handed the cup to Pansy. The woman drank it quickly.

"It will ease her pains and her mind," Mary Frances said quietly to Courtney.

Courtney resisted the urge to ask for a little for herself. "This is my first time seeing this," she said. "I guess I'm scared."

The midwife motioned for Courtney to sit next to her. "The best way to endure your first time is to keep busy." She glanced at Lavinia and Hallie who were talking in the corner. "They have been through this many times on their own and with others. You can help me, which in turn helps Pansy and yourself."

"Great." She sank down on the floor. "I appreciate anything to distract me."

Mary Frances poured more herbs and had her grind them. When the next contraction came, it didn't seem to hurt Pansy as much. When the young woman knelt on the mattress, Courtney rubbed her back and the balls of her feet.

She didn't really notice the passing time until Hallie sent her outside for a few minutes to rest. She was stunned to find the sun had nearly set. She used the outhouse, then went in the kitchen to splash water on her face.

The rectangular room looked much as hers did at home, except for the boxlike object sitting across from the stove. She crossed to it and pulled the handle.

"Oh my Lord!" She stared, openmouthed. There was a block of ice inside, along with butter, milk and other foods. "It's a refrigerator!"

She slammed it shut and raced upstairs. When she burst into the room, all three women turned to stare at her.

"Sorry," she said, then motioned to Hallie to join her in the corner.

"What is it?" the other woman asked.

"I was in Pansy's kitchen. There's this box thing, with ice in it."

Hallie shook her head. "You're the one always talking about modern contraptions. Haven't you ever seen an icebox before?"

"No. I didn't know they'd been invented yet." She clutched Hallie's arm. "We're ordering one as soon as we get back."

Pansy gasped.

"It's time," the midwife said.

The women gathered close. Courtney was given the linens to hold, which was good. She didn't think she was up to anything more complicated. Lavinia and Hallie stroked Pansy's arms as she braced herself in the odd-looking chair. Mary Frances tied an apron over her long dress, then knelt in front of Pansy.

The scent of the herbs filled the rooms. Someone had lit the candles. The sound of their breathing synchronized until Pansy groaned. Mary Frances spoke to her in an unfamiliar language, but the words were soothing. Lavinia and Hallie took turns blotting her brow.

Courtney stared at her, willing her to be all right. Pansy glanced at her and smiled feebly. "You look worse than I feel," she said.

"Gee, thanks."

Pansy closed her eyes suddenly and pushed. Her face tightened with effort, her breathing stopped, then came in pants.

Time seemed to stand still in the room. A gentle breeze stirred at the windows, but the drapes protected the candles. Pansy cried out, then the midwife announced she could see the baby's head.

Courtney didn't want to watch, but she couldn't turn away. The head came out slowly. Before the shoulders appeared, Mary Frances reached under the chair to stroke the baby's cheeks, nose and mouth, then up from the chin. As the shoulders slipped out, she turned the baby. The rest of the body came free. The faint cry of a newborn filled the room.

"Is it all right?" Pansy asked, her face wet with sweat.

"He's perfect," Mary Frances assured her.

A prayer had been heard and answered. The baby was a boy.

"He's got your eyes," Hallie said. Courtney wanted to know how she could tell.

He was red and slimy, but not as ugly as she'd

feared. She passed over the linens and was surprised to find herself feeling a little weepy.

Soon the baby was wrapped up tightly and in his mother's arms. Courtney helped Hallie and Lavinia clean up. It hadn't been all that messy. There was less blood than when she'd gutted the chicken.

The mattress was placed back in the bed and they slid the large piece of furniture to its place in the center of the room. When Pansy was settled under the covers, with her baby nursing at her breast, she held out her hand to Courtney.

"Thank you," she said, quietly. "Thank you for being with me. When your time comes, I'll be there."

Courtney couldn't speak. Her throat tightened and words refused to come. She nodded instead, and squeezed Pansy's hand.

When Mary Frances collected her herbs, Courtney helped her carry them to her wagon. The birthing chair had already been strapped down in the back. Unlike the other women, she wouldn't stay to help Pansy. Her work was finished.

"Is it what you expected?" the midwife asked.

"I thought there would be more pain, I guess. I worried she might die. This was very different."

"Don't be afraid," Mary Frances told her. "Of course women die, but not all. And babies are stronger than we think."

They walked outside into the darkness. "How will you find your way home?" Courtney asked.

The midwife pointed to the sky. "It will be dawn soon and I know the trail. My husband's waiting for me." Her smile was contagious. Courtney grinned and found herself thinking about Matt. She wished she could tell him what had happened.

Courtney set the bag of herbs in the small wagon. "Is there a way to prevent pregnancy?"

"Yes. Several. I tell women they need to time their babies. Be with your husband many times in the fall. Have babies in the summer."

"Why?"

"So I can come help. In the winters, the storms keep me away. It's difficult to have a baby alone. Especially the first time."

Courtney shuddered. "Perish the thought."

Mary Frances walked around to the far side of her wagon and searched through several containers. She picked up a small jar, put it down, then found the one she wanted. She handed it to Courtney.

"Mix a spoonful of this with equal parts of vinegar and water," she said. "Use it after you've been with your husband." She shrugged. "It helps prevent childbearing. Can you time your cycle?"

"Yes."

"The week in the middle is the most dangerous time. Use this before and after in that week. When you run low, send Roger to me and I'll give you more herbs."

"Thank you," Courtney said as she took the jar. "You can't know how much I appreciate this."

"I can. We're all afraid the first time." The midwife smiled.

"If this is a rude question, you don't have to answer it, but why is your name Mary Frances? I would have thought you'd have an Indian name."

"I spent the first six years of my life in a Catholic orphanage before being returned to my home. I use Mary Frances because my real name is difficult to pronounce."

"That makes sense." Courtney clutched the jar to her chest. "Thank you so much for this."

"You're welcome." Mary Frances climbed into her wagon and took hold of the reins. "Enjoy your husband and I'll be with you next summer."

Courtney watched her leave. She stared at the jar, then at the departing wagon. There was a chill in the air. It was nearly fall already.

Courtney heard voices from inside the house and she walked toward them. She'd made friends today. Whatever happened in the future, she'd bonded with these women. For as long as she lived, she would remember the birth of Pansy's first son. The thought of having her own child wasn't as terrifying as she'd thought it would be.

Before she stepped into the house, she glanced up at the sky. The first hint of pink stained the eastern horizon. Was Matt staring at the same fading stars? Was he thinking of her? Did he miss her as much as she missed him?

As she closed the door behind her, she wondered how long it would be until she could return home . . . to Matt.

16

Courtney allowed the horses to slowly pick their way along the rough terrain. She wasn't very good at driving the wagon, but she realized now she would have to ask Matt to give her more lessons. Not being able to control a wagon in 1873 Wyoming was about as foolish as not being able to drive a car in 1996 Los Angeles.

She felt the sun warming the top of her head. Her shadow was almost nonexistent. She didn't have her watch anymore, but she would judge the time to be close to noon. She was still heading in the right direction—home.

She'd only been gone ten days, but it felt like months. She missed Matt. Being with him, talking to him. Surprisingly, she also missed the ranch. She wondered about the garden. It must be overflowing now. And the chickens. Had they noticed someone else was feeding them? Roger didn't know all the secret places to look so there would be extra eggs to collect. Miss

Piggy liked having her ears scratched and two of her piglets were tame enough to hold. Roger wouldn't know any of that, either. He'd probably rushed through her chores, eager to get back to his own.

She glanced at the bright blue sky. Three days of rain had kept her with Pansy longer than she'd wanted to be. Then she'd waited an extra day to make sure the ground was dry. Plants soaked up the moisture. The grasses were green, the leaves on the cottonwoods were bright. A few flowers still bloomed, despite the approach of fall. Hallie had decided to stay longer with the baby, but Courtney had been eager to get home.

Courtney shifted on the hard seat of the wagon and tried not to hold on to the reins too tightly. Pansy's younger brother had escorted her nearly halfway back to the ranch. She'd told him she could go the rest of the way on her own. She fought the occasional trickle of fear. She had her rifle. She would be fine. She smiled to herself. Okay, she was willing to admit she'd feel a tiny bit better if she had a cellular phone, but who was there to call?

The rough wooden fences were the first hint that she was nearing the ranch. She slapped the horses with the reins and they quickened their steps to a trot. Her bottom slapped hard against the unpadded seat, but she didn't care. She wanted to see Matt.

The terrain became familiar. She recognized the cedarwood trees and a couple of large boulders. In the distance, longhorn cattle grazed. Finally she passed the knoll where she'd spent so many afternoons waiting for the storm to come take her back. She barely gave it a glance.

A man on horseback rode toward her. She raised her hand to shade her eyes and squinted. She couldn't make out his face, but his shape was familiar.

She raised her hand and waved. "Matt!" she called loudly.

He swung his hat in the air. His horse broke into a canter. When he neared, she reined in her horses and waited for him to join her.

"Matt," she said again, softer this time.

"What the hell are you doing out here by yourself?" he demanded. "Where's Hallie?"

His blue eyes snapped with temper, but she only smiled. She read worry in the lines around his mouth and knew his anger came from concern. She studied the familiar planes of his cheeks, the line of his jaw. His hair had grown well past the bottom of his collar. The clean-cut cowboy had turned into an outlaw. A ripple of desire flowed through her body. She liked the change.

"Hallie wanted to stay another week with Pansy and the baby and I wanted to come home. Pansy's husband will bring her back. I had an escort nearly halfway to the ranch. I knew I could find the rest of the way by myself and I did."

He was slightly above eye level. When Jasper danced closer to her wagon, she placed her hand on Matt's rock-hard thigh. "Aren't you happy to see me?"

"Dammit, Courtney, you could have gotten lost or hurt or—" Matt threw the reins over Jasper's head so they dangled to the ground, then he swung off the saddle. The trained horse stood in place while his master circled around him to the wagon and stared at her. "Oh, I missed you," he said, his voice thick with emotion.

"Me, too."

She slid toward him on the seat. He wrapped his arms around her and lifted her to the ground. With fingers that felt as if they were trembling, he untied the ribbon holding her bonnet in place and pulled it free.

"Now I can see your face," he said.

Their gazes locked. His mouth tilted up slightly at the corner before turning into a full-blown smile. Her toes curled, while a tingling feeling swept through her body.

He touched her face as if relearning her features. His fingertips brushed against her cheeks, then across her mouth. One hand slipped behind her head to cup the neat coil of hair resting there.

"What happened to your braid?" he asked.

"They taught me how to put my hair up and I showed them how to make a French braid."

He leaned around her to stare at the bun. "I like it."

"It would never do for everyday," she said. "Strands keep coming loose. Hallie says I'll get better at keeping it neat, but I'm not sure if that's true."

They stared at each other. He studied her features while she reacquainted herself with his. She rested her hands on his broad chest, absorbing the heat of him and the rhythm of his heart. "I feel as if I've been gone a month," she said. "I've got so much to tell you."

"I've got things to *show* you. It wasn't the same without you. Everyone missed you. Roger's been moping around. Jonathan brought some more supplies, then went back to town. Even the chickens have missed you."

"Really?"

"Yeah. They hardly ever try to peck Roger."

"He just doesn't know how to treat them," she said.

His nearness was as intoxicating as the whiskey had been those many weeks ago. His masculine scent mingled with the fragrances of the grasses and the trees and the flowers. Her thighs trembled as if she'd been running for hours. Suddenly she couldn't catch her breath.

He read her mind before the thought even came to life. Even as the first whisper of the image of his lips pressing against hers formed, he lowered his head and touched her mouth with his.

It had been too long. Desire flowed smoothly into the empty spaces of her heart. Like cream combining with melted chocolate, it created a sweet and steamy heat.

She clung to him, squeezing his broad shoulders, raising herself on tiptoe to get next to him, to feel him against her. He, too, seemed to want to be close. He wrapped his arms around her waist and hung on tight. She breathed his name against his mouth, letting her eyes slowly slip closed.

He kissed her with the hungry passion of a man long denied. His lips devoured hers, his tongue probed for entrance. She parted for him, traced him, tasted him, and when he would have retreated, she nipped at him, making him groan low in his throat.

She moved her hands to his back, then up to his hair. The long strands slipped through her fingers. He rotated his hips against her. The long skirt and two layers of petticoats prevented her from feeling his arousal. Still she moved her pelvis in time with his.

He tilted his head, then dipped deeper, taunting her, tempting her to follow him back, to tease him as she had been teased. Her heart thundered like stampeding horses; her skin heated, as if she'd been burned by the sun. Her breasts swelled and that place between her legs ached as her body rushed to swell and dampen in anticipation.

When she thought she might faint from lack of air, she pulled away from his kiss. They were both panting. Matt rested his forehead against hers. His eyes were closed and she could see the individual lashes fanning his cheeks. Her heart stirred at the sight of something so delicate on a man so strong.

"Do you mind if we walk the rest of the way?" he asked. "It would hurt too much to ride in this condition."

She laughed. "Fine by me. I'm feeling a little achy myself."

They shared a glance of understanding and promise. A thousand questions leaped to mind. Would they make love tonight? Had they become close enough friends to risk sharing bodies again? It would be different if they did. Before, the sexual act had been their bond. Now they were tied through the ranch and their affection for each other. Physical intimacy would strengthen that tie until they united as one. What then of her plans? What then of the mysterious storm that might be able to sweep them into the future?

She didn't ask any of the questions. She didn't have the answers and she doubted Matt did either. They would simply have to handle the situation as it occurred.

He handed her Jasper's reins. While she walked the gelding in a circle so he was facing in the correct direction, Matt took control of the horses hitched to the wagon. They headed toward the house.

On the way he talked about all that had happened while she'd been gone.

"I've been working on a septic system," he said. "The design is simple. I wouldn't have to modify much from what we're used to."

"What *you're* used to. I've never used a septic system in my life."

"If you wouldn't mind pumping water into a holding tank, you could have a flush toilet."

She stopped walking and stared at him. "Really? You mean like indoor plumbing?"

"Sure. Piping exists. After pumping water into a holding tank, gravity would be enough to make the toilet flush when you pull the handle. The difficult part has been figuring out what to use as holding tanks. Jonathan said something about trains, and I realized the boilers would be perfect."

He touched her arm to urge her forward. "I'd hoped to

get something going before winter, but it's too late. The ground will freeze up before we get everything dug. We'll have to hold off the septic system until next spring."

"Wow, a flush toilet inside. Talk about heaven." It had been months since she'd used indoor facilities. "Now if only you could build me a vanity with a nice marble sink."

"And a shower," he said.

"Of course." She sighed. "A shower."

He gave her an odd look, as if he wanted to say something, but when he didn't, she remembered Pansy's kitchen.

"They've invented iceboxes," she said. "I saw one. It's this box thing, on legs. Ice sits in it and keeps things cold. It's not a refrigerator, but it's pretty close. Hallie says we'll need an icehouse, but it shouldn't be difficult. Imagine our very own refrigerator."

"I'll get Jonathan right on it."

"What would we do without him running all those errands for us?" she asked as they neared the barn. "I hope he's going to get something from his investment in this ranch."

"He's going to be rich."

She thought about the handsome gambler. Jonathan was always alone. He never talked about his past or any women he'd known. Occasionally she caught him staring at her in a way that assured her he wasn't secretly gay. Maybe he hadn't found the right women yet. She didn't know much about courting rituals in the Old West.

"Maybe he'll finally find someone and settle down," she said. "He needs a nice girl."

"I don't think a nice girl would have him."

"Because he's a gambler?"

Matt nodded. "It's not a very respected profession."

"I suppose not, but it's very romantic. At least it always was in the old Westerns."

They stopped in front of the barn. Everything was as she remembered with one or two exceptions. The vegetables had nearly doubled in size. She stared at the rows of healthy plants. "Hallie told me how to start getting everything ready to be put up," she said. "By the time she gets back, we'll be ready to go."

"There are still some fresh berries," he said. "We could go collect them before they're gone."

She knew Matt was busy from the moment the sun came up in the morning until long after it set. The first winter snows weren't that far off and he wanted to be ready. So his offer to take some time off was unusual. It made her want to kiss him again and feel his arms around her.

"I'd like that," she said.

Before she could say anything else, Roger ran out of the barn. He jerked off his ragged hat and skittered to a stop in front of her. His bright red hair stuck up in several directions, and he looked as if he hadn't had a bath since long before she and Hallie had left.

But his pale eyes beamed with happiness. "Nice to have you back, ma'am."

"It's nice to be back. Your mother is staying with Pansy for a few more days."

"I figured she might. She likes little babies." He glanced at the wagon and the couple of baskets sitting in the back. "I can take your things inside if you'd like."

"Thanks, Roger. That would be great."

The teenager beamed.

Matt motioned to the horses. "See to them, and to Jasper."

"Yes, sir."

The boy leaped over to the wagon and scooped up the baskets and few jars Hallie had tucked in the back to tide them over. She was terrified that they would starve before she returned. Courtney kept telling her that she could feed the three of them for a few nights, but Hallie had been skeptical.

Before she could move to follow Roger inside, Matt grabbed her hand. "I've got a couple of things to show you," he said, leading her into the barn. "I've been working on some designs for a brand."

A small room had been added at the back of the barn. Instead of windows, there were shutters that opened to let in the light. On the battered workbench were several long metal poles. At one end was the brand. He pointed to a piece of wood nailed to the wall. He'd burned one of each of the designs. The dark scorch marks clearly outlined the pattern.

She'd always thought of brands as simple. A letter with a bar under it. Maybe two letters together. These were functional, yet complex. Multiple combinations of letters. An *S* with stars at the four corners. An *S* in a diamond frame. There was an entwined *M* and *S*, but the brand that drew her attention was the one burned in the middle of the wood. The *C* and *M* were on top, the *S* in the middle underneath. The supports that held the brand together had also burned through, though unevenly. The effect was their initials surrounded by the suggestion of a heart.

"Do you like it?" Matt asked, when she touched her finger to the brand.

"It's wonderful. Would you really use it?"

She was asking about more than the brand, although she wasn't exactly sure how much more. The air was heavy with anticipation and emotion. Matt's blue eyes darkened.

He nodded slowly.

She released the breath she hadn't known she was holding. "I'm glad," she whispered, then felt as if he'd handed her an unexpected gift.

They walked toward the house. Matt brought her up to date on the cattle. The large herd had been split. A few animals weren't adjusting well to the new location, but for the most part the cows had been quiet.

She paused to pluck a few vegetables from the garden and to check on the chickens. The roosting animals barely glanced at her, although she thought they might have been happy to have her back.

"I've been doing some work in the kitchen," he said as she walked into the pantry.

She paused and stared. "I would guess so."

A large metal drum had been mounted on the wall next to the stove. Pipes ran in and out of the drum, some stretching under the stove, others disappearing into the wall.

"What is it?"

"A water heater."

She moved closer and reverently touched the side of the drum. "I would kill for hot running water. How does it work?"

"You pump in cold water and the stove does the rest. I haven't got it hooked up to the kitchen yet," he said. "I need a little more time."

She smiled. "It's a wonderful idea."

"I've got to give the men instructions for the rest of the day," he said. "I'll be right back."

When he'd left, she set the vegetables on the counter and returned to the pantry to collect one of her aprons. It felt good to be back. She liked her own kitchen. She would like it more when she had an icebox. She glanced around, trying to figure out where exactly she would put it.

In the corner, she decided. Maybe they could get a nice little plant for the top. An icebox. Oh, maybe they could even make and keep ice cream. Did they have that yet? She would have to remember to ask Hallie when she returned.

Courtney hummed under her breath as she filled a

bucket with water and set it on the stove. She collected wood from the pile, grabbed kindling and matches and quickly had a fire burning brightly. Matt had been eating with the cowboys, so everything was pretty much as she'd left it.

In less than ten minutes, she'd made coffee, washed the vegetables, and was slicing them into a large pot. She added seasonings, then went to the springhouse and cut down a piece of meat. When the stew was cooking, she investigated the fresh berries someone, probably Roger, had left on the table. There was enough for two pies. After giving the simmering stew a quick stir, she moved into the pantry, collected two pie pans and ingredients for crust, then stepped back into the kitchen.

The water heater was big and ugly, but she couldn't wait until it was working. The thought of hot water on demand made her mouth water. She wondered how long it had taken Matt to figure out the design, then make it work with his limited tools and supplies.

Courtney crossed to the window and stared out at the yard. Her husband was talking with one of the cowboys.

Her husband.

Despite all their problems, she'd always thought of Matt that way. She'd easily slipped into the language of marriage. It was the emotional commitment, the ability to compromise, and the day-after-day contact that she'd had trouble with.

Watching him, the way he stood so tall and strong, knowing that whatever he said it would be honest and fair, she wondered why on earth she'd wanted to divorce him. Had she been afraid of what loving him would mean? Did she love him?

Today, in this time, there were so many confusing issues. Was the storm going to come back? If it did, would he go with her? She wasn't stupid. She could see that he loved it here. He fit in. Perhaps that was the storm's purpose. To set right an error. But was she supposed to have come back, too, or was that all a mistake?

She continued to stare out the window and knew she might never get the answer to her question. She couldn't put their lives on hold forever, either. She had to commit or she had to walk away.

She and Matt had discussed not being lovers again until they were best friends. The real issue was different. Were they married? If they were, then they needed to treat their bonds as sacred. If they weren't, then it was time to part. The days of living with a half commitment had to end eventually.

Were they married? It was hard to believe she'd been the one asking for a divorce. Looking back, her reasons sounded so selfish and immature. Neither of them had been willing to compromise. She'd wanted to, but she'd been afraid. Was that what the divorce had been about? Was she simply trying to get Matt to see her side? Had she been trying to get his attention?

She had his full attention now, although for very different reasons. What was she going to do with it?

Before she could decide, he finished his conversation with the cowboy and started toward the house. She turned from the window. When he entered the kitchen, she was already rolling out the pie dough.

"Dinner smells good," he said, pouring some hot water into a basin and washing his hands.

"It's just going to be stew. There isn't time for anything else. We'll have to have baking powder biscuits. I'll start bread in the morning."

"Sounds good. The cowboys' cook doesn't seem to want to make more than beans and sourdough bread. I offered him vegetables from the garden, but he just blinked at me and turned away. I asked the men, and they don't seem to mind."

She expertly transferred the piecrust to the pan and crimped the edges. Berries went in next, then she sprinkled on plenty of sugar. She plucked up one of the berries and offered it to Matt.

Instead of taking it with his fingers, he leaned forward and took it in his teeth. His tongue brushed against her skin and she trembled with desire.

"Delicious," he said as he finished drying his hands.

She took a deep breath and tried to turn her attention back to the pie. Apparently she was the only one who had felt the electricity leap between them.

She added one more spoonful of sugar, then put the top crust over the pie and secured it to the bottom one. After making several cuts so that the steam could escape, she put both pies in the oven.

The coffee was ready. She poured two cups and carried them to the table. Matt sat across from her and grinned.

"What's so funny?" she asked.

"Just you. Three and a half months ago you couldn't boil water. Now you're at home in this antiquated kitchen. You've been back less than an hour and half. Dinner is ready, you've made pie and coffee and are discussing when you'll next bake bread. I didn't know you had it in you."

"I didn't either," she admitted. "I was terrified when we first came here. I hated it. But now it's not so bad. I've learned things. There's a rhythm to this life that isn't so terrible."

"How's Pansy's baby? Everything go okay?"

She smiled and took a sip of her coffee. "It was great, Matt. I thought Pansy would bleed to death and the baby would die, but it wasn't like that at all." She leaned back in her chair and recalled the loving support that had filled the dimly lit room. "There's a midwife named Mary Frances. She's a healer. She knows herbs and different kinds of potions. She gave Pansy something to quiet the pains. I was very impressed."

"So it wasn't like those pioneer movies?" he asked.

Her smoky gaze met his as she chuckled. Matt loved to make Courtney laugh. He liked the little lines that formed at her eyes, and the sound of her amusement.

She cupped her mug in both hands. "Not at all. I've never seen a baby born before, so I can't say how different it was from modern medicine, but it seemed sanitary. Everything was washed."

She wasn't afraid anymore. He could see that. But was she willing to have a baby herself? Was he willing to take a chance with her? Would it be so easy when it was Courtney's time?

"How did Franklin take it?" he asked.

"He was a wreck when we got there," she said. "After the baby was born, he seemed relieved, if a little pale."

Matt wondered how he would react to the same situation. The thought of something happening to Courtney made his stomach clench and his heart stop. He wouldn't want to be responsible for that. He would pay any price to keep her safe.

He desperately wanted a child of his own. Several children. A few boys to inherit the ranch and a passel of girls just like their beautiful, sassy mother.

Have my baby.

The words hovered at his lips but he didn't speak them. Their joy in each other was too new. But he ached for her. Ached to hold her. Be with her. Not just for sexual satisfaction but because he was a better man when he was part of her.

She continued to tell him about her week. About all the modern things Pansy had in her house that she, Courtney, wanted to order. About the baby and how she'd gotten pretty good at changing him, although not having disposable diapers was a real drag. She laughed and talked, her hands a fluttering accompaniment to her words.

He drank coffee, also drinking in the sight and sound of her. Instead of making her look older, the upswept hairstyle highlighted the perfect oval shape of her face. Her wide eyes sparkled with humor.

He stood up and held out his hand. "I've got something to show you," he said.

"Oh, a surprise. What is it?"

"You'll have to wait and see."

She slipped her hand next to his. Her skin was warm, but not as soft anymore. She worked hard and had the calluses to prove it. He liked her new hands better. He liked her better.

He led the way down the hall. Once he reached their bedroom, he stepped to one side and motioned to the far wall. A large window looked out onto several trees and a pasture.

She walked to the window and reverently touched the glass. "It's so light in here," she said, and clapped her hands together. "We can see without a lamp. I can make curtains and a matching rug. Maybe even a quilt for the bed. It will be beautiful. Thank—"

As she turned to smile at him, she noticed the large closetlike structure jutting out from the corner of room. "What is it?"

He shifted uneasily. "I probably should have asked you before I did it."

"Did what?" She tried to get around him to the door, but he stepped in front of her.

He cleared his throat. "I figured we'd build out on this room when we added another bedroom. In fact this whole half of the room"—he motioned to the area near the new wall—"could be closed off."

She peered around him at the wooden wall. It hadn't been painted yet. He hadn't had time. The design had taken him nearly a day. Jonathan had helped, although the gambler had thought he was wasting his time. He hadn't believed any woman would be excited about something as stupid as this.

"Is it a closet?" she asked.

"Not exactly." He opened the door and stepped back.

She looked inside. A pipe came out of the wall at shoulder level and ended with a metal disk that had been punched with holes. There was a drain in the floor. A chain dangled a few inches above a hook.

Courtney stared at the device, then at him. "I don't understand."

Damn, maybe Jonathan had been right and it was a stupid idea. "It's a shower," he said lamely. "You pull the chain to open the valve. Hook it here." He tugged on the chain. Instantly water flowed out of the metal disk like gentle rain. He looped the bottom of the chain over the hook. "That holds it open. The tank is about twenty-five gallons. It won't get too hot because it's not directly over the stove, but it's pretty warm."

He glanced at her. She was still staring at the shower, but her mouth had parted. He cleared his throat. "There's no water pressure so it doesn't flow very fast. I'm still working on that. When we get the septic system installed it can drain into that, but for now it goes back to the stream."

She put her hand under the water, then touched her wet fingers to her lips. "You did this while I was gone?"

He shrugged. "I've been thinking about it for a while. I know how much you've missed taking a shower. I miss it, too. Once the water tank is full, it takes about three hours to heat up. Probably a little longer in the winter." He cleared his throat again. "You don't have to use it if you don't like it."

"Don't like it? Matt, it's wonderful."

She looked at him and he saw the happiness reflected in her eyes. And something else. He stared at her. "Courtney, are you crying?"

She blinked several times, then nodded. A single tear slipped down her cheek. "This is the nicest thing anyone has ever done for me. It's the most thoughtful, perfect present. Better than jewelry or perfume or . . ." Her voice caught.

"Or chocolate?" he asked.

She smiled through her tears. "Much better than chocolate."

"I've never seen you cry before," he said, not sure what to do. Courtney had come through time, she'd battled rainstorms, chickens, a cranky stove, the fear of childbirth, and loneliness. None of that had made her cry. Why this?

"Are you all right?" he asked.

Instead of answering, she stepped into the spray and raised her face to the water. It flowed over her, instantly soaking her dress and apron.

"You're getting wet," he said, in case she didn't notice.

"I don't care."

She stepped out of the spray long enough to kick off her boots and drop her apron to the ground.

"What about your dress?" he asked.

She turned slowly under the spray. "It needs a good washing anyway. This is a lot easier than lugging buckets of hot water outside."

She reached up and pulled the pins from her hair. The long blond strands tumbled to her waist. She looked at him. Her face was wet, her lashes stood up in spiky clumps. Drops of water clung to her cheeks and lips.

"Did you try this?" she asked.

"I didn't take a shower. I just made sure it worked."

She reached out and grabbed his shirtfront, then glanced down. "You have ten seconds to take off your boots and belt, cowboy, or they're getting a shower, too."

He did as she asked without ever taking his gaze from hers. When he straightened, she grabbed his shirtfront again and pulled him into the tiny room. The warm water soaked through his shirt and ran down his chest toward his engorged groin.

Her expression turned serious. "Thank you, Matt," she murmured. She wasn't standing in the spray, so the moisture spilling from her eyes came from tears.

"Ah, Courtney, don't cry."

"You shouldn't worry," she said. "I'm crying because I'm happy."

A single tear paused by the corner of her mouth. He bent down and touched it with the tip of his tongue. Her arms came around his waist and she pressed herself against him. As the warm water rained down on them, he claimed her mouth with his.

17

As soon as his lips brushed hers, she felt herself go up in flames. The heat flared between them and was fueled by the memory of the last time they'd made love. Courtney sucked in her breath and was shocked when she didn't inhale steam.

She clutched at him, needing him, wanting him with every part of her. Her breasts swelled, the secret place between her thighs ached. She clung to him, to his shoulders, then his back.

Even as his tongue entered her mouth, she was tugging as his shirt, pulling the wet material from his trousers. The thick cotton didn't cooperate. He tilted his head to deepen the kiss. His tongue stroked hers quickly, making her blood run faster. Her heart pounded in her chest.

At last she jerked the soggy material free. She fumbled for the front buttons, but the wet material resisted her efforts. She slipped and pushed and pulled, but the buttons stayed stubbornly closed.

He encountered the same problem with her bodice. She felt his fingers at the base of her throat. His fore-arms brushed against her breasts, making her whimper.

He broke the kiss long enough to stare at her dress. "I can't get the buttons undone," he said, frustration deepening his voice.

"Me either."

The water continued to spill over them, a soft warm rain that dripped off hair, chin and fingers. Droplets ran down her chest and back. Her soaked petticoats clung to her legs.

"Damn poor planning," he muttered.

She lowered her gaze to his groin. The proof of his desire pressed toward her. She touched him through the layers of clothing. He was wearing trousers Hallie had made. Courtney reached for the first button. It came open easily. She quickly released the others, then reached inside and pulled his erection free.

Matt groaned and closed his eyes as she stroked him. The water made him slick as she grasped him and moved quickly from base to tip. Back and forth, back and forth, creating a rhythm designed to drive him wild. Her breathing increased in time with his. She wanted to watch his face, to gauge his reaction to her ministrations, but shc'd couldn't tcar hcr gazc away from her hand on his body.

Her fingers barely encircled him. His arousal flexed in her loose grip as the blood surged, making him even harder. She forced herself to glance at his face. His expression was intense, almost pained. As if sensing her attention, he opened his eyes. She read the need there.

He reached out and touched her breasts. Through the wet fabric, he stroked her hard nipples. Sweet pleasure arced from the taut points to her groin. Both his hands teased her, pinching lightly. She felt her knees start to give way, but she forced herself to keep standing.

She moved her hands faster, urging him to give in to the pressure she felt building inside him. He groaned, then grabbed her wrist and pulled her away. Before she could protest, he hauled her against him and kissed her deeply.

They clung to each other, writhing in need. Tongues dueled, fingers clawed at uncooperative clothing. She slipped her hand under his shirt and touched his bare back. He began to pull up her long skirt and petticoats. Then she remembered what he would find underneath.

She giggled softly.

He raised his head and looked at her. "If you're laughing, I must be doing something wrong."

She shook her head. "At Pansy's there wasn't time to keep rinsing out my two pairs of panties."

His blue eyes darkened. "So you're not wearing any at all?"

"Almost. Pansy gave me a new pair of pantaloons she'd made."

He grimaced. "So when I get your skirt up, I'm still going to be defeated by pantaloons?"

"Not exactly."

She giggled again, then reached for the first button on his shirt. By concentrating, she was able to push the button through the wet fabric. It popped free. She pressed her lips against his warm skin and licked off the water.

Matt pulled up the last layer of petticoats and fingered the delicate fabric. "I don't want to tear it."

"You don't have to."

"But how—"

Before he could finish the question, she placed her hand on top of his and drew his fingers down her belly. She shivered at both the contact and the anticipation.

He slipped past the gathered fabric, past her covered curls to the open slit at the center.

Matt sucked in his breath. Courtney did the same when his questing fingers sought and found her most sensitive place. He touched it gently, circling, then lightly brushing over the tiny point of pleasure.

"Hold up your skirt," he instructed gruffly. She grabbed the wet fabric. Water continued to pour down upon them, a warm benediction to their act of love.

She braced her legs to keep her balance as his magic caresses taunted her sanity. All she could think of, all she could focus on, were the feel of the individual drops of water and the continuous movement of his fingers.

Her vision blurred. She blinked until she could see his face, on the tight line of his mouth. He stared at the place where his hand touched her. She looked down, seeing little more than his wrist disappearing under yards of fabric.

His erection still jutted out from his open trousers. She shifted the wet fabric in her arms and reached for him with her free hand. Instantly his gaze sought hers.

They stared at each other. His fingers continued to circle around and over, occasionally dipping into her waiting dampness, then moving back to the place of her pleasure. She stroked him along his silken length. She brushed her thumb over his sensitive tip and made him arch his hips toward her.

She watched his mouth part as his breathing increased. Fire lit his eyes. She knew her face reflected her feelings as well. Her heart pounded faster and faster. She couldn't catch her breath. Between her legs, the powerful, aching need built until every part of her trembled. Her muscles began to tighten.

Matt sensed the change, the promise of release. He moved faster. She swayed toward him, barely noticing that the water had finally run out. The small shower was silent, except for their breathing and the dripping from their clothes.

When she was so close she could almost see the moment of her release, he stopped. Before she could cry out her protest, he pulled her hand away from him and grasped her hips. He braced himself in the corner of the shower and pulled her up against him. She wrapped her legs around his waist then slowly slipped onto his erection.

He filled her completely, touching deep inside. Her muscles convulsed, almost sending her over the edge. Neither moved. He kissed her cheeks, her eyelids, then her lips—a slow, thorough kiss that explored every inch of her mouth, stroking her into a restless frenzy.

Only then did he grasp her hips and raise her slightly and let her slide back along his length. The next time was quicker, his hips flexing to add to the movement. She clung to him, helpless to do more than absorb the sensation. Faster and faster until her control was lost and she gave in to the swirling vortex of release.

Even as her body rippled and contracted around his, he groaned out her name. She felt him stiffen inside her. His release fueled hers and she found herself lost in sensations unlike anything she'd known. At first she thought the shower had started again, then she realized the moisture on her face came from tears of ecstasy.

They held on to each other until their bodies relaxed and their breathing returned to normal. He let her slip to her feet, then supported her while she caught her balance.

"Matt, I—"

"Shh." He touched a finger to her lips. "You don't have to say anything. I understand."

Did he? She didn't. She'd never felt anything so powerful in her life. The connection astounded her. Even now, she felt as if they were sharing one body. She felt his movements, his pleasure.

He opened the shower door and helped her out. They dripped on the floor as they tried to get out of their wet clothes. The thick fabric continued to defeat them. Finally Matt got his shirt off and slid down his trousers. He grabbed a towel and dried his hair.

Courtney unfastened the buttons on her bodice. She stared at his body as it slowly returned to normal. She'd never understood what it must be like to be a man. To have passion so easily detected by anyone who bothered to look. Unless someone touched her intimately and felt the telltale dampness of her arousal, no one could know what she was thinking or feeling.

She moved her gaze lower, to his strong legs. The lines of his muscles were as pronounced as ever. The dark hair only emphasized his strength. She sucked in a breath at the thought of all that strength making him plunge inside her. The sharp intake was filled with a sweet scent. Something familiar. She sniffed the air.

"The pie!" she shrieked.

"I'll get it," Matt said.

He wrapped the towel around his waist as he hurried from the room. She started after him then realized she was still dripping on the floor. Concentrating, she unfastened the remaining buttons, then tried to slide the wet dress down her sleeves. The thick fabric didn't cooperate. She was out of one sleeve but caught in the other when Matt returned.

His long hair hung in his eyes. He brushed it away. "They're perfect," he said. "Golden brown and bubbling. I set them on the counter to cool and stirred the stew." He crossed to where she was standing. "Let me help."

He grabbed the cuff of her sleeve and tugged it down. Then he reached behind her and untied her petticoats. She pushed the whole soggy mess to the floor and stepped free.

"Showering with one's clothes on in 1873 is a big mistake," Courtney said. "I must remember to note that for my memoirs." She reached for one of the towels and wrapped it around her dripping hair. After piling it on her head, she glanced at him. "What?"

He pointed at her. "Very interesting contrast of styles."

She looked down. She was wearing a twentieth-century bra with nineteenth-century pantaloons. "Pretty silly, huh?"

"I don't know. I find it kind of sexy." He moved close and drew her to him.

She placed her hands on his shoulders. "Thank you," she said, then pressed her lips to his chest. "For the shower and everything else. It's wonderful. The most thoughtful thing anyone has ever done for me."

He rubbed his palms up and down her back. "Hallie is going to think we're crazy."

"She already does."

"I think she likes us."

Courtney smiled up at him. "I think you're right, but when she's with her family, I bet she keeps them howling with laughter at the odd things we do."

He stepped away. "You'd better get out of those wet things." He grabbed a towel and walked over to the window. A couple of nails stuck out from the wood. He covered the window with the towel. Light still filtered into the room.

She took off her bra and pantaloons, then grabbed the wrapper hanging on the row of hooks. She crossed to the dresser and picked up the mother-of-pearl brush Jonathan had given her.

"What else happened while I was gone?" she asked. She moved to the bed and sat down. After pulling the towel off her hair, she began to draw the brush through the wet strands.

"Jonathan and I went over the breeding program. We're trying to choose a few of the strongest cows to mate with the blooded bulls."

"You're going to have to keep track of all that information," she said. "I could help you with that. I was always very good at flow charts."

Her wet hair provided a shield. She pushed it aside so she could see him. He stood at the head of the bed, clutching the bedpost with both hands. The intensity of his expression frightened her.

"Matt, what's wrong?"

"Nothing," he said quickly, then shook his head. "That's not true." He took a step toward her, then sat on the edge of the mattress. He tried to smile, but it didn't reach his eyes.

"Matt?" She stretched out her arm and touched his hand. He grabbed her fingers and squeezed hard.

"I'm glad you came back," he said. "I didn't think you would."

"Where would I go?"

He stared at their joined fingers. "Away from here. To town. I thought you might decide to try New York or Boston. I thought the storm might come and you'd disappear."

"I wouldn't leave you like that." She didn't want to think about the storm. It confused her. For so long she'd dreamed of its return, of going back to her own time, to her life and all that was familiar. But nothing was simple anymore. Matt loved it here. She knew in her heart he wouldn't want to go.

"How *would* you leave me?" he asked.

"I don't want to," she said softly. "I've changed. I see now that I used my old life to hide. I kept busy, running from place to place because standing still gave me time to think. I used my things to keep from feeling lonely. I had lots of acquaintances because friends were dangerous. They might begin to see the real me. The scared little girl who lost her mother and never recovered. The teenager who didn't understand how to fit in and got good grades so at least the teachers would provide approval. The grown woman who specifically chose her career so that no part of her was on the line artistically."

"What are you talking about? You created beautiful movie posters."

She smiled sadly. "I assembled them. Someone else's artwork. Someone else's words. Someone else's concept. I merely put the pieces together. I never took risks. I never put myself on the line. Even in our marriage. It wasn't the real thing. We were part-time playmates."

He leaned forward and took the brush from her hand. He settled behind her and brushed her hair. "I wish you could see yourself as I see you. I see a sweet-natured woman who has enough humor to laugh at her mistakes, who isn't afraid to work hard. Someone who genuinely cares about other people. You talk about hiding behind your things. Here you have very little and you're doing all right. Sure we both miss some conveniences, but you're not giving yourself enough credit."

"Maybe. I just wish I were more like you."

"Me? I doubt that. I'm just some cowboy with more guts than sense. Smart people don't try to make their living not being thrown off bucking horses."

She turned so she could see him over her shoulder. "Now who isn't giving himself enough credit?"

He gave her a half smile. "Okay, I'll admit we've both changed since we got here."

"Whatever happens, I don't regret this," she said. "I wouldn't give up a minute of this time."

He stared at her for several minutes, then cleared his throat. "I, ah, got something for you while you were gone." He stood up and walked to the dresser. "It's not anything new, but I thought you might like it back the way it was."

He opened the dresser drawer and pulled out a small cloth bag. He unfolded the top, then tipped it so her gold chain spilled onto his palm.

"You fixed my necklace. Oh, Matt, thank you."

She stood up and took it from him. The individual links had been fitted back together. "I've missed this," she said, pulling her damp hair over one shoulder and handing him the necklace. "Can you fasten it please?"

When she presented her back, he slipped the chain over her head and settled it against her neck. She touched the smooth links.

"Let me see," he said when he was done.

She turned slowly, pushing her hair out of the way. The chain disappeared into the collar of her wrapper. She untied the garment and let it fall off her shoulders, baring her to her breasts. Matt's gaze swept over her bare chest before settling on the jewelry around her neck.

"Back where it belongs," he said.

"It's our grubstake."

He grinned. "Where did you hear an expression like that?"

"In a movie." She pulled up the wrapper and tied it at her waist. "Was there any news on the Sears catalog?"

Matt pulled his jeans off the hook and dropped his towel. She admired the lean line of his flank as he stepped into the denim. "It exists. I've ordered one. It should be here in about three or four weeks. You can pore over it all winter and we'll place an order in spring."

"Hallie wants a sewing machine."

"I know. I thought we'd get one. I asked about washing machines, but no one has heard of them. I'll try to figure out some kind of wringing device this winter. And maybe a tub with agitators that are turned by a crank handle."

She returned to the bed and sat down. "That would be heaven."

He started out of the room. "I'll stir the stew."

Courtney picked up the brush and ran it through her hair. With her free hand she touched her necklace. For the third time that day, tears sprang to her eyes. She blinked rapidly to hold the moisture back, all the while knowing she didn't deserve Matt. She never had.

As she felt the flat links of the necklace, she glanced at the shower jutting into the room. He had so much work with the cattle and preparing for winter, but he'd built a shower because it was important to her.

She stared at the beautiful brush in her hand. Jonathan had a way of picking out lovely things, but living in this century had taught her that possessions weren't as important as she'd once imagined. She didn't need them to feel special. Matt did that just by smiling at her.

She looked at the pile of wet clothes still on the floor. She would have to pick everything up and hang it outside where it would dry. They'd never made love like that before. Wildly, giving in to the need of the moment. She liked it. Maybe they could—

She caught her breath. What about birth control? She wasn't on the Pill anymore. She thought about the herbs Mary Frances had given her and the instructions for their use. It was the middle of her cycle. She should have used it before as well as after, when in fact she hadn't used it at all. Was it too late?

She started to stand up, then she sat back on the mattress. If she didn't do anything and she and Matt remained lovers, she could get pregnant. Was she prepared for that? She counted months on her fingers. If she got pregnant today, the baby would be born in May. The worst of the storms were over by then. The women could come be with her. Hallie would be here.

She thought about what Pansy had gone through and was surprised to discover she wasn't as afraid. The thought of being a mother made her nervous. Would she know how to act? Yet the terror was gone. If nothing else, Matt would be a terrific father. And if he was right, their child would inherit a cattle empire.

She heard his footsteps in the hall. "The stew is simmering," he said, and handed her a large paper-wrapped package. "This was waiting at the mercantile in town. Jonathan said you ordered it."

"I did." She set her brush down and picked up the package. The paper crinkled. "Hallie is making a fancy dress out of the blue silk. But it won't fit well without the right underwear." She grimaced. "I can't believe I'm giving in on this."

"On what?"

She glanced at him and smiled. "Have a seat and I'll show you."

He settled on the mattress, fluffed the pillows, and leaned against the headboard. His chest and feet were bare. He rested his left wrist on his bent knee. Dark hair fell to his eyebrows.

"You look like a barbarian prince," she said as a powerful wave of desire swept over her. She dropped the package on the bed.

"Are you my slave or my princess?"

"Which would you prefer?"

She'd expected him to smile, but his expression turned serious. "Always my princess, Courtney. I never think of you as less."

Her throat tightened. She took a step toward him. "Matt."

He waved her away. "But if you were my slave, I'd order you to open your package naked."

A thrill shot through her. Did he mean that? Did he want her naked? "As you wish," she said quietly, and unfastened the tie at her waist. She shrugged the wrapper off her shoulders and let it fall to the ground.

He stared at her as if he'd never seen her before. A blush started somewhere around her toes and worked its way up. She felt her nipples tightening.

"Your body's changed," he said.

She glanced down and patted the side of her leg. "I know. Can you believe it? After years of fighting the same ten pounds, they're finally gone. I've got the thighs I've always wanted. The irony is I wear a long dress all the time and no one knows."

"*I* know." His voice sounded hoarse.

She tossed her head, sending her hair back over her shoulders. Placing her hands on her hips, she sauntered over to the bed. "I'm your princess at heart, but just for this minute, let's pretend I'm your slave. What would you have me do?"

"Just standing there is pretty good." He swallowed hard.

She smiled. Already the physical proof of his desire pressed against the button fly of his jeans. She moved closer, until the front of her thighs touched the mattress. "Surely there's something that would bring you pleasure, master."

"Show me what would bring *you* pleasure," he commanded. "Touch yourself as you would have me touch you."

"I couldn't," she said without thinking. What he asked was too intimate, too personal.

Her gaze met his. She could feel her cheeks flaming. He continued to stare at her, not asking, not even demanding, simply requesting. She reminded herself that this was Matt and she'd been the one to start their sensual game.

She moved her hands across her belly. She shivered. Desire flowed with the beating of her heart. Not just from the touch of her hands on her sensitized skin, but from the look in his eyes. The intensity, the stark hunger that grew as her hands slipped higher toward her breasts.

She cupped herself. The shape was familiar. She touched herself there when she bathed or adjusted her bra. But this was different. Sensual. She could read his thoughts, or perhaps they were simply her own. She pinched her already taut nipples between her thumbs and forefingers.

He groaned. "Jesus, Courtney."

He started toward her. His foot hit the package and it crinkled. He glanced at it. "What did you buy?"

"Huh?" She blinked to clear away the sensual fog. "Silk pantaloons, a camisole, and a corset. There are some stockings, too."

"Put them on."

She thought about protesting, then saw him reach for the buttons of his fly. She was wet and her body one mass of quaking need.

By the time she had the package open, he was naked, once again sitting on the bed, leaning against the headboard. His position of one leg bent, one leg stretched out, left little to the imagination. She could see the dark arrow of hair bisecting his belly. His dark curls emphasized the strength and size of his erection.

She lifted out a pair of stockings first. They were shorter than she was used to and would only come to the top of her knees. They felt like finely knitted cotton and had a delicate diamond pattern in the weave.

She waved them. "Do you want me to start at the bottom and work my way up?" she asked.

"What else do you have to show me?"

She dropped the stockings and picked up a chemise. At least she thought that's what it was called. This one was white and so delicate the fabric was transparent.

Lace edged the short sleeves and scooped front. She held it up for Matt's inspection. He stared at it for a long time. She tried to gaze at his face, but again and again her attention was drawn to his thighs and the swollen male flesh. She wanted to touch him and taste him. Without stopping to consider the consequences, she repeated the words he'd spoken to her.

"Show me what would bring you pleasure."

Without speaking, he slid his hand down his leg. He moved to his erection and closed his fingers around the engorged length. He moved back and forth slowly. She watched, mesmerized. She didn't know she was holding her breath until she exhaled and gasped for air. Her belly clenched, her fingers relaxed. The chemise drifted to the floor.

"Come here," he commanded.

She reached toward him. He grabbed her around the waist and settled her on top of him. Her aching center trapped his hardness between them. She rocked her hips, taunting them both. He tangled his fingers in her hair and pulled her head down.

His kiss was hot and hungry, a dance of lips and tongues. Even as the need between them spiraled out of control, he pulled back. He cupped her breasts, then teased her nipples into quivering peaks.

"I never thought I'd meet anyone like you," he murmured, then kissed her chin. He trailed down her neck. She arched her head back to let him have his way with her.

Her hands rested on his shoulders. She felt the tightness of his muscles. Still she rotated her hips, rubbing his hardness with her hungry center.

With one quick shift, he had her under him. He nudged her thighs apart, then entered her. His hand slipped between them and he gently rubbed her.

"It's never been like this," she gasped. "Not just the

sex." She arched against him as her body collected itself in anticipation of release. "All of it."

"I know."

He thrust deeper and faster, moving his fingers in time with his hips. She was caught in a whirlwind of sensation, panting, grasping at him, begging him never to stop.

As she felt herself falling into paradise, he spoke her name. She forced herself to open her eyes and look at him. His features were taut with his pleasure.

"I'll always love you," he said.

Before she could say anything, he shook his head. "Don't say anything. This is enough."

It wasn't, but she understood his fears. He didn't want her speaking in the passion of the moment, only to regret the confession later.

She wanted to tell him it wasn't like that. She knew her heart, at least she was beginning to. Then it was too late to protest. She fell off the other side. She couldn't think, couldn't breathe, could only feel. As Matt followed her, she promised herself she would prove her affection in actions so when the time came, he would be willing to listen to her words.

18

The first brown leaves fluttered to the ground. Matt tilted his hat back on his head and watched them. The mornings had turned cold. When he saddled Jasper, their breath formed small clouds in the chilly air. By afternoon it warmed up, but not as much as in the summer. Fall had come to Wyoming.

"Be winter soon," he said.

Jonathan glanced at the tree. "We'll have our first snowfall by the end of the month. According to Old Man Daniels, it's going to be a mild winter."

"How does he know?"

Jonathan grinned. "No one is sure, but he's usually right. Something about the size of the beaver dams and the thickness of the rabbit pelts. The animals know before we do."

And they don't even have satellite photos, Matt thought, missing the Weather Channel on cable. It would be nice to be able to see a storm front approaching instead of depending on Old Man Daniels and his beaver dams. Still, being without cable television was a small price to pay for this life. Except for a few inconveniences, he had everything he'd ever wanted.

He glanced around at the grass-covered land and the cattle grazing contentedly. He had plans. As soon as there was extra money, he wanted to buy more land. Jonathan thought he was crazy, but the gambler was willing to admit Matt knew more about cattle.

They'd already culled the herd and sent a couple hundred head East. Both had put the money back into the ranch. As Matt worked the land and Jonathan was merely an investor, Matt got a salary in addition to his share of the profits. With that money, he planned to buy Courtney whatever she wanted from the Sears catalog. He had some ideas for other improvements for the house.

They rode around the quiet herd. Up ahead, by a finger of the main stream that fed the land, Matt saw several dark shapes lying on the ground. He swore under his breath and urged Jasper into a canter. Jonathan followed close behind.

"Damn it all to hell," Matt growled as he reined Jasper to a halt and slid to the ground.

Half a dozen cattle lay dead. He examined their stiff bodies and the color of their tongues. Jonathan remained on his horse and moved up wind.

"What happened?" the gambler asked.

"Poison," Matt said. "Lupines or maybe . . . ," He glanced around, then grabbed a plant by its base and jerked it out. "Larkspur." He swore. "I told the men to dig these plants out when they saw them."

"You might as well try to harvest hay with a pocketknife," Jonathan said. "You're running cattle on hundreds of acres. You can't kill every weed."

"I could with a good weed killer," Matt said under his breath.

"What?"

"Nothing." How could he explain the concept of a weed killer to a man born and raised in this century? He stared at the dead cattle and felt a spurt of frustration. It didn't have to be like this. It was a simple procedure: Destroy the poisonous plants and the cattle won't eat them. He would talk to the men again, but he knew that Jonathan was right. It would be a difficult battle to win without the help of chemicals that probably hadn't even been invented yet.

Matt grabbed Jasper's reins and swung into the saddle. "Maybe we could hire some extra help next spring," he said, thinking aloud. "Have them go through the main pastures."

"Sounds expensive."

"So are dead cattle."

Jonathan nodded slowly. "You've got a point."

They headed back for the ranch. Even as they discussed their plans for the winter, Matt continued to think about the dead cattle. With these six, they'd lost nearly fifty head. There had to be a better way. He grimaced. It was the price of having all he'd ever wanted, he supposed.

"Courtney will appreciate a mild winter," Jonathan said.

"Only if it's mild enough not to snow at all." Matt glanced at his friend. "Plan to visit frequently. She'll be going out of her mind for company."

Their gazes met for a moment, then Jonathan looked away. Matt saw guilt tighten the other man's features and felt a twinge of it himself. He shouldn't have asked the gambler to come out to see Courtney. Matt knew how Jonathan felt about her. It must torture him to spend time in her presence and know that she only thought of him as a friend.

"Jonathan," he said.

His partner shook his head, as if warning him not to say anything. "She seems more settled than when she first arrived."

"She is." Matt stared at the ground. "Hallie's been a great teacher. Now that Courtney understands how to deal with the stove, the garden, and the livestock, she's finding that she fits in."

Or maybe it was their relationship, he thought with contentment. They were finally a real married couple. At night, every night in fact, they cuddled and talked about their day. They spent long hours discussing dreams and plans. She had finished her first quilt. It wasn't much to look at, but she'd learned several stitches. She'd sketched out a design for another quilt, this one more complicated. She talked of selling them in the city.

Then, when the lantern burned low, they made love. Sometimes slow, sometimes fast. Sometimes she teased him by putting on just her bra and panties and prancing around the room. Other times she was a nineteenth-century seductress, in cotton and lace, with her hair high on her head and ribbons trailing down her back. Always she was giving . . . responsive, calling out his name as he carried her to the heights of ecstasy.

In the morning they exchanged secret smiles over breakfast. He went out to work the cattle with a light heart and a soul warm from her affection.

He drew his eyebrows together. Since that first day she'd come home from staying with Pansy, they'd been lovers. But they hadn't talked of love. Since he'd found the courage to say the words once, he hadn't wanted to say them again. He didn't want her responding automatically. He wanted her to say them of her own accord. Because she felt them. He needed her to love him back as much as he needed to draw his next breath, but he was willing to wait until she was sure her feelings came from the heart.

As they neared the ranch, the smell of jam filled the air. Matt inhaled deeply. "Hallie said she'd found a couple of bushes still filled with berries. She didn't put all of them up for jam. We'll be having fresh pie tonight."

"No one makes pie like Hallie Wilson."

Both men urged their horses into a canter. When they came in view of the house, they saw a large pot dangling over an open fire. If it was a clear day, Hallie preferred to make jam outside. She said it was hot work at the best of times and a body could keel over from the heat if trying it indoors. Matt didn't like the women working close to the fire. He worried about their long skirts so he and Roger had constructed a stone ring to protect them.

Hallie stood next to it now, stirring the hot liquid. Courtney poured in sugar. Behind them was the first of the three boilers he'd ordered for the septic system. They wouldn't be able to put it in until next spring, but Courtney swore she didn't mind. He wondered if she'd still be saying that after a week of real winter. Hallie thought the whole idea was crazy, but she was used to that with them. Besides, the housekeeper confessed to having grown real fond of the kitchen's hot water pipe.

The women saw them and waved. Matt and Jonathan waved back, then headed for the stable. "Are you planning to come to town before winter?" Jonathan asked.

"I hadn't, but I can if it's important. Why?"

The gambler dismounted and handed his horse to Roger. "The Laramie County Stock Association is having a meeting. You said you wanted to join. This would be a good time."

"You're right. We have to register our brand, too." The original heart-shaped design had been modified to include Jonathan's last initial. The S and H entwined inside a large C.

"They haven't built the Cheyenne Club yet, have they?" Matt asked, remembering stories the oldtimers used to tell.

Jonathan stared at him, then slowly shook his head. "I never heard of any Cheyenne Club. When are you expecting it?"

"In about—" Matt stopped talking and glanced at his friend. The other man's expression was unreadable. "I thought I'd heard someone mention it to me once. I must have been mistaken."

Roger returned for Matt's horse and led Jasper back to his stall. Jonathan folded his arms over his chest and leaned against the entrance to the barn. He pulled a cigar out of his inside coat pocket and sniffed it. "You're not from California, are you?" he asked.

"Why do you ask?"

Jonathan handed Matt the cigar. "You're not from anywhere around there or anywhere I've ever been. You know things you shouldn't know. I've seen it with the cattle. You know what's going to happen. Maybe I shouldn't even be asking. After all, I've thrown in with you. If you're wrong, I've lost a lot of money."

Matt held his gaze. "I'm not wrong."

"How do you know?"

"I can't say."

Jonathan shoved his hands in his pockets. "Courtney, she's like you, too." It wasn't a question. "That's why she didn't know anything about keeping house. Hallie thinks she's a little touched in the head, but it's not that, is it?"

"No."

The gambler grimaced. "It's probably best if you don't tell me. I don't want folks thinking I'm crazy, too."

"They won't."

Jonathan hesitated, as if he were going to ask

another question, but instead, he moved off toward his small two-room house. Matt stared after him. Had Jonathan guessed the truth? If he had, he wasn't going to say anything about it. For a moment he considered confiding in his friend, then he shook his head. He and Courtney had already decided it would be best if no one knew.

Roger came out of the barn and cleared his throat. He rubbed his hands against his wool trousers. "About them cattle," he said hesitantly.

"How are they doing?"

"Two died this morning."

Matt swore under his breath. When Roger flinched, he walked over to the boy and patted his back. "It's not your fault. We both knew their wounds were turning septic. I'd hoped they'd pull through, but they didn't."

Together they walked to the pen behind the barn. Several cows had been injured. Run-ins with thorns, broken tree branches, and predators didn't always kill them. Matt brought the mobile cattle back to the ranch to recuperate. It was a frustrating job. He didn't have access to any medical equipment or drugs.

Matt leaned against the railing and stared at the cattle. Three had been mauled by a wolf. The first one had died the same day. Now the other two had gone. It would have been so simple, he thought, frustrated. All they needed was a decent dose of antibiotics. The infection hadn't spread. But he hadn't had anything to give them. The wounds had gotten worse and the cattle had died.

He slammed his hand against the railing. "It shouldn't be like this," he muttered.

"I'm sorry, Matt. I did the best I could." Roger sounded as if he blamed himself.

"It wasn't your fault," Matt told him. "I wish there was something we could have done. If only—"

He sucked in a deep breath. That "if only" was another price of living here. He didn't have access to modern medicine, which meant more cattle were going to die needlessly.

"Courtney, watch out!"

Hallie's cry cut through the afternoon. It was followed by a loud scream.

Matt and Roger took off together toward the sound. As Matt rounded the side of the barn, he saw flames crawling up the front of Courtney's long skirt. Even as panic gave him a burst of speed, she fell to the ground and rolled to extinguish the fire.

He was at her side in a second. His heart thundered in his chest and his hands were shaking. "Courtney, are you hurt? Are you burned?"

He tugged at her skirt. The still-smoldering fabric singed his gloves. He patted it thoroughly, then inspected her petticoats. They were untouched.

She sat up slowly and shook her head. "I'm okay, Matt." She gave him a quick smile. The stink of burning cloth filled the morning. Roger hovered in the background.

Hallie crouched beside her. She grabbed Courtney's hand and squeezed it. "I told you to dampen your skirt. You could have been killed. Or worse."

Matt had never seen the housekeeper so upset. He shared her fear. "Dammit, Courtney, I can't lose you now."

Courtney shuddered. "I know. I'm sorry. I wasn't paying attention. It won't happen again."

Hallie grimaced. "Always with your head in the clouds."

Matt rose slowly and pulled off his gloves. He held out his hand. Courtney took it and stood up. She glanced at the front of her skirt. Part of it had burned nearly to her knees. His heart still raced. He could taste the dread. He wanted to haul her close and never let her go, but he was shaking too much to move.

Courtney gave him a quick smile, then glanced at Hallie. "I'm sorry. Really. But I'm okay. I'd better change into something else."

She started for the house. Hallie sighed, then turned to the fire. The housekeeper began scooping the hot jam out by herself. "Go help your mother," Matt told Roger. The boy hurried to her side.

Matt slowly walked toward the barn. As he did, his mind echoed with Courtney's scream. His gut clenched. He remembered how she'd burned herself that first night. That was bad enough, but today she could have died.

At the cattle pen, he stared at the few remaining cows and wondered if they would survive. In this primitive time there weren't any guarantees. For any of them. He couldn't keep the cattle safe and he couldn't keep Courtney safe.

A coldness swept through him like a blizzard gale. He shuddered and felt the chill clear down to his soul. Life was fragile. He didn't know why he hadn't seen that before. If he couldn't keep Courtney safe, she might die. How would he survive that? How would he live with the pain of being without her or the guilt of having killed her?

He knew he wasn't thinking logically, but he couldn't help himself. He glanced at the sky, searching. It took him a moment to realize he was looking for the mysterious storm that had swept them here. After months of praying she wouldn't leave him, he wanted to find a way to send her home. To safety.

Courtney got up to slice the pie, but Hallie shooed her away. "I told you to rest," the housekeeper said.

"I'm not an invalid," Courtney said, then returned to the table and cleared plates. Roger jumped up to help her, but she speared him with a look that had him quickly settling back in his seat.

"I didn't get burned," she continued. "It was just the dress. I'm fine."

Except for the sound of Hallie's knife hitting the small plates as she served the pie, the kitchen was silent. No one responded to her claim of being in good health. Okay, so she'd had a scare. Just thinking about the fire made her want to swoon. It had been a mistake not to dampen her skirt. She wasn't stupid. She would make sure the mistake didn't happen again.

Courtney glanced at Matt. Her husband sat in his usual place at the head of the table. But something else was wrong. She could feel it.

Normally conversation flowed at dinner. He and Jonathan discussed their plans for the ranch. If the gambler wasn't with them, they all talked about their day, the change in the weather. Something. Silence was unusual. It made the tiny hairs on the back of her neck prickle.

Jonathan handed her his plate and smiled. Some of her concern faded. Surely if there was something terrible going on with the ranch, he would know. But he'd been cheerful all evening. It was Matt who wasn't talking.

She understood Matt was still concerned about her. Having her dress catch on fire had been unnerving. But he was treating her as if she were dying of some wasting disease.

When the plates were cleared, she poured everyone more coffee, then looked at her husband. His blue eyes were dark with an emotion she couldn't read. As she circled behind him, she placed her left hand on his shoulder. He reached up and touched her fingers.

"Matt?" she asked softly. "What's wrong?"

He released her hand. "Nothing."

Courtney put the coffeepot back on the stove and leaned against the counter. He was acting so strange. Maybe it wasn't just about the accident. Had he guessed her secret?

She placed her hand on her still-flat belly. They'd been lovers for five weeks. Every night they'd joined together and every morning she'd ignored the jar of herbs Mary Frances had given to her. Had she been tempting fate, or had she secretly wanted to get pregnant?

She suspected it was the latter. After all, she knew the consequences of unprotected sex. The corner of her mouth tilted up as she thought of the tiny life growing inside her. She wasn't sure when she'd gotten pregnant. Sometime in the first couple of weeks, she thought. So the baby would be born in May. Pansy and Mary Frances would come be with her when it was her time. She wasn't afraid.

The best part was she didn't have to use those hideous rags now. Whenever she'd read about how people in the Old West had so many children, she'd thought they were crazy. Her teachers had said it was to have help with the family businesses, but Courtney knew the truth. Women kept getting pregnant so they wouldn't have to use rags. She would be willing to bet that the birthrate declined in direct proportion to the rise of the disposable sanitary napkin.

She smiled, but then her smile faded. Did Matt know she was pregnant and was he angry about it? She couldn't imagine that. After all, he'd been so excited last year when her period had been late and she'd thought she might be expecting. He'd been crushed when she'd gotten her period. Of course he would want a child. So what was wrong with him?

"You going to eat standing up?" Hallie asked, thrusting a plate at her. "Or are you going to sit at the table like good civilized folk do?"

Courtney grinned, took the piece of pie, and returned to the table.

"There's cream if you want some," Jonathan said, pushing the small china pitcher toward her.

"No, thanks." The mental image of thick cream made her stomach stir. She quickly took a bite of pie. The sweet fruit settled her belly and she breathed a sigh of relief.

"We lost half a dozen more cattle to larkspur," Jonathan said. "Matt and I found them today."

"Oh, Matt." Courtney sat on his right. She covered his hand with hers. "I'm sorry. No wonder you're upset. What are you going to do about it?"

He stared at the table. "There's nothing to be done. We can't dig all of the poisonous plants out, although, by God, I'm going to try. There's no weed killer, no antibiotics, no drugs. How the hell do you people live?"

The room was silent again. Courtney glanced around the table. Everyone stared at Matt. Her husband glared back, daring them to defy him.

She squeezed his hand. "Matt, you—"

He jerked free of her grip. "Dammit, Courtney, I can't keep you safe here."

"What are you talking about?"

His mouth twisted, as if he were in pain. He glanced around the table, then settled his gaze back on her. "Jonathan is in love with you."

Disbelief filled her. She looked uncomprehendingly at her husband's best friend. Jonathan stared at Matt. She didn't know what either man was thinking.

Courtney felt her cheeks flame with embarrassment. Roger pushed back his chair and raced out of the kitchen without saying a word. Jonathan cleared his throat as if he were about to speak, but he was silent. He continue to stare at Matt, his expression unreadable.

In the stove a piece of wood snapped. The coffee bubbled. Courtney didn't know what to say. She cleared her throat. "Jonathan Hastings has been a good friend to you. He's taken care of all of us. If you're accusing us of . . . of—"

She couldn't even say it. Tears filled to her eyes. She blinked them back. "Oh, Matt, how could you think that of me?"

He got up and walked over to the counter. With his back to the room, he braced his hands on the edge of the sink. "I'm not. I know that nothing has ever happened between you. I also know how Jonathan feels about you. I want you to leave with him."

"What?" She sprang to her feet. Her chair shot out across the room and bumped into the far wall. "What the hell are you talking about? What kind of sick game is this? Are you saying after everything we've been through, you want a divorce?"

"No! Never that!" He spun to face her. Pain tightened the lines of his face. "I love you, Courtney. But I can't keep you safe here. Don't you see? Six cattle were poisoned. The two that were mauled by a wolf died this morning."

"I'm not a cow."

"What about what happened today? You could have burned to death."

Out of the corner of her eye she saw Jonathan rise, but he didn't move away from the table. Slowly she took a step toward Matt. "It was just an accident," she said softly. "I wasn't hurt at all."

"But you could have been." He crossed the room to her and grabbed her upper arms. "Don't you see? I can't help you here. In the city you'll have servants and doctors. You'll be safe. Jonathan will keep you safe. Out here, we're isolated. Anything could happen to you." He shook her. "Dammit, Courtney, I don't want you to die."

Jonathan started for the door. Matt released her and started after him. "Wait," he called. "Don't go. Help me convince Courtney to go with you."

The gambler shook his head.

"But you want her," Matt insisted.

"Not like this."

The back door closed behind him. When Courtney looked back at the table, she saw Hallie had gone to her room.

Courtney stared at her husband. "What's wrong with you?" she asked. "You've never acted like this before. Nothing is going to happen to me."

"You don't know that." His hands were tight fists at his side. "There's no penicillin, no surgery. Anything could kill you. I couldn't stand that."

At last his pain made sense. She crossed the room and touched his cheek. "I don't want to lose you either, Matt. But we can't know what's going to happen. If this was our own time, one of us could be hit by a car. I lived in Los Angeles, for heaven's sake. I could have died in an earthquake or been a victim of a drive-by shooting. You could have been thrown and broken your neck at the rodeo."

"It's not the same. At least there you'd have a chance if your were hurt." His gaze bore into hers. "I want you to leave with Jonathan."

"No. I won't leave you. I want to be with you. I love you." She'd been holding the words in for several weeks, waiting for the right time. This wasn't how she'd planned to tell him, but under the circumstances, it was probably best.

He flinched as if she'd slapped him. "Don't," he said hoarsely. "Don't care about me at all. I want you to go where it's safe."

"It's better for us to be together," she said. "Can't you see that?" She held onto her temper because she knew he was hurting. "Besides, something could happen to me in the city just as easily. There are diseases, plagues."

"It will be easier if you go."

Her control snapped. "You bastard. Easier for you, you mean. You don't give a damn about me. This is all about you and your precious feelings. You think you can send me away and forget all about me."

"No. It's not like that."

"It's exactly like that. You get to keep your heart in one piece. You don't have to risk exposing everything. You once said you loved me, but that's not true. You want to hold back and protect that last little corner of your heart. Go ahead, Matt. Send me away. But if you do, you'll have to live with the fact that you're nothing but a coward."

19

Courtney grabbed her shawl and stepped outside. She'd been at the ranch nearly five months and the darkness at night still shocked her.

She stood at the rear of the house until her eyes adjusted to the inky sky and faint illumination from the moon. Light spilled out of the kitchen window, but she refused to look in that direction. She didn't want to see Matt or talk to him right now. She was so furious, she was shaking.

Her head told her he wasn't thinking straight. He was reacting to the death of the cattle, his concerns about the coming winter, and probably half a dozen things she didn't know about. That hardly gave him the excuse to act like an idiot, but rationally, she understood his actions.

Emotionally, she was devastated. How could he want what was easiest? Hadn't their time together meant anything to him? She closed her eyes and fought against the dark gaping pain in her chest. She couldn't believe he was willing to send her away. Is this what he'd felt when she'd taken the easy way out and served him with divorce papers? She was going to have to apologize for that.

At least she'd grown enough to change. All this time she'd been fighting her own feelings. She'd worried about doing the right thing, about what their marriage really meant. She'd stared into her soul and faced the demons residing there.

She'd learned things about herself, too. Ugly things. That she had been afraid and acted out of fear. That she'd married Matt because with him, she didn't have to risk a *real* marriage. That in the deepest, furthest corner of her soul, she hadn't expected the marriage to last.

She didn't want to face her own shortcomings, but she had. She'd fought the fears and she'd won. Now, when she was willing to risk it all, when she was willing to lay herself bare before him, he was the one running away. He was the one who was afraid.

Her temper exploded. She wanted to hit someone, preferably Matt. Barring that, she wanted to scream at the unfairness of it all. How dare he do this to her?

She stalked away from the house toward the barn. After a few feet the darkness swallowed her up. She slowed and tried to pick out the different buildings. Behind the barn, in a grove of trees, she saw Jonathan's small house.

Heat flared on her cheeks as she remembered Matt's suggestion that she run away with the gambler. How could he? She bit her lips to still their trembling, then hurried toward the light spilling from the small front window.

She knocked on the door and stepped back. Within seconds, the door opened.

Jonathan stood silhouetted by the glow of the lamp. He loomed above her, a tall, broad masculine shape.

Funny, he was so physically similar to Matt, but she never thought of the two men as being anything alike. Jonathan was a product of his time. In her mind, he was different from the men she had known. Not just in the obvious ways, but also in the way he thought and acted toward women. He would never accept her as his equal. He couldn't. Equality was a hundred years away.

He moved back and held the door open. She stepped into the front room. When the house was being built, they'd discussed making it larger, with a kitchen and second bedroom, but Jonathan had refused. He always ate with them, but he spent most of his time in town. He had two good-sized rooms, a parlor in front with a bedroom in back.

Courtney had been in his house dozens of times. She'd never thought anything about it. But now, as he motioned for her to sit on the smooth velvet settee and he took the chair across from her, she felt awkward and self-conscious.

There was a fire in the big stone fireplace. Flames silently consumed the dry wood, filling the room with a pleasant smoky scent and warming the air. She was pleased that her accident hadn't done more than ruin her dress. At least she wasn't afraid of fire. That would make living here a problem.

She continued to study the room. Several hook rugs had been scattered on the floor. There was a buffet against the far wall, but little in the way of personal effects. She couldn't escape the feeling of nervousness. Her hands twisted together and she tried to still the movement.

"I came to apologize," she said at last.

"There's no need."

"Yes, there is." She raised her gaze to his. The single lamp was on a small table by the door. He sat in front of it and the shadows concealed his expression. She wanted to know what he was thinking, then decided it was probably best if she didn't. "Matt respects you, Jonathan. He cares about you. You've been a good friend to both of us. He would never deliberately do anything to jeopardize that relationship. Tonight he was—"

"I know he's afraid of losing you," Jonathan said, cutting her off. "At first he was afraid you would go away. Now he's afraid you're going to die."

She nodded. "I know. I've tried to explain that sending me away doesn't automatically keep me safe. Besides, where's the joy if we're apart?"

He sucked in his breath.

She raised her head and stared at him, but her gaze couldn't pierce the darkness. "Jonathan?"

"I've wondered about you and Matt," he said, nothing in his voice giving away his emotions. He sat easily in the chair, his hands still, his posture erect. "I know you're not from Los Angeles. I know there's a mystery. Whatever it is, it bonds the two of you."

She was surprised. How much had he guessed? "Obviously, it doesn't bond us well enough," she said.

"Any man would fear losing you," he said.

She dropped her gaze to her lap. "Jonathan, don't. Please."

"I must." He rose to his feet, crossed the small room, and sank down beside her on the settee. Before she could stop him, he'd taken his hands in hers.

She stared at his fingers as they stroked her skin. The sensation wasn't unpleasant. Now that he was next to her, she could see his face, the hard, handsome features, the light burning in his dark eyes. His hair brushed against his shoulders. Matt had finally given in and asked Hallie to cut his, but not Jonathan.

The gambler was a nineteenth-century man with all the danger and rawness of that era flowing through his veins. Some part of her might respond to that, but she knew she was only kidding herself. What seemed different and exciting now would quickly get tiresome. She didn't have the right personality to be chattel.

"Matt spoke the truth," he said. "I love you, Courtney. I have from the moment you walked into the saloon trying to pass for a man."

He drew her into his arms. The shawl slipped off her shoulders and pooled around her waist. Their legs bumped. He held her gently but firmly, and she found herself clutching his shoulders. She wasn't sure if she was trying to push him away or move closer.

"I think you like me," he murmured, his mouth close to her ear.

"Of course I like you. We're all friends. Good friends." But instead of sounding sensible, she was breathless.

"Perhaps you could learn to care for me." He brushed his lips against her cheek. "Come away with me," he whispered. "I'll take you anywhere. Paris, London. I've got money. You won't want for anything. I'll show you the world."

Before she could refuse, he kissed her. She let him because, well, it was pleasant and she was curious. She let his hands span her back and move slowly down her spine. She traced the breadth of his shoulders and the powerful muscles in his upper arms.

His head tilted as his mouth brushed against hers. The fleeting contact teased her. His lips were smooth and warm. Unfamiliar, as was his scent. Not unpleasant, just different.

Her eyelids fluttered shut and she concentrated on the feel of him so close to her. She wondered what it would be like to have him touch her intimately. As if reading her mind, he moved his hand from her back to her waist. An innocent act considering they still had their mouths closed. But something inside Courtney shrieked at the violation. She opened her eyes and pushed him away.

He studied her for a moment, then smiled regret-fully. "I'd hoped you were swooning with delight. Apparently my expectations were too high."

"It's not you, it's me." She drew in a deep breath. "I care about you, Jonathan. I care about you as a very good friend. I hope we can always be friends. But I'm in love with my husband. As badly as he acted tonight, I can't change my feelings for Matt."

"I understand. At least you didn't say you loved me like a brother. I don't think I could have stood that."

His tone was playful, but she saw the pain in his eyes. For one brief moment, she felt a flash of regret. A relationship with Jonathan Hastings would have been uncomplicated, if only because he wouldn't engage her emotions the way Matt did.

"You're far too handsome for me to want you to be a close relative," she said, hoping to tease away some of his hurt. "And I was very tempted."

She leaned forward to brush his mouth with hers, but this time he stopped her. He placed a hand on her shoulder. "Please. You have no idea what you do to me."

His mouth twisted and for a single heartbeat, she saw the ragged edges of his battered soul. "I'm sorry," she whispered. "I never meant—"

He brushed off her apology. "If I have to lose you to someone, I'm glad it's Matt. He deserves you."

"Explain that to him. He doesn't even want me." She drew her shawl up over her shoulders. "What a comedy of errors we are. The three of us could be living out some Shakespearian play."

"You've read Shakespeare?" he asked, obviously surprised.

She cuffed his arm. "Dammit, Jonathan, I might not have a penis, but I do have a brain. Yes, I've read Shakespeare."

Courtney had the unique pleasure of watching

Jonathan blush. The color climbed up his cheeks and he actually looked away from her.

She grinned. "I shouldn't have said the *P* word, huh?"

"It's quite all right," he said formally, as if they were in a fancy parlor having tea.

"This is why it would never have worked," she said. "I'm not subservient enough."

"There's another reason. Does Matt know about the baby?"

She stared at him. Her mouth opened, but no sound came out. She cleared her throat and tried again. "How did you know? I haven't told anyone. Not even Hallie."

"I suspect she knows, too." He shrugged. "It wasn't hard to figure out. There haven't been the usual discreet rags drying behind the house."

"Oh." Now it was her turn to be embarrassed. "No, I haven't told him. I was going to soon, but now . . . "

Now she wasn't sure what to do. If Matt didn't want her around now, what would he think when he found out she was pregnant? He would be even more concerned.

"He loves you, Courtney. He'll come around."

She smiled at him. "How come you can read my mind?"

Dark eyes flared with need. "I know everything about you."

She squeezed his hand, then rose to her feet. "Good night, Jonathan." She walked to the door and left the small house.

As she stood in the darkness outside, she knew there was one thing Jonathan didn't know about her. He didn't know that she'd come through time. It was too far-fetched for anyone to believe. She barely believed it herself.

She headed back for the house. Light still shone

from the kitchen window. She wondered if Matt was waiting for her.

She wasn't quite ready to face him yet, so she walked slowly. She could see faint outlines of the buildings and the bunkhouse in the distance. The cattle were quiet.

They'd made a life for themselves in a very short period of time. She wouldn't have thought it was possible. When they'd first come here she'd hated everything about this place and time. She wouldn't have thought she could ever stop missing her condo or her little red sports car, but she barely thought about them at all. There was little she missed, although she regretted that the stable probably assumed she'd stolen her rental horse, Rocky.

As she neared the house, she glanced up at the sky. She was beginning to learn the constellations. She inhaled the sharp air and knew winter was on its way. Soon snow would cover the ground and she and Matt would face the toughest task of all.

She knew in her heart they could make it if they tried. If they believed. If they both loved. But did they? She paused by the back door and figured it was time to find out.

But when she stepped into the kitchen, instead of her husband, she found Hallie cleaning up from dinner.

Courtney paused in the doorway to the pantry. "I'm sorry you had to hear all that," she said.

Hallie gave her a sympathetic smile. "Living in other folks' homes means you hear things that aren't meant for outside ears. You and Matt are easier than some I've known." Her smile faded. "He asked me to tell you that he'll be sleeping in the barn tonight."

Courtney caught her breath. She felt as if she'd been stabbed. "He's gone?"

Hallie put down her dishrag and walked over to

place her hand on Courtney's shoulder. "It's not so very far." Her brown eyes widened with sympathy. "Matt's a good man. He cares about you."

"So I've been told." Courtney leaned against the door frame and closed her eyes. "Just not by him."

"Can't say that I blame him for holding back on you."

"What?" Her eyes snapped open. "You're taking *his* side in this?"

"I'm not taking anyone's side. I'm just pointing out that you took your time in settling down around here. You can't blame a man for being cautious."

"But I'm settled now. I like it here."

"And you wouldn't want to go back, no matter what?"

Hallie saw more than she should. Courtney stepped away and hung her shawl on the hook. Did she want to stay here, no matter what?

"I don't know," she admitted.

"It seems to me that you need to know your own mind before you go demanding Matt make up his."

Courtney smiled faintly. "How did you get to be so smart?"

"Just born with it."

"I'm lucky to have you. Thank you for everything." Courtney gave her a hug and walked through the parlor to her bedroom. She stared at the double bed and wondered what it would be like to sleep in it alone. It hadn't been but a few minutes and she already missed Matt. Why was he doing this to them?

She fought the urge to go to him and demand they work this all out. Hallie was right. She *did* have to know her own mind before she confronted Matt. She had to be sure she was willing to give everything. That even if the storm returned, she would want to stay with her husband. Because she knew that no matter what, he wasn't going back.

*   *   *

Matt sat in the barn for a long time. It was cold and the smell of the horses bothered him, which it almost never did. He'd slept in barns before. When times were hard on the rodeo circuit, he'd been grateful to sleep anywhere that was wider and longer than the bench seat in his truck.

He stared out the open door at the light still on in Jonathan's house. He owed his friend an apology. There was no excuse for what he'd done. He didn't like knowing he had the ability to be so thoughtless and cruel.

He got to his feet and walked out into the night. When he reached the small house, he hesitated before knocking. What was he going to say? Then he figured the words would come to him.

He pounded once, hard, then waited. Jonathan opened the door and stepped back, silently inviting him inside. Matt searched his face, looking for anger, but the gambler's poker face was unreadable.

Once inside, Matt refused a seat. He shoved his hands into his pockets and rocked back on his heels. "I came to say I'm sorry. I had no right to tell Courtney how you felt about her. Not like that."

Jonathan walked to the buffet and pulled out a bottle of whiskey and two glasses. He poured a healthy shot into each, then handed one to Matt.

"No need to apologize. Courtney already did it for you." Jonathan tossed back his drink.

Matt did the same and told himself the burning in his belly came from the liquor and not jealousy. "Courtney was here?"

Jonathan nodded once. "You might as well know everything. I asked her to go away with me."

The world jerked once, nearly throwing Matt off his feet, then settled back to normal. The pain in his chest deepened. He could barely breathe, let alone speak, but he forced the question out. "What did she say?"

Jonathan crossed the small room and grabbed him by the front of his jacket. The two men were the same height and were able to stare each other directly in the eye. "You damned fool. What do you think she said?"

"She's not going?"

"Of course not." Jonathan shook him once, then released him. He crossed to the fireplace and stared at the flames. "You might as well know the rest of it. I kissed her."

The snapping of a log was the only sound in the room. Matt had stopped breathing. He wanted to pound his fist into the other man's face until all that remained was a bloody pulp. He wanted to crush him like the slimy vermin he was. He wanted—

"She doesn't want me. She never has."

The words broke through his jealous haze. He blinked to clear his mind. "What happened?"

Jonathan shrugged. "The same thing that's always happened between us. Nothing. Courtney's right. This is like some damn play. I love her, she loves you. You love her but you want her to run away with me."

He turned around and stared at Matt. "You're a fool if you let her go. You'll never find another woman like her, no matter how long you search."

"I know," Matt said hoarsely. "But I'm terrified something will happen to her. I'm so afraid."

"So you're willing to lose her now to keep from losing her later? I thought you were smarter than that, Matt. Haven't you figured out that some fears are worth facing?"

"It's not that simple."

Matt wondered if he could explain what he was feeling. Jonathan made it sound so simple. Loving Courtney had always been easy, but it had never been safe.

Unfortunately it was all that made sense in his sorry life. From the first moment he saw her, he'd been lost.

He walked to the buffet and poured another shot of whiskey. He swallowed it in one gulp and tried not to remember. It was too late. The memories crowded together, like balls on a billiard table. They bumped into each other, cracking and racing until his head ached.

"The first time I saw her, I thought she was about the prettiest woman I'd ever seen," Matt said slowly. "By the time I walked her to her hotel room later that night, I knew I was in love with her. I would have married her then, but I figured suggesting it so early would scare her away."

He glanced at the gambler. Jonathan stood in front of the fire, facing the room. Pain etched deep lines in the man's face. Matt told himself to stop talking, but the words came of their own accord.

"I worked the rodeo circuit and she lived in L.A. We barely saw each other. She talked about compromising, but I didn't want to listen to that. I suppose I knew if we compromised, the risk of losing her would be higher. If we stayed together too long, she would see the kind of man I am. She would know that I don't deserve her. It was easier to meet for weekends, to have half a marriage instead of none at all. Then she asked for a divorce."

He still remembered the pain of that phone call. The crack in her voice and the rushing he'd heard in his ears. It wasn't the long distance connection, it was the sound of his hope draining away.

"I told her yes, because she deserved more than I could give her. But when the time came, I couldn't sign the papers. I couldn't let her go. Then we were here and I had a second chance."

"If you let her go, you never were worthy of her," Jonathan said. "She loves you. Any fool could see that."

"What if I destroy her? What if I can't keep her safe?"

"There are some things no man can control."

Matt knew that in his heart, but he was so frightened of something horrible happening to her. It was easier to let her go. But, as she'd said in her rage, that was the coward's way out.

"I don't know what to do," he said miserably.

"Yes, you do."

Jonathan crossed the room and entered the bedroom. Matt followed. He was surprised to see an open suitcase on the bed. "You're leaving?" he asked.

"I've got some unfinished business back home."

"In Boston?"

Jonathan nodded. He opened the dresser across from the bed and pulled out several shirts. "I'll be back. It might take some time, maybe a year." He glanced up. "Don't go taking on any partners while I'm gone."

"You don't have to do this."

"It's not just for you and Courtney." He shook his head. "Some of it's for me. I can't stand looking at her every day knowing she belongs to you. Besides, I haven't seen my family in years." He walked over to Matt and extended his arm. "Put my profits back into the cattle. When I come back, we can settle up."

The two men shook hands.

"I didn't expect to win her," Matt said.

Jonathan stared at him. "There was never a contest. You always had her."

Matt left the house and started for the barn. Maybe Jonathan was right. But that didn't help Matt. He still didn't know what he was going to do with her.

Or worse, without her.

20

Courtney adjusted her skirt as she flopped down on the back step. The sun was bright in the afternoon sky, but it wasn't as warm as it had been a couple of weeks ago. She told herself it was the natural changing of the seasons, but irrationally a part of her wondered if it was really because Matt still slept in the barn.

In the last three days, she'd barely seen him. He'd taken most of his meals with the cowboys. He was up and working by dawn and didn't get back until long after the sun had set. Without lights to guide him, she wondered how he even found his way back to the house, but as they weren't speaking, she couldn't really ask him.

Jonathan had left. The gambler had told her he was heading home to Boston. She wondered if his unfinished business included a woman, but she'd thought it would be rude of her to ask. So she'd hugged him for a moment and made him promise to come back. She'd grown used to having him around; she would miss him.

Now she and Hallie were alone. Roger skulked in for

meals, then he was out the door. She wondered if the teenager understood what was going on. Even though he was nearly a man, he didn't deal well with the prospect of his familiar world collapsing.

Courtney stared out at the trees and the cattle grazing in the distance. Hallie's words were never far from her thoughts. She had to be sure. She had to know. Was she willing to stay with Matt, no matter what? If she was, then it was time to fight for him. If she wasn't . . . She shook her head. If she wasn't, she didn't know what she was supposed to do.

In an odd way, Matt's reaction made sense. She remembered the stories he'd told her about how he'd grown up. His father had been little more than an itinerant worker, going from ranch to ranch. Matt said the man drank a lot. It would have been difficult for Matt to develop self-confidence under those conditions. No doubt he heard his father's discouraging voice in the back of his mind. No matter what he did, it wouldn't be enough to silence the past.

But he'd prevailed despite that. He'd made something of himself on the rodeo circuit. She might not know all the details of scoring points and earning money, but she knew only the best were invited to the National Finals Rodeo every year and Matt had gone three years in a row.

She leaned against the closed back door and turned her face toward the sun, then swallowed the lump that formed in her throat. How much had she interfered with his dream?

The question hurt more than she'd expected, but she was determined to be honest with herself. She'd refused to even discuss ever living on a ranch. She hadn't liked visiting him in tiny towns, so he'd often flown to Los Angeles and stayed with her. It wasn't just the time away from practice she felt guilty about. It was the money. He'd had to buy a ticket to fly to be with her. When they were together, he rarely let her pay for anything. How much of his dream had she selfishly stolen?

He must have been so torn between what he wanted to do with his life and being with the woman he loved. She believed he loved her as surely as she believed winter would follow autumn. He was afraid. He finally had everything he wanted and he didn't feel that he'd earned it. He didn't think he was good enough.

What did she want?

Courtney sighed heavily. She wanted to be happy. She wanted to belong. She glanced around at the outbuildings, at the barn, and at the injured cows in the corral behind it. If the storm came back right now, what would she do?

Indecision filled her, then, as quickly as it had come, it faded away. She would stay, because *this* was where she belonged. She didn't understand the forces that had brought her here. Perhaps time travel was a phenomenon of nature that no one ever talked about. Perhaps it was related to the power of love. For whatever reason, she and Matt had been given a second chance together. She would be a fool to waste it.

A flicker of movement caught her attention. She glanced toward the chicken coop and saw a large snake slithering under the fence toward the chickens. She always missed a few eggs, but she was damned if she was going to let that bull snake get any.

She stood up and stepped into the pantry. Her rifle was leaning in the corner. She always kept it loaded and ready.

"There's a bull snake after the chicken eggs," Courtney called. "I'm going to shoot it."

"Don't just leave it in the yard," Hallie said, sticking her head in from the kitchen. "I don't like dead snakes."

"I could bring it to you live."

Hallie smiled. "Get on with you."

Courtney went outside. She saw the snake heading for the coop. After taking aim, she pulled the trigger slowly. The recoil jerked the rifle in her arms. The chickens squawked and scattered. Roger came running from the barn.

"What happened?" he asked.

She pointed to the now dead snake. Blood poured from the place where its head had been.

Roger's pale eyes widened. "Golly, I didn't know you could shoot that good." He sounded impressed.

Her belly lurched. "Roger, could you get rid of it for me?" she asked, taking deep breaths of air. She'd been processing chickens for the last couple of months and was even getting used to the sight of blood. But in the last couple of weeks, she'd gotten queasy. It was probably the pregnancy.

"I'll take care of it," the teenager said, and stepped inside the fenced yard. Courtney headed back to the house.

She stopped and looked back at the dead snake, then she started to laugh. She laughed so hard, she had to bend over and rest the butt of the rifle on the ground or she would have dropped it.

She'd killed a snake without even giving it a second thought. She hadn't screamed, she hadn't called for help, she'd done it herself, because by God, no one but her was going to mess with her chickens.

When the laughter faded, she straightened and stared up at the sky. "I would say that I've adjusted," she said aloud, then hurried toward the house. She knew exactly what she had to do.

Matt urged Jasper forward. The cow pony circled the small herd. Matt figured he could keep this up for the rest of the day, but eventually he would have to go home.

What would happen when he got there? He would have to find the strength to convince Courtney to leave. He didn't think he would survive being without her, but he had to do what was best for her, not himself. She was all that mattered.

Over the last three days, the pain in his chest had grown until each breath was agony. At times he wondered if this was worth it. Should he even bother with the ranch? Maybe he should take Courtney to the city himself. He could find work.

But the thought of being closed up and confined by buildings made his skin crawl. He didn't like cities. Never had. This was where he belonged. Besides, if he wasn't around, she could find someone better. Someone who deserved her.

As if his thoughts alone had conjured her from thin air, he glanced up and saw her riding toward him. Her bay horse cantered easily and she rocked with the motion as if she'd been born to the saddle. She wore her cream felt cowboy hat. Her long braid bounced against her back. She was riding astride, with her skirts pulled up to her knees. He was used to seeing her in less, but somehow, the sight of her bare calves was erotic.

A thrill of gladness eased the pain in his chest. Before he could stop himself, he waved at her. As she rode closer, her beauty overwhelmed him. Sometime in the last few days he'd forgotten how she took his breath away.

She reined in her horse about ten feet from his and dismounted. He did the same and they walked toward each other. When they were close enough to touch, they stopped.

He stared at her, at her familiar face, her hazel eyes fringed by pale lashes. Her mouth was unsmiling, but the corners tilted up. She had freckles on her nose. She hadn't bothered to pull on gloves and he could see the scars on her hands from her burns, a few cuts, and some bruises. She worked hard these days. How she must miss her old life.

"I'd forgotten you were beautiful," he said without thinking. "I always forget. When we're apart, I tell myself I'm imagining it, so when I see you, it shocks me."

A faint blush stained her cheeks. "You make my toes curl when you smile. You always have. It's embarrassing. Like having a crush on a rock star."

His hands balled into fists. He wanted to touch her, but he held himself back. Her words might ease his pain, but they didn't change reality. He had no choice; he had to send her away.

As if she read his mind, her soft expression hardened and her mouth turned down. "You were always the most stubborn man." She bent over and picked up a blade of grass. She turned it in her fingers, studying it from all sides. "I killed a snake today."

"What? A rattler?"

"No. Just a bull snake. It was going after the eggs, or maybe even the chickens. So I shot it." She glanced at him. "Maybe I should have tied it onto Rocky's saddle like a banner. Like that book *The Old Man and the Sea.* Then you could have seen my trophy and believed."

He didn't want to hear this. It was too dangerous. He could survive almost anything except losing Courtney and that was the one thing he had to do.

He turned away from her and started up the slight rise. Several cattle grazed in the distance. A couple of them raised their heads and stared at him, then returned their attention to their meal.

"The longhorns don't look as funny as I thought they would," she said, her voice right behind him.

He kept going up the rise and she kept on following him. When he reached the top, he stopped. "What do you want?" he asked.

"I want you to listen. Look at me, Matt."

He did as she requested. She was a few feet away. Her hat shaded her eyes, but he could feel the intensity of her gaze.

"I shot the snake without even thinking about it," she said. "I went in the house and got the rifle. I didn't question what I was doing, I didn't stop to consider anything. I just did it." She raised her arm and motioned toward the grazing cattle. "This was never my dream. I admit that. I adore five-star hotels."

He smiled faintly remembering her squawk of outrage when they'd stayed at a small place outside Denver and the owner had told her she could get her breakfast at the fast-food restaurant across the highway.

"But it's my dream now," she said softly. "Because it's yours. Because this is what makes you happy and this is where you belong. I don't belong in any time, I belong at your side. If that's here, in 1873, then so be it. I'm your wife, Matthew Stone, and I'm not leaving you."

He desperately wanted to believe her. He needed to believe her as much as he needed to draw his next breath. But he couldn't. It wasn't right. He didn't deserve her.

She must have sensed his thoughts. She stamped her foot in frustration. "Dammit, Matt, listen to me. Quit being such a stubborn hick cowboy. I'm not leaving. I don't know the right words to convince you of the fact, so I'm going to stick with what's simple. I am not leaving. I'm going to stay here, glued to your side until you believe me. I love you."

He flinched as if she'd slapped him. Love. Dear God, let it be true. It would be enough, if she loved him just a little.

"I know you don't think you're worthy of me," she said softly.

The pain returned to his chest, sharper than before. He stared at her. She'd stripped him of everything. He was naked before her.

"You're right," she continued softly. "You don't deserve me. Not because of who you are or how you were raised, but because of what you're doing today. You're afraid to give your whole heart. It's easy to hold that last piece back. I know because I did it, too. I held back because I didn't think it was forever. It's safe to hold back. Then, whatever happens, you still have a piece of yourself left alive. But it doesn't work that way."

She took a step toward him. She raised her hand to wipe her cheek and he realized she was crying. Courtney never cried. He shook his head. That wasn't true. He'd made her cry when he'd built her the shower. Lately, sometimes she cried when they made love, as if the passion overwhelmed her.

"You're holding back, too," she said, her voice shaking. "You're holding back by saying you're not good enough. But you can't keep all your feelings in check, so you're scared. And now you're trying to send me away. But I w-won't go." A sob broke the word.

He started toward her. She held up her hand. "No. Don't come near me. I have to say all of this. I want you to hear everything." She wiped her face again and drew in a deep breath. He could see the tears running down her cheeks. "I love you, Matt. With every part of me. No matter what happens, I'm committed to you. You have to do the same thing. You have to believe. I could die tomorrow, but so could you. We can't live our lives in fear. We have to believe. As long as you think I'm going to walk out on you, you get to hold some part of yourself back. But love isn't like that. I need you to love all of me with your whole self. You have to give that much so you can receive all my love. No more hiding."

Pain radiated out from both of them, making every fiber of his being ache. A single step of faith. Did she ask for too much?

He closed his eyes against her tears and tried to search his soul. Could he risk it? Could he lay himself bare? Could he not?

In that moment, he knew the truth. Courtney was his world. Without her, there was no life. He loved her. If the price was risking it all, he would pay it gladly, ten times over.

He opened his eyes and started toward her. But instead of his wife, he saw the violet skies on the horizon. His heart stopped and the pain returned. He wanted to rage against the injustice. Not now. Not when he could finally claim her as his own.

The earth grew still and in the distance a silent turquoise tornado swooped toward them. He glanced at Courtney. She was staring at him. She hadn't seen it. She didn't know it was coming. All he had to do was wait and it would take her back to where she belonged. But he didn't want to let her go.

Sacrifice warred with need. He loved her. If he loved her, he would want her to be happy. In her world, her time. In the future.

He looked at Jasper and Rocky. Both horses dozed under the darkening sky. They didn't seem to notice the rapidly approaching storm.

"Matt?" Courtney asked. "Are you all right?"

He nodded.

The chill became noticeable. She rubbed her hands up and down her arms. "What on earth?" She turned and saw the storm.

"It's returned," he said, though the pain made it hard to speak. "It's time. Go back."

She glanced from the storm to him. Her eyes were wide. "I belong with you," she said.

"No. You've never belonged here. Go back to your life, Courtney. You want to. Everything you care about is there. Think about it. Running water, flush toilets, microwave ovens."

The tornado swept closer and closer. He didn't remember it moving this quickly before. He started backing up, not wanting to be caught in its power. He wanted to stay where he was.

She took one last look at the storm, then started toward him. "I belong with my husband," she said. "I'm not leaving you."

He grabbed her shoulders and pushed her back. "You'll never be happy here."

The storm was nearly upon them. The temperature continued to drop. He felt as if they should be shouting to be heard over its fury, but the silence made them whisper instead.

"Don't make me go back," she begged. "I love you. I need to be with you."

"It's better this way. I want you to leave."

She glared at him. "Can't you for once in your life be selfish?"

He smiled sadly. "Not about you, Courtney. I'll always love you."

She swallowed hard. Tears darkened her eyes. "If you really loved me, you wouldn't let me go."

With that, she turned away from him and started for the storm. He knew the moment she stepped into its powerful winds. Her hair whipped around her face and her skirts billowed like sheets on wash day.

All the hurt he'd felt before, all the questions, all the agony, exploded inside him. The pain was so intense, he stared down at his chest, expecting to see an open wound. There was nothing. He touched his chest. He could feel the hollowness inside. He knew he would die without her.

"Courtney, no," he yelled into the silence. "Don't leave me. I love you. I need you."

Her smile was bright enough to light the night. She moved toward him.

At least she tried. But the storm held her firmly in its grasp. She flailed her arms, as if against a strong current, but she seemed frozen in place.

"Matt, help me. I can't get out!" Her voice was frantic.

"I'll come with you." He began to run toward the tornado.

"I don't want to go back," she screamed. She struggled against the mysterious force. "I want to stay here, with you. Get me out."

She pushed against invisible walls. Her clothes continued to whip around her. Tears flowed down her cheeks. "Matt! Help me!"

The storm began to retreat. He broke into a run, but he wasn't fast enough. She was being carried away.

He whistled for Jasper. The gelding trotted toward him, apparently unconcerned about the huge turquoise tornado directly in front of them. He mounted the horse and kicked him into a gallop. The storm ducked and turned, carrying Courtney farther and farther away. She continued to scream for him to help her escape its clutches.

Matt bent low over his saddle and reached for his rope. He prayed as he never had in his life. Words of need and hope and love tumbled over each other in his mind. For one brief moment, the storm froze in place. Matt raised his arm high and released the rope.

It sailed across the oddly colored sky, then hovered in the air. The tornado whirled in place. The silence overwhelmed him. His heart filled with love and hope. The prayers flowed from him. It was if by the sheer force of his will the rope began to move toward her again.

Courtney surged toward him. She lifted her hands and the thick rope slipped down them to settle around her waist. Slowly, gently, he pulled her toward him. The storm resisted his efforts. Jasper backed up, drawing her closer. Then the tornado seemed to give up. It released her and swirled away.

When she was free from the storm, he jumped to the ground and ran toward her. They embraced. She clung to him as if she would never let go. He prayed she wouldn't.

"Matt," she breathed against his chest.

He touched her hair, her face, then stroked her back.

"You're here," he said, barely able to believe his good fortune. "You didn't go back."

"I couldn't. I love you."

He held her tightly against his chest. The wound had miraculously healed.

"I was so scared," she said. "I couldn't get out and I thought you were going to let it take me away. I wouldn't have survived without you."

He touched a finger to her mouth to silence her. "I love you, too," he said slowly. "I love you with my whole heart. The good parts, the bad parts, even the parts that are afraid. I'll do my best for you. Every day. We've been given a second chance. How many people get to say that?"

"Oh, Matt." She pressed her lips against his. "I'll never leave you."

They stood there for a long time. Her kiss was sweet. He felt as if he'd been tested by fire and come through stronger. There were no guarantees, so he would savor each day as a gift.

When he raised his head and looked around, the

storm was gone. He still didn't understand the forces that had brought it into their lives, but he was grateful.

"I love you," he said again.

She smiled. "All of me? No matter what?"

"No matter what."

"Even if I get old and gray?"

He grinned. "Especially then."

"What if I get fat?"

"More of you to love."

She'd lost her hat in the storm. He could see her hazel eyes. They brightened with secret knowledge. "Good, because I'm about to get very fat." She took his hand and pressed it against her belly.

He sucked in a breath. His heart filled until the joy was overwhelming. "Courtney? Are you sure?"

She nodded. "Hallie says I have childbearing hips. I think she meant it as a compliment, but that's not how I took it. But it means I'll be fine. I want to have bunches of children, Matt. I want them to grow up on our ranch and be happy."

He couldn't contain his feelings. He swept her up in his arms and swung her around in the air. "I'll love you forever," he announced to the world.

"That's a long time," she said, then smiled. "But you already know that. I warn you, I want every modern convenience as soon it's invented. I want a washing machine and a car and a radio. Oh, Lord, how long do we have to wait for television?"

Instead of answering, he kissed her. And instead of asking more questions, she kissed him back.

Epilogue

Two minutes until midnight, December 31, 1899

"You can't have fireworks in the snow," Jason said as he climbed on the front porch railing.

"Uh huh. Grampy says we're gonna have 'em and the snow means they're safe." Matt Stone III, all forty pounds of him, ran to Courtney and leaned against her legs. "Isn't that right, Grammy?"

She touched his blond hair and smiled. "That's right. Now it's nearly time. You want to sit on my lap?"

The boy nodded. She helped him crawl up, then settled him on her skirt and leaned back in the chair. Her daughter-in-law, Sally, held the youngest of the grandchildren—a perfect, beautiful little girl named Courtney after her doting grandmother.

Courtney smiled at the thought. She'd never thought about being a grandmother, and then when she'd told Matt she wanted a bunch of kids, she'd sort of been kidding. Yet here it was, all these years later. She'd had seven boys.

"What are you grinning at?" Matt asked as he settled next to her.

"I was thinking about your sperm," she said.

"What's sperm?" young Matt asked, then stuck his thumb in his mouth.

Sally rolled her eyes and grabbed her oldest's hand. "Grammy isn't going to explain about that tonight," she said, giving Courtney a warning look.

Matt laughed. "You still shock them."

"I can't believe how repressed our children and their wives are," she said. "We certainly didn't raise them like that. I told the boys everything about sex."

"From the number of grandchildren we have, they obviously listened."

"Oh." Courtney leaned back in her chair and smiled. "I suppose you're right."

"So what about my sperm?" he asked, taking her hand in his and bringing her palm to his mouth. He kissed her, then touched the tip of his tongue to her skin.

As always, a shiver of anticipation swept through her. "We had seven boys, Matt. I really thought you'd give me at least one girl. But you must only have little boy sperm."

His blue eyes, still bright and alert even though he'd turned sixty the previous year, darkened with regret. "I'm sorry, too. I would have loved a little girl just like her mother." He leaned close and whispered in her ear. "As soon as everyone goes to bed, we could try for one."

She slapped his arm. "I went through the change years ago."

"I know, but the trying's the best part."

She smiled at him, then touched his face. They'd been through so much together. Sometimes she looked around the ranch and didn't recognize it as the same place Matt had won during that poker game. The four-room house now had three stories, with more bedrooms than she could count. Jonathan and his family lived about half a mile away, although they had joined them for the New Year's celebration.

She glanced around the wide porch at the crowd of children, in-laws, and friends. She found the old gambler and smiled at him. He raised his glass in salute. Time had mellowed them all.

"It's time!" someone called. The first of the fireworks exploded in front of the house.

"At least we don't have to worry about the roof catching fire," Matt said, stretching his legs out in front of him.

"The Fourth of July fire was a small one," she reminded him. "The boys had it out in no time."

"You're so calm about everything," he said.

"I've learned to be."

They held hands as fireworks lit up the night. "Reminds me of our storm," Matt said as violet-hued sparks drifted to the snow.

"Hmm, it does." They'd never seen that mysterious storm again. Perhaps it had simply been sent to set something to right. They would never know, but Courtney didn't mind. She'd had a wonderful life.

Molly climbed up on her lap. "Tell me a story," the four-year-old demanded, then stuck her thumb in her mouth. Little Matt joined his cousin, as did Jason.

"Tell us," they demanded, "'bout waves and pictures in the air."

"All right," Courtney said. "A long time from now, when you're as old as Grampy and me . . . "

The children giggled at the thought.

"There are going to be many wonderful things. Microwave ovens that cook food in a quarter of the time. Why, you can bake a potato in six minutes."

The young grandchildren obligingly gasped in disbelief. Her grown children looked on and smiled indulgently. They were used to their parents' strange stories about a future where objects flew and man actually set foot on the moon.

Courtney looked at Matt and he winked. They knew the truth. They knew about all the wonderful things yet to be invented and the changes that would sweep over the land. They also knew about the power of a love so strong, it could survive a real test of time.

"Do we have a date for later?" Matt leaned over and asked.

She cuddled her grandchildren close, then smiled at him. "I'm yours, cowboy. For always. Just like I promised."

Escape to Romance
and
WIN A YEAR OF ROMANCE!

Ten lucky winners will receive a free year of romance—*more than 30 free books*. Every book HarperMonogram publishes in 1997 will be delivered directly to your doorstep if you are one of the ten winners drawn at random.

*M*Harper Monogram